ONLY YOU

Also by Denise Grover Swank

The Wedding Pact Series

The Substitute
The Player
The Gambler

ONLY YOU

DENISE GROVER SWANK

FOREVER

NEW YORK   BOSTON

Copyright © 2016 by Denise Grover Swank
Excerpt from *Until You* copyright © 2016 by Denise Grover Swank
Cover design by Elizabeth Turner
Cover image from Shutterstock
Cover copyright © 2016 by Hachette Book Group, Inc.

Forever
Hachette Book Group
1290 Avenue of the Americas
New York, NY 10104
hachettebookgroup.com
twitter.com/foreverromance

Originally published as an ebook.
First mass market edition: October 2016

Forever is an imprint of Grand Central Publishing.
The Forever name and logo are trademarks of Hachette Book Group, Inc.
The publisher is not responsible for websites (or their content) that are not owned by the publisher.
The Hachette Speakers Bureau provides a wide range of authors for speaking events. To find out more, go to www.hachettespeakersbureau.com or call (866) 376-6591.

ISBNs: 978-1-4555-3976-5 (mass market) 978-1-4555-3977-2 (ebook)

Printed in the United States of America
OPM
10 9 8 7 6 5 4 3 2 1

ONLY YOU

Chapter One

This place is a piece of shit." Kevin Vandemeer stood in the front yard of the two-bedroom home he'd purchased sight unseen, running his hand over his head.

"Well, of course it is," his sister, Megan, said.

He turned to her, his mouth dropping open. "You purposely found me a piece-of-shit house? I know I was an asshole when we were kids, but this seems excessive for payback."

She shook her head in annoyance. "Stop being a drama queen. You said you wanted a flip house. This is a house to flip."

"That I could *live in*." He punctuated the last two words with his hand.

"*Noooo*, you said to find you a house that would make a good investment."

He swung his hand toward the two-story bungalow. The bright blue paint had peeled off in massive chunks. The covered front porch ran the length of the front of the house, although the right side dipped down, probably because the right pillar was missing. It had been replaced with several concrete blocks, then a few bricks, and finally, on top, a canned good. He took a step closer. "*Is that a can of pork and beans?*"

A grin spread across her face. "See? Your first dinner in your new home."

His gaze swung back to her. "Megan..."

She put her left hand on her small, rounded belly. He hadn't seen her since Christmas, and he'd had a hard enough time dealing with the wedding ring on her finger, much less the fact that she was pregnant.

"Kevin, look." The teasing tone was gone, seriousness replacing the merriment in her eyes. "I know it seems daunting, but you needed a project after everything...and this seemed like it would take up a lot of your time."

He ignored the *after everything* lead-in. He was starting to regret telling his sister about his latest breakup. "My new job is going to take up plenty of my time. *This* place is going to take the rest of my life. How did this even pass inspection?"

"Well..." She sounded insulted. "It didn't."

"What the hell are you talking about, Megan?"

"It's a flip house, Kevin. You take what you get and make the best of it."

"It looks like the whole place is about to fall into a sinkhole."

"It's not that bad."

"Let me be the judge of that. I want to see inside." He paused, horror washing through him. "Tell me you've been inside."

"Of course I've been inside." But she sounded unconvincing.

Well, shit. There was no telling what kind of mess he was going to find in there. Might as well find out what twenty-two thousand dollars in cash had bought him. Although in hindsight, that should have been a major clue. He'd chalked it up to the cheaper cost of living in the Midwest. Now he felt like an idiot.

Buying the house had seemed like a good idea at the time. He'd come back to his hometown because he needed a change. After twelve years in the marines, his second tour in Afghanistan had been enough to convince him he was ready for civilian life. So it had seemed fortuitous when his lifelong best friend practically begged Kevin to come work with him.

Kevin hesitantly took the executive contractor job even though he felt significantly underqualified. He'd protested that he didn't know the first thing about overseeing a construction project, let alone one as big as the shopping mall Matt had taken on.

"I need someone who can organize the financial end and watch the overspending. You may not have been a drill sergeant, but you sure as hell act like one. You're perfect," Matt had said.

Kevin had accepted the job for a variety of reasons. One, it was as different as he could get from trying to root out the Taliban in small Afghan villages. The horrors he had seen would haunt him to his dying day. And, two, he wanted to be part of his niece or nephew's life as well as have a chance to get closer to his sister.

After seeing the hellhole she'd bought him, he was reconsidering the second part of number two.

"Keys." He reached out his hand and she placed two keys in his palm.

"I'm not sure you need them, though. The lock on the front door doesn't exactly work."

"Then what exactly does it do?"

She gave him a hopeful grin. "Sits there and looks pretty."

This situation was going from bad to worse. "Am I going to find a homeless man sleeping in my basement?"

She cringed. "More like a family of squirrels in the attic."

Releasing a groan, he stomped across the front yard, tripping on an exposed tree root and nearly falling on his face.

"Be careful," she called after him. "The front yard is like a minefield."

"Thank you, Captain Obvious."

She laughed, and he made his way up the steps. At least they were made of concrete and looked fairly stable.

He paused, taking in the sight of the first house he'd ever owned. What the hell had he been thinking? His life had gone to shit—there was no denying that—but why had he trusted his sister to find him a place to live?

But, after *everything*, he'd wanted something familiar. Plus, his sister had recently moved back to Blue Springs, Missouri, after living in Seattle for years. After her entire wedding fiasco, he'd realized he barely knew her. Last summer, she'd shown up three days before her wedding with the man everyone presumed to be her fiancé. But he'd turned out to be a guy she'd met on the plane ride home. Kevin had kicked himself for months afterward, telling himself if he'd been more active in his sister's life he would have known that the first guy was an asshole and the second was an imposter. She seemed happy now, but he planned to be around to see if it was really true.

Megan called after him. "Be careful on the...second board."

His foot fell through a porch slat and tossed him forward,

the front door breaking his fall, until it swung inward and he fell on his face flat on floor.

"*Megan.*"

"Yeah...the porch has some wood rot. The boards need to be replaced."

"And my ankle?"

"God, I know men are babies, but you were a marine, Kevin Vandemeer. Isn't your motto Live free or die?"

"It's Semper fidelis. Always faithful. And you better be damn glad I'm faithful to not killing my only sister."

"In case you start to reconsider, just remember I'm giving you a niece or nephew in a few months."

"In the spirit of this sibling bonding time, I think it's fair to tell you that's the only thing saving your ass at the moment."

"Come on, Kevin. Don't be so cranky."

"*Cranky?*" He rolled to his side and glared back at her. "You think I'm *cranky*? You just pissed away over twenty thousand of my money!" He realized his voice was rising, but he didn't give a shit.

"Let's just go inside and I'll show you it's not as bad as you think it is, so stop being so cranky."

"I'm not cranky!" Somehow he suspected the inside was worse, but he was good and stuck now. And, speaking of stuck, he sat up and jerked his foot out of the hole, pulling off his shoe in the process. "*Goddamn it!*"

She grinned at him from the bottom of the steps. "Well, if the shoe fits..."

"Not funny." He crawled over to the hole and pulled his cell phone out of his jeans pocket, shining the flashlight down into the abyss. He found his shoe, but next to it was a pair of black beady eyes that shined back at him before whatever it was scurried for the corner. He jerked backward and pointed to the hole. "What the hell is *that*?"

She cocked her eyebrows. "It's a hole. I'm so glad all those years in the marines taught you some valuable discerning skills."

"There's something alive down there!"

She leaned her head back and groaned. "You are such a baby. It's probably a raccoon or a possum." Then she stomped up the steps and reached for his phone. "Give me that."

"I don't think you should be messing around with a wild animal in your condition. What if it attacks you?"

She knelt on the porch next to the hole. "I doubt it's going to jump out and chew off my face. And even if it does, I don't need my face to give birth. You'll just be stuck looking at the grisly scars during the holidays. Now give me your phone."

He knew that look from when they were kids. She wasn't budging until he caved, so he saved them both time and handed her his mobile. "Don't drop it. I've heard raccoons are like pack rats."

"But what if he needs to watch raccoon porn? I wonder what that's like...do they show lady raccoons doing the nasty in a trash can?" She leaned forward and shined the flashlight on his phone into the space, then she lay down on the porch and reached her arm down into the two-foot-wide space.

"What the hell are you doing, Megan?" he barked out in a panic. "You're going to get bitten!"

She sat up, holding a tiny gray kitten in her hand. "I think your data plan is safe." She held the now mewling animal in her hand and lifted it in front of her face. "What do you think, cutie? Do you want Kevin's phone?"

She cuddled it close to her chest and gave him the phone. "Get your shoe and I'll give you the grand tour after I pee."

"Does this place even have running water?"

"Ha. Ha," she said in a dry tone. "People in Africa would call this a palace."

"Twenty-two-grand money pit is more like it."

He was totally screwed.

Chapter Two

H olly Greenwood sat in the shade of the trees in her back-yard, surrounded by flowering shrubs, her feet in the baby pool her cousin Melanie had bought weeks ago as a joke, saying they were living the good life now that they had ac-quired a swimming pool for their grandmother's house—the home they now shared.

Holly had to admit it helped cool her down as she watched Melanie's rambunctious Chihuahua burn off some energy, and it wasn't just the late June temperature she needed help cooling down from. Her boss had been in a *mood* today, es-pecially after Holly had presented her decorating plans for a fund-raiser and Nicole had found a mistake in the budget. Holly had an associate degree in hospitality, but Nicole Van-demeer had experience that was far more valuable.

Holly wanted to own her own wedding-planning busi-ness, and after years of working at a local hotel, she'd jumped at the chance to work beside one of the best event planners in the area. Holly told herself the experience she was getting was worth putting up with Nicole, but some days made her question her fortitude.

A bee landed on the Chihuahua's nose, but the dog batted it away, then gave chase.

"Killer, leave that bee alone. You're going to get stung."

The dog ignored her and started to bark.

"Killer, *come*." The last thing Holly needed tonight was Mrs. Darcy—the neighbor who lived immediately behind her—to call the police because Mel's five-pound dog was barking. Any other night Holly would try to play peacemaker, but between Nicole's attitude today and her grandmother's dementia, she'd lost whatever incentive was left in her.

Her visit with her grandmother at the health-care center after work today was still weighing heavily on her mind. Grandma Barb had been having more and more frequent bouts of memory loss, but completely forgetting Holly was her granddaughter was a new development.

The dog suddenly stopped barking and ran to Holly, sitting next to her chair and waiting for a treat. Holly chuckled. Her cousin had trained Killer to obey commands with pieces of deli turkey. Now he expected rewards for his obedience. Holly only had a bag of Cheetos, so she pulled one out, broke off a small end, and tossed it to Killer while she popped the other end in her mouth. Killer scarfed his treat then barked, begging for more.

Dinner of champions.

On nights when Melanie worked, Holly rarely found the gumption to cook for herself. If she was feeling good about the day, she'd make a sandwich or a salad, but more and more lately she came home exhausted and frustrated, and she resorted to whatever she could grab.

She had eaten several more Cheetos, the crumbs dropping

all over her shirt, when her phone vibrated. She almost didn't answer, not feeling up to dealing with Nicole. She was known for calling at all hours of the day or night, but tonight she was scoping out a competition's party. What if it was Happy Dale Retirement Community calling about her grandmother? They had given her a sedative before Holly left, but what if it hadn't calmed her down? Holly sighed in relief when she saw her cousin's name on the caller ID.

"Hey, Melanie."

"How was your day, Sunshine?"

She smiled, even if the nickname made her a little sad. Their grandmother had nicknamed them Sunshine and Storm Cloud. Holly had been Sunshine for her bright and shiny disposition, while Melanie had been more waterworks and moodiness. "It sucked."

"I had a feeling your presentation to Nicole would be stressful, so I left you a surprise in the fridge. Did you find it yet?"

Holly hopped out of the lawn chair and padded across the lawn to the house, the dog on her heels. "No."

"I'm crushed," she teased. "I made your favorite."

She gasped when she pulled the refrigerator door open and saw the foil-covered casserole dish on the top shelf. "You didn't!"

"I did. Lasagna."

"Mel..."

"It's not that big of a deal. You've had a few bad days and junk food is your comfort food. At least eat something with *some* nutritional value."

Killer started barking in front of the living room window.

"Killer, be quiet!"

"What's he barking at?" Melanie asked, sounding worried. "One of the older women on the neighborhood watch said some cars had been broken into. Is the front door locked?"

Melanie was prone to exaggeration, but Holly had heard rumors of the break-ins, too. She walked over to the window and noticed a U-Haul parked in the street. "It looks like someone's moving in next door. I didn't know that junk pit had sold."

"Seriously?" her cousin asked, annoyed. "I told you about this last week. Hot single guy. Remember? You were busy working on that wedding proposal and you kept nodding and saying, 'Uh-huh.' I *knew* you weren't paying attention."

"Wait." Holly shook her head, trying to remember the conversation. Her cousin had been rattling on and on about the house next door, but Holly had been so focused on the McHenry wedding design she'd tuned her out. "You *met* him?"

"Okay," Melanie conceded, "so I don't know that he's hot, but I *do* know that he's single. The Realtor made sure to tell me."

"So?"

"*So?* You need to get back into dating world. Your vagina's probably shriveled up by now."

Holly groaned. "Not this again."

"Maybe you should burn off some of that work frustration in the bedroom," Melanie teased. "They say hate sex is hot."

"I'm pretty sure you're supposed to hate the person you're having sex with, not someone else. And I'm not having sex with anyone."

"So you're becoming a nun?"

"No, I've been reconsidering my priorities."

Melanie laughed. "Maybe you can piss off our new

neighbor and then have sex with him. Have you seen him yet?"

"No. Oh, wait." Holly looked out the window again and saw movement in the trees. "A guy just walked from the van into the house."

"Is he hot?"

She craned her neck to look, but the limbs from the overgrown trees in the yard obstructed her view. "I have no idea. His back is to me and the trees are blocking him."

"Go out and get the mail."

"*What?*"

"Walk to the curb and get the mail!"

"I can't do that!"

"Why the hell not? You walk to the street, get the mail, and walk back in. And you just happen to cast your gaze over to the house next door. You have to look somewhere. Play it cool, Holly."

"I've never played it cool in my life. When I get embarrassed, I can't make eye contact. You've lived with me for nearly twenty-five years. You know this."

"What's there to be embarrassed about? Getting one's mail isn't a criminal offense. That's only if you steal someone else's. Oh! You could take his mail out of his box and take it to him to introduce yourself. Say it was delivered to us by mistake."

"I'm not going to do that!"

"Well, you don't have to—yet. We'll save that as a last resort. I can't see you committing a felony without a few drinks first."

"Melanie!"

"Are you getting the mail yet?"

"No. I'm still inside talking to you." If she craned her neck any more she'd have to visit the chiropractor to get her spine realigned, but it was all for nothing. She couldn't see a thing.

"That's good. I'll provide your cover. Then it won't be awkward if he catches you staring at him. You just keep talking to me on the phone and lift your hand in a tiny wave. Now go!"

Holly opened the front door. "I hate you right now."

Melanie laughed. "No, you don't. I made you lasagna."

Holly had a feeling she was going to regret this, but she walked down the front steps anyway. "Aren't you supposed to be working?"

"I'm on break."

"You just started your shift an hour ago!"

"Never mind me—have you gone outside yet?"

"I'm halfway to the curb."

"Do you see him?"

"How could I see him?" she whispered, hoping her voice didn't carry. "I'm walking away from our house."

"Ever hear of looking over your shoulder?"

"I thought the whole point of this endeavor is to spy on our new neighbor without making it look like I was spying on him."

"Holly." Melanie groaned. "Why do you have to be so literal?"

She stopped at the curb and opened the mailbox door, keeping her gaze down.

"Well?"

"I'm getting the mail, Melanie!" She held the phone to her ear with her shoulder and pulled the stack of envelopes from the box.

"Will you just look at his house already?"

"Yeah...*Oh*!" she squealed in excitement.

"I knew it! He's hot, isn't he? Does he have his shirt off?"

"No. I just got a fifty-percent-off coupon to Bath and Body Works."

"Oh, my God, Holly. You're killing me."

"I'm almost out of Wild Honeysuckle shower gel. And obviously you love it, too, since you've been using it."

"Will you focus? Look at the freaking house!"

Holly darted her eyes up and saw a pair of denim-covered legs walking out the front door and toward the truck. The view of the top part of his body was obstructed by the tree limbs. "I can see him," she whispered, her face feeling warm. "He's got long legs."

"Don't get me wrong, legs are nice, but at the moment, I'm more interested in the top half. What's he look like?"

"I can't see his face," she hissed, standing in the street with her shoulder shoved up to her ear. She watched him hoist a box out of the truck. "The overgrown trees are hiding him. Can I go inside now?"

Melanie groaned. "No. That's not enough. We need more information."

"He drives an old truck and wears jeans that hug his butt," Holly said as she took several steps toward her house. He was carrying the box through his front door. "He has a very nice butt."

"I knew it!" Melanie shouted in her ear. "And it's an ass. Even twelve-year-olds are too mature to say 'butt.' What else do you see?"

"Nothing. He's gone inside and so am I."

"That's a great idea! Follow him inside."

"Not *his* house. *Ours.* Are you crazy?"

"No, I suppose you wouldn't. That's okay."

Holly pushed out a breath of relief that her cousin was going to let this go.

"You need an excuse."

"Melanie!" She shouted as she walked through the front door.

"Oh! I know! The lasagna. Take it over as a *welcome to the neighborhood* offering."

Holly gasped. "You traitor! You didn't make that lasagna for *me*! You made it for me to take to him!"

"Calm down. I had no idea he was moving in today— only an idiot would move into that house—but why not use it to your advantage?"

"If you think he's an idiot, why do you want me to meet him?"

"Maybe he's an adorable idiot . . . with a rippling six-pack. I mean, he *is* flipping the house. Hot construction guy . . . no shirt . . ."

"Am I meeting him for me or *you*?"

"You, Sunshine. I'm with Darren right now, remember? Besides, no one said you were looking for your future husband. You're just looking for a good time. Now go."

Holly tossed the mail on the kitchen counter. "I'm not sharing my lasagna."

"It's a huge dish, Holly. You don't have to take him the whole thing. Just take part of it."

She didn't answer.

"Come on. You know you want to . . ."

She did. Kind of. But the thought of walking over with a casserole filled her with dread. All she needed was a large L painted on her forehead. The whole move reeked of desperation.

"I'll clean up the dishes for a week," Melanie said.

She leaned her butt against the kitchen counter. "Two."

"Are you kidding me?" Melanie asked in disbelief. "Why am *I* paying the price for *you* to meet a guy?"

"I'm perfectly fine sharing my lasagna with Killer."

"When I come home I'm taking that lasagna over to him myself. *All of it.*"

She would, too. Holly let out a guttural growl. "*Fine.* But if I do this, you can't bug me about not dating for an entire month. I'm marking on the calendar in the kitchen in case you forget."

"Okay. One month, but you have to make an effort to talk to him, otherwise you can't hold me to the date part."

"And how do you know I won't just tell you that I did?"

"Because you're a terrible liar. I'll know."

Holly pushed out a sigh. "*Melanie...*"

"Text me when you get back." Then she hung up.

Grumbling, Holly pulled the thirteen-by-nine casserole dish out of the fridge. The question was how to take it to him. Cut some out and put it on a plate? That would look tacky. She *could* give him the entire thing.

No freaking way that was going to happen.

She found an eight-by-eight dish in the cabinet, then cut what looked like an eight-inch square in the pasta. The transfer was a disaster. Picking up a piece that big was unmanageable, and the lasagna broke in half. She put both pieces in and tried to pat them back together, but it was obvious it wasn't whole. It was also obvious the lasagna hadn't started out in the original dish—one look at the one-inch gap on one side was proof enough of that. She popped it in the microwave for five minutes while she started to throw together a salad, then stopped. If she wanted to impress him, salad wasn't the way to do that. And damn her, but she did kind of want to impress him. She grabbed two beers out of the fridge and put them in a small brown bag. The microwave dinged and she pulled out the lasagna, trying to smash the cheese over the gaps, then gave up and covered the entire mess with aluminum foil. She tossed a plastic fork and a napkin into the brown bag with the beers, then took a deep breath and headed out the door.

Why was she doing this?

She glanced back at the messy kitchen, pots and dishes from Melanie's cooking filling the sink.

She *hated* doing dishes.

Killer followed her out the door, then let out his displeasure when she shut the door before he could get out.

"I'll be back, you big baby," she said to the door, then started across the yard, the dog's angry yaps following her.

Great.

She stood at the bottom of his porch, looking up at the partially open front door and listening to her cousin's disgruntled dog. The casserole dish was burning her hand and she was having serious second thoughts. Her new neighbor was going to think she was a nutcase—which she was, courtesy of her cousin. All she had to do was dump this off, then head home. Sure she was supposed to try to talk to him, but she'd drop off the food, exchange a few pleasantries, then leave.

Easy-peasy.

She quickly climbed the two steps to the porch and sidestepped the hole in front of the door. This place was even more of a disaster than she'd thought. She rapped on the door frame and waited. Killer renewed his barking efforts and she glanced over at her house, worried that Mrs. Darcy would hear him and call animal control.

"Hey."

She whipped her head around, her breath catching when she saw the man standing in the doorway. He had to be the most good-looking man she'd ever seen. He was tall—tall enough that she had to tilt her head to look up at him—but the view was worth the effort. His dark brown hair was

cropped short, but the unruly short waves suggested he was
growing it out or needed a trim, and while she didn't care for
men with beards, the few days' growth of stubble on his face
made her fingers itch to touch it. His chest and shoulders
filled out his light gray T-shirt, and the previously noticed
dark jeans clung to his hips. Never in her twenty-nine years
had Holly reacted to man like she was now. She was literally
tongue-tied.

His chocolate brown eyes swept from her face, down her
body, then back up again as he stood in place waiting for her
to say something.

She'd heard of women doing this, acting like an imbecile
over a man, but not her. Never her.

"Can I help you?"

"I...uh..." she stammered.

Lines creased his forehead as he frowned. "Are you
okay?"

Oh, my God. She was making an utter fool out of herself.
She cast her gaze to the floor, trying to get herself together.
Say something, Holly. Anything. The hole in the porch floor
caught her attention. "I can't believe you're actually moving
into the Miller house. It's falling apart."

The blood rushed to her face. *Oh, my God. Did I really
just say that?*

He laughed, but it sounded pained. "So I've noticed."

Why was she so awkward? Why couldn't she be more
like Melanie?

He shifted his weight, his shoulder leaning into the door
frame. "Unless you're a very generous Jehovah's Witness,
I'm guessing that's for me?"

"Uh...yeah..." She looked down at the dish in her hand,
now all too aware that it was still hot. She tried to shift it
from her palm to her fingertips, the dish tipping sideways. It

started to fall and she tried to catch it with her forearm, but the man grabbed it from her hand.

"Whoa. Runaway casserole." He chuckled. He stood in front of her now, so close she could smell his musky shampoo mixed with his sweat, which wasn't as bad a combination as she would have expected. In fact, it was quite the opposite. Her chest tightened and she forced herself to take a natural breath.

"Yeah..." *Jiminy Christmas, Holly. Get yourself together.* "It's lasagna."

"Even better."

"I didn't make it." Brilliant. Just freaking brilliant.

He laughed and lifted the loose foil. "So you got a frozen lasagna from Costco and stuffed part of it in this casserole dish and brought it over to impress me?" He grinned at her, his gorgeous brown eyes dancing.

"What? No!" Oh, God. Could she just turn around and go home now? Did this constitute talking to him?

He watched her, waiting for further explanation.

"I...uh..." Then she remembered the bag in her hand and shoved it out toward him, punching him in the stomach. He released a soft grunt.

Could this get any worse? She started to take a step back, but he shifted the casserole dish and grabbed her arm, pulling her forward until his chest stopped her. She rested her free hand on him, feeling his hard muscles under her palm.

Oh, my God. She was touching his chest. His sexy chest.

Panic washed through her and she tried to jerk away, but he held her firmly in place. She hadn't dated in a while, and she knew a lot of the new dating apps had changed the rules. Did bringing a man food mean she wanted a booty call? She was going to *kill* Melanie.

She narrowed her eyes, then said in a haughty tone, "I'm not ready to sleep with you yet."

An amused grin spread across his face. "While I'm happy to hear that's on the agenda for later, that's not why I'm holding you *now*. You were about to step into the hole." He tilted his head toward it.

Her eyes sank closed and her face combusted.

He dropped his hold on her arm and took the bag, moving slowly like she was a skittish animal. "What's in the bag?"

"Beer." She couldn't bear to look at him, instead taking a couple of steps backward while making sure to avoid the hole. "Yeah...I...You're busy...."

"I can't accept your store-bought lasagna," he said, sounding serious.

Who didn't eat lasagna? "What? Oh...you don't eat meat? *Oh!* It's not store-bought. My cousin made—"

"It looks like there's enough for both of us. I figure maybe we should have dinner together before we hop into bed."

"What? *Oh.*" This had moved well past disaster and was quickly moving into *relocating to another state to avoid ever seeing him again* territory. Her breath caught again at both his suggestion and the way he was watching her now—a mixture of curiosity and interest. Well, *hello.* She'd just let him know she was thinking about sleeping with him. Still, she'd never had a man look at her with such intensity, and a shiver ran down her spine.

His eyes held hers and she felt herself melting.

"There's only one fork in the bag." That was brilliant. Why was she still standing here? *Run!* But her feet had somehow become disconnected from her brain.

His grin turned wicked. "We can share."

Her face burned at the thought of their mouths touching

the same utensil. Her eyes shifted to his mouth and she suddenly wondered what it would be like to kiss him. Would he hold her tightly to his chest like he had moments ago?

Oh, my God. She had just turned into every clichéd woman she'd made fun of since high school. What the hell was happening to her? Without another word, she spun around and ran back to her house, her foot catching on a tree root and making her stumble. She looked back at him, horrified to see him watching her, his amusement mixed with confusion.

When she got inside the house, she shut the door and locked it, wondering if she could convince Melanie into building a six-foot privacy fence to run the length of their property.

Because there was no way she could ever face that man again.

Chapter Three

~

Kevin watched the cute blonde run back to her house next door, tripping on a tree root on the way. He couldn't help noticing the way her jean shorts clung to the curve of her ass. He was still standing in the same spot—grinning like a damn fool—when he heard her door slam.

Stand your ground, marine.

He let out a loud sigh and went back inside, casserole dish in hand. He was used to women falling at his feet, but there was a vulnerability to his neighbor he didn't usually see in the women who came on to him, and he was intrigued. Intrigued enough to consider dropping his self-imposed six-month break from women.

And that was a bad thing.

If he'd learned nothing else from his last breakup, he had learned that he had absolutely *terrible* taste in women. He'd had a string of disastrous relationships, but the horrifying end of his last relationship had brought him to the conclusion that it was time to reevaluate his love life along with his career choice. So as he made the shift into civilian life, it seemed like a good time to shake up everything and self-impose a ban on women. He had plenty of other things to focus on: working on his house, re-acclimating to life in his hometown, and helping Matt reorganize his company.

"Did I hear someone at the door?" Megan asked, coming out of the bathroom, the kitten in her hand.

He lifted the casserole dish. "My neighbor."

Her eyebrows lifted. "Oh, yeah? The little old ladies in the neighborhood already looking out for you?"

He considered telling her the truth, but she'd give him more grief about his no-women rule. "Something like that."

He looked around his house and groaned, suddenly scared—and, after everything he'd seen, it took a lot to scare him. But he had a feeling this place was going to suck up more money than anyone realized. "Okay, let's get this tour started."

Cuddling the kitten with one hand, Megan waved around the room with the other. "This is the living room."

The hardwood floor needed to be refinished, and the window moldings were small and skimpy, not to mention lumpy and chipped after multiple layers of paint. "Okay..."

Megan shot him a glare. "This room is easy. Refinish the floor, repaint, add new trim, and you're good to go."

He shook his head, then headed toward the kitchen.

The dining room walls were covered with blue-and-pink floral wallpaper. The four-foot-tall built-in cabinets surrounding the window were impressive, but the ugliest glass and brass light fixture he'd ever seen, which was currently hanging off center in the room, had to go.

"The dining room."

"It's hideous."

"Of course it is. But it only needs cosmetic changes, although I think we should get an engineer out to see if that wall is load bearing." She pointed to the wall separating this room from the living room. "You could tear it down for an open floor plan."

"Someone's been watching too much HGTV."

Ignoring him, she led him past a staircase, stopping at a door underneath the stairs. "This leads to the basement, but we'll check it out later."

The way she announced it made him worried about what was down there.

"And here is the kitchen."

He followed her through a small door and stopped in his tracks. "Oh, my God."

She gave him a tentative smile. "I know it looks bad, but it can all be fixed."

"Bad?" He moved into the room and spun in a circle. "You think this is *bad*? This is a freaking train wreck." He took a breath, then wiped sweat from his forehead. "Why is it so hot in here? Is the air-conditioning not on?"

"About that..."

"What?" His voice was hard, but she seemed undeterred.

"There is no air-conditioning, and the furnace probably needs to be replaced."

"Megan!" His voice boomed in the small room. "What the hell have you done?"

She moved in front of him, the kitten still cradled in her arm. "I know it's daunting, but you have no idea how much money you can make off this house. I did my homework. You can hire someone to do most of it and still make thirty grand profit."

That caught his attention. "How do you know that?"

"I had three contractors come in and make bids."

He took a step back and ran a hand over his head. "Why the hell didn't you lead off with that?"

She laughed. "Because it was more fun watching you freak out."

He looked at the place with a new appreciation, although there wasn't a single redeeming quality about the kitchen. Half the drawers were crooked, obviously broken, and several of the cabinet doors were missing. The pink laminate counter was stained and chipped. The sink was a shallow, scratched-up stainless-steel bowl. The range looked like it was original to the house—about fifty years old—and there was no dishwasher. "This room is a disaster."

"You can put in a new one for ten thousand."

"That's a third of the budget you mentioned."

She shrugged. "Kitchens sell."

"Where am I going to come up with thirty thousand dollars? I used up most of my savings to get this place. I've only got ten left."

"We'll figure it out." For the first time she looked uncertain. "I'll help you, Kevin."

"How are you going to help me? You're pregnant."

"Yeah, I'm pregnant, not an invalid. I can do things and I can give you money. As a business partner."

"Megan."

"Look, the fund-raising position I took at the food pantry phased out when they merged with the community center, and most places don't want to hire a pregnant woman." She held up a hand when he started to protest. "Yeah, I know it's illegal, but the fact is that I haven't applied anywhere. I'm still trying to decide if I'm going to stay home for a few years after the baby comes, so it didn't seem fair to apply for a job I might only stay at for a few months."

He gave her a pointed look. "So you're telling me that you're bored? And you saw my house as a project."

"No. I saw it as a chance for you do something that will make you some money and keep you occupied since you've sworn off women." She bumped her shoulder into his arm. "Besides, no woman would ever want to come home with you to this dump."

He was beginning to regret sharing his no-women policy with her. "Very funny."

"What's done is done. Let's just figure out how to fix this place up and make it livable."

Still carrying the kitten, Megan took him upstairs to see the two small bedrooms and bath. The bedrooms had holes in the walls, and the bathroom shower was covered in so much mildew Kevin was sure the EPA should have been called in. But the bedrooms and hallway had hardwood floors that only needed refinishing and the bathroom looked like a simple gut job.

"How the hell can I live here?" he asked, staring out the front bedroom window at the U-Haul in the street. "Especially if I'm renovating it."

"You told me you didn't bring much furniture. A mattress, a few chairs, and a bunch of boxes. You won't have much in the way."

"I meant here with all the construction. This place is hardly livable as it is."

She shrugged. "I guess it's up to you. You can always live with Mom and Dad."

His irritation rose. "The purpose of having you look for my house was for the express purpose of *not* living with Mom. Not even for one night."

"You can live here *and* work on it. People do it all the time. Trust me on this."

He tried to open the window but met resistance. He gave it a good jerk and the window shot up, making him stumble backward.

This house was one giant piece of shit. But now it was *his* piece of shit. Maybe he could make this work. Megan was right—he needed something to do to keep him preoccupied. "Okay. I'm game to try this."

"That's the spirit!" Her phone rang and she pulled it out of her purse, cringing as she headed down the stairs. "It's Mom. I forgot to mention that she wants to come see your new house."

He shook his head. "No way."

"You think I want her knowing I picked out this dump for you?" She laughed. "I'll stall her, but you owe me," she said as she walked to the door.

"Not by a long shot, sis. You owe *me*. And I plan to collect. Big-time."

She turned around and reached up on her tiptoes to kiss his cheek. "I love you. You have no idea how happy I am you're home."

He grinned. "So Mom will have someone else to obsess over."

She tilted her head, mischievousness in her eyes. "Well, there's that, too."

"Sorry to be the bearer of bad news, but you'll trump me every time with that little niece or nephew of mine."

"For now." She walked out onto the porch.

"What's that mean?"

She turned back to him, grinning. She was up to something, of that he was sure, but damned if he knew what it was. "Oh!" She handed him the sleeping kitten in her arms. "Your first pet."

"I am *not* keeping this kitten. I don't do pets."

She headed to her car, not bothering to look back. "Whatever you say."

She gave him a wave as she drove away, then he looked down at the kitten, who had snuggled into his arm.

He was in deep shit.

                    *   *   *

Holly shut the door behind her and pressed her back against it as she covered her face with her hand and groaned. She'd acted like a complete and utter idiot. But she'd never see him again, right? Sure, her neighbors were friendly and were in everyone else's business, but he was going to fix it up and move on.

At least she sure as hell hoped so.

Her phone dinged in the kitchen, alerting her to a text. She stomped toward it, her irritation with her cousin mounting with each step. Melanie had sent three texts, all saying the same thing: *Well???*

Holly texted back. *I'm going to kill you.*

Melanie texted back within seconds. *Did you talk to him?*

Yes. That one word said so much, yet nothing at all.

It had been a long time since she'd been this humiliated, and it didn't sit well. Holly had spent a long time outgrowing the gangly, awkward girl from high school, and this situation reeked of her past. She opened the refrigerator and pulled out what was left of her lasagna, pissed all over again.

She cut out a piece with more force than necessary, trying to figure out whom she was more mad at—her neighbor, her cousin, or herself. Which was utterly ridiculous. Why would she be angry with her neighbor? What had he done other than manhandle her to keep her from breaking her leg on his porch and be better looking than a person had a right to? She decided she could be angry with him on principle alone.

Her phone rang seconds later with her cousin's ringtone. She put her plate in the microwave and turned it on, trying to decide whether to answer or not. Her anger won out. "I mean it. I'm seriously going to kill you," she spit out after putting her phone on speaker and resting it on the counter.

Melanie laughed. "What happened? Start at the beginning."

Holly opened the fridge and grabbed a beer. "I made an utter fool of myself, that's what happened."

"Let me be the judge of that. Tell me what happened."

"Aren't you supposed to be working?"

"We're not busy at the moment, and Scott's covering the bar so I could call you. Quit stalling. Is he sexy?"

"He's…" *Hot, sexy, stunning, mind-alteringly gorgeous.* "…okay."

"How old is he?"

"I don't know, maybe early thirties." She popped the top off her bottle.

"Married?"

"No ring."

"He must be hot. You looked!"

"Only because I knew you'd ask."

"You liar. What's he look like?"

"He's short, fat, and bald."

"Try again."

Holly took a long drag of her beer, sorting through her options.

"Holly!"

"He's tall, dark, and handsome, okay? He's everything you could ever hope for."

"Me? Why not you?"

"I made a fool of myself, Mel." Her defeat seeped into her voice. "I can never, ever face that man again. I'm just about to Google-search how to build a six-foot privacy fence."

"Oh, Hol." Melanie sighed. "It couldn't have been that bad."

Holly wandered over to the table, picking up a photo of a wedding bouquet. "It was worse than bad."

Holly had been planning weddings since she was a kid, but she'd never met a man worth taking a risk on with "I do." Sure, it had been a couple of years since she'd had a serious relationship, but she'd been okay with that. Until now. Why did she feel so unsettled?

"It's okay to love somebody, Hol." Melanie's voice was warm and soft. "You don't have to chase everyone away."

"Says the woman who won't go see the woman who raised her." Holly's voice was sharper than she'd meant it to be, but Melanie's comment stung more than she cared to admit. "I saw Grandma today."

Melanie was quiet for several seconds. "So? You see her almost every day after work."

"She was worse today."

Melanie remained silent.

"Mel, she's deteriorating fast. Don't you want to see her at least one more time before she forgets us both?"

Of the two girls, Melanie had had a rougher time putting their grandmother into the health-care facility eleven months ago. As far as Holly knew, Melanie had seen her only a handful of times, and Holly had guilted her into two of them.

"She misses you, Melanie. She asks for you."

"I can't see her like that, Holly. I just can't. She's not the woman who raised us."

No, the woman who'd raised them had been strong. She took in two frightened, traumatized girls—ages five and six—when she thought she was done raising children. Instead, a year after she'd lost her husband to a heart attack she'd lost her only two sons and their wives in a fiery car accident, and taken in her two orphaned granddaughters.

Holly didn't remember their grandmother falling to pieces after the tragedy. Her only memories were of Grandma Barb's strength and compassion—the nights she rocked Holly for hours when she woke up crying for her parents. Dealing with the responsibilities of two young, rambunctious girls couldn't have been easy for a woman in her fifties, especially after losing her own children, but she'd welcomed the girls with open arms and a heart full of love. Grandma Barb's house was small, and they'd financially scraped by most of their lives, but Holly had always felt loved.

Melanie had felt equally secure in their little family, but when Grandma Barb was diagnosed with dementia, Melanie couldn't handle it. Always the more practical of the two, Melanie had started shirking responsibilities over the last year, quitting her job at an insurance agency and becoming a bartender at a local bar. Holly knew she was acting out, but it left most of the responsibilities of Grandma Barb's care on Holly's shoulders, as well as most of the household bills. And while Holly understood this was Melanie's way of dealing with another tragic loss, it didn't make things any easier.

"I know, Mel. But she's fading fast. I think you'll regret it if you don't see her." Holly felt a twinge of hope when her cousin remained silent. "Tomorrow's your day off. We could go together after I get off work."

Melanie pushed out a long breath. "I'll go, I promise. Just not tomorrow. But I noticed how you changed this from being about you to me. If I have to go see Grandma, when are you going to agree to consider having a real relationship?"

"I have enough to keep me busy," Holly said. "I don't need a man."

"No woman *needs* a man," Melanie teased, "but they have some very nice fringe benefits. Speaking of fringe benefits, I'm going out with Darren tomorrow night."

Melanie was probably using her date as her excuse not to go see their grandmother, but Holly knew better. Still, she was too tired to call her on it. "What is this? The fifth date?"

"Sixth." Holly heard the grin in her voice. "But who's counting?"

But Holly heard the hopeful tone in her cousin's voice. Melanie was falling for the guy, and hard. She didn't understand how Melanie could fall for someone so quickly, although she'd seen it happen to several friends after high school.

Maybe it was because Holly had never fallen for a guy at all. Not for lack of trying. She'd dated back in college, but no one had ever clicked. She'd spent a year with a guy in her degree program at the local community college, but she'd finally broken up with him after he'd confessed he loved her and she couldn't reciprocate.

She'd psychoanalyzed the crap out of herself, so she knew there was some merit to her cousin's statement. Holly had attachment issues that had been caused by her parents' death, but the truth was, she remembered little of her parents—which made her feel guilty as hell. Living with Mel and Grandma Barb in this house was pretty much all she'd ever known. And while she'd love to find a man to have a family with, she wouldn't settle, either. What few memories she had of her parents were of them happy and in love.

She wouldn't settle for anything less.

Chapter Four

⌇

Kevin wasn't sure what to expect when he showed up at the job site of Osborn Construction at eight o'clock the next morning. The unfinished outdoor shopping area was a multi-block strip mall with concrete exterior walls and metal studs inside. Several of the workers were milling around, while a guy was arguing with the driver of a flat-bed trailer loaded with supplies. Kevin felt completely out of his element.

Granted, he was a bit off center anyway. Between the shock of his new house and the woman who'd shown up on his doorstep, he hadn't found the peace he'd hoped being back home would bring. But last night he'd told himself he just needed to start his new job, then he'd find his center and it would all work out.

"Kevin!"

He turned to see his lifelong friend striding across the lot toward him. "Matt."

When Matt reached him, he pulled Kevin into an embrace, thumping his back. "Good to see you, man."

"Good to see you, too."

Kevin looked around at the activity, then turned back to his friend. "I think I should remind you that I don't know the first thing about running a construction company."

"Like I told you, you don't need to know construction. You just need to keep us organized and sort out the financials. Since Dad died the day-to-day running of the business has all gone to shit."

Matt smiled when he said this, but Kevin could see the pain in his friend's eyes. "Where do you need me first?"

"You sure you don't mind starting today?" Matt asked. "You can wait until Monday, so you can, you know...get settled."

Kevin laughed. "Believe it or not, I'll be more settled here."

"Then let's go to the office." Matt waved to a small trailer. They walked the short distance, passing the truck driver, who was now unloading his cargo. Matt opened the door and motioned for Kevin to climb the two steps up. He stopped short when he saw the mess. While Matt had warned him that the office was unorganized, he hadn't expected *this*.

Kevin didn't do unorganized.

But he reminded himself that was why he was there.

After his initial shock, he noticed a young woman sitting at a desk with a phone pressed to her ear. Her free hand tugged on her long auburn ponytail, the color a sharp contrast to her black tank top.

"That's Carly," Matt said, walking in behind him and closing the door. "She's the receptionist, bookkeeper, and the token woman in the crew."

She covered the mouthpiece and grinned up at Matt as she mouthed, "Watch it."

"Carly, this is Captain Kevin Vandemeer. Our new CFO."

Then she turned to Kevin and her smile widened. "Well, *hello*, Captain Vandemeer. Are you a pirate? You can pillage me any day of the week."

Kevin laughed and gave her a nonflirtatious smile—he hoped. Two months ago, he would have reacted much differently. But he was surprised how quickly he'd gotten used to ignoring women's attention—with the exception of the sexy blonde on his doorstep last night. He'd chalked that up to a momentary lapse brought on from the shock over the state of his house. He chose to ignore the fact that he'd thought about her all evening after Megan left. Or that he'd thought about putting the rest of the lasagna onto a paper plate and returning the empty casserole dish so he could see her again.

But now Carly was watching him like he was the cherry on a hot fudge sundae, and he needed to make it clear he was unavailable. Especially since they would be working together. "Just Kevin," he said, trying to maintain a bit of distance in his voice. "I ditched the *captain* when I left the marines."

"No dating the employees, Carly," Matt said, narrowing his eyes. "You know the rules. We don't want our new employee filing a sexual harassment complaint on the first day."

She leaned forward, her hand still over the mouthpiece. "If he's telling me what to do, that technically makes him my boss. You never said I couldn't date the boss."

"Yeah, because I knew you had your eyes set on that new electrician and you were never interested in me. But hands off Kevin. He's here to get this place organized. The mess is enough to scare him away. We don't want you adding the final straw."

She rolled her eyes, then turned her attention to the phone. "Yes, I'm still here." Then she started talking about a shipment of sheet metal.

Matt leaned into Kevin's ear. "She's a bit headstrong, but she's better than the last bookkeeper. She just up and left us, for no reason at all."

Kevin was wondering if he should give that option serious consideration himself. The small trailer was piled with stack upon stack of papers. There were even stacks on the floor. "What did you have in mind?" Kevin asked. "You have someplace you want me to start?"

Matt grabbed a laptop off a second desk, which was piled with even more papers, and handed him the computer. "I've had Carly set you up with an employee e-mail and grant you access to all the programs. Look everything over and see if you can get it under control."

"Have you considered a bonfire?" Kevin asked, lifting an eyebrow.

His friend laughed, but he looked pained. "Dad ran it all, and you know how territorial he was. While he officially made me a partner five years ago, he never shared his organizational system, which meant I didn't know shit when he died. Right now, I'm splitting my time between running the site and the administrative part, and it's just not working. Both sides are falling apart." He turned his back to Carly and lowered his voice. "I can run the crew as long as I'm out there." He pointed his thumb toward the door. "I need someone to run the business."

"No offense, Matt, but don't you just need an office manager?"

"No. I need a CFO—someone to fill Dad's shoes. I know you haven't been around to see it, but we've had incredible growth over the last ten years. Dad built this company into a multi-million-dollar corporation. And while he may not have taught me how to run it, the truth was I wasn't much interested in the money part. I'm more of a hands-on guy."

"And you're running your multi-million-dollar corporation out of a trailer?"

Matt shrugged. "We have an actual office, but right now it's easier for me to run everything on the job site."

"I have to warn you, I may have double-majored in accounting and finance, but I didn't use it all that much in the Afghan mountains. I'm not sure I'm the salvation you're hoping for."

Matt clamped his hand on Kevin's shoulder. "I know you, Kev. You don't do anything half-assed. You're exactly who I need."

He shook his head, taking in the fire hazard Matt called his on-site office. "I'll give it a try."

"There you go! That's the spirit." Matt squeezed his shoulder, then dropped his hand. "I need to get out there. I'll check on you later. Do you have plans after work?"

"No," Kevin said hesitantly. "Why?"

Matt laughed. "I don't plan on taking you to the circus. Don't look so scared."

Matt knew how much Kevin hated the circus—especially clowns—but the circus comment was a little too close to home after what had happened with his last girlfriend. He couldn't stop his cringe.

Pointing his finger in Kevin's face, Matt laughed. "There's a story behind that look that I'm dying to hear. But it can keep until tonight with burgers and beers. Tyler's coming. You in?"

"Tyler?" He hadn't seen their other best friend in several years. "Yeah. Hanging out with you guys is half the reason I moved back."

Matt opened the door and had started down the steps before he turned back. "You have no idea how happy I am that you're back. And not just for this."

Kevin felt the same way, even with the daunting task. He knew it was going to take days or weeks to make sense of the books, and he knew it should have scared him, but he felt energized. He loved staring into the face of a daunting task and conquering it. Which he was ready to do with Matt's business.

He was still warming up to his house.

He'd barely gotten started when his cell phone rang. While he was expecting an apology call from his sister, he was surprised to receive it minutes before nine a.m. He'd have bet money she would wait until after lunch. Then he looked at the caller ID and groaned.

"Hello." There was no avoiding this call.

"Is this how you greet the woman who gave you life?"

"Hello, Mom."

"You were supposed to call me last night, Kevin. I want to see this secret house of yours."

He sat back, the old metal office chair creaking. "Well... things came up." He'd expected this call, too, but there was no amount of preparation that could get him ready to deal with his mother.

"I haven't seen you since Christmas, Kevin. What could be more important than seeing your mother?"

"It was a long drive from San Diego, Mom. I wanted to be fresh when I saw you."

"Fresh? I saw you covered in slime when you came from my body. How could anything be less fresh than that?"

"*Mom.* That definitely falls under TMI." He was going to be traumatized by that mental image for weeks to come.

"Surely you're fresh now, so why haven't you called me yet?"

Fresh while living in his house? Not likely. At least he had hot running water. "I'm at work. I started my job today."

"Oh…" Her voice faltered. "I thought you started next week."

"Matt said everything was a mess, and I was eager to start getting things under control."

He knew she would suggest coming over tonight. He had to nip that in the bud before it came up or he'd be even deeper in the *bad son* hole. "How about we meet for coffee this afternoon?"

She hesitated. "Why can't I come over to your house?"

He considered telling her that he had plans with his friends, but that would never fly. "My air-conditioning is out. I don't want you over in my stuffy house." Partially true. The air-conditioning would work when he had it installed.

"We're supposed to have a heat wave next week. Maybe you should stay with us until it's fixed."

"How about we discuss it at coffee? We can meet at Starbucks. What time works for you?"

"Um…" He could tell she was trying to decide whether to concede the battle for the sake of winning the war. No one ever accused his mother of being faint of heart. "I can get away at four," she said. "But it's your first day. Will you be able to leave?"

"I'm not even supposed to be here today. I'm sure Matt won't mind."

"Then I guess I'll see you at four."

Which meant he had seven hours to prepare himself.

He spent the rest of the morning digging through Osborn Construction's QuickBooks and bank accounts. He'd only glanced through the past two months, but, thankfully, the electronic files seemed to be in better shape than the physical paperwork. The stacks seemed to be more of a filing issue. Still, he was concerned about what he'd found so far.

At noon a food truck pulled up to the lot and everyone took a break, Kevin and Carly included. After her flirtatious beginning, she had settled into business mode, showing him the way they handled things and how to get into files and accounts. He'd thought the trailer was stifling with its meager window air conditioner cranking out semi-cool air, but he realized how good he had it when he stepped out into the ninety-degree heat.

"How's it going?" Matt asked, walking over to the line already forming at the authentic Mexican food truck. "You still have all your hair, so I take it as a good sign you haven't pulled it out."

Kevin grinned, wiping the sweat from his brow. "It's slow going, but so far, it's nothing I can't handle." He nodded to construction workers lined up in front of him. "How many guys do you have on the job site?"

"Right now, we're running about twenty. We're waiting on the city inspector to look over some electrical work before we move on to the rest of the wiring and let the masons finish some of their brick- and stonework. The other guys are spread out over three other smaller jobs." He looked out onto the shopping mall and pride filled his eyes. "The shopping center doesn't look like much now, but I promise it will when we're done."

"I trust your vision." Matt had sent him photos and links to some of the work he and his dad had done, and every bit of it looked high-end. Kevin had no doubt he could pull off the execution. It was the finances he was worried about. "You think you and I could sit down next week and go over everything I find?"

Matt gave him a blank look. "That bad, huh?"

Kevin shook his head, kicking himself for even mentioning it. "No. It just seems smart for me to go through it all with you and tell you what I find. After that, we can decide where to go from here."

Matt pushed out a sigh of relief. "Whew. For a moment I thought you were going to tell me we were in trouble."

Kevin forced himself to remain expressionless. From what he'd seen, he was worried it might actually be true. "Do you mind if I look at the historical financial records? Older, completed projects? The ones your dad ran so I can get a feel for how he handled everything." When Matt looked worried, Kevin gave him a smile. "No sense reinventing the wheel, right? It sounds like it worked for your dad for years. I'll just figure out what he did and duplicate it."

"Yeah...sure. They should all be in the main office. I'll warn you, though, it's all on paper. Dad didn't believe in computers. Having everything digital is fairly recent, and only because Dad's accountant put his foot down and in-sisted."

"Maybe I can look at it tomorrow." They moved closer to the window and Kevin studied the handwritten menu board while he asked, "Do you mind if I take off a little early to-day? My mom's having a coronary that I haven't seen her yet, so I suggested we meet this afternoon for coffee."

Matt burst out laughing. "I wouldn't want to be you right now, Kev. Knowing your mother, you're going to pay for that for quite some time."

He groaned. "Yeah, I know. ..." Now he just had to figure out a way to get her to agree to wait to see his house.

Matt shook his head. "God speed, my friend. You're go-ing to need all the help you can get."

"Tell me something I don't know."

Chapter Five

Nicole Vandemeer expected punctuality, something that consistently challenged Holly. She had no trouble showing up on time for client appointments, but the mornings she came in knowing she had a desk full of paperwork to tackle, she often arrived five to ten minutes late. While there was no doubt that the paperwork and the estimates were important, Holly loved the planning—coming up with the colors, and the flowers, and the themes. She poured a great deal of her heart into her work, and she was proud of what she did. The paperwork and accounting were just a necessary evil. So Holly was proud of herself for showing up on time—on a Thursday, no less—only to discover that her boss hadn't even come in yet.

For the millionth time, she considered quitting, but she couldn't bring herself to do it. Not only was she gaining invaluable experience, but her salary had also increased. Which meant Holly was good and stuck, especially since she was now making enough money to pay for her grandmother's private room at Happy Dale Retirement Community. If she quit, her grandmother would have to go back to sharing a room—something that would be difficult for her since her dementia had worsened.

She'd just have to try harder to be on time and make her boss happy. At least until she'd built up her reputation enough to support herself and her grandmother. But the thought was more depressing than she cared to admit.

She got busy working up a cost proposal for a potential wedding client, but by nine forty-five Nicole still hadn't come into the office. Holly was worried, especially since Nicole had a ten o'clock appointment. Nicole liked to give herself plenty of time to prepare before a meeting, and she'd hinted that this one was more important than usual. Nicole was meeting with a mother and daughter who were unhappy with their current wedding planner. The problem was that the wedding was less than a month away. Nicole had casually mentioned that they wanted to change everything, which sounded like a nightmare. But Nicole insisted it would be a coup d'état in the Kansas City event-planning world.

Holly might understand the appeal of this wedding if Nicole had shared the clients' names. But she'd kept them under lock and key, as though Holly would steal them from her, which was utterly ridiculous.

Nicole's paranoia was just one more reason for Holly to get her experience and run.

All Holly knew was that Nicole had insisted that this meeting had to go perfectly, and now she hadn't even shown up yet.

To expel some nervous energy, Holly straightened up the small office, made a pot of coffee, and finally called Nicole at nine fifty-two.

"Nicole, is everything okay? Did the meeting get canceled?"

"No!" Her boss sounded panicked. "I was on my way to pick up some pastries, and on my way back, I was in a minor accident."

"Oh, my God. Are you okay?"

"I'm fine, and my Navigator only has a small dent in the fender, but this police officer insists that I have to stay and fill out a report."

"Do you want to cancel the meeting?"

"No!" Nicole shouted. "It's too late to cancel. Just stall them until I get there."

Then she said, her voice fainter, "Yes, Officer. I am taking this very seriously." But Holly suspected she meant the meeting and not the accident report.

Holly cast her glance toward the front door, her breath catching when she saw a middle-aged woman at the office door. "Nicole, they're already here."

"What? They're early! Tell them I'll be there as soon as I can."

Holly hung up and placed the phone on her desk, then smoothed the wrinkles from the lap of her pale-pink skirt. The woman walked through the door, a younger version of herself following behind her.

"Good morning," Holly said, using her most cheerful voice. "Welcome to Distinctive Events. Nicole has been delayed, but I'm Holly, and I'm more than happy to get you some coffee or tea while you wait."

The younger woman's full lips pursed into a pretty pout. "Does she know how rude it is to keep her clients waiting?"

Holly clasped her hands together so the younger woman wouldn't see them shaking. Nicole had been so irritated with her lately that Holly wouldn't put it past Nicole to fire her if she screwed this up. "Yes, of course. Your meeting is very important to Nicole, but the truth of the matter is that Nicole was just involved in an auto accident."

The older woman's eyes flew open. "Oh, dear. Is she all right?"

"Yes, she insisted it was minor and that she's fine, but she's been detained giving the police report. She's quite upset about the delay and hopes to be here very soon."

The older woman waved her hand. "Of course. The important thing is that she wasn't hurt."

The glint in the younger woman's eyes suggested she didn't necessarily share the same opinion.

But the mother didn't seem to notice. She offered her hand to Holly. "I'm Miranda Johansen and this is my daughter Coraline."

Holly took her hand, appreciating the woman's firm shake while trying not to fawn over the woman. She recognized her name. Miranda Johansen was one of *the* hottest up-and-coming wedding-dress designers. Her collection in New York the previous spring had been the talk of the wedding design world. And since Holly had spent two-thirds of her life poring over bridal magazines, she knew the names of all the top designers. "Ms. Johansen, I'm honored to meet you. Your spring collection was amazing."

The woman's eyes lifted. "You attended the show?"

"No, but I saw the photos of the impressive gowns. I love the way you've updated classic styles with a contemporary edge. Pure genius." Holly turned to Coraline. "You're so lucky your mother is designing your gown." Then she paused and glanced back at the bride's mother. "I'm presuming you're designing your daughter's dress."

"Yes." Miranda sighed. "Although it's taken multiple designs to make Coraline happy."

"I can't help it if you don't get me, Mother," the daughter said through gritted teeth. While she looked like a younger version of her mother—dark hair, pale skin, bright green eyes—it was clear the two had completely different personalities.

"Can I get you something to drink?" Holly asked, hoping to defuse the situation. Nicole wouldn't be pleased if her clients were bickering when she arrived. "Coffee, tea, water?"

"I'll take a nonfat latte," Coraline said, her gaze on the photos on the walls. "With extra foam."

"I'm so sorry. While we have an espresso machine, we don't have a milk frother." Holly braced herself for Coraline's reaction.

The woman shot her a look of disbelief.

"Regular coffee will be fine for both of us," Miranda said, giving her daughter a warning look. "With cream and sugar."

Holly nodded. "I'll be right back."

She grabbed her phone off her desk and hurried to the small back kitchen, sending her boss a text.

They're here and I'm serving them coffee.

Good. I hope to be there in ten minutes.

Oh, please God, let that be true. She poured both cups, placing them on saucers on a silver tray, along with a bowl of sugar cubes and a small pitcher of cream. Presentation was everything with their more prestigious clients. With that in mind, Holly placed several chocolate biscotti on a small plate, then carried the tray out to the small client table in the corner where Miranda was sitting, her legs crossed and tucked to the side of the chair. She reeked of sophistication and class, and Holly felt way out of her league. She couldn't even fathom having as much money as half her clients had, but she was really good at faking it.

Coraline was prowling the perimeter of the small office, although there wasn't much for her to look at. She stopped, her attention drawn to a photo of the first wedding Holly had planned.

"This is quite lovely," the bride-to-be murmured, leaning closer. "Was this one of Nicole's weddings?"

Coraline was staring intently at the gorgeous photo, the sunlight catching on the fresh-fallen snow making it look like the field outside the botanical gardens' chapel was strewn with tiny crystals. The red roses in the bouquets of the bride and her two bridesmaids were deep and rich. But it was the look on the bride and groom's faces that always made Holly pause—so full of love and devotion. For a brief moment, Holly considered saying yes, but her pride wouldn't let her. "No, that was a wedding I planned. It was a lovely day, which was a relief since I had less than two weeks to pull it together."

Miranda turned to look at her with new interest. "Oh, really?"

Oh, crap. There was no way she wanted Coraline as a client. Not to mention Nicole would make her life a living hell. "Nicole and I planned it together, of course," she amended.

Miranda stood and moved closer to the photo. "I saw this in the *KC Weddings* magazine. I don't remember Nicole being listed as the planner." She turned her attention to Holly. "What part of this wedding did you work on?"

It was difficult to deny something she was so proud of. "Almost all of it."

"And you put this together in less than two weeks?" Miranda asked.

"Some of it was already done."

"Which part?"

"The couple had set the date."

Her carefully groomed eyebrows lifted. "And that's it?"

Holly pressed her lips together, then said reluctantly, "Yes."

"Do you have more photos?" Coraline asked, now interested. "A portfolio?"

She had one online, which was how she had acquired some of her wedding clients since she'd begun working for Nicole, and she handed Coraline her tablet so she could view the photos. "Nicole really is amazing. Her events have been featured in both *HERLIFE* and *435* magazine."

"How many weddings has she done?" Coraline asked, sliding her finger across the screen as she whizzed through the photos. Maybe that was a good thing. Maybe she hated what she saw.

"Distinctive Events has only been open since last November, so we've only seen a few weddings to completion at this point, although we have over a dozen in progress."

"*We?*" Coraline asked, lifting her gaze to Holly's. "You share the work equally?"

"Well, no."

"How many weddings are you overseeing and how many is Nicole?"

Holly clasped her hands in front of her, trying to keep from fidgeting. "I'm overseeing them all, but Nicole—"

Coraline turned to her mother. "I want her." She pointed her finger at Holly.

Miranda sighed, but she cast Holly a curious glance. "Coraline, darling. We're here to see Nicole."

Coraline tapped her three-inch-heeled wedged sandal. "Well, Nicole's not here, is she?" she asked in a snotty tone.

"She'll be back any moment, I promise," Holly said, taking a step forward. She had to turn this around quickly or Nicole was going to kill her. "Why don't I pour you a cup of coffee while you wait?"

"That's a good idea," Miranda said, grabbing the silver pot and pouring it into a cup. "And while we wait, tell us how you reserved the Powell Gardens chapel in less than two weeks. They are notorious for being booked out months in advance."

"Uh…a lucky fluke." Holly's pulse picked up. They weren't going to let this go. "And I had a friend who knows the director of the gardens."

"How did you deal with shuttling the guests from the parking lot to the chapel?"

Oh, shit. "Horse-drawn sleigh."

Coraline's eyes widened. "What?"

Holly waved a hand as she released a nervous chuckle. "I had a friend who brought his horses. The gardens couldn't guarantee that they'd have the path clear, especially since it was still snowing, so I got permission for Dillon to bring his horses and sleigh." Holly had simplified the process and had glossed over the multiple phone calls and pleading required to make it happen.

"Did the sleigh have bells?" Coraline asked.

Holly fought the urge to cringe. "Yes, but you said the wedding is in a month, correct? You couldn't have anything like that, of course, and, given the fact that we don't typically have snowfall here in the Kansas City area, we could never plan on something like that. The entire wedding was kismet."

Miranda turned to her, resting her hand on her knees. "Do you have photos of your other weddings?"

"Yes, but—"

Coraline handed the tablet to her mother. "They're just as good."

Miranda took her time scrolling through the album.

"Nicole would love to plan your wedding. In fact, I think she already has some ideas."

Coraline tilted her head. "What are they?"

"I...uh...I'm not sure."

"What would *you* do?"

Holly's tongue lay at the bottom of her mouth.

Coraline's eyes narrowed. "If you don't start talking, we'll walk out the door. We have an appointment at eleven thirty with Tender Moments, and they are taking us to lunch at the Plaza."

Miranda's silence confirmed everything her daughter said.

Shit, shit, shit. Holly had two options: try to keep them here and possibly accidentally steal Nicole's client, or let them walk and lose them for certain. Which was bound to piss her boss off less?

She took a deep breath and grabbed her notebook and a pen, then perched on the edge of her desk. "I'm presuming you have the venue booked."

A triumphant smile spread across Coraline's face. "Yes, Stonehaus Vineyard in Lee's Summit."

"An outdoor wedding?" Holly asked in surprise. "In July?"

Coraline gave her a challenging look.

Holly wanted to tell her good luck with the ninety-degree heat and melting guests and push her out the door, but she also wanted to keep her job, which was in peril whichever path she took.

Where in God's name was Nicole?

"And the reception?"

"The same place. Outdoors."

Well, double shit.

"It's an early-evening wedding," Miranda added. "Five o'clock."

Holly forced a smile. "Well, that helps with the heat a bit, doesn't it? How many guests?"

"Three hundred."

She wrote the information they'd given her in her notebook, trying to stall. "Do you have anything else planned?"

"I have my dress," Coraline said.

"And the bridesmaids?"

"I've changed my mind about theirs."

The blood in Holly's veins turned to ice.

"I see." And she did. All too well. Coraline was a spoiled brat who changed her mind at the drop of a dime. "How many wedding planners have you worked with?"

Coraline looked taken back by the question, but Holly gave her a direct gaze.

"Four," Miranda finally said. "We just fired the last one this weekend."

"And may I ask why?"

"Difference of opinion."

What was Nicole thinking? This was a train wreck. It was just a matter of *when* the cars would all pile up over the course of the next month, not if.

"I'll be honest," Holly pushed out, sure that she was going to be writing her letter of resignation when Nicole finally returned. "I'm not sure I'm the planner for you."

Both women's eyes grew wide.

"My goal is to make sure that my brides have the best possible experience. I want them to have the most perfect wedding, no matter what their budget. So I need my brides to trust me, and, in turn, I need to trust them."

Coraline's nostrils flared. "Are you saying you don't trust me?"

"No, I'm saying that you have to be certain you want to work with me, then you need to trust my judgment. You've seen my photos and you're still here, so you liked what you saw, but I'll be honest, planning a wedding of the quality you're sure to be looking for with three hundred guests in less than a month is next to impossible."

"But there's a chance you can do it?"

"You have absolutely nothing else arranged?" Holly asked, trying to hide her dismay.

"We have a photographer," Miranda said, watching Holly intently. "Coraline fired the rest."

"See, here's the thing," Holly said, moving closer to her. "If you work with me, you can't keep firing people. I will bring on the people I think will work best given what you want and the difficult time constraints."

"You're wanting *me* to give *you* full control of my wedding?" Coraline asked in a condescending tone. "Are you insane?"

"Probably, but that's exactly what I'm saying. I'll sit down with you and find out the tone and feel you're looking for. I'll show you what I have planned, and if you accept, I'll give you the wedding of your dreams. But it all boils down to trusting me."

In truth, Holly couldn't see Coraline trusting anyone. Which meant this was a lost opportunity, but she could live with that. She wasn't going to grovel at this spoiled brat's feet. Even if she lost her job over it. She was certain she could get back her position as an assistant manager at the Marriott. Then if she got a second job, she might still be able to pay for her grandmother's private room. She'd be exhausted, but it wasn't like she had much of a social life anyway.

"I think I've heard enough," Coraline said, lifting her chin. "I knew this hole in the wall would be a waste of time."

Holly had to make some attempt to salvage this. "As I said before, Nicole already has some ideas in mind. If you'll wait for her to get here, she would love to share them with you. I'm sure you'll find her more...acquiescing than I am."

Miranda's eyes narrowed.

"No, I've heard enough. Come, Mother." Coraline spun as though she were on a fashion-show runway and strutted toward the door.

Miranda stood and gave Holly one last look. "It was lovely to meet you, Holly. Do you have a card?"

"Yes." Holly tried to hide her surprise at the request. Coraline had made her intentions clear. Nevertheless, she grabbed a card off her desk and handed it to her. "I wish you the best of luck with your search."

The older woman grimaced. "Thank you. I think we'll need it."

Holly watched the two women walk out, Nicole walking in seconds later. She stood in the open doorway, looking out into the parking lot.

"Was that Miranda Johansen and her daughter?"

Holly's back tensed. "Yes."

"*And they left?*"

"I tried to keep them here."

Nicole looked torn between coming into the office or chasing them down. Propriety won out and she shut the door behind her. "What happened?"

Holly sat in her office chair and took a deep breath. "Coraline saw the photo of the Ginsburg–Huffman wedding on the wall. She wanted to see what else we had done, so I gave her the tablet and showed her the photo gallery."

"She didn't like what she saw?"

"Oh, she liked it too well. I told her that you had come

up with some lovely ideas, and if they would only wait, you would share them."

Nicole bristled. "How did you know if I had any ideas or not?"

"Please, Nicole. When did you ever go into a meeting unprepared?" When her boss didn't respond, she continued. "They wanted to know if I had any ideas to pitch them."

"You stole my client?" Nicole demanded.

"No! I told them to wait, and when they insisted I do something or they would leave, I started asking questions about what they did have in place." She gave her boss a pointed look. "Did you know they only have the venue, the photographer, and her wedding dress? And literally nothing else. An outdoor wedding and reception at Stonehaus Vineyard. For a big, fancy wedding—in less than one month—that's insanity."

"So you sent them away?"

"No, I told them that I wasn't a good fit for them and they needed to wait for you. But Coraline threw a temper tantrum and left."

Nicole sank into her office chair. "So we lost them."

"Honestly, Nicole, I think they would have done us more harm than good. That wedding is a disaster waiting to happen."

"That is my decision to make," Nicole said in a chilly tone. "Not yours."

"I did the best I could. I'm sorry."

She sat still, waiting for Nicole to fire her, but the woman pushed out a sigh and reached for her phone. "Maybe I can save this."

"They have a lunch date with Tender Moments at eleven thirty."

Nicole scowled. "Well, then we can definitely kiss this wedding good-bye."

"I hope you're not kissing *my* wedding good-bye." A tall, lanky blonde woman laughed as she walked in the door.

"Oh, Bethany!" Nicole gushed, clasping her hands together. "It's so lovely to see you!"

Bethany smiled. "I was in the neighborhood so I thought I'd drop by for a visit."

Nicole shot Holly a glare. "Now's not a good time for an in-office chat. How about we go for coffee?"

Holly turned to her computer screen and rolled her eyes.

"Sounds wonderful." Bethany's attention was drawn to the photo that had captured Coraline's attention minutes ago. "This is beautiful. Did you organize this, Nicole?"

Holly cringed, preparing for the backlash.

"No. That was Holly." Her answer was clipped.

"I've always wanted a winter wedding."

Nicole brightened at that. "If everything works out, we can plan the wedding of your dreams. But obviously, there are quite a few things to work out. Let's go talk about it over coffee."

Bethany beamed; her dazzling white teeth in her perfect smile nearly blinded Holly.

That's exactly the kind of woman my neighbor would probably go for.

She'd tried her best to forget him and had succeeded while dealing with the potential wedding clients from hell. So where had that thought come from?

Nicole looped her purse over the crook of her arm. "Holly, I have no idea how long I'll be out. Bethany and I have a lot to discuss. I need you to work on the Hicks estimate and then we'll discuss the other predicament when I get back."

Holly watched the two women walk out. But her humiliation from the night before was back in full force, mingling with her fear over her future.

Because she was fairly certain she might be out of a job by the end of the day.

Chapter Six

Kevin considered going straight to the coffee shop after work, but Matt had taken him on a tour of the mall after lunch. If he was going to stand by his pretense of looking fresh for his mother, he needed a shower.

When he got home the kitten was mewling in the laundry room that had been attached to the back of the house, off the kitchen. He'd picked up a bag of kitten food, some milk, and cat litter on the way home, although he had no idea why he was taking care of the cat. But the alternative was to take it to the animal shelter, and that wasn't happening. So he was the temporary caretaker of a tiny gray kitten until he could find some other poor sucker to take it.

He scooped up the kitten, groaning when he saw the vinyl floor. "How did such a tiny thing make such a disgusting mess?" But then he wasn't all that surprised. The night before, he'd fed the poor thing some of his lasagna.

He thought he'd given himself enough time to get

everything done and be at the coffee shop a good five minutes early. Instead he arrived right at four and found his mother waiting at a table, a notebook in front of her. She looked up at him and stood, tears filling her eyes. "You're really here."

He was fairly certain she didn't mean at Starbucks. "I'm here."

He gave her a warm hug, and she clung to him for a few seconds longer than he'd expected before she dropped her hold and looked strangely devoid of emotion.

Despite the fact that she drove him absolutely crazy, he loved her. Nicole Vandemeer would go out of her way to help her children. Unfortunately, she rarely asked if the help was needed.

"You look lovely today, Mom."

She beamed, tugging at her lightweight jacket. "Thank you. I have to say, my day started off terribly, then progressively improved. Now that I'm here with you, it's nearly perfect."

"What happened this morning?" he asked as they got in line in front of the counter.

"First I was involved in an accident on Seven Highway—"

That got his attention. He reached for her elbow and looked her up and down for signs of trauma. "Are you okay? Why didn't you call me?"

She reached up to pat his cheek. "Kevin, I'm fine. It was very minor. In fact, my car is still driveable."

"Thank God."

"You're such a sweet boy to worry. But that was the lesser of my morning evils."

"Oh?"

"That ridiculous girl lost my biggest client to date. You

have no idea what doors the Johansen wedding could have opened for us." They moved forward a few steps, under an air-conditioner vent, and she swept back several stray hairs that had blown onto her cheek.

"Your assistant?"

She frowned. "Of course. Who else? I was tied up with the accident and she had one job: keep them there until I got there. How could she screw up something so simple? And on top of that, she tried to steal them from me. Can you imagine?"

"Every time I've talked to you over the last few months, you've done nothing but complain about your assistant. Why don't you just fire her?" But he also knew his perfectionist mother. She rarely thought anyone was up to her impossible standards and would clone herself to do the job if possible, yet when someone came close to hitting her standards, Nicole became defensive and threatened.

His mother took a breath and something flickered in her eyes that Kevin couldn't read, confirming he might be on the right track. "It's not that simple."

"Seems pretty simple to me."

But before she could respond, the barista took their order. Kevin insisted on paying for the drinks, and they settled at a table close to the windows.

His mother made a show of getting comfortable, then leveled her gaze on him. "I want to know more about your house. Megan won't tell me a blessed thing. But then she was always an obstinate child, defying me simply for the joy of driving me crazy."

"It's a small two-bedroom, one-bath house. It needs a little work."

"So what's the big deal? Why can't I see it?"

"It's still a mess. ..."

"Please..." She dramatically waved her hand. "Whenever I visited you, your apartments were always impeccably clean. Even your bedroom when you were a kid was neat as a pin."

"Like I said...I'd like to fix it up a little before you make a judgment."

Her gaze leveled on him. "What has your sister done?" She shook her head, releasing an exaggerated sigh. "I knew that girl would get you into trouble."

His mother was saying exactly what he'd been thinking the previous night, but sibling loyalty trumped the truth. "Matt agrees it will be a good investment."

Her scowl returned. "I have no idea why you agreed to work in construction. You could always come work for your father at the engineering firm."

"I don't want to work at Dad's firm. Besides, Josh has taken charge and he's doing a great job."

"Josh is your father's son-in-law. You are his son and heir. If you want the company, it's yours."

He didn't try to hide his shock. "You'd have Dad fire the father of your grandchild?"

She shuddered. "Of course not. Don't be ridiculous. He would merely be...reassigned."

Kevin shook his head. "From what Dad has said, Josh has worked his ass off to turn the company around. He's earned his place there. I would never dream of screwing him out of it."

She frowned. "Kevin. Language."

"My language is far less insulting than your suggestion."

"I would never suggest moving Josh out, but surely you two could share responsibilities. He works long hours—maybe he'd like someone to take part of the load so he can spend more time with Megan and the baby."

When she put it that way, he could see her point. Perhaps his mother's biggest problem was her delivery, not her intent. "It's a moot point. I don't want to work for Dad. I never did."

"So you'd rather work for Matt's father's company?"

"You know Matt's father died less than a year ago, so it's Matt's company now. He asked for my help and I like the challenge. It's a fresh start and I'm helping a friend."

"But are you making very much money?"

He shouldn't have been surprised she asked, but he was still offended. "Enough."

"Well..." She smoothed her skirt as she planned her next attack. She looked up with a forced smile. "I suppose this is an opportunity for you to *explore your options*"— she used air quotes—"or whatever you kids call it these days. I have high hopes that you'll realize it's time to take on your other responsibilities."

"What does *that* mean?"

She stared at her cup for a moment. "If you're ready to have your own home, then you're ready to consider settling down."

He laughed. "You think I'm going to the Power and Light District to get drunk every Friday and Saturday night?"

"No." She scowled again. "I mean marriage. Children."

He'd hoped Megan's pregnancy would curb her "I need a grandchild" mantra, but he should have known better. "I think I'll take it one step at a time."

"You're thirty-three years old, Kevin. You're not getting any younger. All your things"—she pointed her finger in the air and made a squiggly motion—"are going to die and leave you childless."

Kevin choked on a mouthful of coffee, sputtering it down his shirt. "You mean my *sperm*?"

She cringed. "Such coarse talk, Kevin."

And *things* with a hand motion was any better? "Mom, I'm not sure where you're getting your biology facts, but my sperm are good for decades to come."

"Kevin!"

He shrugged. "You brought it up."

"It's time to consider starting a family."

He fought the urge to groan. Definitely time to change the subject. "The Royals had a five-game winning streak. I'm thinking about taking Dad to a game next week."

She narrowed her eyes. "So you refuse to have this discussion?"

"I'm focusing on other things, Mother. My job. My new house. My new niece or nephew. Maybe when I feel settled with everything else, I'll be ready to consider marriage." But he didn't see that happening for a very long time, not that he wasn't open to it. He just didn't want to settle for the wrong kind of woman—the women he typically dated.

She pushed out a breath and gave him a tight smile. "Of course you know best."

He steeled his back. "But? What aren't you saying?"

Instead she patted his hand. "Always so suspicious. Since I can't bring dinner to your house, then I insist you meet your father and me for dinner tomorrow night."

"Sure."

The smile she bestowed on him made him nervous

"Oh, look at the time." She grabbed her purse and stood. "I'll text you the details about dinner tomorrow." She started to leave, then turned back to him. "Oh, I hope you don't have plans for Saturday afternoon. I need you to come to Megan's baby shower."

"What?" he asked in dismay. "Is it a couples shower?"

"No, but you're playing bartender. I'll let you know

when to show up." Then she walked out the door with a tiny wave.

He already regretted agreeing to dinner. But expecting him to come to a baby shower? He'd seen that look on his mother's face before.

She was definitely up to something.

Chapter Seven

Holly was glad when Nicole left early for the day, even though Nicole hadn't said another word about losing the Johansen wedding. In fact, she'd been in an exceptionally good mood after she'd come back from her appointment with Bethany this morning, and Holly figured she was in the clear. Then she said she was leaving early to meet her son and she'd see Holly in the morning.

Holly had spent another hour working on a menu proposal for a client's wedding when her phone rang.

"Distinctive Events, Holly speaking."

"Holly, this is Miranda Johansen."

Her breath stuck in her chest and she sounded slightly wheezy when she said, "Miranda. How was your meeting with Tender Moments?"

"It was wonderful. The two planners catered to Coraline's every whim."

Was she calling to jab the knife of losing the job in deeper? "How wonderful for you."

"No, it's not wonderful at all. In fact, it's far from wonderful."

Holly blinked in confusion. "I'm sorry?"

"Catering to Coraline's every whim is exactly why we're in our current situation—three and a half weeks away from a wedding that has nothing but a venue, the photographer, and a dress."

"I'm not sure—"

"I want you to plan the wedding."

Holly leaned back in her chair. "What?"

"I need someone to stand up to my daughter and tell her no."

"With all due respect, Miranda, isn't that your job?" The words were out before Holly could reel them back in. "I'm sorry. That was inappropriate."

"No," the woman said quietly. "You're right. But you have to understand, I've spent too much time neglecting my daughter for my career and now that we're close again, I don't want to destroy that. Our reconciliation is too fragile."

"So you need someone to be the bad guy."

"Yes."

Holly released a short laugh as she rubbed her forehead. "I'm not sure why you think I can perform that role. I assure you that I make a terrible bad guy."

"No, you set Coraline straight this morning and you were absolutely right. Then you stated your opinion moments ago."

"Moments ago, I spoke without thinking. It was incredibly rude."

"Yet it was absolutely correct."

"Miranda, your daughter made it clear she didn't want me. And if Tender Moments wowed her, there's not a chance this will work."

"It's my money paying for the wedding. It's my decision."

"But my job is to wow the bride, even when the mother is paying for it. I need to know that Coraline is happy with me."

"She will be once you present your plans to her. She loved every wedding photo she saw in your portfolio."

"What if she fires me?"

"She can't. I'll draw up a contract that states once I sign on the dotted line, termination is impossible."

Holly paused, actually considering it. Maybe her grandmother's dementia was contagious.

"But termination will be impossible on both sides."

So there *was* a catch. She was stuck with them until the end. "I understand how this could benefit *you*, but how would this be in *my* best interest?"

"I'm willing to pay more than Nicole had mentioned when we first spoke."

"Miranda, I'm going to be honest, which is probably incredibly stupid in this situation, but I have no idea what figure Nicole mentioned. She's been very guarded about everything regarding your meeting."

"But you said you knew about her ideas."

"I had no idea what she had planned, but I knew she'd walk in prepared. She wants your wedding. She'll be furious if you offer it to me. So if I accept, I'll be dealing with an angry boss, an ungrateful, demanding bride, and ulcer-inducing time constraints to pull off a three-hundred-guest wedding that is worthy of the *New York Times*. What could possibly entice me to say yes?"

"A ten-page spread in *Modern Bride* magazine."

That could do it.

Miranda lowered her voice. "Between you and me, *I* fired the last planner. She'd catered to every one of Coraline's crazy ideas. I found out about the spread last week and I knew her Victorian cowboy theme would sink my career. I need someone who can not only pull this off, but make it the wedding of the year."

A spread in *Modern Bride*? The talk shows often pulled planners who had been featured in the magazine to host segments. The more exposure Distinctive Events got, the better chance they had to get higher-profile clients. Nicole would be thrilled.

Who was she kidding? Nicole would be furious, but she wouldn't dare fire her over this. She couldn't afford to, but that still wouldn't stop her from making Holly miserable. "What kind of budget am I looking at? I'll need to pay extra to make things happen this close to the wedding."

"An obscene amount. I need this spread for my own business. They'll be featuring Coraline's dress as well as the bridesmaids' gowns."

"I thought the bridal party didn't have dresses."

"They don't, but once we lock down a theme, I'll make the dresses accordingly. So what do you say?"

She was insane to consider it. This was going to be a three-week-long nightmare. Still, it was an opportunity she couldn't pass up. "I'll do it. I'm up for a good challenge."

"Perfect. I'll have my attorney draw up a contract and e-mail it to you tomorrow morning. You can bring it with you to my home tomorrow afternoon to discuss ideas with Coraline."

"I look forward to it."

Miranda laughed. "You might think so now, but you'll earn every penny I'm paying, and even then you'll probably wonder if it's worth it."

Holly sighed as she hung up the phone. Had she just made a deal with the devil?

* * *

By five thirty, Holly had finished working up her proposal. She locked up the office and headed to the retirement center, her stomach twisting into knots. Seeing her grandmother agitated and confused the day before had upset Holly more than she'd cared to admit. The doctors and nurses had warned her the day was coming when her grandmother wouldn't know her at all, but last night had been the first time Holly had seen it for herself. And it was only the beginning. But she had high hopes that today would be a good day, and she had brought her leather-bound scrapbook.

"Good evening, Holly," one of the nurses greeted her, squatting next to an elderly man in a wheelchair.

"Hey, Betty. How's Grandma today?"

The silver-haired nurse offered her a warm smile. "Better today. She's been asking for you. You can find her in the dining room."

"Thanks."

"How's that wedding coming?" Betty stood, moving behind the chair and grabbing the handles. "The one with the bride who'd been sick."

"Oh. The Murphy wedding." One of Holly's brides had had a cancer scare, but everything had worked out in the end. The couple had turned the ceremony and reception into a celebration of life as well as the beginning of their new life together. "The wedding is next weekend. Everything's coming along perfectly. She picked the strawberry cake."

"Ooh! I want to see photos!"

Holly smiled. "I'll make sure to bring them."

She found her grandmother at her usual table, sitting

next to several of her friends. Grandma Barb looked up and smiled, her eyes lighting up with happiness. "There's my Sunshine!"

This was the woman who had mothered her. Who had been the rock she'd clung to almost her entire life. Tears filled Holly's eyes as it fully hit her all that she'd be losing when Grandma Barb would no longer recognize her.

But she blinked them back, offering her grandmother a bright smile as she sat in an empty chair at the six-person table. "Hey, Grandma. How's the Jell-O today?"

"They put oranges in it today. Delilah hates oranges, don't you, dear?" she asked the woman next to her.

The woman wrinkled her nose. "Can't stand them." She patted Grandma Barb's arm. "Is this your granddaughter? She's lovely."

Delilah must be new. The ever-changing resident roster was more depressing than usual today. Holly forced a smile. "Thank you. I've been told I look just like my grandma when she was young."

Her grandmother laughed. "I had hair just as blonde and eyes just as bright green. But you should see her cousin, Melanie. She's the spitting image of her mother with her coal-black hair. No one ever mistook these two for sisters. They were as different as night and day in both looks and spirit."

"I can't wait to meet her," Delilah said. "When will she be by?"

Grandma looked down at her plate, so Holly jumped in. "Melanie has a new boyfriend and she had a date tonight."

"You don't say," her grandmother responded. "You hadn't told me that."

Holly forced herself to stay calm. She'd told her grandmother several days ago.

"Maybe she'll bring him by," Delilah volunteered. "Do *you* have a boyfriend...what was your name?"

"I'm Holly, and no, no boyfriend." She set her leather binder on the table. "But I get to plan weddings, so I'm perfectly content living vicariously through other people's love lives." She laughed. "Even if it makes me sound a bit like a stalker."

"You brought your notebook," her grandmother said.

Holly smiled. "You'd been asking and I hadn't brought it in in ages. There's quite a few more weddings in it now."

Grandma Barb turned to Delilah. "She's been planning weddings since she was a little girl. She used to cut photos out of magazines and paste them into notebooks." Her grandmother stroked the leather cover. "She's got a nicer cover now, but they're still just as lovingly planned."

Holly's face flushed. "I have photos, too, but Grandma prefers the cutouts. I like to start out with them as I'm trying to put it all together." Nicole wasn't a fan of Holly's pages of cutouts. She was surprisingly digitally advanced and preferred for Holly to show her clients digital images, saying Holly's scrapbook pages were too elementary-school looking. But the scrapbook pages were still Holly's favorite part of planning the wedding. And at least her grandmother appreciated them.

The women spent the next ten minutes flipping the pages of Holly's binder. When they finished, Delilah begged Holly to bring in her photos next time.

"You should see the photos of the glass chapel," her grandmother gushed. "With the snow and the red flowers. She even had sleighs."

"Oh!" Delilah exclaimed. "It sounds lovely."

An aide took the women's trays and Holly walked her grandmother back to her room.

Grandma Barb sat in a wingback chair and leaned over and patted the chair next to hers. "Sunshine, have a seat."

Holly sat down, her stomach twisting into a pretzel again. Her grandmother sounded serious, and she rarely sounded so grave.

Her grandmother grabbed her hand and held on. "I don't remember what happened yesterday when you came to see me."

Holly shrugged, forcing a smile. "I don't remember what I had for lunch today. It's not that big of a deal."

"Yes, Holly. It is."

Her grandmother sounded so earnest that a lump clogged Holly's throat. She nodded.

"I worry about you," she said. "You lose yourself in everyone else's love. When are you going to have your own?"

Holly forced out a sigh. "Grandma, I'm happy. Other than my sometimes difficult boss, I love what I do. I give couples the weddings of their dreams. Why can't that be enough? Why do I need a man?"

"I never said it *can't* be enough. I spent the last twenty-five years without a man."

"Because of me and Melanie?" Why had that never occurred to her?

"No!" her grandmother protested. "Because the love I had with your grandfather ran so deep it was enough to fill me, even after he passed. Besides, I had you girls and I would have never given up a single moment of my time with you for something that would have paled in comparison to what I had with your grandfather."

"But I have you. And I have Melanie. I'm full up on love, Gran."

Her grandmother slowly shook her head. "No, Holly. You're afraid of love."

If Holly hadn't known better, she would have suggested her grandmother had been talking to Melanie. "I'm not afraid of love. Look how much I love *you*."

"But you've never been *in* love."

Holly stared at her in surprise. "I've had boyfriends."

"It's not the same thing." She squeezed Holly's hand. "I've watched you your entire life, Holly. I know you, girl. You keep your heart locked up in a tower like Rapunzel. If you want your fairy tale, maybe you should come down from the tower instead of waiting for your prince to find you."

Either scenario was ridiculous. She wasn't looking for love, and she saw no reason why she should. She had enough on her plate with her job and trying to keep her boss happy. But she wanted to appease her grandmother, so she said, "Okay, Gran. I'll think about what you said."

Now if she could only ignore the image of her sexy next-door neighbor that had suddenly popped into her head.

Chapter Eight

~

Kevin was more than ready for a beer when he arrived at the bar and grill in downtown Kansas City. He'd spent the last hour at the hardware store making a list of all the things his kitchen was going to need.

Make that two beers.

Both of his friends were already at a table and his friend Tyler stood to greet him, pulling him into a gruff hug before setting him loose. "Good to see you, Kev. Glad you're back."

Kevin grimaced as he scrubbed the top of his head. "Well, the jury's still out on that one."

Tyler sat back down, and Kevin sat next to a worried-looking Matt. "I know things are probably a mess—"

"Not your books," Kevin said, shaking his head. "Let's just say I'm never letting my sister make a real estate investment for me ever again."

Matt burst out laughing. "From everything you've told me, it sounds like a great investment. That neighborhood is up and coming. Just let me come over and take a look. It's probably not as bad as it looks."

"I suspect it's worse." Time to change the subject. He looked across the table at his friend. "So, Tyler...I hear you're a lawyer now in a big fancy office downtown."

"He won a big case to get him that big fancy office," Matt said, flagging down a waitress.

"That big case paid for my condo in the Plaza." He grinned. "Which impresses my dates." Kevin was pretty sure Tyler didn't need help impressing women. He never had. He'd been the player of the three of them. His dark hair, dark eyes, and dark complexion had always grabbed the attention of all the girls in high school and college.

"I thought you decided to give up dating for a while," Matt countered. "After Sheila."

Tyler's brow lowered and he took a drag of his beer, obviously wishing to change the subject.

Kevin wanted to ask more about Sheila, but Tyler looked like he needed another beer or three before he'd talk. The waitress came over, and Kevin ordered a beer before turning to Matt. "What about you? How's it going with your girlfriend? Aren't you living together?"

Tyler spit out his beer in a burst of laughter.

Kevin gave him his full attention. "So there's a story there?"

Matt cringed. "I think we need a few more rounds before I'm ready to spill *that* story. I'd rather talk about your house."

"I think I'll just take some gasoline and a match to my house. Put it out of its misery."

"You going to live with your mom?" Tyler asked. "Is she just as scary as she was when we were in high school? How are you going to bring your dates home?"

"Easy. I *won't* be bringing home any dates. I'm taking a break from women."

"You're kidding."

"No. I'm like a magnet that attracts crazy women." All the more reason for Kevin to stay away from his next-door neighbor. She definitely hadn't acted normal. Based on several of his previous girlfriends, Kevin's crazy meter was very broken. He'd been blindsided in his last three relationships. So if Kevin could spot *her* brand of crazy, that was definitely a bad sign. So why had he thought about her half a dozen times today?

His two friends chuckled while the waitress set down Kevin's glass. "You boys ready to order?"

Tyler flashed her a grin. "I want a burger and fries, and get one for my friend over here." He motioned toward Kevin.

"Same for me," Matt said, handing her the menus.

Kevin laughed. "I confessed to having terrible taste in women, not terrible taste in food."

"You haven't had a burger until you've had one here. And as for the women..." A grin spread across Tyler's face.

"What?" Kevin asked. "You don't believe me?"

"Oh, we believe you," Matt said. "But I suspect you're on the farm team when it comes to crazy ex-girlfriends. Tyler and I are in the big leagues."

A smug grin plastered Kevin's face. "I've got the story to top all stories."

Matt leaned back, wearing a smirk. "Okay, Vandemeer. Give it a go. Tell us your crazy-ex story."

"You want the short and dirty version or gory details?" Kevin asked.

"What are we? Middle-school girls?" Tyler asked.

Matt's eyes lit up. "All the gory details."

Kevin sighed. "Wrong answer. Here's what I *will* tell

you—we moved in together after Christmas and that was the first time I realized her obsession with the circus."

"Cirque du Soleil?" Tyler asked.

"No. Barnum and Bailey."

"Oh, shit." Matt groaned. "You and clowns..."

"Yeah, I about flipped my shit when she moved in and unpacked a box of clown dolls."

"Dude," Matt said. "You let her stay?"

"I was trying to be mature about it."

Tyler laughed. "Because having a clown-doll collection is so mature."

"Touché." Matt chuckled.

Kevin narrowed his eyes. "Since when did you start saying things like touché?"

Matt leveled his gaze, the corners of his lips twitching as he tried to look serious. "I'm trying to be mature. Like you with the clown dolls."

Releasing a loud groan, Kevin picked up his beer. "Never mind. There's no fucking way I'm telling you why we broke up."

"Fine," Tyler said, leaning forward. "Don't tell him, but don't think you're getting out of telling me."

Kevin took a long gulp of his beer. "I found her with a clown."

Tyler's eyes bugged out. "When you say found her with a clown..."

Kevin took another drink. "I mean in the biblical sense."

His friends burst out into laughter.

"Yeah, laugh it up. I was traumatized."

Matt wiped the tears from his eyes. "No wonder you've sworn off women. It's a wonder you didn't become a monk."

Tyler laughed. "Okay, I'll admit you're in the big leagues of crazy exes, but you're still a rookie."

"There's no way in hell you can top that."

"Want to bet money on it?" Tyler asked.

"It's too subjective," Matt said. "All our stories are bad."

"I'll go next," Tyler volunteered. "You know that I'm not a believer in relationships. But then I met a woman who intrigued me enough for me to ask her out several times. But then I noticed things started going missing in my condo. Little things. My comb. A tie. You know how socks disappear in the wash? My underwear went missing. But I still wasn't putting things together. She never wanted me to go to her place, but one day I stopped by to surprise her. I knocked and the door was cracked open. At first I was worried someone had broken in or she was in danger, so I walked in to make sure she was okay. But then I found her home office...or, rather, her stalker room."

"What?"

"Every wall surface was covered in photos of me. Her computer screen was frozen on an image of me getting out of the shower. Naked. Then I found all my missing things scattered around something that resembled a shrine in her closet."

Kevin shook his head. "What a nut job."

"I broke up with her, of course, right after I notified the police, but she refused to leave me alone. She kept turning up. At my office. At my house. At a ball game I went to with Matt. She sat down at my table in a restaurant when I was on a date. The last straw was when I woke up tied to my bed. I filed a restraining order."

"Jesus." Kevin groaned. "That's freaky."

"She was harmless," Tyler said. "Just annoying."

Matt picked up his glass. "She tied you to your bed, dude!"

Tyler shrugged. "She wasn't going to hurt me."

"Still, it freaked you out enough that you haven't dated since," Matt said.

"How long ago was that?" Kevin asked.

"Three months."

Kevin shook his head. "Have you ever gone *three days* without a woman?"

"No." Matt chuckled. "Which explains his crankiness and his blue balls."

"You're a fine one to talk," Tyler said. "If we're awarding prizes, then you get first place."

Matt's smile fell. "It's a prize I can do without." He looked behind him. "Oh, look, here comes our food."

The waitress set down the plates and as soon as she walked away, Kevin turned to his friend. "Good stall, but I told my story so you're telling yours. Start talking."

Matt's grin fell. "I thought Sylvia might be the one. She moved in and things seemed to be going well—even though it was weird she didn't have any friends or family. But then one night we were in bed—"

"And they weren't sleeping," Tyler added with a grin.

"Let's just say I was preoccupied, when the bedroom door burst open and several members of the SWAT team came pouring through the door and the bedroom window. They arrested both of us and hauled me outside—"

"Naked as the day he was born, but with part of him still at full attention." Tyler winked.

"Then they arrested us both on bank-robbery charges."

"What?" Kevin gasped. "Was it the wrong apartment?"

"No." Matt shook his head. "They had the right place and the right girl. Sylvia was really Paula and had robbed a string of banks in Iowa six months before. She figured she could hide out with me for a while, then start a new life—without me. Thankfully, I was cleared."

"That sucks, man," Kevin said.

Matt shrugged, but Kevin could see the pain in his eyes.

"So we've all sworn off women?" Kevin asked.

Both men studied him. "Looks like it," Matt said. "We should start a club. The Losers."

"Nah." Kevin laughed. "It's like when we were kids. Remember the Knights' Brotherhood? Sixth-grade year. We swore to help damsels in distress."

"We also swore to kill fire-breathing dragons," Tyler said.

"Only now we're avoiding them," Matt said.

"Turns out they're one and the same." Tyler winked. "The dragons, not the damsels."

"Maybe we're cursed," Kevin said. "My sister and her friends believed their weddings were cursed. What if our entire lives are cursed when it comes to women?"

"We're not cursed," Tyler scoffed.

"Maybe we are," Matt said, looking unhappy with the idea. "All three of us have had extraordinarily bad experiences with women. Maybe this is our sign that we're destined to be bachelors."

Tyler gave him a wry grin. "Hey, I've never wanted to get married. But now I'm not even sleeping with women."

"So it's a Bachelor Brotherhood," Kevin said, and for some weird reason the face of the woman next door popping onto his front porch sprang into his mind. No, *that* was never going to happen. The sooner he let that idea go, the better. "I always wanted kids, though."

"Your sister's having a kid," Tyler said. "Just borrow hers."

Kevin lifted his eyebrows. "I don't think it works that way. I'm pretty sure Megan's the maternal type who won't let her kid out of her sight until it's twenty-five."

Matt looked down at his plate. "I wanted kids, too."

"Maybe we're wrong," Kevin said. "Maybe we've just had a run of bad luck."

"All three of us?" Matt asked. "When was the last time any of us have had a normal girlfriend?"

They all remained silent for several seconds.

"Tina Lebowsky," Kevin said, pointing his finger at Matt. "She was normal."

"You dated her for three weeks our junior year of high school. I don't think that counts. Especially since she joined a commune after she graduated."

"I've dated plenty of normal women," Tyler said.

"How would you know if they were normal?" Matt countered. "Your crazy ex was the only woman in the last few years you even called your girlfriend."

"Just goes to show you really can't trust *any* woman."

The thought of spending his life alone was depressing, but Kevin had bigger things to worry about than his love life. And besides, there were worse things than being a bachelor the rest of his life.

Like not having a life at all.

Chapter Nine

After Holly came home from visiting her grandmother, she changed into a pair of shorts and a tank top before she sat in the backyard with Killer. She was on her second glass of wine, pinning things on her phone's Pinterest app to get ideas for Coraline's wedding, when she heard a car pull up to his house. After Holly's chat with her grandmother, she was frustrated that she kept thinking of her new neighbor. She barely knew him and the encounter had been painfully embarrassing, but she couldn't ignore the fact that she'd felt something with him that she'd never felt in her life.

She was curious. That was all.

At least that was what she told herself when she nearly jumped up to see if it was his car, but she forced herself to keep her butt in her chair, despite her inner argument that she should at least make sure it wasn't another car break-in. But her job responsibility won out. She didn't need to have the entire wedding planned out until she knew what Coraline and Miranda wanted, but she had to go to the meeting with at least a few broad ideas. So far nothing was coming to her, which had her slightly panicked. Holly's work was very much muse driven, and now was *not* the time for her muse to take a break.

She was jumping down a rabbit hole of outdoor-reception pins when she heard her neighbor talking on the other side of the fence.

"Yeah, I saw her. She still wants to come over, but I think I've held her off for now. ..." Then his voice faded as he went back inside.

She sat back in her chair, horrified to discover she was straining to hear his sexy voice through the open windows of his house.

What in the world was wrong with her?

She closed her laptop and stood. "Come on, Killer. Let's go inside."

He was distracting. That was all. She definitely wasn't interested in him. Not when he surely thought she was a bumbling idiot.

She set her computer on the dining room table and poured herself a third glass of wine from the box in her refrigerator, jumping when she heard a sharp rap on the front door.

Killer looked up at her, then took off to investigate, his high-pitched barking piercing her ears.

"Killer, stop!"

Who could be knocking at her door? The break-ins fresh on her mind, she set down the glass and grabbed a baseball bat that Melanie kept in the kitchen for security measures before moving to the front window to peer out the curtains.

There was a man on her front porch.

She considered not answering, but the man was sure to

have heard her yell at the dog, who was still yapping at her feet.

"Killer! Stop!"

She wedged herself between the dog and the door before she opened it, her jaw dropping when she saw her new neighbor.

He looked even sexier tonight in his white button-down shirt and his low-hung jeans. His hair was neater, and the scruff on his face from the night before was gone. And his smell...she was close enough to tell he smelled delicious.

His gaze took her in, moving head to toe in a slow sweep and back up again, taking in her bare legs and lingering on her breasts before lifting to her face.

She self-consciously lifted her hand to the hair escaping her messy bun. "Uh...hi. What are you doing here?" Oh, shit. Had she said that out loud?

He laughed and she loved how his eyes lit with amusement, his lips tilting up slightly. "I thought I'd bring your dish back over." He lifted the container to prove his intent, and she felt her cheeks burn.

"Oh."

"Are you about to run off to a baseball game or should I be concerned?"

"What? Oh." Then she remembered the bat in her hand and she tossed it into the house. The loud thud when it hit the hardwood floor made her cringe. It also made Killer jump and start barking again. She stepped onto the porch, pulling the door closed behind her and bumping into his chest.

"Sorry," she murmured, feeling like an idiot. How did this man make her lose her head? Although she was sure the wine wasn't helping the situation.

He grabbed her arm to steady her and she found her hand resting on his chest again. This time she didn't pull away, instead looking up into his eyes, which had focused on her mouth.

"We're making a habit of this," he said, his voice so low it rumbled his chest under her fingertips.

She sucked in a breath, still looking up at him. "Sorry."

A mischievous look filled his eyes. "I'm not complaining."

She realized he was still holding the dish in one hand, but his hand on her arm had moved to the small of her back.

What in the world was she doing? This went against every rule she had for dating. No physical contact until the second date, and even then it never went past momentary hand-holding and a short kiss good night. It definitely didn't include plastering herself to the front of a stranger.

She tried to take a step back but the door blocked her escape, which ordinarily would have worried her but instead sent a raging fire through her blood. Her body's reaction confused her, and she chalked it up to the wine. She'd never been so turned on by a man, and she wasn't sure how to handle it. She had to make him leave and soon, or she'd probably do something she'd regret.

"Thank—" Her voice came out raspy, so she pressed her lips together then tried again. "Thank you for bringing back the dish."

He grinned. "It was one of the best lasagnas I've ever had, but don't tell my mother or she'll make me suffer for the rest of my life."

She chuckled, surprised that she was starting to feel at ease, which was equally surprising since they were still as close as they were a few moments ago. "Surely she can't be that bad."

"You'd be amazed." But then he took a quick step back,

putting a couple of feet between them and moving like he'd just been caught doing something wrong. "Thanks again for bringing me the lasagna."

Something had changed, although Holly couldn't put her finger on what. "Yeah, no problem."

Then he abruptly turned and walked down the steps before he looked back at her, his warm smile returning. "I'm Kevin, by the way."

Butterflies fluttered in her stomach at that smile—when was the last time she'd had butterflies?—and she was certain she was smiling back like the fool she was, but damned if she could stop it. "Holly."

If possible, his smile grew even brighter. "Nice to meet you, Holly." Then he turned around and walked toward his house.

Holly turned the doorknob to go back inside, her eyes still on him, only vaguely aware that the door wasn't opening. She pushed harder, her shoulder banging into the wood. What the—? She tried to turn the knob before the truth hit her: she had locked herself out.

Kevin stopped at the bottom of his steps and looked back at her and smiled.

She gave him a small wave, her mind reeling. No need to panic. She'd just walk around and go through the back door.

Oh, shit. She'd locked the back door when she'd gone in, worried about the car break-ins.

Now what should she do? She considered calling Melanie, but Holly's phone was inside. For one brief moment she thought about asking to borrow Kevin's, but she quickly dismissed the idea. She'd already looked enough like a fool. No need to add more evidence. Besides, it was pointless. Melanie wouldn't be able to come until she took her break in another hour or two.

Although Holly knew it was probably a long shot, she set the casserole dish on the porch and checked under the flowerpot on the top step of the porch. It was their usual hiding place for the spare house key, but Melanie had used it a couple of weeks ago, and Holly was fairly certain she hadn't replaced it. Sure enough, the only thing Holly found under the clay pot was an earthworm.

That left the dining room window. The lock had been broken for months, and she and Melanie had never gotten it fixed. Now she just had to climb through it.

Granted, it had been a few years—or fifteen—since she'd tried crawling through the window, but it had worked the last time she and Melanie had locked themselves out of the house. Of course, they'd been teens, but surely it was like riding a bike.

But first she had to get it open. Walking around the side of the house, she realized that climbing through a four-foot-high window had been less intimidating when she was fifteen. Of course, her older cousin had boosted her up.

She could still do this. She just needed something to stand on.

Thankfully, Kevin had gone back inside his house, so she didn't feel so conspicuous going into her backyard to grab a bucket Melanie kept by the water spigot. Flipping it upside down, she set it under the window and climbed onto it, adjusting her feet to get her balance. Once she was centered, she grabbed the lower edge of the window and tried to lift it—without success. The window was stuck. She put more weight into it but it still didn't budge, and she nearly fell off the bucket.

The "*Shit!*" that came out of her mouth was much louder than she'd intended, making her cringe. She hadn't meant to shout. A quick glance around confirmed that she was still alone, with the exception of Killer, who was now barking at the dining room window instead of the front door.

"Killer! Stop that right now!" she hissed, peering inside at the dog, but when he saw her, he began barking in earnest.

Time to try a different tactic. She lifted her arms over her head and braced her hands on the top part of the window frame and pushed. It budged a slight bit, but not enough even to get her fingers through the opening at the bottom. Standing on her tiptoes, she gave a hard shove, but the bucket underneath her bare feet wobbled to the side.

"*Shit!*"

Holly tried to grab the window, but her fingers slipped, and she knew she was going to hit the ground. She squeezed her eyes shut, her body tensing as she prepared for impact, but she found herself stopped mid-fall by two strong arms and a very solid chest.

"Is this your first breaking and entering?"

She opened her eyes to look up into Kevin's face, his eyes dancing with amusement.

The only thing that could save her now was if the earth opened up and swallowed her whole. Only she was sure she couldn't get that lucky.

Kevin set her back upright on top of the bucket and took a step back.

Holly figured she had two choices. One, she could die of embarrassment on the spot. Or she could laugh at her situation. She couldn't look any worse, right? "Is it that obvious?" she teased.

"Well, I'm no expert, but I think the first rule of breaking and entering is to be quiet about it."

"You heard me?"

"To be fair, I was next to my kitchen window, which is open and only ten feet from the scene of the crime."

Her face flushed. "I locked myself out."

He laughed. "I figured as much...unless you're brushing up on your criminal skills, and if so, I suggest you think about another line of work."

She smiled, surprised she didn't feel more embarrassed. He made her feel at ease, even though his proximity heated her body several degrees.

She motioned to the window. "It's stuck. The humidity must have made the wood swell. I only got it to budge a crack."

"No spare key, huh?"

"No, my cousin didn't put it back and there's no way she can come home for at least an hour or more."

He glanced at the window. "Let me have a try."

She climbed off the bucket, and he moved it out of the way before he put his hands on the top window and pushed. The frame shimmied, then finally slid up a few inches before he pushed again, the frame sliding easily all the way to the top.

Kevin grinned as he turned to face her. "I take it climbing through the window is next."

"Yeah." But there was no way on God's green earth she was going to let him see that. She had to save *some* of her dignity. "Thanks for your help. I've got it from here."

He shook his head. "Now what kind of gentleman would I be if I didn't see this all the way through? Especially since I'm the reason you're locked out."

"I've done this before," she said. "I don't need any help."

"You routinely climb through windows? Maybe I should reassess your potential life as a criminal."

She laughed. "Okay, so maybe I was fifteen the last time I tried this. But how hard can it be?"

He grinned. "Fine. I'll let you climb in on your own, but I

insist on sticking around as a spotter. You know, in case you get stuck."

She lifted her eyebrows. "Are you suggesting I won't fit through the window?"

His face paled. "God, no. I just meant…"

She laughed again. "I know what you meant. I'm just giving you a hard time. But I really don't need your help. Thanks for everything you've already done." Then she gave him a tiny wave for good measure.

He grinned, obviously recovered from his embarrassment, and took several steps backward. "I'll just stay over here on my property. It really is a great spot. A great view."

Ignoring the flush on her cheeks, she put her hands on her hips. "You're really not going to leave, are you?"

His grin spread, lighting up his face. "Not a chance."

Stifling a groan, she moved the bucket back under the window. How was she going to do this gracefully? There was no way she could hike a leg up and straddle the window, which left a very unattractive option.

Crap. She was going to have to dive in.

Holly glanced over her shoulder. "I've got this. Don't you have a wall you need to tear down or something?"

He laughed, crossing his arms over his broad chest. "It can wait."

Great.

Taking a deep breath, she placed her hands on the windowsill and lifted her body as though she were mounting a balance beam, just like she'd learned to do during the gymnastics section of her eighth-grade gym class. Only now her head was at the top of the window opening.

Two strong hands encircled her waist, lifting her up. "Put your feet in first."

"I said I could do it," she said, trying to sound irritated, which proved difficult when all she could think about was the fact that her shirt had lifted slightly and his left hand was on her bare skin.

"Trust me," he said, kicking the bucket out of the way. "I would have loved nothing more than to see you attempt this on your own, but it doesn't feel right since I'm the reason you're locked out in the first place. So just lift your feet and put them through the window and I'll slide you in as gracefully as I can."

While she would have preferred to stand her ground, this seemed the least embarrassing route, not to mention that he was touching her. While she tried to convince herself that his touch was not a good thing, her body protested otherwise.

"Will you let me help you, Holly?" he asked, his voice low.

As her back pressed to his chest and her feet barely touched the ground, she could think of something else she'd like him to help her with. "Yes," she said a little too breathlessly.

Then he lifted her several feet up and she gave herself a mental shake—*You're supposed to be sticking your feet through the window.*

While this option might be the most graceful, she still felt awkward as she lifted her hips to get her feet through the opening. Once her lower legs were through, he gently slid her in until she rested her butt on the windowsill. He dropped his hold but hovered close as she dipped down and slid in the rest of the way.

Holly turned around, surprised to see that he had backed up a couple of feet.

"Thanks for your help," she said, wondering what the appropriate response was in a situation like this.

He lifted his shoulder into a half shrug. "It's the least I could do. Now that you're safe and sound, I'll head back home. If you get locked out again, I'm your guy."

She laughed. "Thanks again." But then she felt incredibly lame. She'd already thanked him.

He gave her a wave, then disappeared around the corner. And suddenly she was rethinking everything.

Chapter Ten

On Friday morning, Holly woke up unsettled. It didn't help that her dreams had been filled with her new neighbor who'd turned out to be as nice as he was sexy—a deadly combination if she was determined to stay on the celibate route. But she reminded herself that she had far more pressing issues—like keeping her job.

She'd considered calling Nicole to fill her in on her conversation with Miranda Johansen last night, but she'd thought the news was probably better delivered in person. In the end, Holly decided to put it off until the next day. But now it *was* the next day and there was no way around it.

So she'd stopped and picked up muffins from the bakery, Nicole's favorite—lemon poppy seed—and arrived at work fifteen minutes early, in plenty of time to start a pot of hazelnut coffee. She returned to her desk and checked her e-mail, her thoughts drifting to her run-in with her next-door neighbor last night.

After he'd gone back home and she had spent the rest of the evening obsessing over every little thing he'd said and did. Just like a stupid middle-school girl.

What had happened to her?

But in the light of day, she'd decided this was all Melanie and their grandmother's fault. Holly never would have noticed him if they hadn't planted the seeds in her head. But there *was* something about him that made her want to see him again. If she did, would that be so bad?

She sent Melanie a text before she changed her mind.

I want to bring our new neighbor dinner tonight. Can you make something?

It was only nine o'clock, so Holly didn't expect an answer for at least another hour or so. She definitely didn't expect Melanie to text back immediately.

YES!

Holly's phone rang seconds later. "You must have changed your mind if you want to bring him dinner."

"Maybe? I don't know. He brought back your dish and seemed nice enough." She decided to spare her pride and keep getting locked out to herself. "By bringing him dinner, I can snoop a bit. I'm curious about his house."

"His house?" She snorted. "Snooping is more my forte than yours."

Holly laughed. "Maybe you're rubbing off on me."

"One can only hope, but I doubt it. You like him. There's no reason to be ashamed of it."

"Okay, maybe I am a tiny bit interested. ..."

"I knew it! Don't worry. I'll make him something good. Something to warm him up. Something to get his engine going."

Holly laughed even as a blush rose to her cheeks. "Slow down, there. Instead of making something high-octane, maybe stick to something cool. I'm pretty sure that house is still un-air-conditioned."

"Good thinking."

Holly hung up, and moments later her boss walked through the door.

"How was your evening?" Holly asked, looking up from her computer.

"It was interesting." Nicole sat in her chair and put her purse into the bottom desk drawer, not bothering to look at her.

This wasn't a good sign. "Was the Henry party as bad as you thought it would be? Were you right about them using frozen appetizers?"

Nicole bit her lower lip, hesitating for several seconds, and it was clear she was fighting the urge to spill the details. Her love of gossip won out and she spun around to face Holly. "It was beyond tacky."

"Did they really have a mariachi band?"

"Yes! Can you believe it?" Nicole's face lit up as she told Holly all about the party, describing how the organizers got it all wrong.

Holly let her talk for several moments, dreading breaking the news about the Johansen wedding to her boss. This was the Nicole who had hired her—the friendly woman who had promised to teach her the ropes, but who had become progressively standoffish the more Holly learned and grew. When Nicole had finished her story, Holly said in a cheery voice, "I brought you a surprise."

"Oh?" Nicole looked genuinely shocked.

"I'll be right back." Holly disappeared into the back and returned with a small tray that held a cup of coffee prepared the way Nicole liked it—one tablespoon of hazelnut creamer—and a small plate with the muffin. She set them on her boss's desk, then stepped back and smiled. "This is to help make your morning better after yesterday."

Surprise filled Nicole's eyes before she took a sip of the coffee. "Oh, this is lovely. Thank you."

Holly returned to her seat, then took a deep breath. "Miranda Johansen called me yesterday afternoon after you left."

Nicole's eyebrows shot into her hairline. "What?"

"She said they met with the designers at Tender Moments and, while Coraline loved them, Miranda worried they were *too* agreeable."

"What does that mean?"

"It means that Miranda Johansen wants to hire Distinctive Events to plan her daughter's wedding."

"Distinctive Events or you?" Nicole asked, her tone short.

"I'm your employee, Nicole. My clients are ultimately yours. Besides, I tried to suggest that you be the lead planner, but Miranda insisted I take charge."

"I'm sure you worked *very* hard at trying to convince her." Sarcasm bled through her boss's words, filling Holly with disappointment. She missed the woman who had hired her.

Holly took a breath. "Honestly, Nicole, I don't want to do this wedding. In fact, I told Coraline I wouldn't be a good fit. But Miranda said that was the reason she decided to hire me. Because I wouldn't kowtow to her daughter."

"That's ridiculous! Our job is to give the client what she wants!" Nicole sputtered in disbelief.

"There's something else you should know." This was sure to tick her off even more. "*Modern Bride* magazine is doing a ten-page feature on the wedding."

"*What?*"

"Miranda's concerned that any additional changes by her

daughter will produce embarrassing results. She wants me to come up with a plan and stick to it."

Nicole looked skeptical.

"I asked her what kept Coraline from firing me, and Miranda said she was drawing up a contract stating that I can't be fired, but I can't quit, either. However, once we decide on a plan, what I say goes." Nicole remained silent, but she seemed more interested. "She also said she would be quite generous with the fees. And that her budget amount is 'obscene.'"

Nicole's mouth pursed. "I think maybe we can work with this."

Holly couldn't help smiling, although she was pretty sure this was a fool's endeavor. "Miranda said she would send a contract this morning and she wants us to come to her house this afternoon to discuss the plans."

Her eyes widened. "We? I'm sure she asked for you."

"I may be planning the wedding, but she's hiring *Distinctive Events*. This is a huge win for the company, Nicole. I think you should be part of this."

Nicole's back stiffened. "No, Holly. She wants *you*."

"I would still feel better if you sat in on the first meeting." That was only a partial truth. It was more to cover her butt should things go south later, which had a very strong possibility of happening. But it also might appease her boss if she was part of the planning. Holly would have enough stress dealing with the difficult client without adding a difficult boss. "You're an expert at dealing with clientele. And, if nothing else, your presence shows that the wedding has the attention of the complete company team."

"Well...I see your point when you put it that way. ..." She took a sip of her coffee. "Has she sent the contract yet?"

"There was nothing when I checked five minutes ago, but

let me look again." Holly spun around and checked her e-mail files. "It showed up a couple of minutes ago. Would you like me to forward it to you?"

"Yes. I'll have one of Megan's friends go over the contract for me." She picked up the phone and made a call. "This is Nicole Vandemeer calling for Blair Hansen-Lowry and it's time sensitive. Is she available?" She paused. "Thank you. I'll hold."

Nicole opened her e-mail and the file, scanning the screen as she waited.

"Blair? No, not to worry. Megan and the baby are fine." Nicole's voice softened. "I need you to go over a contract for me. ... Yes, I know you're a divorce attorney, but surely you can look this over. ... Yes, that's doable. I'll send it right away. And is there any chance you can look it over before noon? I realize that's only a few hours away. Did I mention that I currently have you in charge of a game at Megan's baby shower tomorrow? *But* I can switch it to Libby." A wicked smile lit up her eyes. "Very good. I look forward to hearing back from you." She hung up and looked over her shoulder at Holly. "She was hesitant, but agreed to glance it over, and if it's too complicated she'll recommend someone else to review it."

Holly had to appreciate the way Nicole could get people to do what she wanted, and the mention of the shower reminded her that Nicole had been driving herself crazy getting ready for her daughter's party. "How are things going with the shower planning?"

"Everything is in place, but Megan still stubbornly refuses to tell me the sex of the baby."

"Maybe she doesn't know yet."

"She *claims* she and Josh don't want to know, but I'm sure they are doing this to spite me. I'm certain she told my mother, but she swears she doesn't know, either. I wouldn't put it past Megan and my mother to use this against me in some kind of prank at the shower."

Holly had gotten to know Megan since she'd moved back from Seattle, and Holly had recognized that she had a mischievous spirit. And as for Gram—as everyone called Nicole's mother—Holly had met her, too. Nicole's paranoid concern wasn't outside the realm of possibility.

"I wanted to announce the baby's sex at the shower. Many of her friends will be there, as well as her aunts and cousins."

"And some of your friends."

"Well, yes..."

Nicole seemed flustered by her statement, although Holly wasn't sure why. She hadn't hidden the fact that she'd planned her daughter's shower during her second trimester purely to host it in her recently updated backyard. It was the perfect opportunity to sign on more clients. Still, maybe Holly could use this to her advantage.

"It would have been great to make a big production of announcing the baby's gender." The fact that Nicole had some really great ideas had never been in question. That was part of the appeal of working with her.

Nicole turned around to look at her, seemingly surprised to have a coconspirator. "*Yes!* That's what I've told Megan." Her face lit up. "Why don't you talk to her?"

"Me?"

"You know each other. Maybe you can convince her to give up this foolishness."

"But..." Was she insane? "You want me to just call her and ask her if she's having a boy or girl? I haven't talked to her in over a month."

"Of course not. Warm her up with something else first. Tell her what you'll be wearing tomorrow."

Holly froze. "Why would Megan care what I'm wearing tomorrow?"

"So she can tell you if it clashes with her outfit." A smile spread across Nicole's face. "I need you to help at the shower tomorrow."

Holly stared at her in disbelief.

"Millie Leopold will be there and I know for a fact she's planning a huge engagement party for her daughter. We need to impress her."

"But this is Megan's baby shower."

Nicole rolled her eyes. "Yes, I know. And if you can find out the baby's gender by three, I can make sure the cupcakes coordinate."

She was serious. But she was also in a slightly better mood. This was a way for Holly to earn her way back into Nicole's good graces. Besides, it wasn't like Nicole was going to give her the option of saying no.

"Okay," Holly said, knowing there was no way to get the baby's sex out of Megan but she'd at least make an effort.

"Perfect!" Nicole clasped her hands together. "Distinctive Events has scored the wedding of the year." She paused and took a sip of her coffee. "Things are definitely going my way."

Chapter Eleven

$\sim$

Kevin arrived at the restaurant at seven p.m. sharp and was surprised when he didn't see either of his parents' cars in the parking lot. His mother had texted the time and location that afternoon and had made him promise to be on time. Maybe they'd parked around back.

"I'm meeting my parents," he told the hostess after he'd gone inside. "The reservation is probably under Nicole Vandemeer."

The hostess's eyes lit up and she gave him a knowing grin. "Right this way, Mr. Vandemeer."

"Are my parents seated already?" he asked, following her.

"You're the first to arrive." She motioned to a white-cloth-covered table in a dark corner. A rose in a small vase and a lit candle were in the middle of the table.

He looked around, then back at her. "None of the other tables have flowers and candles."

She covered her mouth with her hand, doing a poor job of trying to hide her smile. "This was specially ordered."

"Okay…" He rolled his eyes as he sat down. Leave it to his mother to make a production out of meeting for dinner.

"Can I get you something to drink to start you off, Mr. Vandemeer?"

If his mother went to this much trouble, it was a safe bet she wouldn't approve of him getting a beer. And he was mostly here to appease her. "Water for now."

"We'll have it right out."

He looked around the room, wondering if he was too dressed up. He hadn't been to this restaurant before, but his mother had told him to wear a dress shirt and tie. He'd obeyed but paired it with jeans. He couldn't conform too much or she'd get suspicious.

He really wanted to be back at his monstrosity of a house. He was about to tear out the kitchen. Matt had given him step-by-step instructions, and Kevin had almost psyched himself up to do it. He'd try to make this quick and then head back home.

After five minutes, a waiter had brought him his water but his parents still hadn't arrived. He had pulled out his phone, ready to call his mother, when the hostess returned with a woman who looked vaguely familiar.

The tall blonde was dressed in a clingy teal dress and heels. She stopped next to his table, her eyes lighting up as she waited for him to react. Finally, she laughed. "Kevin Vandemeer, you look *amazing*."

"Uh…" He stood. She obviously knew him. "So do you."

She tilted her head and gave him a coy smile. "You don't remember me, do you?"

"I'm sorry…" Who the hell was she?

"Bethany, silly. Bethany Davis. From high school."

Oh, crap. He knew her, all right. "Wow. You haven't changed." Outwardly anyway, but he already suspected she hadn't changed much on the inside, either. She'd always been empty-headed, but he had to admit that she *did* look amazing.

Based on the pleased smile that lit up her face, he'd said the right thing. She rested her hand on his arm and squeezed, like she was picking out a melon at the grocery store. "You've definitely filled out."

He took a step back and looked around. Where were his parents? "Are you meeting someone here?"

She giggled. "I'm meeting *you*, silly." Then she sat in the seat across from him.

He frowned. "My mom and dad—"

"Aren't coming." She set her shiny leather purse on the seat next to her. "Your mother set this up."

He took a breath and pushed it out before he sat across from her. "I'm sure she did."

"Wasn't that sweet of her?"

"Ah...*sweet* wasn't the word I was thinking," he said, his voice tight.

She laughed, a high-pitched noise that sounded like a cross between Tinker Bell and scratching metal. "She said you were shy so we'd surprise you. Funny, I don't remember you being very shy."

"I guess some things have changed after all." Damn his interfering mother.

She held up her hands, flashing her shiny, long red nails. "Now I have to tell you that I'm on a very restricted diet. Very holistic."

"Okay..."

"And you have to eat it, too. I can't be around unholy food. But your mother said it wouldn't be a problem."

Unholy? Did she mean food that hadn't been blessed? "Of course she did." He remembered that Bethany had always been quick to try the latest fad or craze. If the past thirty seconds were any indication, it was going to be a long dinner.

The waiter started to walk by and Kevin grabbed his arm. "I'll take a scotch on the rocks." He needed alcohol to get through this and he needed it fast. "Bethany?"

She put her hands on the table and gave the waiter a patient look. "Now this is very important. I want a glass of Pinot Gris, but it has to be from New Zealand."

"Miss, we don't have a Pinot Gris from New Zealand, but we have several fine vintages from France and California."

She sighed and rolled her eyes. "The California, then." She turned her gaze to Kevin. "I only drink wines from English-speaking countries. It's part of my holistic approach. I believe the grapes can hear the language spoken around them." She spread her arms wide, then brought her hands together, tapping her fingertips. "And that language is absorbed into the grape and then into the wine. If you drink a wine from a country you don't understand the language of, it will upset your system because it's *literally* bringing foreign elements into your temple." She pressed her palms together and smiled softly.

The waiter stared at her, his mouth parted, then looked down at Kevin with fear in his eyes.

Kevin knew exactly how he felt. At least the waiter could run away. "I need you to make mine a double." Then he added, "And bring the menus. *Right away.*"

The waiter walked away and Bethany gave him a curious look.

"I'm starving. I'm working for Matt Osborn now, with his construction company. Remember him?"

She nodded. "Your mother mentioned it. That's so sweet of you."

"Excuse me?" Oh, God. What had his mother told her? He picked up his water, wishing he already had his drink. He might have to call a cab when this was all said and done.

"Putting your life on hold and helping him out in a bind like that." She shook her head and stared at him in awe. "You're like a living saint."

"I'm definitely *not* a saint."

"Aww...and so humble, too." She took a breath, her eyebrows rising as her eyes danced. "You know how sometimes you just *know* things? Like it's just fate? That's us. We're going to make beautiful babies, Kevin Vandemeer."

What the hell? He spit his water across the table, putting the candle out.

Bethany was up in an instant. "You poor dear! Are you choking?" She stood behind him, leaning forward and draping her arms down his chest, and began stroking his abs. "I know the Heimlich."

He pushed her arms off his shoulders. "That's not the Heimlich."

"Are you sure? I've given it to several men and none of them said it wasn't."

He stood. "Excuse me. I have to go to the restroom to dry my shirt."

"If you like, we can go back to your place and you can take it off there."

"Yeah, that's okay." He pointed over his shoulder with his thumb. "I think I'll just go to the men's room."

"Don't be so silly." She pushed him back down and grabbed the napkin off the table and dabbed at the wet spot, letting her hand linger on his left pec. "You must lift weights."

He grabbed the napkin from her hand. "You know, it's really not that wet. It'll dry. Have a seat and tell me what you've been up to."

She looked torn, as though trying to decide if she should be upset or pleased, but pleased won out as she sat down. "*Well*...I'm a licensed masseuse."

"You don't say."

"I have magical crystals that exude an electromagnetic energy that fills my touch with healing powers. I'm sure you felt them when I touched you a moment ago. Sometimes it can be a bit jarring."

Where the hell was his drink? "I totally feel jarred."

She smiled. "I have my own holistic center. I have so many customers I might have to expand."

"Wow. Really?" People actually believed in this crap? "How many?"

"Well...maybe ten? My mother is always complaining about the amount of people tromping up and down her stairs to the basement."

"You still live with your mother."

"I'm still waiting for my center to take off."

"I see."

The waiter brought their drinks and Kevin held up his hand and took a big gulp, then said, "Bring me another."

"Another double?" He leaned close to Kevin's ear. "You won't be able to drive, sir."

"Yeah, I know," he whispered. "I'll get a ride."

"All right, then."

Bethany gave him a questioning glance.

"He was filling me in on the specials."

"But I didn't hear them."

"It was mercury-filled sea bass. I told him to find something else."

Her gaze followed the waiter and her lips pressed into a pout. "But that sounds interesting."

Kevin drained his glass, his chest already warming. He

looked into her startled face. "I was thirsty. It's hot working outside all day."

She nodded. "It's important to hydrate."

He was going to kill his mother.

The waiter came to take their order, bringing Kevin's drink with him. Bethany leaned forward. "I would love to hear more about your mercurial sea bass special." She tilted her head, her eyes narrowed as she focused. "Exactly how temperamental were the fish? I'm worried they were too stressed."

Kevin choked on his drink again and Bethany gave him a look of concern.

"I really think you should let me do a crystal cleansing on you."

He finished the drink, then set the glass down with a bang. "I want a moody fish dinner."

The waiter looked startled. "The best I can do is salmon grilled on a cedar plank."

Bethany shook her head. "No, Kevin. I think you have too much strife in your life to get the mercurial fish. You need something calm and soothing. Like smashed potatoes."

Kevin paused, trying to keep a straight face. "But I would think the potatoes would be stressed from the smashing."

"Oh, dear. I hadn't considered that." She turned to the waiter. "What is your mellowest meal?"

"I...uh..." he looked back at Kevin, giving him a look that said *traitor*. "I would say it's the spaghetti and meatballs. It makes me think of *Lady and the Tramp*. Something that cute is soothing."

Bethany nodded. "Yes, I agree. We'll take two of those."

Kevin ordered another drink, then listened to Bethany talk about crystals and how they harnessed the earth's energy and how she insisted on giving him a private reading.

When their food and his third drink arrived, he hoped she'd focus on her meal, but she then went on to describe her holistic diet, the purest foods being Swiss cheese and angel food cake. For obvious reasons.

"Where did my mother dig you up?" Kevin blurted out. The alcohol had loosened his inner censor.

"Oh, she planned my engagement party."

"*To me?*" He nearly dropped his fork in his instinct to run and never look back.

She laughed. "No, silly. To my ex-fiancé."

"What happened to him?"

She pursed her lips. "He moved to Hong Kong."

Kevin had to wonder if that was far enough to escape her clutches. "Did my mother meet yours at the country club?"

"Yes!" She squealed. "How did you know?"

His mother, if nothing else, was predictable. He stood. "If you'll excuse me for a moment, I need to go to the restroom."

"Of course."

He disappeared down the hall and pulled out his cell phone, calling his sister. "Megan. I need your help."

"Kevin?" She sounded worried. "Are you okay? What's going on?"

"I'm stuck on the blind date from hell and now I'm drunk as shit and can't drive home. Come get me."

She chuckled. "I can't believe you agreed to a blind date."

"I didn't. It was thrust on me. Thrust—I bet Bethany likes that word."

"Where are you?"

His mind fixated on the word *thrust* and for some reason the thought of his neighbor came to mind—lying on his bed, as he—

"*Kevin.* Focus. *Where are you?*"

He blinked. God, he was such a lightweight. He used to drink his friends under the table. Now, he was drunk as shit on three drinks. Okay, they were all doubles, and he hadn't had more than a few beers at a time in months, but still.

"Kevin!"

"Café Rustica. On Seven Highway."

"Oh, nice place. Totally date worthy. You really wanted to impress." He heard the grin in her voice.

"*Mom* wanted to impress. She set this whole thing up."

She laughed. "No kidding. This has her stamp all over it."

"So will you come get me?"

"I owe you, remember? Sit tight and I'll be there in about ten minutes."

Bethany was watching for him when he got back, concern in her eyes. "Are you okay? You were gone so long."

"I think maybe that spaghetti was just as cantankerous as the fish, if you know what I mean."

She gave him a blank look, then her eyes widened. "Oh…your bowels."

He shifted in his seat. "Funny thing. My sister, Megan, called while I was in the restroom and said she needs my help. It's an emergency."

Worry filled her eyes. "Oh, my. Is she okay? What's the emergency?"

Crap. What was it? "She needs my help picking out a name for her baby."

"Shouldn't her husband help her with that?"

"His names are ridiculous. He wants to name him Pickle."

"Oh, dear. That's terrible." She gave him a pout. "I was hoping to come see your new house."

"Maybe another time." He flagged down the waiter and asked for the bill.

She leaned over the table, her voice sounding husky. "So

do you want to pick me up tomorrow night or should I meet you somewhere?"

"*Excuse me?*"

The waiter brought the check then ran off, looking over his shoulder at Bethany. Kevin pulled cash out of his wallet instead of using his card. He didn't want to wait a second longer than necessary.

"Our next date."

"Yeah." He grimaced. "Let me get back to you on that. Matt said something about me pulling a few evening shifts." He hated lying, but in this instance it was better than telling her *Never, because you're batshit crazy.*

She reached across the table for his hand. "Well, at least give me your number so I can call you."

He tried to look nonchalant as he pulled his hand from hers, sure he wasn't as smooth as he hoped, given his inebriated state. "Why don't you just give me yours? I'm kind of old-fashioned and want to be the one to call."

"Oh! Okay." Her face lit up and he felt bad, even though he was more than a little creeped out by her. She reached into her purse and handed him a business card. He wasn't all that surprised to see that it was covered in sparkles.

"Crystal Living Center," he read.

She pointed to the card. "That's my cell-phone number. I have my phone with me all the time."

"Got it." He didn't feel right just leaving her here at the table, yet he didn't want to lead her on even more. His manners won out. "Would you like me to walk you to your car?"

She radiated with happiness. "Of course."

Guilt washed through him as he walked her out into the hot, humid evening, but there was no turning back from this now. The only other alternative was to try to let her down gently. He stopped at the back of her car, feeling slightly less drunk but nowhere close to being ready to drive. "It was great getting to see you again, but I'm going to be honest— I don't think I'm ready for a relationship yet."

"Oh." The light in her eyes dimmed and he felt like a jerk. Damn his mother.

"See, I'm at a weird phase in my life right now. I think I need to figure out me and where to go forward before I start something with someone."

Her smile returned. "You *think* you need to wait?"

Well, shit.

Before he could react, she kissed him hard on the lips, then took a step back. "Challenge accepted."

Challenge? Shit! "Bethany!"

But she had already gotten into her car and given him a little wave through the side window.

Frustrated, he spun around, almost falling over from his screwed-up equilibrium, and headed straight for his sister's car, which had just pulled up to the curb in front of the restaurant.

She was giggling when he climbed into the passenger seat. "Is that your date? She's very pretty."

"She's batshit crazy—on a level that astounds even me. And that's saying something."

She took off her sunglasses and gave him the once-over. "She must be crazy if *you* drank too much to cope, Mr. I'm Always in Control. How many drinks did you have, anyway?"

"Too many."

"That much is obvious." She slid her glasses onto her nose and shifted her car into gear. "You want me to take you home or to Mom's so you can lynch her?"

"As tempting as the lynching is, home."

She shot him a grin. "Oh, I was really looking forward to the lynching."

"I can't believe she did this. I had no idea. She told me to meet her and Dad for dinner, and instead Bethany showed up."

Megan turned onto the main street. "Oh, *I* believe it. She's desperate for you to get married and have kids. She's tired of waiting so she's taking matters into her own hands."

"By setting me up with a crazy woman?"

"Why are you so surprised? Crazy doesn't recognize crazy."

Oh, my God. She was right. He was crazy, too. Otherwise he would have seen the signs in Lacy and all the previous crazy girls before her.

Unaware of his inner turmoil, Megan moved on to another topic. "How was your first couple of days working with Matt?" Megan shifted her gaze to him, then back to the road. "I hadn't thought about him owning a construction company. Does that mean he's going to help you work on the house?"

He leaned his head back into the seat and wished Megan's car would stop spinning. "Matt's given me some pointers, but I haven't had a chance to do anything yet. I've been too busy returning dishes to my cute neighbor and going on blind dates with women our mother picks out."

She grinned. "I want to hear more about your cute neighbor."

"There's nothing to tell." He closed his eyes. Last night he'd argued with himself all the way home from his dinner with his friends. He'd convinced himself to dump the rest of the lasagna, rinse out the pan, then take it over to her—and then made himself go home before he molested her right there on her front porch. What kind of guy would he be if he hadn't helped her climb in her window? Of course, checking out her ass and touching the bare skin of her abdomen had been a bonus. But tonight with Bethany had been the reminder he needed to stay the course of the Bachelor Brotherhood. "I'm giving up women. They're all bonkers."

"Hey!"

"You bought me a piece-of-shit house without my consent. You qualify as crazy."

She paused. "I suppose I deserve that."

"I have to have a talk with Mom. Setting me up on blind dates is unacceptable."

"And throwing me a baby shower I don't want *is*? Not to mention that she's hounding me to tell her if it's a boy or a girl. Why can't she accept that Josh and I don't want to know?"

"You're comparing my situation to a *baby shower*? Please. That date ranked up there in the top three worst dates *ever*. She's into crystals, and nonfighting food, and English-speaking wine."

"*What?*"

He shook his head. "Whatever. My date was *way* worse than a stupid baby shower."

She pulled up to a stoplight and stared at him in disbelief. "Are you kidding me? You saw the fiasco she made of the family party before my wedding. And we won't even go into the fiasco at Blair's wedding shower. This is a bigger disaster."

"Give me a break," he scoffed.

"Fine. You think it's not so bad, then you come to the shower and see for yourself."

"To a baby shower? No way." He was still trying to get out of playing bartender. If Megan found out their mother had roped him in, she'd make sure there was no way he could get out of it.

"Then good luck on your second date with Crazy Pants."

He sat up. "What's that mean?"

"It means come to my shower, and I'll get Mom to back off."

He scoffed his disbelief. "You can't get her to promise that."

She rested her hand on her belly. "No, but her grandbaby can."

His eyes narrowed. "Now *you're* crazy."

"Trust me on this." They drove the rest of the way in silence until she parked in his driveway. "Hey, how's your kitten doing?"

"It's not *my* kitten, and it's doing just fine. I locked it up in the unfinished basement this morning since it's hot as hell in my un-air-conditioned *piece-of-shit house*."

A grin spread across her face.

"It's not funny, Megan."

"Kevin, just trust me on this, okay?"

"No." He opened the car door and stomped up to the front door.

"Kevin!" She followed behind him, then took his keys as he fumbled with the lock. She got the door open, then looked down at the porch. "You fixed the hole."

"I can't have Girl Scouts suing me after they break their leg when they show up trying to sell me cookies, can I?"

"You have months until it's Girl Scout cookie season."

He groaned and leaned his head against the door frame, but she pulled him into a hug.

"Trust me."

"You keep saying that, but I'm still in a shit hole."

She laughed and kissed his cheek. "Josh and I will come help you on Sunday. If you come to the shower on Saturday."

"That again?"

She gave him an ornery smile.

He was figuring out that his little sister was used to getting what she wanted. No sense making it easy for her. "I'll think about it."

"I'll take that." Then she kissed his cheek again and walked down the steps. "Now go drink some water and take some aspirin. You're gonna have a killer hangover tomorrow."

Dammit. She was right.

He was going to kill his mother.

Chapter Twelve

Holly should have been happy. The lawyer had deemed the Johansen contract good, and the meeting with Coraline had gone better than expected. Nicole had seemed pleased when they left, and had even insisted that Holly was the perfect designer for the wedding.

So now she sat at her kitchen table with her laptop open and a notebook full of ideas. Surprisingly, it had all come together fairly quickly. The vineyard had been the key; that and a photo of Coraline with her fiancé that Holly had seen at Miranda's house.

Coraline and Donald had met in Italy and attended a wine tasting at a vineyard for their first date. The wedding dress Miranda had designed was the clincher. It was a classic design—a tight-fitting dress made of satin with sheer net over the back with cloth-covered buttons. The bottom had a slight flare like a mermaid style. Miranda explained that she had kept the dress simple, to fit in with Coraline's ever-changing themes. Holly planned to suggest that Coraline wear a veil with Italian lace to help pull the dress into the theme.

An outdoor Tuscan-themed wedding could work perfectly with the venue, the dress, and the bride's surprising sentimentality when she discussed her first date with her fiancé. But, just as importantly, Holly was certain she could pull it off in the three-week time frame. And it would photograph well for both the wedding photos and the magazine spread.

If Miranda lived up to her end of the bargain of keeping Coraline from changing her mind after she'd given her approval, and Nicole remained happy, this could end up being an amazing opportunity.

So she had no reason to be sitting at her kitchen table feeling unsettled. Especially when her unease had nothing to do with her job and everything to do with the guy next door.

Melanie had come through on her end and made pasta salad and pita sandwiches, placing them on their nicest Target plate. Not only could Mel cook, but she styled food as well. She was definitely wasting her talents as a bartender. But Holly couldn't quite bring herself to take the plate next door.

She gulped down the rest of her wine as her practicality warred with some deep, dark desire. But desire for what, exactly? A relationship? A romp? She didn't know him well enough to want a relationship with him, which meant this yearning had to be chemistry. That was a good thing, right? She'd never felt it with anyone else before, and honestly, who knew if she ever would again. Her friends—who had all gotten married and were having kids—used to talk about how a guy would make them weak in the knees, but that had never happened to Holly until Kevin.

And damned if she wasn't curious about what else he could make her feel.

Before she could change her mind, she grabbed the plate and marched over to his house, knocking on the door. As she waited, she glanced over at the driveway and realized his car wasn't there.

A hot guy like Kevin didn't stay home on Friday nights.

Feeling like a fool, she went back home and poured another glass of wine before she sat at her dining room table, photos of bouquets and wedding cakes spread around like scattered flower-girl petals. For the first time she allowed herself to admit her discontent. She wanted to experience the happiness that filled her wedding couples. She didn't even need her own happily-ever-after. She was willing to try a happily-for-now.

Killer started barking, pawing at the front window. Pushing out a sigh, Holly went to investigate. What if someone was breaking into one of the neighbors' cars? Or, worse, into their house?

At first she couldn't see what Killer was barking at, and then she saw an older SUV parked in Kevin's driveway. The overgrown trees blocked part of her view, but she saw a man walking to the front porch and a woman in a loose-fitting dress following behind. Did he have a girlfriend?

Unable to stop herself, she opened the front door and moved to a wicker chair on her small front porch. She could see two figures in front of Kevin's door, embracing. Then the woman went down the steps and stood at the bottom, turning back to him before she walked back to her car, and Holly suddenly realized she had just turned into a stalker. She was literally spying on her neighbor.

That man was screwing with her head.

She went inside and stared at the images on her table. For

the first time ever, she couldn't get excited about her job. She couldn't work on celebrating someone else's love when she was overcome with a loneliness she'd ignored for too long.

Holly grabbed her wineglass, then called the dog. "Killer, let's go outside." Then, as an afterthought, she grabbed the box of wine and headed out the back door.

The eager dog bolted past her on the way out. Holly planted herself in a chair, dangling her feet into the wading pool. It was too hot to be outside, but she needed her Zen spot and the water helped cool her off. She finished her half-empty glass, then poured another.

Who *was* she tonight?

Leaning her head back against the chair, she closed her eyes and breathed in the scent of the roses and the honey-suckle her grandmother had planted years ago, letting her mind wander. Of course he had a girlfriend. Gorgeous guys like Kevin weren't single. On the bright side, maybe this meant she'd unlocked some secret door to her libido. She could look for someone else.

Killer suddenly released a low growl, sounding totally unlike himself. Holly jerked upright, knocking her glass off the arm of the chair and onto her lap. Shrieking from the shock of the wine drenching her skirt, she scrambled off the chair as she realized she could only see Killer's butt. His front half was on the other side of the fence that separated her yard from her new neighbor's. At the same time, she heard a man shouting and then the startled shrieks of a cat.

A cat?

Killer's growl deepened and his back legs scratched at the ground beneath him in an effort to get through the hole. "Killer! No!" she shouted, dashing toward him. "Come!"

The dog was more enticed with what was on the other

side of the fence than the possibility of turkey and puffed-cheese snacks. The rising squalls of the cat seemed to encourage his efforts, and he pushed himself the rest of the way through just as she reached him.

"Shit!" a male voice shouted on the other side of the wooden privacy fence.

Killer's growls turned to barking, and the cat now shrieked in panic.

"Killer!" She ran for the gate to the front yard, fumbling with the latch before getting it open. She didn't wait for an invitation, just opened her neighbor's gate and burst through.

Kevin was standing in the middle of the yard with his back to her. The dog was barking at his feet, and a small gray kitten perched on top of his shoulder, its back arched.

"Killer!" she shouted in horror and started to run for him, but Kevin turned at the sound of her voice and she froze, her heart jolting at the sight of him.

He was even more sexy than the last two times she'd seen him. How was that possible?

He studied her, too, and she realized he might not recognize her. The times he'd seen her she'd been in shorts, makeup free, and sporting a ponytail or bun. Now she was in her work clothes—minus her shoes—and her hair was down, hanging several inches below her shoulders.

The sight of the bleeding scratch on his cheek caught her attention, pushing her into action. "Oh, my God. I am so sorry!" She scooped the dog off the ground, holding him close to her side as she looked into his face. "Killer! Bad dog!"

She turned her attention to Kevin again, close enough to see that his eyes were a darker brown tonight, and they looked slightly unfocused.

The kitten on his shoulder looked panicked and dug his claws deeper into Kevin's shoulder, making him cringe.

"I am *so* sorry," Holly gushed. "Killer's not mean, I promise. He's so small he likes to bluff everyone."

"I noticed that last night." Kevin pried the cat off his shoulder, giving an additional tug to get its claws free of his blue dress shirt. He wore a tie, too, a dark gray charcoal. So he dressed up for dates. That only intrigued her even more. "I think he found someone smaller to intimidate." He got the kitten free and held it close to his chest, the animal's feet dangling free.

Holly's last defense against him slipped away. The sight of the tall, strong man cradling a tiny kitten was impossible to resist.

Killer started barking again and Holly turned him around to look into his face. "*Stop.*"

The dog lowered his gaze and stopped barking.

"He likes turkey," she said in response, then realized how random it sounded. "He belongs to my cousin. She trained him with deli turkey."

"The one who made the lasagna?" When she nodded, a slight grin tipped up the corners of his mouth. "Then I might be able to overlook the attack."

Attack? "Oh, God! Did he bite you? He's never bitten anyone before!"

"Oh, no. Wrong choice of words. You'll have to forgive me." His grin turned sheepish. "I'm more than a little drunk."

"Oh."

He frowned as though deciding he shouldn't have been so blunt, so she piped up. "I'm slightly tipsy myself."

"Bad day?" he asked.

"No, actually a good one." Probably the best she'd had with her boss since she'd first started working for her.

"So a celebration?"

She couldn't very well tell him she'd been drinking because of him. "Yeah. You?"

"Coping skills."

The woman had brought him home, then left him while he was drunk. Did they have a fight? It seemed rude to ask, yet she was dying to know. "Because of your girlfriend?"

He snorted. "I don't have a girlfriend."

Because they broke up or because they weren't together in the first place? She decided to be bold and ask—figure out her chances here—but he reached up to his cheek, gently patting the scratch.

"You need to clean that," she said, taking a step closer to look it over, but the dog started barking again. She looked down at him. "*Stop.*" The dog obeyed and she continued. "Who knows what germs are in that kitten's claws?" she said, feeling more courageous than her usual self. *Thank you, wine.* "We can't have your pretty face getting eaten by flesh-eating bacteria."

His eyes danced with amusement. "You think I have a pretty face?"

She laughed. "I find it interesting that you pick up on *that* part of the sentence and not the flesh-eating bacteria."

"Does your dog always obey you?"

"Obviously not, or he wouldn't have gotten back here in the first place."

The amusement in his eyes faded, turning dark and sultry. "I'm glad he did."

She looked away, suddenly unsure of herself. But his face was still bleeding and needed attention and, honestly, it was her fault. If she'd been paying attention, Killer might not have gotten through the fence and scared his cat. "Do you have a first aid kit in your house?"

He laughed. "I don't have shit in my house."

"So that's a no?" She grinned. "Come over to mine and let me clean you up."

He looked uncertain, and she realized she may have over-stepped her bounds.

"You don't have to…I…"

His eyes found hers. "I don't want to leave the cat." He lifted it slightly. "I've been gone all day and just got home and now it's shaking. …" His voice trailed off, then he laughed. "If my friends could hear me now. I think this is the literal definition of pussy whipped."

Her cheeks heated up and he stared at her in amazement. "How do you do that?"

"Do what?"

"Look so sexy and so innocent at the same time."

Her blush deepened, but she told herself that he was drunk and didn't know what he was saying. "You can bring your kitten with you, if you want. Or I can bring the first aid kit over here."

"What about your dog?"

"If he continues to terrorize the cat, then I'll shut him into Mel's room or put him in the backyard. But I think he'll just get used to him…or is it a her?"

"I'm not sure."

"You don't know if it's a boy or girl?"

He looked embarrassed. "I can't tell."

She laughed. "The vet didn't tell you?"

His eyes widened. "Shit. I suppose I need to make an appointment." When he saw her surprise, he said, "The kitten came with the house."

"You negotiated it into the contract?"

"No, I found it under the front porch."

Realization hit her. "Oh. The hole."

He sighed. "The hole."

"It was trapped down there? Poor baby." But his actions told her a lot about his character, even if the way he protectively held it now hadn't. An unexpected heat washed through her, pooling in her core, and she told herself it was the alcohol. "Bring the cat and I'll clean you up."

She didn't give him a chance to answer, just turned around and headed to her house, leaving him to follow or not.

Chapter Thirteen

If he'd had any hesitation, watching her ass in that tight peach skirt as she walked away would have wiped it away. He was a hypocrite. He'd just sworn off women, yet he was *literally* chasing after her. It wasn't like anything was going to happen. She'd put antibiotic ointment on his face, then he'd go home and rip out his kitchen cabinets.

Yeah, right.

The kitten released a soft mewl and he held it closer to his chest. He wasn't sure whether to be happy or upset that the cat had dictated his decision, but it was terrified. He couldn't lock it up in the basement again. First chance he got, he was calling his sister to come and get it.

Holly led him to her front porch and he followed, keeping his gaze on her ass when she bent over to put the dog on the floor. She held his front legs off the floor and looked into his face.

"You be good, Killer. Or you'll be shut in your mommy's room." But her voice was anything but firm.

"Does he understand you?"

She dropped her hold on Killer and rubbed the top of the dog's head before she stood. "I like to think so, but, honestly, he's spoiled rotten." Her gaze lingered on his cheek. "Why don't you sit at the kitchen island and I'll get the first aid kit."

She disappeared up the stairs but her dog stayed behind, looking up at him like he was dinner. Or maybe it was staring at the cat. At least it had stopped barking.

Kevin sat on the bar stool and took the opportunity to look around. The house was a little bigger than his, but it was cozy and well kept. The living room, dining room, and kitchen were all one open space. The wood floors had been refinished, and the kitchen cabinets had been painted a crisp white and topped with black granite counters. It was apparent the house had been redone.

The dog turned its attention toward the stairs. Holly had come back down carrying a white plastic box, which she set on the counter, but he was more focused on her silky cream blouse—how it clung to her breasts and revealed her cleavage peeking out of the deep V. His gaze dropped and caught a wet spot at the bottom edge of her skirt. It looked fresh and he thought to ask what happened, but he got distracted watching her legs when she turned to the cabinet and reached up on tiptoes to pull out two glasses. She filled them with ice water, then handed one to him. "I think you need this."

He took it from her and drank several gulps, if nothing else to cool down his rising libido.

She took a sip of the water and went to the back door. "Killer, go outside." The dog ran out the door, and she turned back to him and grinned. "I think the kitten's been traumatized enough."

"Won't he go back through the hole into my yard?"

"I don't think so. He only went through to get the cat."

She moved to the sink and washed her hands.

"Did you buy your house already updated?"

She laughed as she tore off a paper towel and held it under the running water. "No, I've lived here since I was a kid. It's my grandmother's house. My cousin and I just live in it. We're the ones who remodeled everything."

"Just the two of you?"

She shrugged. "It started out of necessity my senior year of high school. The house was falling apart and we couldn't afford to hire all of it out. Some we had to leave to professionals—like the electricity—but we did a lot ourselves. We gutted the kitchen. We did it a step at a time." She paused. "We probably look like amateurs to you."

He gave her a wry grin. "I don't know the first thing about remodeling a house. It seemed like a good idea at the time."

"You'll figure it out. We didn't know how to do anything in the beginning." She grinned up at him, her eyes twinkling. "A helpful hint: YouTube will become your best friend."

"Maybe you could show me a thing or two." It slipped out before he could reel it back in. He lifted his hand to his temple as he cringed, bumping into hers as she held a wet paper towel on his cheek. "I didn't mean it like it sounded. I really meant..."

She grabbed his hand and held on to it for several seconds as a teasing glint appeared in her eyes. "I know."

She'd been so tongue-tied the past two times he'd seen her, he loved seeing her like this. She was different than the women he usually dated. Less jaded and less sure of herself—in a good way. Lacy and the others had always thought he was a sure thing, but he'd known they were a sure thing, too. He had no idea where he stood with Holly—she could finish cleaning his scratches and toss him out on his ass. But he found the uncertainty of it all intriguing.

She released his hand, then opened the first aid kit to grab several alcohol squares. "This is probably going to hurt." She ripped one open and dabbed at his cheek.

He flinched when it stung. "Sorry."

"I noticed you shaved." She looked up at him. "I like it."

It shouldn't have mattered what she thought, but it did. "Thanks."

She continued to stare at him, her eyes darkening to a forest green as they fell to his lips. She was less than a foot away and the urge to kiss her burned in his chest.

She broke the gaze, looking down at the bloodstained wipe in her hand. "I don't think it will scar."

"Think of the stories I could tell if it did."

She tossed the square onto the discarded wrappings on her counter, then lifted her gaze and grinned. "Why do I think it might be embellished?"

"Because you are a very smart woman."

Her smile faded slightly. "Maybe not as smart as I should be."

Was she sorry she'd invited him into her house? "What do you mean?"

Her answer was to close the distance between them and kiss him.

It was the last thing he'd expected. Her lips pressed against his, warm and bold. Her hands rested on his shoulders, her fingertips digging in. Her tongue skimmed his bottom lip, and he lost all restraint. He wrapped his free arm around her back and pulled her to his chest.

The cat released a panicked cry.

He pulled back and looked down at the kitten squashed

between them, then back up at Holly, worried that the moment had been broken and she'd change her mind.

She picked it up from his arms and put it on the floor, then turned back to him, moving between his parted legs. Placing her hand on his uninjured cheek, she trailed her fingers down to his neck. He forced himself to remain still. The hesitancy in her touch told him this was unlike her, and he planned to let her make the call as to where this went.

Her gaze held his as her hand skimmed back up, the pad of her thumb brushing his lower lip, and his groin tightened.

"I've wanted to do that since last night," she whispered.

"Do what?" His voice sounded husky, even to his ears.

"Kiss you."

She'd said she was tipsy. Was she drunk? He didn't think so. Her coordination opening the alcohol pads and wiping his scratches had been on point. Was *he* too drunk?

She leaned forward again, her lips softer this time. His mouth parted and her tongue found his as she pressed herself to his chest, still soft and gentle.

Need surged through him and he wasn't sure how long he could restrain himself. But then she grabbed the back of his head, deepening the kiss as her tongue became demanding.

Wrapping an arm around her back, he crushed her to him as he took over, the need to have her closer overtaking all thought as his hand tangled in her hair. He kissed her until she pulled back, her chest heaving with breathlessness.

She looked up at him with eyes hooded with desire. "Do you have a condom?"

Her bluntness startled him, then it didn't. She'd been straightforward in everything else so far.

But her confidence faded at his hesitation. "I'm sorry. That was... if you don't want—"

There was no way in hell he could let her think he didn't want her, and the best way to assure her was to show her. He grabbed her hips and pulled her close again, his mouth finding the nape of her neck and skimming up to her ear. "I very much want."

"I don't have..."

"I do." His mouth found hers again, hot and demanding. Her hands rested on his chest, her fingertips sliding downward as though itching to explore.

His hands were still on her hips and he tugged her shirt free from her skirt, then over her head, and dropped it onto the floor. Her ivory satin bra and the creamy breasts peeking over the edges of the cups drew his attention. His hands returned to her hips, and he started to pull her close again, but she resisted, reaching for his neck.

"You look sexy in a tie," she murmured as she worked on the knot.

He grinned. "I don't wear them very often."

Her gaze lifted to his, her eyes dancing. "Then I'm happy I saw it." She got the knot free and left the tie hanging from his neck before she turned her attention to the buttons on his shirt.

He was aching to touch her, his erection throbbing against the tight confines of his jeans. His fingers dug into her hips in an effort to keep them still while she worked, but when she'd reached his lower chest he let his hands wander, lightly skimming her sides.

She shuddered and sucked in a breath, lifting her eyes to his. The pure lust he saw there tested his control.

"Do you want me to finish that?" he asked, sounding rougher than he intended. She was equal parts bold and hesitant, although he wasn't sure if her hesitation was because they were practically strangers or if she was rethinking her impulsiveness. He wanted to be sure she was all in this, because once he took over, he wasn't sure he'd maintain her seductive pace.

Her fingers slid a button free of its hole while she kept her gaze on his face. A grin tugged at her lips. "Impatient?"

The need to cover her mouth with his and demonstrate how impatient he was warred with his control. "You have no fucking idea."

She paused, her eyes widening, then a new confidence washed over her, her smile turning sexy and mischievous.

"You have no idea how much I want you, do you?"

She finished the last button and lifted her head, her lips parted as she stared up at him.

He grabbed her hand and placed it over his erection, his hand covering hers.

Her hand rubbed the length of him and he squirmed as his jeans made his confinement painful. She slid her hand free and found his belt, unfastening the buckle and pulling it open. Then she concentrated on the button, working it loose. Before he realized what she was doing, she had him unzipped and slid her hand inside the band of his underwear, finding his erection.

That was his cue to take over.

He shot to his feet, leaning over to devour her mouth. She hooked a hand around his neck, pulling closer as his tongue found hers. Grabbing her hips, he lifted her onto the counter, pushing up her skirt and pressing himself against her.

She gasped in surprise.

Slow the fuck down, Kevin.

Taking a step back, he paused to study her face. Was he moving too fast? But she was already reaching for the back of his head, lifting her mouth to his.

He unclasped her bra, then slowly slid the straps over her shoulders and down her arms, the bra falling to the floor and exposing her breasts.

God, he wanted her.

"If you want to do this in a bed, we need to go now or I can't make any guarantees we'll get there."

Her pupils dilated before she tugged on his neck, then kissed him with an intensity that took his breath away. But then she leaned back, her eyes hooded. "I've had fantasies about having sex on a counter, but we should use the bed. Melanie is coming home early tonight."

Scooping her off the counter, he tightened his arms around her as she wrapped her legs around his back. "Upstairs?"

"Yes." She lowered her mouth to his neck, her lips brushing his pulse point.

When he got to the top of the stairs, he paused.

"The room on the left."

He turned his back to the partially closed door and pushed it open, letting her slide down his body as he backed up to her bed.

He cupped her cheek, searching her eyes for any signs that she'd changed her mind. But she broke his gaze and lowered it to his chest, placing her hands on his shoulders and pushing his shirt down his arms. The shirt hadn't hit the floor before her hands were on the waistband of his jeans, tugging them down over his hips.

"Wait." He stilled his hands, then slid his wallet out of his pocket and removed a condom. He tossed it on her nightstand and pulled off his jeans. Turning her back to his chest, he unfastened the button on her skirt, then slowly unzipped it, pushing the fabric over her hips and letting it pool on the floor at her feet.

He took a moment to study her, naked except for her ivory lace panties. Placing his palm on her abdomen, he tugged her backward, her back flush to his chest, the small of her back pressing against his erection. He stifled a groan at the contact, pausing to get control before he cupped her breast with his free hand, his thumb lightly brushing the tip of her nipple.

She released a low moan that shot pure need straight to his erection.

His hand slid lower, underneath the band of her panties, skimming lower until it was between her folds. "God, Holly. You're so wet."

She didn't answer, just pushed herself into his hand and leaned her head back, her eyes closed as he stroked her. He watched her react to his touch and he fought to keep control.

As though reading his mind, she took a step back and slid her fingers under the band of her panties and pushed them over her hips, letting them fall to the floor. Then she walked toward him and pushed him down so he was sitting on the edge of her bed. Placing her hands on his chest, she pressed him back onto the bed.

He watched her, letting her take the lead for the moment. From the hesitation in her eyes he suspected she was the kind of woman who waited until the fifth date to sleep with a guy. He had no idea why she chose to pick him to be adventurous with, but he felt like the luckiest bastard on the planet.

She grabbed the condom from the nightstand and opened the package. She searched his face as she hesitated at the tip. He pushed out an involuntary breath, his erection twitching in anticipation. She gave him a sexy smile as she slowly rolled the condom on, wrapping her other hand around him and stroking down.

Gritting his teeth, it took everything in him to lie still and wait to see what she had planned next, but she seemed unsure again, so he sat up and tangled his hand in her hair, then kissed her hard. She kissed him back with an urgency of her own.

He flipped her onto her back, gathering her wrists in his hand and pinning them to the pillow over her head. He searched her face, relieved that the lust in her eyes told him she was still onboard. He covered one of her legs with his own and placed his hand on her abdomen, sliding over her mound and between her folds again, stroking slowly. She lifted up to his hand, releasing a low moan. His mouth skimmed her breast, teasing her nipple with his tongue until she writhed under his touch.

His knee nudged her legs apart and she wrapped her leg around his back, keeping her gaze on him. Her mouth parted as she watched him with anticipation.

He wanted her now.

Releasing her hands, he lifted her ass up to meet him, then slid into her with one stroke, her tight walls squeezing around him as she took him in. He paused, waiting for his control to return.

But Holly had other ideas. She lifted up, letting him slide deeper, then grabbed his hips and pulled him even closer, squeezing around him again.

He leaned his head back and groaned. "Oh, God, Holly. You feel so good."

She rolled her pelvis against him, and looked up at him with hooded eyes, her skin flushed.

"You're going to kill me," he forced out through gritted teeth. Bracing his hands on either side of her head, he lowered his mouth to her nipple.

She pulled his head up, her eyes desperate. "Don't die yet."

He pulled back and filled her again, and she grabbed his shoulders, her fingers digging in.

"No. Don't stop."

He dropped his head next to hers and let go of his control, pulling back and pushing into her over and over. He lifted up onto his forearms and watched as she came undone, her nails digging into his back as she cried out. He came seconds later, completely losing himself in the moment, losing himself in her.

Kevin collapsed on top of her and it took him too long to figure out he was crushing her. Rolling to the side, he looped his arm around her side, surprised at his need to still be close to her.

Her eyes were closed, her chest heaving as she fought to catch her breath. The sun had set, turning the glow in the room to a soft golden red. Her eyes opened slowly and she cast a cautious look toward him.

He leaned over and kissed her, still feeling the urge to be close. He stared into her emerald green eyes and he knew without a doubt this was the woman he wanted to spend the rest of his life with.

And that was when he knew he had officially lost his mind.

Chapter Fourteen

What the hell was wrong with her? Holly had just slept with a man who was practically a stranger, yet she had no regrets. Not one. It had been the most amazing experience in her life.

But that didn't mean she didn't feel slightly awkward with this man she hardly knew collapsed on top of her.

And then he rolled to his side and kissed her. He could have just gotten up and left, but he gave her a kiss full of gentleness and the promise of more. More sex. More him. Possibly a relationship.

Possibly a relationship?

She was in unfamiliar territory. Was she supposed to entertain him? They'd just had a workout. Should she offer him water? Or a snack?

She decided to be honest. "Um...I've never done this before."

His eyebrows lifted. "Had sex?"

"What?" She sat upright. "Oh, my God! You think I was a virgin?"

He sat up and wrapped an arm around her back. "Holly, I was teasing. I know you weren't a virgin."

She gasped, her face heating. "Oh, my God. Because I acted like a slut."

"Holly! No!" He lifted his hand to her cheek, searching her eyes. "Relax. In no way, shape, or form do I think you are a slut. Yes, you were forward—"

She scrunched her eyes closed. *Oh, God.* She wanted to hide under the bed.

"Holly." His voice was so insistent she cautiously opened her eyes. "You have no idea how sexy you are, do you?"

Her breath caught in her chest. Was he messing with her?

His thumb stroked her cheek. "I don't want this to be a one-time thing."

"You don't?" Oh, Lord. That sounded needy.

"God, no. This was amazing. And I want to do this again." He kissed her, his mouth more demanding than before. "Maybe soon."

"So you're in this just for the sex?"

His eyes widened in horror.

She laughed. "I'm the one teasing now."

He pulled her close and kissed her again, his hand tangling in her hair, and she was surprised that she was ready to do this again *right now*. But she heard a noise from outside the room, so she put her hand between them, cocking her ear toward the door.

"What's that?"

He grinned and shifted against her. "If you don't know what that is, then maybe you were a virgin."

She rolled her eyes. "Not that. The noise. There have

been several car break-ins in the neighborhood, and I'm sure I left the front door unlocked."

His body tensed, his smile instantly gone. "Could it be your cousin?"

She shook her head, growing more worried. "No. Killer's barking and it's his stranger bark. He knows the sound of her car."

He was out of bed in an instant, reaching for his jeans. "Stay in here and leave the door shut." His voice was low and tight.

Her pulse increased. "You think someone is really in my house?" she whispered.

He pulled up his jeans and fastened the button. "That's what I'm going to find out."

"Kevin, that's crazy. I'll just call the police."

"They won't get here fast enough, and there might not even be anyone down there. I'll be right back. Stay here."

She jumped out of bed, but he had already shut the door behind him. Her heartbeat throbbed in her temple as she padded to her dresser and pulled out an oversized T-shirt and pulled it over her head, straining to hear anything downstairs.

The door opened and she jumped, but Kevin stood in the opening, cradling the kitten, which looked tiny in his large hand. "I found your intruder."

She pushed out a breath of relief. "I forgot about the kitten."

"I think I owe you for a lamp he knocked over."

She took the cat from him and cuddled it against her chest. "I'm sure we can come up with some kind of barter for it."

"I was gone for five seconds and you covered up all the good parts." He moved closer and cupped her bare butt cheek with his hand. A grin spread across his face. "Well, maybe not everything."

"Are you hungry?

His eyebrows rose playfully.

"For food."

"If it's half as good as the lasagna, then that's a yes."

"How about pasta salad and turkey-avocado pita sandwiches?"

His eyes lit up. "I hardly had anything at my dinner from hell, so yes, please."

The mention of his dinner reminded her that a woman had brought him home, yet he claimed he didn't have a girlfriend. She wanted to ask him more, but decided that, at least for tonight, she didn't want to know. "Then come downstairs."

She squatted and picked up her underwear, setting the kitten on the floor, but when she stood, he took her panties and tossed them onto the bed.

"Uh-uh. I like you this way." He grinned. "Easy access."

She considered protesting—Melanie really could show up at any time—but the jolt of excitement that skated along her nerves decided for her. Tonight was about living dangerously and taking chances.

He snagged his shirt off the floor and followed her. When they reached the bottom, she spun around and grabbed his hand as he started to fasten the buttons. "Nope. If you get easy access, then so do I. You can wear the shirt, but no buttoning it." To prove her point, she placed her free hand on his stomach, her fingertips tracing along his abdomen. She couldn't believe she was touching him so freely, so wantonly. She'd always held back in her previous relationships. She barely knew Kevin, yet he made her feel safe and confident to explore him.

He grabbed her hand and held it still against his chest. "If we're eating, then you better stop touching me or I'll give you your fantasy on the counter."

Her breath stuck in her chest as her core throbbed at the image in her head, but he'd said he hadn't eaten much earlier. Better to feed him so he wouldn't be distracted later.

She'd had no idea she had this wanton side, but she liked it. She didn't want to question it. He was still holding her hand, so she tugged him toward the kitchen.

"You go sit down," she said as she pulled a plate from the fridge.

"Are you eating, too?"

"Yeah, I didn't have dinner yet." She grabbed two forks from the drawer and handed him one. "*Bon appetit.*"

He picked up one of the pita sandwiches and took a bite. "I'm not sure this is possible, but I think it's better than the lasagna."

"I keep telling Mel she's wasting her time bartending. She needs to open a restaurant."

"Or become a private chef."

She laughed. "She's into taking chances lately—she might actually try it if you suggested it to her."

"So if she takes chances, I'm guessing you like to play it safe."

She stopped, fork midway to her mouth. She considered protesting, but what was the point? "We're both scarred from the same incident, yet we've handled it very differently." When his eyebrows rose in question, she continued. "I already told you that we're cousins. Our fathers were brothers, and our parents were together when their car was hit by a semi on the highway. Grandma Barb took us both in and raised us."

Sympathy filled his eyes. "Holly, I'm sorry."

"I was five. Mel was six. I barely remember them."

"I'm sorry for that, too."

She shook her head. "I don't feel sorry for myself."

He watched her. "I would have guessed that about you."

Laughing, she shook her head. "There's no way you could have guessed that."

"You'd be surprised."

She wasn't sure what he saw, but she felt the need to set him straight. "This"—she waved her hand between them— "is very unlike me."

He grinned. "I guessed that, too."

He didn't say the same, not that she expected him to. But it made her feel relieved that she'd gone into this with eyes wide open.

She lifted her sandwich off the plate. "So what made you buy the Miller house?"

"My sister bought it for me."

She paused, midbite. "Wait. You never saw the house?"

"Nope. I told her to buy me a house that would make me a profit when I sold it in a year or two, and this is what I got."

"You didn't know it was a money pit?"

"No. But knowing my little sister, she's up to something. I just haven't figured what it is yet."

"So she's conniving?"

"Not as conniving as my mother, and she usually chooses to use her power for good instead of evil." He grinned. "But enough about my family and my money pit. I want to know more about you."

She hesitated. If she told him she was a wedding planner, he might turn around and run. She'd been on a few dates since starting her job, and commitment-phobe men tended to think that she must be desperate to plan her own wedding. She suspected Kevin wouldn't be like that, but she really liked him. She didn't want to screw this up before it even began. "After our parents died, Melanie and I moved in with Grandma Barb, who had only been widowed a year."

"Was it hard for her to take in two little girls?"

"No." She gave him a soft smile. "She was so devastated about losing her two sons that I think having the two of us helped with her grief. And we needed her. She was a very loving and affectionate grandmother."

"Was?"

Her eyes burned. "She's been in Happy Dale Retirement Community for the last year with dementia. She's herself a lot, but sometimes she doesn't even know who I am."

"What about other grandparents? Cousins?"

"She and Melanie are all that I have left." She realized how pathetic she sounded. Time to change the subject. "But I have a job I love even if I have the boss from hell. I'm happy." Mostly.

"How did your boss earn her title?"

"Boss from hell?" she asked with a grin. "I can't do anything right in her eyes—at least not for the last few months—yet she loves to try to take credit when I do something well. I was sure she was going to fire me yesterday. She had a big client coming in, but she showed up fifteen minutes late. I had to keep them occupied until she got there and they started asking questions." She sighed. "The next thing I knew, they wanted me to do the job. As expected, she was furious, even though, as the owner, she's still making a lot of money."

"It's not your fault she couldn't show up on time. She should be grateful you salvaged it."

"She doesn't see it that way. But I'm there to gain experience, then I'm quitting and starting my own business. If all goes well with this big job, it might happen sooner rather than later." Curiosity filled his eyes, and she knew he was about to ask what she did. Time to change the subject. "How much work have you gotten done on your house?"

He shook his head. "Not much."

"Do you have a plan?"

He laughed. "Other than gut the kitchen and bathroom, put in an air conditioner and a furnace, and repaint everything, no."

She grinned. "Would you like me to take a look?"

"Sure."

She started to walk past him, but he looped his arm around her waist and pulled her next to him. "Whoa. Where are you going?"

"To get dressed so I can look at your house."

He slowly shook his head, a sexy smile lighting up his face. "My house isn't going anywhere. We can look at it tomorrow. I have better plans for now." His arm wrapped tight around her back and pulled her to his bare chest. She fell into him, and his mouth captured hers, kissing her senseless.

He leaned back and looked into her eyes. "Holly."

She lifted her gaze, still dazed by his kiss.

"I really like you. I want to see what happens between us."

"Me, too."

He brushed a strand of hair from her cheek, staring into her eyes. As she watched him, something tightened in her chest.

"Are you still hungry?" she asked

A grin spread across his face. "You have no idea."

"I can make you something else."

"Everything I want is right in front of me."

Holly was thinking the exact same thing. And that scared her more than she liked to admit.

Chapter Fifteen

$\frown$

Kevin woke to find Holly still asleep, lying on her side facing him. The kitten was batting at his head, and he picked it up and put it down at his feet, but it decided it was playtime. The clock read close to seven thirty, which meant the cat had been good longer than could be expected. If nothing else, the thing needed its litter box.

After three rounds of sex, he knew Holly was exhausted. She'd gotten worried when her cousin hadn't come home, but she'd finally gotten a text that her cousin was spending the night with her boyfriend. Which made him regret not insisting on taking her on the counter.

He slid out of bed and stepped into his jeans, then hurriedly shoved his arms into his shirtsleeves. The kitten had discovered Holly's hair and was about to pounce on it when he scooped it up and carried it downstairs.

A dark-headed woman sat at the kitchen counter, nursing a cup of coffee. She turned her head to look at him, a slow smile spreading across her face.

"Please tell me you live next door."

He cocked his head. "Um…yes?"

"So was it the pasta salad or the pita sandwich that won you over?"

"Excuse me?"

"Last night's dinner. I made it for Holly to take to you."

He smiled. "She won me over before I even saw the dinner."

"She's a good person and she's been through a lot. She deserves a great guy, if you get what I'm saying."

"I'm not sure if I'm a great guy, but I do want to get to know her better and I have no intention of hurting her."

"I suppose that's all you can promise, isn't it?" There was a sharp edge in her voice, which he suspected had nothing to do with him and Holly. She stood and walked to the sink with her coffee cup, wobbling slightly. "There's definitely no promises in life."

"Are you okay?"

"No. But thanks for asking." She enunciated her words like a drunk person trying to appear sober. "I'm going to bed."

She walked past him, over to the dining room table, glancing down at the papers spread across the top. "The wedding's going to be gorgeous."

"Excuse me?"

"Her wedding. It looks a lot like the ones she used to plan when we were little."

She was planning her wedding? He walked over to the table and, sure enough, there were pictures of cakes and flowers and dresses scattered around. If she wasn't planning a wedding, she was definitely obsessed with one.

Holly's cousin started for the stairs, but then Kevin remembered her earlier remark and called after her, "You said you made dinner for Holly to bring to me?"

"Yeah. I pushed her to take you the lasagna, but last night's dinner was all her. She called me and told me she wanted to use it to win you over."

His eyes sank closed and disappointment washed over him. He'd thought she was normal. He could have sworn she was normal. Yet she'd begun planning her wedding—*their* wedding—before they'd even slept together.

He'd broken his six-month ban to sleep with a crazy woman. This was a disaster.

The kitten squirmed on his arm. "I have to take the cat to do its business and get to work."

"On a Saturday?" she asked at the bottom of the steps, sounding skeptical.

"Yeah. New job and all."

"Yeah...right..."

He didn't give her time to call him on his bullshit, instead practically running across the front yard to his house. It occurred to him as he entered the house that he'd left it unlocked, which wasn't a smart move if there really were car break-ins in the neighborhood. Jesus. Had she made that up, too, so she'd look helpless and he'd stay to take care of her?

He took the kitten to the laundry-room litter box, afraid to let it do its business outside. Trying that last night had been what had gotten him into this situation.

How was he going to get out of this? He really liked her, but what sane woman planned her wedding before her first date? Still, he hated to just ignore her. Was there a kind way to say: *Sorry, I made a mistake. I didn't realize you were batshit crazy*?

He pulled out his phone and considered calling his sister to take him to pick up his car, but he needed advice, too, and he didn't exactly trust her decision-making skills at the moment. Instead he sent a text to Matt.

Any chance you can pick me up and take me to my car at Café Rustica?

It was early enough that he didn't expect Matt to respond immediately.

I have a T-ball game at 9. I'll pick you up in fifteen minutes and you can help me coach.

Coach a T-ball game? Why not? If nothing else, he could leave the house and avoid any awkward encounters with Holly.

I'll be ready.

He took a quick shower, hoping the calming effect of the water would help him figure out what to do.

Sex with Holly had been the best he'd ever had. And then the time they had spent just talking made it even more perfect. He'd thought she was what he'd been looking for— that puzzle piece that just fit—but that damned wedding planning—

Why couldn't women just be normal?

The kitten looked up at him through the shower door and mewled.

"Yeah, I know, buddy. Life sucks."

He finished showering quickly and tugged on a fresh pair of jeans and a T-shirt, then tromped downstairs. He needed to get Megan to take the cat or admit defeat and give it a name. He wasn't ready to go that far yet.

A rap on the door made his heart stutter. Had Holly come over looking for him? But the door opened and Matt poked his head inside. "I'm a few minutes early, so I thought I'd come in and take a look at your project."

Kevin snorted. "You mean disaster."

Matt made a quick walk-through, silent the entire time until he ended up at the front door.

"Give it to me straight," Kevin said, his back tense.

"There's a lot of work to do, but your sister has a good eye. I think it's a good investment." He clamped his hand on Kevin's shoulder. "Let's get some doughnuts and coffee and eat them on the way to the field, which will give you plenty of time to tell me why you have the wild look in your eyes. We'll stop by your car after the game."

"Worried I'll take off and skip the game?"

Matt crossed his arms. "Nope. I know you're too smart to break a commitment to your boss."

A sardonic grin spread across Kevin's face. "Well, that's your first mistake—assuming I'm smart. It only took twenty-four hours before I broke our pact and jumped straight into the fire."

Matt laughed, dropping his arms to his sides. "Ha! You didn't waste any time, did you?"

He grimaced. "I blame it on the alcohol." Only he'd sobered up quite a bit before he'd carried her upstairs.

Matt released a sigh. "We *all* want to blame it on alcohol. Let's go, and you can fill me in on the ugly details."

Kevin put the kitten in the basement with fresh food and water, then locked up the house and cast a long look at Holly's bedroom window before he climbed into Matt's truck.

"What happened?"

"I also give partial blame to the blind date my mother set me up on."

Matt started laughing. "I definitely need more coffee. I could swear I heard you say you let your mother set you up on a blind date."

"I didn't *let* her do anything. She tricked me into it. I thought I was meeting her and Dad."

"She fixed you up with your neighbor?"

"No. She fixed me up with Bethany Davis from high school."

"What? No way. Is she just as crazy as she was back then?"

"Even more so."

"How'd your mother find her?"

"I'm guessing the country club. She's sure using it to her advantage since she coerced Dad to join a few years ago."

"So you went home with her?"

"God, no. Why would you think that?"

"Dude, you're doing the walk of shame to your car. Or in this case, the drive of shame."

"My car's still in the parking lot because I got drunk off my ass to make it through the dinner. I had to call my sister to come get me."

"Bethany didn't offer to take you home?"

"Oh, she offered, all right. I gave her a hard pass."

Matt laughed. "Is that why you're so grumpy? You got blue balls?"

Kevin sat back in his seat, his mood getting worse by the minute. "That's right, funny guy. Laugh it up."

"So you left one date to go home and hook up with another woman?" Matt whistled. "And I thought Tyler was bad."

"It wasn't like that," he said a little too defensively, cringing at Matt's chuckle. "Megan took me home and I took that damn cat out back to pee."

"Why didn't you just let it use the litter box?"

"Dude, I was drunk, okay? Obviously I wasn't thinking straight."

"Obviously..."

"Holly's dog got through the fence to chase after the cat and she followed it back." Was that all staged, too? To give her an excuse to talk to him?

"And then...?" Matt prompted.

"Then I saw her...she was still in her work clothes. This

tight peach-colored skirt that clung to her ass and a low-cut top that showed off her…"

"And you were drunk. …"

"She said she was, too. She'd had a good day."

"And you made it better?"

Maybe, but he had to have fucked up her morning just leaving like that. What if there was some logical explanation for her wedding photos everywhere? What if she was helping a friend? "Her dog freaked out the cat and it scratched my cheek. Holly saw the scratches and offered to get her first aid kit. So I went over to her house and she cleaned up the scratches."

"And then?"

"And then one thing led to the other and I had the best night of my life." He realized it really had been. He'd never connected with someone that quickly. He took a deep breath, trying to fight his rising panic. "I think I just fucked up."

"Nah, it was one hookup. You can jump back on the womanless wagon. Call it Day One of your new virginity."

That wasn't what he'd meant. What if he'd made a mistake about leaving her this morning? What if he had thrown away something that could have been amazing?

But Matt continued on, unaware of his inner dilemma. "What made you realize she was crazy?"

"I found wedding photos."

Matt's eyebrows lifted. "She's married?"

Kevin shook his head. "No, like she was planning one. Cutouts from things she'd found online—you know: flowers, cakes, dresses."

"One of those, huh?"

"But she didn't seem like it last night. In fact, she seemed like she thought I was just going to get up and walk home." His panic increased. "Oh, Jesus. I really fucked up."

"Well, hold on. Maybe not. Could they have belonged to someone else? Didn't you say she lived with her cousin?"

He paused to recall his conversation with her cousin, his heart sinking. "She does, but her cousin was the one who pointed them out. She said they were Holly's. She said it was the wedding she'd wanted as a kid."

Matt cringed. "That sure sounds like a woman desperate to get married to the first man who comes along."

"Her cousin said Holly asked her to make dinner so she could bring it to me."

"I thought she showed up in your backyard to get her dog. Did she happen to have the dinner with her?"

"No."

"Maybe she tried to bring it over while you were gone? But look at it this way: she's at home on Friday night, trying to land you with a tuna casserole."

"Pasta salad and turkey-and-avocado pita sandwiches."

He turned to look at Kevin. "Are you shitting me? Was it good?"

Kevin pinned his gaze on him. "Amazingly good."

Matt shook his head. "It doesn't matter. What matters is that she's some kind of looney tunes who set her sights on you the day you moved in. She brought you a lasagna, for Christ's sake." Matt turned to face him. "Take it from someone who knows all too well—when they want to rush to play house, all kinds of red flags are flying. Don't be an idiot and ignore them."

"Yeah…"

"And don't worry about working on your house. After the game, I'll follow you home and we can spend the rest of the day working on ripping your house apart."

"Only until three or so. I have plans."

"Another date with your neighbor?" Matt laughed. "What's she bringing you tonight? Steak and baked potatoes?"

Kevin frowned. "I promised my mother that I'd go over this afternoon."

"After she set you up on a blind date with Bethany Davis? I would totally blow it off on principle alone."

"Like hell you would." Kevin laughed. "Your mother would hand you your ass on a platter. And it's not just her. I promised my sister."

"What's so important? A family dinner?"

Kevin considered lying, but Matt already thought he was an idiot. He couldn't make it much worse. "A baby shower."

Matt burst into laughter. "You are so whipped. And you aren't even married. You need to stay away from women until you can grow a pair." Chuckling, Matt tilted his head toward Kevin. "And you definitely need to cut your losses with your neighbor."

Unfortunately, Kevin was sure they were talking about two very different losses.

Chapter Sixteen

Holly woke up to an empty bed: both Kevin and the kitten were gone. Granted, it was after nine—she hadn't slept so well in years—but still, she should have found some sign of him. She went downstairs to see if he was down there or had left some kind of note. Nothing.

There had to be some kind of logical explanation, but damned if she could come up with one.

She started a pot of coffee, then looked at her phone to see if he'd sent her a message, which was ridiculous. She'd never given him her number.

He really had walked out on her.

She let Killer out, then grabbed her day planner and sat down at the counter, looking at her notes for the day. The day before, Nicole had given Holly a list of things to pick up before she showed up for the shower. With any luck at all, Nicole wanted Holly to help with the setup and then she could go.

But her thoughts kept turning back to Kevin. "Why did

he pretend this was something when I'd made it so clear I didn't expect it to be more?"

"Isn't it obvious?" Melanie asked behind her, sounding groggy. "Men are dicks."

Holly frowned. "Mel."

"It's true and you know it."

"I *don't* know. Kevin was gone when I got up."

"So he didn't come back after all."

Holly's face jerked up. "You saw him?"

"I'd just come home. He said he had to take his cat to do its business in the litter box."

Holly pushed her hair from her face, totally confused. "What time was that?" They'd woken up around three a.m. for their last round. Had he gotten out of bed before that and she hadn't realized it?

"About seven thirty."

"This morning?"

"Well, yeah." Her brow lowered.

"Why were you home already? You said you were spending the night."

Melanie grabbed a mug and poured herself a cup of coffee. "When a man and a woman like each other, sometimes after they've dated a few times, they have sex. Or, in your case, they just have sex." Her snotty tone was totally unlike her.

"Melanie, what's going on?"

"I broke it off."

"With Darren? What happened?" Holly got out of her seat and pulled her cousin into a hug.

She rested her cheek on Holly's shoulder. "He's an asshole. All men are assholes."

"Oh, Mel. I'm sorry. You really liked him."

"I liked him. Past tense. Now I loathe him."

"He obviously didn't deserve you."

"Just like Kerwin doesn't deserve you."

"His name is Kevin, and maybe he has a good explanation," Holly said. "Maybe something came up."

"And maybe monkeys are going to start flying out of my ass. Accept it, Holly. Men are assholes unworthy of our attention. We should vow to live lives of celibacy."

After what Holly had experienced with Kevin the night before, celibacy was the last thing on her mind.

"I know that look." Melanie said, pointing her finger into Holly's face. "You're going to give him another chance."

"But what if he has a good reason?"

"He couldn't leave a note?"

There was one last place she hadn't checked. She ran to the front door and looked for a note on the porch or taped to the front door. Nothing.

"Face it, Holly. He got what he wanted. He's moved on."

"You're right. He got what he wanted." The truth was harder to accept than she'd expected. If it had been half as good for him as it had been for her, wouldn't he want to see her again? But, then again, he was a gorgeous man. Maybe hopping in and out of beds was what he did. She was sure he had his choice of women, and the woman on his front porch last night was Exhibit A. Besides, she had little to base his performance on. She'd slept with three other men, and two of them hadn't exactly been live wires out of bed, let alone in it.

Horror rushed through her head. What if it was her? What if *she* sucked at sex and just didn't know it?

"Okay," Melanie said slowly, wrapping her arm around Holly's shoulders. "I don't know what you're thinking right now, but you're obviously overanalyzing it." She led her to the bar stool and pushed her down. "Let me get you a cup of coffee. That will help put things in perspective."

She leaned her elbow on the counter and rested her forehead in her hand. "That I got dumped by my own one-night stand?"

Melanie started to pour coffee into a cup.

"What if I completely suck at sex?"

"You realize that's, like, nearly impossible, don't you?"

"I don't know any such thing. It's not like you get a grade card at the end of a relationship. Attentive Girlfriend: B-plus; Cooking: D-minus; Sex: F."

"Don't be ridiculous." Mel handed her the coffee, along with a bottle of creamer. "Sex would be broken down into multiple categories, just like that row of checks, misses, and dashes for 'needs work' on our grade-school report cards. You know—Blow Job: plus; Doggie Style: dash; French Kissing: minus; with 'too wet and sloppy' in the comment box."

A renewed wave of horror washed through her. "Oh, my God. I suck at sex."

Melanie looked up at her in exasperation. "How many times did you do it?"

"What?"

"You know. How many times did he get off?"

"Melanie!"

"Just answer the question."

Holly's face burned. "Three."

Melanie rolled her eyes. "Trust me. He thought you were good. Otherwise he would have been out the door after the first time."

"Are you sure? Maybe he figured he should get it while he could."

"Please. I saw the guy. He could have a woman in his bed every night of the week."

"Is that supposed to make me feel better?"

Melanie gave her a piercing gaze. "Believe it or not, yes."
She leaned closer. "You said you didn't expect more than
just last night, right?"

"Well, yeah..."

"You wanted a round of great sex, and you got it, right?"

"I didn't put it that way—"

"Was it good?"

Holly blushed. "Yeah."

"All three times?"

Her blush deepened. "Yeah."

"Well, there you go. Three rounds of amazing sex to tide
you over until you dip your toe back into the asshole pool.
It's better than what I got."

Holly had been waiting for this opening. She'd known
Mel would get there eventually. "What happened?"

"He turned out to be a complete ass, okay?"

"Mel, I'm sorry."

Tears filled her cousin's eyes. "Why can't I find someone
to love me, Hol?"

"Oh, Mel. *I* love you."

"It's not the same."

Her grandmother had said the same thing. "I know. But
you need to love you first, Mel."

A hateful look covered Melanie's face. "If that's not calling the kettle black. You won't even get pissed off that a
man just slept with you and lied to you all because you don't
think you deserve him."

Holly gasped.

"Tell me I'm wrong."

Tears stung her eyes, mostly because her cousin was being so blunt, but also because she could see some truth in her
words. She didn't think she deserved him.

"Promise me you won't fall for some bullshit line he

gives as an excuse. Because he lives next door and he's going to have an opening in his schedule. Ten to one he comes crawling back like the slime he is, trying to weasel another go at you."

"Melanie, I never expected it to be a *thing*. I thought it would be a one-night stand."

"Exactly. A one-night stand. Which means it's over."

Holly closed her planner and headed for the stairs. "I have to take a shower."

"Holly…" her cousin called after her. "You know I only tell you this because I love you and want the best for you. A quick roll in the sack is good every now and then, but if you sleep with him again, your heart's bound to get involved. And that will *not* end well."

She knew that all too well, too.

"You deserve to have a *great* guy, Holly. Don't settle for an asshole."

"You need to listen to your own advice," Holly said without malice.

A wobbly grin lifted Mel's lips. "Maybe I told myself the same thing this morning."

Holly pulled her cousin into a hug. "I love you, Mel."

"I love you, too." She dropped her hold. "Now you can run away like you always do."

"No I don't—" She stopped, because she could see Mel was right about that, too. It had never occurred to her that avoiding relationships was also running away from them. "But in this case, I really do have to go. Nicole's daughter's baby shower is this afternoon."

"Do what? Her daughter's *baby shower*?"

"When your boss jumps, you ask how high."

"No, you find a new boss who doesn't ask you to jump at all."

With any luck, she'd be able to start her own business in a few months. But her cousin misunderstood her silence, and when Holly started to argue, Melanie patted Holly's cheek. "That's okay, little grasshopper. One fight at a time."

The day Holly quit would be more like Armageddon, but she'd worry about that later.

Chapter Seventeen

Kevin was thirty-three years old. Old enough to tell his mother no, yet here he was parked in front of his parents' house, about to play bartender at his sister's freaking baby shower.

He turned with a glare when his sister rapped on his passenger window. She jerked open the door. "Suck it up, buttercup."

"It's a baby shower, Megan. It's for a bunch of gossipy women."

"That's a sexist statement, Kevin Vandemeer. You think a man's responsibility ends as soon as he's deposited his sperm?"

He cringed, the statement hitting a little too close to home. "No."

"Whoa," she said, her teasing gone. "What happened?"

"Why do you think something happened?"

"Because you look exactly like Dad did when he ran over the family dog."

"I didn't—"

"Every minute you stay out here with me is a minute you don't have to be with Mom." She grinned. "Maybe that will help loosen your tongue."

"Fine. It's about a woman."

"Your date last night? Yeah, I remember. I picked you up." She paused. "Oh, my God. You're not having second thoughts about her, are you?"

"No, it's my next-door neighbor."

Her eyes flew open and she looked more eager than he expected. "Oh? The cute one you mentioned last night."

"That's the one."

She waved her hand. "So, wait. Did something happen last night?" When he gave her a questioning look, she added, "Was she the one who brought you dinner the first night?"

He grimaced, acknowledging her leap.

She gave him a mock punch in the arm. "Hey, we Vandemeers are more than just a pretty face."

"I'm not sure I'd be including me in the smart gene pool anymore."

"Oh, God. What happened?"

"I slept with her."

Her smile fell. "But you just met her." She shook her head, grimacing. "Sorry. You're both consenting adults"— her gaze jerked up to his—"it was consenting, wasn't it?"

"Oh, my God! You really think I would do that?"

"Not you, you idiot." She smacked his arm again. "You were drunk as a skunk last night. Maybe you leaped before you looked and now you feel like you rushed things." Then she hastily added, "Or maybe she took advantage of the situation and now you feel trapped." But she looked like she didn't believe the last one for a minute.

"Save your sympathy. *I* was the asshole."

"What did you do?"

He groaned and leaned back in his seat. "For some reason she thought it would be a one-time thing. And she admitted she didn't randomly sleep with guys. And I didn't mean for it to happen, but she was just so damn sexy. ..."

Megan grimaced. "Okay, maybe tell this story without so many details."

"Oh, I love the details!" A familiar voice said. "And here I thought this baby shower would be boring as hell."

Megan spun around and squealed. "Libby!" She pulled her friend into a tight hug, then set her loose. "Look at your cute little tummy. I've grown as huge as a whale in the last month since you've seen me."

"Huge?" Libby asked, shaking her head. "Please. But enough baby talk. I want to hear Kevin's juicy details."

"Do you even know what we're talking about?" Megan asked.

"If *you* don't want to hear something from your brother, it has to be about sex."

"He found himself a girlfriend," Megan said.

"Haven't you only been home for three days?"

He groaned. "She's not my girlfriend."

"Why?" Libby asked. "What's wrong with her?"

"Nothing. *At first.* She seemed sweet and normal."

"Normal is so overrated," Libby said.

"Not for me," he said. "I've had my share of crazy."

"So she's pretty, sweet, and normal," Megan said. "I fail to see a problem."

Kevin narrowed his eyes. "I'm pretty sure I never said she was pretty and I never said she was sweet. How do you know she's those things?"

Megan looked momentarily flustered before she said,

"Last night you said she was cute. And you slept with her. That's a given."

Something wasn't adding up here. "You know about my past girlfriends, so sweet is definitely *not* a given."

Libby waved her hand. "Forget about that and move to the good part: You slept with her?"

"Oh, my God." Kevin groaned. "Yes, I slept with her."

Libby put a hand on her hip. "I also fail to see the problem."

"I spent the night at her house, but when I got up this morning, I found a bunch of wedding photos spread across her dining room table. Cutouts. Like she was planning a wedding."

"Ouch," Libby said. "Little early in the relationship to be planning your wedding."

Megan closed her eyes, then opened them, staring at him for a moment as though carefully choosing her words. "What did she say when you asked her about it?"

"I didn't ask."

Megan narrowed her eyes. "What do you mean you didn't ask?"

"I woke up before she did and I had to take the cat home to the litter box—"

Libby gasped. "*You* have a *cat*?"

But Megan glared at him. "You didn't."

Libby shook her head. "I can't believe you have a cat."

Megan shot her an exasperated look. "Libby, focus." Then she turned her steely gaze back on her brother. "*Please* tell me you didn't."

Kevin cringed. "I panicked."

Libby's eyes flew open as she realized what Megan had figured out. "Oh, my God. You snuck out?"

"Her cousin saw me," he said a little too defensively.

"That's supposed to make it better?" Megan demanded, getting irrationally pissed. "You are such a fucking idiot." Then she stomped off to the house.

He turned to Libby. "Why's she so mad?"

"Well...I would say she's offended for all womankind, but I agree she's taking it a tad bit personally."

"Matt thought I did the right thing."

Libby snorted. "Matt Osborn?"

"Yeah..."

"Did you ever wonder why he's still single?"

"How would you know...?"

She shook her head. "I know things. But your sister's wrong. You're not just a fucking idiot, you're also an asshole."

"I already said that I was."

"It obviously can't be said enough."

"What should I do?"

She laughed. "You're asking *me* for advice?"

"You three girls are the only ones I *can* ask. Megan's pissed, and Blair's liable to kick me in the nuts. That leaves you."

"Aww...so happy to be your first choice."

"Well?"

"You're screwed." She started toward the house.

"Libby!"

She stopped and turned around to face him. "Okay, fine. What do you want out of this? Absolution? Because that's not happening."

"No. I don't know." He ran his hand through his hair. "I'd like to find out if she was really planning a wedding with me, I guess."

She put her hand on her hip again. "You realize how incredibly egotistical that sounds, right? You're presuming a woman who knew you for three days was already planning your wedding? You're just *that* awesome."

"When you put it that way..."

"So presuming she's halfway normal and it wasn't your wedding, what outcome are you looking for?"

"Another chance with her."

Libby burst into laughter. "That ship has sailed, Kevin."

He tried to ignore the heavy feeling in the pit of his stomach. "But what explanation could she possibly have for those pictures?"

"I don't know. Maybe she's helping a friend plan her wedding." Libby looked back at the house. "Hell, think about your mother's job. Maybe she's a wedding planner."

"Oh, God. I'm an idiot."

"I thought we'd all accepted that as a given."

"I have to apologize."

"That's a good start." She grabbed his forearm and dragged him into the house. "But right now you have to deal with your mother."

Chapter Eighteen

Holly's boss was more high-strung than usual.

"I think the tables are too close together." Nicole looked up at Holly, hesitation in her eyes. "Do you think they're too close together?"

"No, I think it's beautiful." And she did. They'd spent two hours setting up the round rental tables and chairs, covering both with white organza that caught in the breeze. The tops were covered with pale yellow and white flowers with plenty of greenery. A table for the elaborate cake and decorations sat under the gazebo, along with a table next to it for Megan's presents. Nicole Vandemeer had the perfect backyard for entertaining—a beautiful pool in the center, a two-tiered deck, and well-manicured landscaping with lots of shade. Nicole's plan was simple elegance, and she'd achieved it. It was equal to any socialite shower, which was exactly what she was going for. "It's very classy."

Nicole clasped her hands together as she surveyed the backyard. "Thank you. I just hope Millie Leopold likes it."

"And Megan."

Her gaze jerked up. "Well, of course." But Holly could see the guilt in her eyes. "I should go inside and see if the string quartet is here yet." She wrung her hands. "They're fifteen minutes late. The guests should be arriving and my son hasn't even shown up to attend the bar." She shook her head. "Doesn't punctuality mean anything these days?"

A string quartet for a baby shower seemed like overkill, but it was Nicole. "I'll double-check the draping on the posts where they are playing. It looked like one was working loose. And the bar's all set up, so all he has to do is show up." The bar also seemed like overkill, but Nicole insisted that the guests needed to be served fresh mimosas. The juice had to be freshly squeezed.

"Thank you."

She disappeared into the house, and Holly walked around to the other side of the pool to check the temporary gazebo Nicole had erected. Seconds later, Megan emerged through the back door, walking toward her as she took everything in.

"It looks lovely, Holly," Megan said as she stopped next to her. But she looked nervous, not that Holly blamed her.

Holly hadn't known Megan very long. After Megan moved back to Kansas City she'd run into Holly often when visiting her mother's office. Megan had invited Holly out to lunch, and the two women became fast friends. However, after the first two lunch dates, Nicole made it very clear she didn't approve of her employee socializing with her daughter. Megan was willing to meet Holly on the sly, but Holly couldn't do it. She hated lying. Even to her unreasonable boss.

She gave Megan a sympathetic look. "I know you would have preferred something much more casual."

"This was my mother's doing, not yours. Thanks for

giving up your Saturday to come help." She glanced over her shoulder, then back.

Holly looked down, feeling embarrassed over her earlier grumbling. "I'm happy to do it. Oh, and by the way, if your mother asks, I called you yesterday and made one last effort to find out the baby's sex."

"Thanks for helping me with that, too."

"Anytime."

Megan hesitated, looking like she wanted to say something, but then she lifted her hand to the silky bow at Holly's neckline, straightening the length. "You look very pretty today."

Holly looked down at her pale-green-and-white-polka-dot sleeveless dress. Was it too much? The full skirt allowed a breeze to cool her down, something important since she'd been outside for a few hours already. Thankfully, the late June day wasn't too hot. "Thank you. But you're the special guest. I'm supposed to stay in the background." She waved to Megan's pale blue dress. "And you look stunning. Pregnancy agrees with you."

"I love being pregnant. I'm really happy." But she sounded distracted as she glanced over her shoulder again.

Who was she looking for? "I can tell," Holly said, surprised by the surge of envy that rose inside her.

Megan turned serious. "There's something I have to warn you about."

Holly chuckled. "That your mother is upset over the string quartet? I know." Then she gave her a sly grin. "I'll see if I can get them to play something contemporary to shake things up. Got any requests?"

"No. That's not it. I did something maybe I shouldn't have done." Megan paused, then grabbed both of Holly's hands, giving them a tiny shake as she stared deep into her eyes. "I just want you to know that you are a remarkable, beautiful woman. You deserve someone special. Insist he treats you right. And if he doesn't, then that's on him, not you, okay?"

Holly's eyes widened. Was she wearing her shame from last night like a scarlet letter? But then, what did she have to feel guilty about, anyway?

Nicole poked her head out the back door. "Megan, I need you for a moment."

Frustration washed over Megan's face as she called out, "I'll be there in a minute."

"*Now*, darling."

Megan looked torn, casting a glance back at her mother, then a guilty one at Holly. "Holly, I don't know how to tell you—"

Holly's phone rang in her dress pocket. "You go deal with your mother while I take this."

"But I—"

As she pulled the phone out of her pocket, she saw the number of the retirement center appear on the screen. "Go. This might be about my grandmother. I need to get it."

"Megan!" her mother shouted. "Now!"

Megan nodded, but she didn't look happy to be walking away, which Holly attributed to concern. Megan knew about Holly's grandmother and her deteriorating health, even though Holly had begged Megan not to tell her mother. Despite Megan's protests, she worried Nicole would think her grandmother's health would be too distracting for Holly to do her job well. Nicole Vandemeer abhorred any signs of weakness.

Megan looked over her shoulder, then back at Holly, her guilt palpable. "I really am sorry," she mouthed as she walked away.

A ball of anxiety churned in Holly's stomach, but Megan took off before Holly could ask what she was sorry for. Was Nicole upset with her? What had she done this time?

But she was more worried about the reason for the phone call. "Hello?"

"Holly?" her grandmother asked. "When are you picking me up?"

Holly blinked in surprise. Had she forgotten an appointment with her grandmother? "I'm sorry, Grandma. I'm helping my boss with her daughter's baby shower."

"Vickie's daughter's too young to have a baby."

"Not my boss from the Marriott. My new boss."

"What new boss? Did you get a new job and not tell me?"

Tears stung Holly's eyes. "No, Grandma. I've had it for almost a year."

"Why didn't you tell me?"

The doctors had told her to mention the present, and if her grandmother got frustrated to let it go. There was no reasoning with her, but it also probably meant she hadn't forgotten a prior arrangement. "Where were we supposed to go?"

"You said you wanted to see *Swan Lake*. I bought the tickets and everything, but I thought they were in my drawer..." Her voice faded. "Who stole my tickets?"

Holly wiped the tears from the corners of her eyes. Her grandmother had saved up to take her and Melanie to see *Swan Lake* when they were in middle school. "Gran, I'm going to ask the nurses to help you look."

"What nurses?"

She swallowed the burning lump in her throat. The quartet was on their way toward her and she had to help them get set up or Nicole would be furious. "I'll find someone to help you, okay?"

But her grandmother hung up on her first.

She called the nurses' station to fill them in, and they assured Holly not to worry, that they would take care of her grandmother.

Stuffing her phone into her pocket, she forced a smile as she greeted the quartet and showed them where they would spend the afternoon. As she watched them, she told herself that there was nothing she could do for her grandmother right now. If anything, Holly's presence was usually more upsetting to her grandmother when she was having an episode. Holly had to trust the staff to take care of her.

But she was still an anxious mess. She needed to pull herself together.

Nicole emerged with a tray of appetizers, looking remarkably calm since the shower was about to start and her son hadn't made an appearance yet. If push came to shove, Holly figured she could fill in at the bar.

Megan made a beeline to her mother and motioned to Holly. Nicole's mouth pinched and she shook her head no. Megan grabbed her mother's arm, looking like she was pleading.

What in the world was Megan doing?

Then she saw him.

Kevin stalked across the deck with a dark expression, heading straight toward the bar area set up at the end of the pool.

The blood rushed from her head to the bottom of her feet and she swayed, feeling light-headed.

Oh, God. No.

Kevin was Kevin *Vandemeer*? She'd slept with her boss's son.

"Miss, are you all right?" the cellist asked in an anxious voice.

She placed her hand on her chest, sucking in a deep

breath. "Yes. I'm fine." But she felt anything but fine. She felt like she was going to throw up.

Megan was hurrying toward her, pure panic on her face. "Holly, let's go inside."

Holly looked into Megan's eyes, putting things together. "Kevin's your brother."

She nodded, biting her bottom lip.

Then new horror washed through her. "Oh, my God. *You know.*" But she said it louder than she'd intended and the sound of crashing glass startled her. She and Megan turned their attention to the sound. Kevin was staring at her, his face pale, while champagne shot out of a bottle spinning around on the concrete patio.

"Oh!" Megan's grandmother shouted from the deck. "You've added a fountain to the party."

"Not now, Mother," Nicole chided, stomping toward her son. "Kevin! What on earth is going on here?"

Megan grabbed Holly's arm and tugged. "Let's go inside."

Libby joined them, looking confused, then she looked back and forth between the two. "*Oh.*"

"Libby," Megan begged.

Libby gave her a push. "Yeah, I've got her—you deal with the fallout."

Megan shot off toward her mother and brother, while Libby looped her arm through Holly's. "I'm feeling a little light-headed from the heat. Will you help me inside?" Libby asked, fanning herself.

"Oh...sure..."

Kevin was walking around the table toward her, but Megan grabbed his arm and held him in place while Nicole went on a rant.

"This party could make or break my career, Kevin. Why

are you just standing there? We have to clean this up before anyone sees the mess!"

Libby ushered Holly into the kitchen, then dropped her hold and went to the cabinet, pulling out a glass.

"I take it that you're Kevin's neighbor?"

Holly cringed, closing her eyes in hopes she could shut the world out. "You know, too?"

"That Kevin acted like an ass? Yeah."

Her eyes shot open. "Oh, my God! *He's going around telling everyone?* Does *Nicole* know?" A new anxiety steamrolled through her head and she fought to catch her breath. "Oh, God. I'm going to lose my job."

Libby handed her a glass of ice water as she guided Holly to a bar stool at the kitchen island. "Whoa. Slow down. First of all, as far as I know, he's not telling anyone. Megan and I found him outside and he was feeling like a first-class asshole. We pried it out of him. And, second, why on earth would Nicole fire you? You didn't do anything wrong."

"I slept with her son!"

"Obviously you didn't know he was her son when you slept with him."

"She won't care."

"Kevin's a grown man who is in charge of his own life; who he sleeps with is his own business. Just like who you sleep with is yours."

"She won't see it that way."

Libby frowned. "No, I suppose you're right."

Panic flooded through Holly's veins. "She can't find out. I can still fix this." She got off the stool and headed to the door.

Libby pushed her back. "Where do you think you're going?"

"To convince Kevin to keep this to himself."

Libby shook her head. "Megan's on damage control. Trust me, she can handle it. Just take a deep breath, then we'll go back out when you feel ready."

"Thanks."

The doorbell rang and Holly started to get up. "Nicole said she was going to put up signs to go through the gate and straight to the backyard instead of through the house. I better make sure they're up."

"I'll check. You just sit here for a moment." The doorbell continued to ring repeatedly, and Libby groaned. "Oh, goody. It sounds like one of Nicole's asshole friends is at the door."

Holly couldn't help grinning.

"If that grin means you agree that her friends are assholes, then I can see why Megan likes you so much." Then she walked into the living room, leaving Holly alone.

Holly stood and moved to the bay window in the breakfast room, checking on what was going on in the backyard. Kevin was squatting next to the bartending table, Megan next to him. Nicole was waving her arms around, while Nicole's mother stood next to them.

She only had to make it through the next two hours, and then she could run home to her boxed wine and her cousin's dog. The damage was done. It wasn't like it could get any worse.

"Of course I saw the sign," a woman said behind her. "But I'm practically family." Holly recognized that voice. She spun around to see Bethany, Nicole's coffee date from the other day—the one wanting to discuss her wedding— standing next to an infuriated Libby. "I'm sure I have free rein of the house."

"Anyone familiar with Nicole knows better than to disobey her signs." Libby scowled with her hands on her hips, obviously not a fan of the pushy woman. "I've been best friends with Megan her entire life, and I'm pretty sure you and I haven't met. How are you practically family?"

Bethany jutted her head back, obviously offended. "Why, I'm Kevin's soon-to-be wife, of course."

Sure enough, there on her left hand was a shiny diamond ring to prove it.

Chapter Nineteen

Kevin watched Holly walk into the house, feeling like he'd just been run over by a steamroller. What was she doing here? Was she one of Megan's friends? Was that why his sister was so ticked earlier?

He started after her, but Megan grabbed his arm and pushed him back. "We have to clean this up, Kevin."

"But Holly—"

"You know Holly?" his mother asked in surprise. "Did you come to the office this week while I was out with a client?"

"Your office?" he asked, his synapses still misfiring in his brain.

"Holly is an event planner," Megan said slowly, enunciating each word so it sank in. "She works with Mom at her office."

"Why are you talking like that?" his mother demanded.

"Because the bottle obviously landed on his head and addled his brain," his sister said, fury in her eyes.

His mother's assistant . . . the wedding photos . . .

How could he have been so stupid? "I have to talk to her."

Megan pushed him into a squat. "No, you have to clean up."

"Why would you want to talk to Holly?" his mother asked, shaking her head. "Oh." Understanding filled the word. "She set up the bar. What did she get wrong?"

Her demanding boss…biding her time…It all made sense now. Oh, shit.

"I have to talk to her."

Megan gave him a look of understanding as she squatted next to him, picking up the shards of glass, then whispered, "Not now. She needs some space."

"Will someone tell me what is going on here?" his mother demanded, her hands on her hips. "Why would you hold a champagne bottle over your head? Is this your childish way of getting back at me because of your dinner with Bethany last night?"

He took a breath, pulling himself together. His mother had it out for her employee, and, just as he'd presumed earlier, most likely out of jealousy and not the ineptitude she continually insinuated. If his mother caught wind that he'd slept with Holly, she might fire her. He couldn't let that happen.

He forced a grin. "Megan dared me."

His mother turned her disapproval to her daughter. "Megan Nicole, I thought pregnancy would make you more mature."

His sister tried to hold back a grin as she stood. "I'm sorry to disappoint you, Mother."

"This is your way of getting back at me for not including Libby in a dual shower, isn't it?"

"For God's sake, Mother." Megan groaned. "It's not always about you. Sometimes Kevin and I do things without giving one thought to what you will think."

Their mother gasped and took a step backward.

"How long has it been since you've been with a woman?" his grandmother asked. She'd been uncharacteristically quiet during the exchange. Of all his grandparents she had always been his favorite, never giving a shit what other people thought of her. Her outfit today was proof enough of that. The septuagenarian was wearing a glittery pink track suit that looked like it was made out of shiny polyester, and she sported a pink stripe of hair that stood out in the snow-white mop on top of her head. She'd become even more bold after the death of his grandfather several years back, much to the aggravation of his mother. Last November, she'd married a yoga instructor twenty years her junior. "Going too long without sex can make a man clumsy. You should have seen Geraldo before we hooked up."

"Gram!" Kevin grinned, his irritation with his mother fading. "I'm not discussing my sex life with you."

"Why not? Later I can tell you all about the orgasmic meditation yoga class Geraldo and I teach." She winked. "We demonstrate it, too."

Kevin could live without the visual, and Megan shuddered.

"Mother!" Nicole shouted. "There are children present!"

Gram looked around. "Where?"

"*My* children."

For once, Kevin was happy for his mother's interference.

Megan jumped in. "Gram, I didn't think you were coming. After the incident with Mom and Geraldo at Christmas, you said you wouldn't be home for a while."

She shot Nicole a glare. "I decided I needed to be here

for my granddaughter's baby shower. Even if I had to leave a seminar in Milwaukee to do it."

"How's Geraldo? I was hoping to see him." Kevin felt a little guilty asking, since he knew his mother did not approve of her mother's quickie wedding in Little Heaven Wedding Chapel in Las Vegas. But he was pissed at his mother and it was an extra dig. Granted, he was acting like an eight-year-old, but the fact that his sister was, too, gave him all the encouragement he needed.

Nicole groaned. "I can*not* believe you are bringing that…*man* into the conversation."

Megan turned back to look at her. "You mean her *husband*?"

His mother shuddered, then lifted her chin. "Your grandmother has yet to produce a marriage license, so I still choose to believe this is simply an act of rebellion."

Gram looked her daughter up and down. "Just as uptight as ever. Geraldo would be willing to give you and Bart a private session." She curled her upper lip. "I couldn't teach you, of course. That would be too weird."

"And it's okay for your new husband—a man younger than me—to teach me how to have an orgasm?"

"Oh, my God!" Megan screeched, stuffing her fingers in her ears. "Stop!"

Kevin was shocked that his mother actually said the word. He'd never even heard her say the word *sex* in reference to the act.

Gram shrugged. "Since Bart can't seem to get the job done, then…sure."

The back gate opened and the voices caught his mother's attention. A panicked look washed over her face, and she pointed her finger at her mother. "No talk about orgasms during Megan's baby shower!"

Gram looked offended. "But it's been proven that pregnant women who have regular orgasms have safer deliveries." Gram turned to Megan. "Now, this is important. Are your orgasms mostly clitoral or G-spot?"

"Gram!" Megan gasped.

"Mother! That's quite enough." His mother did not look pleased.

Kevin popped off the top of another champagne bottle, poured it into a glass, then chugged it down like a shot.

"That is so not fair," Megan grumbled. "I can't rely on alcohol to get through this shower."

He lifted the glass in salute and grinned before taking another drink.

"Megan, you didn't answer my question," Gram said. "Do you know where your G-spot is?"

Megan gave her grandmother a solemn look. "Josh has his own personal map to my G-spot. I'm sure he'll be happy to show me." She glanced toward the guests. "But let's pick this up later, okay?"

"And make sure you're about five miles out of my hearing range first," Kevin said, pouring another glass. He did *not* want to hear about his sister's G-spot.

"Kevin!" his mother chastised. "Save some of that for the guests!" Then she looked around. "Where's Holly?"

The snotty way she said her name made his jaw set. He started to defend her, but Megan jabbed an elbow into his side. "Libby wasn't feeling well, so Holly offered to help her inside."

Nicole placed a hand on her chest. "Oh, dear. I hope she's not going to leave early. I need her for a game later."

"Un-fucking-believable," Kevin muttered under his breath before he finished off the rest of his drink. "Not is she okay, but she needs her for a game."

Megan gave their mother a tight smile. "Libby's fine. I think she was just overwhelmed by how amazing everything looks."

Nicole beamed. "Of course it does." She smoothed her skirt. "Now I need to go greet our guests."

She strutted away and Gram moved closer. "Give me a scotch on the rocks."

"All I have is mimosas, Gram."

"What kind of bar is that?"

"A lame-ass one, obviously." He turned his attention to his sister as he poured his grandmother a drink. "I have to talk to her, Megan."

"Not now—just trust me on this." Her eyes narrowed. "When I figured out what happened, I asked Mom to let Holly go, but she won't let her leave."

Gram looked between the two of them. "What secret are we keeping from your mother?"

"Uh..." Megan gave Kevin a questioning look.

He shook his head in irritation. "Might as well tell her. Half the fucking world knows."

"And Holly is horrified beyond belief at that."

He slammed the bottle down on the table. "*Goddammit.*"

His sister put her hands on her hips, then pushed out a breath. "I'm still pissed as hell at you right now for jumping to conclusions, but we'll fix this. One way or the other. You go walk around the block or something, take a few minutes to calm down, then come back. After everyone's left, you can talk to her."

He wasn't sure he should wait, but he decided to trust his sister on this one. "Okay."

She gave him a little push toward the house. "Use the side gate."

He nodded, bolting for the exit just as his worst nightmare came true.

"Kevin!"

He turned, horror washing through him when he saw Bethany coming out the kitchen door—headed straight for him.

"There you are, cupcake!" She gave him a pageant wave as she hurried toward him.

"What in God's name is she doing here?" he grumbled.

His mother moved to his side. "I invited her, of course. I know you think you're not interested in her, but you really should give her another chance. She might grow on you."

Like a fungus. But he wisely kept that to himself.

Bethany draped herself around him in a lingering hug, then kissed his cheek as she pulled back and looped her arm through his. "Nicole, I know you complain about your assistant, but I found her to be very sweet."

Kevin's heart seized. "You talked to Holly?"

Bethany winked. "I suggested she might be helping plan a special celebration for the two of us...if you know what I mean."

He was so screwed.

Chapter Twenty

Holly stood back by the musicians, but the soothing lullabies they played had yet to calm her. She had moved past *stunned* to *pissed*. It was one thing for Kevin to have left without saying good-bye, but the bastard had lied to her about being single.

The guests were mingling, and her job was to make sure things were going smoothly while Nicole played belle of the ball. Never mind that it was Megan's shower, not that she seemed to mind. Megan used the opportunity to come check on her—often with her friends Libby and Blair in tow—but she'd sent them away, insisting she was fine. And she was. Mostly. She'd slept with Kevin with no intention of anything more. That was exactly what she got.

But for a guy who was engaged, he sure didn't seem interested in his fiancée. After Bethany had greeted him, he'd bolted back to his bartending station. Not that Holly was specifically watching him. Her job was to watch everything, which included making sure the bartending station was stocked and functioning. At least that was what she told herself, because no self-respecting woman would still be interested. Mostly she just wanted to see if he'd squirm. And, from the looks he kept sending her, he was squirming plenty.

Soon Nicole announced that it was time for games. "The first game is to match baby names with celebrities. Holly's going to pass out the papers and pens, but don't look at your paper until I say go. The first one done wins this mystery surprise." Then she held up a white gift bag stuffed with white, fluffy tissue paper, smiling like she was a game-show hostess.

Nicole had an assortment of items waiting for Holly's attention in the back corner of the deck. She looped a wicker basket with a big white satin bow over her arm, but as Holly made her way to the guests, ready to pass out the slips of paper and the pens inside, Kevin intercepted her and reached out a hand.

She shot him a deadly glare. "I've got this."

"Let me help, Holly." His voice was low but firm.

"I don't need your help."

"There's over fifty people here, and I don't have anything to do. Let me help you."

"Kevin," Bethany called out in a singsong, waving at him with a princess wave. She sat at a table with an older woman who looked a lot like her. "Come sit with me, pooh bear."

Holly arched her eyebrows. "Go sit with your *fiancée*." Her tone was snottier than she'd intended.

"She's not my fiancée." He snatched half the stack of papers out of the basket before she could stop him. She considered snatching them back, but she wasn't about to make a scene. With a resigned shrug she lifted the basket so he could grab a handful of pens.

She had to admit that it went faster with Kevin's help. She

kept sneaking glances at him, telling herself it was to track his progress. From the glares Nicole bestowed upon her son, it was obvious she was unhappy he was helping. After Holly had passed out the last form she started back to the deck, but Nicole handed Holly an empty crystal pitcher. "I need you to make some fresh lemonade."

Holly gave her a tight smile. "Of course." She'd hoped to ditch Kevin, but he was hot on her heels.

"Holly, please just let me explain," he said as soon as they went through the kitchen door.

"You really don't have to do that, Kevin." She snagged a bag of lemons from the counter and dropped them onto the island counter. "I told you last night that I had no expectations, so no explanation needed."

He stood at her side. "I didn't know you worked for my mother."

She set the cutting board on the kitchen island and picked up a large knife. She grabbed a lemon and chopped it in half with more force than necessary. "And I didn't know you were her son. So no harm, no foul. Go join your fiancée."

"Holly, listen to me. She's not my fiancée."

She stopped and looked up at him. "Then why does she say she is?" She shook her head.

"She's *crazy*," he said. "I knew her in high school and my mother set me up on a blind date with her last night. That's why I was drunk. I couldn't handle her. I called my sister to pick me up and bring me home."

So Megan was the woman she'd seen him hugging on his front porch. She hadn't been able to see enough of the woman through the trees, but she supposed it could have been Megan. "But Bethany came into the office this week. She told your mother she wanted a winter wedding and the two of them left to plan it."

"Holly, I swear to you, I have no part of it. Before last night, I hadn't seen her since high school. She's flat-out crazy with her crystals and her talking grapes."

Talking grapes? Her eyes darted up to his to see if he was serious. His eyes were pleading with her, but he could be lying to cover his tracks. She returned her attention to the lemons.

"If you don't believe me about the date, just ask Megan. She'll confirm it."

The sound of the knife whacking the cutting board was louder than expected. He was driving her crazy standing next to her like this. Asshole or not, all she could think about was the things he'd done to her body the night before. Never in her life had she felt anything even close to what he'd made her feel, and even though she'd gone into the experience with her eyes wide open, she wasn't prepared for the heartache that stole her breath now. What if she never experienced anything like last night again?

But right now, she had to get him to leave. Because her nerves couldn't handle him so close, the smell of his shampoo filling her nose. "*Fine.* You're not engaged, not that it's any of my business. Thanks for helping with the game. So now that that's settled, see you later." *Oh, Lord. See you later?*

"I'm not done."

She pushed out a sigh, keeping her eyes on the cutting board. "I'm busy, Kevin, and your mother will be pissed if I'm not out there fairly soon." She froze, thinking over what she'd told him the night before. Her gaze darted up in panic. "Oh, God. Your mother...I told you that she's a horrible boss. ..."

He put his hand on her arm and she sucked in a tiny breath, her body reacting to his touch. Apparently her brain had forgotten to tell everything from the neck down that he was off-limits.

But if he noticed he didn't let on, leaving his hand on her bare upper arm. "I'm not going to tell her. Trust me, I know how bad she can be. I feel like I should be apologizing to you for her behavior."

"I'm not an indentured servant. I'm here of my own free will."

"But that's not entirely true, is it?" he asked. "Last night you told me you needed your job to pay your grandmother's medical bills."

"I told you much too much last night for someone who's a one-night stand. Because that's all it was, so I really wish you'd just been honest with me that that was what you wanted, too. I never had any expectations—you know that. Why the deception if you were just going to leave the next morning?"

"I never meant it to be just a one-night stand."

A lump filled her throat. "This morning suggested differently."

"I fucked up, Holly."

She shook her head. "This is all a moot point. It's not like we can see each other anyway."

"Why not?" he asked, looking genuinely confused.

She glanced up at him in exasperation. "Your mother."

His body tensed with anger. "I don't give a damn what my mother says."

"Well, bully for you, but I don't have that luxury."

His eyes widened with understanding and disappointment.

"Yeah," she said, trying to keep the bitterness from her voice. "She would never approve. She has a certain woman in mind for you, and I am definitely not her."

"I don't give a shit." But he sounded less convincing.

"Unfortunately, I do," she said, refusing to look at him.

"That's it?" he asked, sounding angry. "This thing between us is over?"

"Kevin." She shook her head. "This thing between us never began."

"That's bullshit and you know it."

Tears burned her eyes. "I don't have time for a relationship right now. I have a wedding that could make or break my future as a wedding designer that literally got dumped into my lap yesterday. I spent several hours last night pulling a theme and a plan together, but I have three weeks to get all the pieces in place, which will be next to impossible. Add to that your very jealous mother, who wanted the wedding for herself and can't decide if she wants me to fail so she'll feel better or succeed so she can take credit for the clout it will bring her company."

"Holly, you're good. If you weren't she wouldn't feel so threatened by you. Just quit."

"I can't. Not until I've built a solid enough reputation to start my own business. So now I have to endure her belittling and introducing me as her assistant when she and I both know I'm generating more income for the business than she is. I could go back to hotel management and get an additional part-time job to help cover my grandmother's expenses, but I don't want to. Because, my grandmother's private-room fees aside, I really love what I do. I don't want to give it up."

"I don't know what to do here." He sounded like the admission was ripped from his chest.

She shook her head, biting her lip. She started to turn away to get the juicer, but he grabbed her arm and spun her around, pulling her to his chest. He just held her, one hand tangled in her hair, his other arm wrapped around her back, cradling her against him. She tensed, waiting for him to make a move, but he didn't, just rubbed the back of her head with his fingertips. She dropped her guard and let herself sink into him, fighting the urge to cry. How long had it been since someone had just held her, offering her comfort and asking for nothing in return? Not since her parents died and Grandma Barb had rocked her night after night, singing softly to chase away her fears.

But after a few seconds the comfort she felt turned to longing, and she couldn't afford to let herself feel that. She took a step back, already missing his body against hers. She offered him a tight smile. "Thanks for your help. You better get outside."

"Holly."

She shook her head and picked up the knife. "Look, I have no idea why you ran this morning—"

"I ran because I'm an idiot. I saw your wedding photos spread out on the table and I jumped to conclusions. I freaked out and bolted. But all it took was a few hours, and several cups of coffee, for me to come to my senses and realize I'd screwed up."

"You thought I was planning a wedding for *us*?" she asked, slicing another lemon. "I hardly know you!"

He tilted his head, lifting his mouth into a wry grin. "In my defense, it hasn't stopped the crazy woman on the pool deck who said you agreed to help plan a special celebration, which I'm guessing might be her wedding. To me, apparently."

She grimaced. "Yeah, I can see your point."

"Look." He took a step toward her, then took the knife out of her hand and put it on the counter. "This is the second time I've encountered you with a deadly weapon." He grinned down at her. "You could give a guy a complex." He grabbed her shoulders, bending at the knees to look into her face. "If you knew all the insane situations I've been in, you might be more inclined to understand why I automatically went with Door Number Three: the crazy edition. But after just one night with you, I can tell you're not like any other woman I've been with."

"You mean I'm the most sane?" She gave him a teasing grin. "You sure know how to flatter a girl."

"No. That's not it." He looked frustrated and groaned. "I felt something with you I haven't felt before. I don't want to let it go without at least giving it a chance." His voice lowered, turning husky and sending a shiver down her spine. "Tell me you felt something, too."

Damn him. Why did he have to be so tempting? "I did—"

Before she realized what was happening she was in his arms again, his mouth on hers, demanding her response. Her body complied, her desire taking over her senses as her fingers dug into his hair, pulling him closer.

His hand slid up her side, then cupped her breast. His thumb brushed over her bra cup, finding her nipple. Molten desire raced through her veins, but something in the back of her head set off alarms. She had to stop this—now.

She took a step back, out of his hold, her fingertips resting on her lips as she tried to catch her breath. "We can't."

"Because of my mother?"

"I can't risk it."

"What if I talk to her?"

"No! What if she fires me?"

He groaned and ran a hand through his hair, then he turned to her with new hope in his eyes. "What if we just don't tell her?"

"You mean lie?"

"No, just keep it a secret."

"So no one would know? We'd hide like we were ashamed?"

"No. Dammit." He ran a hand through his hair. "I'm trying to make this work."

She shook her head, more disappointed than she'd felt in a long time. "I can't lie. I hate lying."

"Keeping it a secret isn't lying."

"It is to me." She took a step back. "Say we see each other in secret, if nothing comes of it, then your mother never knows and no big deal. But what if something *does* come of it? We hide it from our friends and family? Because no one could know. All it would take would be one slip and your mother could find out and fire me. Do you really want to live in secrecy?"

"But what about your big job? The one you said Mom wanted but could help you break free to start your own business."

She froze, trying to remember what she'd told him. He could run and tell his mother *everything*. "You were paying attention."

His eyes darkened. "I'm not sure what assholes you've been with before, but, yeah, I pay attention."

"You could tell her every word I said—"

"I'm not going to tell my mother anything. So what about that wedding?"

"The Johansen wedding. The bride's mother is a wedding-dress designer and *Modern Bride* is coming to take photos for a ten-page spread. But nothing is guaranteed. First the wedding has to go well, and people have to realize I planned the wedding. …"

"Basically you're saying it's not a sure thing."

She gave him an apologetic smile. "I could have the

chance to leave her in four weeks or four years. I just don't know. What if we see each other and really fall hard? Do you think you could hide that? Or would want to?"

His eyes clouded. "No. If I loved you, I suspect everyone would see it."

His admission surprised her. "Then you agree this can't happen."

A war waged across his face before defeat settled in. "Yes."

"Okay," she said, the disappointment evident even to her ears. "That settles that."

"But I still want to be friends," he blurted out.

She sighed, her heart breaking all over again. "That will never work."

"Why not?"

"You know..." she hedged.

"No. I don't." The seriousness in his eyes caught her off guard.

"This thing between us...I don't..." Her face flushed.

"We're both adults. Why not?" He seemed to grow more confident with each word. "I'm capable of self-control. How about you, Holly?"

Damn him. "Of course I am."

"Then there's no reason we can't be friends. Besides—" he paused as though weighing his words "—I don't know shit about remodeling my house. You said you'd come over and give me your opinion. You wouldn't leave me hanging, would you?"

The triumphant look in his eyes told her he knew he had her. She wouldn't refuse him help and he knew it.

"Fine."

His grin lit up his face, drawing her like a moth to a flame. Dear Lord, what had she gotten herself into?

Chapter Twenty-One

⁓

So Kevin didn't get the outcome he'd wanted, but he could work with the parameters he'd been given. He knew what he wanted, and he'd be patient until he could have it all. But in the meantime, he could still have Holly in his life. Just not to the full extent he wanted. Yet.

After the shower games and the presents were opened, Megan approached him wearing a suspicious look. "Why are you so chipper?"

"Chipper?" he asked, making her a nonalcoholic drink. "In all of my thirty-three years, no one has ever called me chipper."

"Cut the bullshit." She glanced over her shoulder at Holly, who was organizing the opened presents on the gift table. "Even Holly seems relaxed."

He grinned. "It's a beautiful day and I'm basking in the glow of our mother exploiting the upcoming birth of my niece or nephew."

"Wow. How many bottles of champagne have you had?"

"Only the couple of drinks I had after the shit hit the fan."

"You talked to Holly?"

"I explained several things."

She waited a few seconds before she prodded. "And?"

He shrugged, trying to look nonchalant. He loved driving her crazy. "We've decided to be friends."

Her jaw dropped. "You're kidding me."

"Nope," he said with a smug grin.

"She seriously wants to be friends?"

"For now."

"She said that. She actually said the words 'I want to be friends for now'?"

"Not exactly."

"What *exactly* did she say?"

He turned serious and lowered his voice. "Look, I told her that I completely fucked up and jumped to conclusions, but after all the loons I've dated, it had merit. Exhibit A of the Crazy Train Express helped convince her." He tilted his head toward Bethany, who seemed to be pouting because Kevin wouldn't take a break and sit with her. She'd tried to hover around his table, but he'd sent her away, telling her he felt a strong negative presence coming from the bushes behind him and she should save herself.

"So why the just-friends status?"

"Synonyms for the entity in question include Diablo, Devil Incarnate, Master Manipulator, and *your* personal favorite, Knickers—yeah, I know the nickname you, Libby, and Blair use."

"Mom." She shrugged when he gave her a questioning look. "Because she always has her knickers in a wad."

He nodded, then grimaced at the thought of his mother's knickers. "Holly is certain Mom will never approve, and I hate to admit it, but I think she's right. Exhibit A stands as evidence in this as well."

"I wish I could say you were wrong. Holly and I used to go out to lunch until Mom figured it out and put a stop to it. Maybe I can talk to Mom and make her see reason."

Kevin shook his head. "No. I offered to do the same thing, but Holly's worried about the repercussions. And knowing the animosity Mom has toward her, I'm not sure it's unwarranted."

"So you're just going to let this thing between you and Holly go?" she asked sounding dismayed.

His eyes narrowed in suspicion. "Why would you care?"

"Well . . . I . . . I think you'd make a cute couple."

"Yeah . . . I don't think that's it. I knew you were up to something when we walked through the house the first time, then you seemed a little too interested when I mentioned my cute neighbor. This has your mischievous handiwork all over it."

"I have no idea what you mean," she said, looking away guiltily.

"You need to work on your poker face."

She shrugged. "Okay, so at one of our lunches, Holly told me about her grandmother and that she and her cousin still lived in her house. I asked about the neighborhood because I was searching for a deal for you and she happened to mention that the house next door to her was for sale. Cheap."

"So suddenly you had matchmaking bulbs going off?"

"Not necessarily." She flashed him a mock innocent smile. "You just can't put a price on good neighbors."

"Like I'm buying that. For the record, Match-dot-com is a hell of a lot cheaper than that hellhole you bought me."

"Please. If you want more crazies, be my guest. After

Lacy and all the others... you deserved someone good, and decent and sweet. You deserve someone like Holly."

The warmth that flooded his chest caught him by surprise and tightened his voice. "But does she deserve someone like me?"

"Despite your plummet into asshatery this morning, you're a good guy. Just don't hurt her, okay?"

Hurting her was the last thing he wanted.

After the shower ended, Kevin offered to load Megan's gifts into her car. But when he studied the huge pile of presents on the gift table, he shook his head. "There's no way we'll get all of this into your SUV."

"Good thing I showed up with my car," Megan's husband said behind them.

"Josh." Megan's face lit up when she turned to face her husband, and Kevin knew he had to get over the grudge he still held against his brother-in-law. Kevin loved his sister, and she obviously loved her husband. And he obviously adored her. So they'd had an unconventional beginning. After his rough start with Holly, Kevin had a new empathy for Josh's position.

Kevin turned around and held out his hand. "Hey, Josh. Good to see you."

His brother-in-law hesitated before he shook Kevin's hand. "Megan's thrilled you're back in town."

Kevin grinned as he dropped his hand. "But not you?" Then he laughed. "That's okay. I haven't made things easy, but I want to be part of Megan and her baby's life. You make her happy, and it's obvious you love her. I'd like to make a fresh start with you."

Megan's mouth gaped open.

Josh looked at his wife, then gave Kevin a tentative grin. "As long as this isn't some practical joke against Megan as payback for sticking you with that house, I'm willing to let bygones be bygones. It's obvious you've been a good brother looking out for his sister."

Megan hooked an arm around both their necks and pulled them into a group hug. "This is the best gift you could have given me."

Her voice was muffled and Kevin asked in horror, "Are you *crying*?"

"I'm pregnant, okay? Hormones." She dropped her hold on them both and shoved her brother's arm as she swiped at her eye. "Way to ruin the moment."

Josh laughed. "Welcome to my life."

Megan's eyes narrowed as she pointed her finger at her husband in mock warning. "Watch it."

Josh turned to Kevin. "Since we're all bonding here, I want you to know that I told her not to buy that house for you."

"House?" Nicole asked, walking out the back door onto the deck. "Are you talking about Kevin's house?"

Kevin took a step back. "I think that's my cue to leave."

Megan turned to him, horrified. "Don't you leave me here to deal with her alone!"

He graced her with a wicked grin. "Paybacks, Megan. Sometimes they really suck."

* * *

Kevin stopped at the hardware store on the way home from Megan's shower and bought a gas grill and a couple of lawn chairs. His checking account groaned that he had wiser things to purchase, but it was all part of his plan to win Holly over. The steaks and potatoes he bought next were also part of the plan.

He changed clothes, then started the grill, letting the kitten play in the yard. He'd bought a couple of cat toys when he was at the store. It was currently playing with a stuffed mouse that had a bell sewn into its belly, while Kevin plotted ways to get Megan to adopt the creature. Especially since the constant twinkling of the bell was getting on his nerves.

"If you've gotten wind chimes, I have to warn you that the neighbor behind me will be complaining within hours," Holly said as she walked through the back gate. Her hair was pulled back into a ponytail and she'd changed into shorts and a gauzy top with a deep V that showed off her cleavage.

He laughed, taking a drink of his beer before he answered, giving his now racing heart a chance to slow down. She'd come to him, saving him from having to use his excuse to get her to come over. Maybe she really had forgiven him.

"I got the cat a toy. I'm deeply regretting it now."

She grinned, but she stayed close to the gate, looking like *she* was regretting her decision to come over.

"I went furniture shopping." He waved to the lawn chair he was sitting in and the empty one next to him. The chairs were collapsible, with drink holders in the armrests. "You like?"

She laughed, moving closer. "There's a place for your beer. Looks like you got the super deluxe model."

"Yeah, the guy at the hardware store gave them a double thumbs-up. He said you can sit in them for hours and feel like you're in a cloud."

She gave him a curious look. "Do you plan to sit here for hours?"

He took a drag from his beer. "I haven't decided yet. I've had a shitty day, but it just got better." He opened the cooler next to him and pulled out a beer bottle, popped off the top, and offered it to her.

Relief washed through him when she reached for it and sat down. "Not bad. I see you bought an appliance, too." She gestured toward the grill.

"You know what they say about a man and his grill."

"Is it anything like a boy and his dog?"

"It's the grown-up version. And, trust me, you haven't lived until you've tried my steaks."

"You don't say," she murmured, watching the cat as she took a sip from the bottle. "How'd you know I drank beer?"

"You brought me two the first night."

"How'd you know they weren't left over from an old boyfriend?"

His hand stopped, the bottle inches from his mouth. "Were they?"

She laughed. "No. They were mine and Melanie's." She took another drink.

"Hard day at the office?" he asked in a teasing tone.

A wry grin twisted her mouth. "I'd say you have no idea, but then again..." Holly hesitated, then turned to him. "Let's make a deal. We'll try this friendship thing, but we don't discuss your mother."

"But my mother is a huge pain in both our asses. Isn't part of being friends being able to gripe about the people who bug the shit out of you?"

"We'll just have to try." When he didn't answer, she continued. "Kevin, this *friendship* is hard enough. It doesn't feel right to complain about my boss to her son."

If she saw secrets as lies, he understood her aversion to talking negatively about his mother. "No need to make any lifelong decisions now. We'll agree Nicole Vandemeer discussions are off-limits for the time being."

She nodded, her mouth pursed. "Sounds fair enough."

"Have you had dinner?"

She hesitated. "No."

"Then you should stay and have dinner with me. I'm grilling steaks and baked potatoes."

Her smile wavered. "I don't know."

"You've fed me twice; it's the least I can do. Besides, this isn't a date. This is just two friends eating together. Or—if it makes you feel better—you can consider it a bribe."

She looked wary but a twinkle filled her eyes. "A bribe?"

He turned toward her. "Just how handy are you with a sledgehammer?"

Her wariness deepened. "Why do you ask?"

"I thought maybe after we eat, we could do a little demo on my kitchen."

"You want me to help you demo? With a sledgehammer?"

"Well, part of it with a sledgehammer. Some will probably come out with a good kick." When she hesitated, he said, "It's a great way to work off frustration."

Her eyes lit up. "I'm intrigued."

"The potatoes are on the grill and I'll add the steaks in about ten minutes. After we eat, we can take our frustrations out on something productive."

She hesitated.

"Do you have something else you need to do?"

"I don't have any plans for dinner. Mel was trying to get the night off, but it didn't work out. Which is probably a good thing."

"Why?"

She shot him a hesitant grin. "You're not exactly her favorite person right now."

"I guess that's deserved. Any chance I can win her over?"

"I'm not sure," she answered with a shrug. "Once she makes up her mind, there's little chance of changing it back."

Well, great. He'd already suspected that her cousin's approval would be important, just like he'd suspected his mother's was important to her as well. He'd have to figure out how to fix both, but he'd deal with it later. Tonight he was in the clear.

"Do you want to bring Killer over?"

"I'm not sure it's a good idea with your kitten running around. Maybe later." She turned her head toward the non-stop tinkling bell. "What did you name it?"

"I haven't named it yet."

"What?" she asked in horror. She leaned out of the chair and scooped the tiny gray fur ball out of the grass and cuddled it against her chest. "How can this cutie not have a name?"

Kevin had never felt jealous of an animal, but he was feeling pretty envious of the cat's proximity to Holly's breasts. He'd seen them in all their glory the night before, and he had to grab the armrest on the chair to keep himself in place. "How can I name it when I don't even know if it's a girl or a boy?"

"You're just like your sister."

"Excuse me?" he asked. "Are you comparing my niece or nephew to a cat?"

She laughed and he loved the sound, so light and carefree. Her laugh gave him hope they could work this out.

"I *was* going to ask you to help me name it," he teased. "But I wanted to make it as difficult as possible."

"You want me to help name it?" she asked in surprise.

He hadn't planned it, but now that he'd suggested it, it felt right. "Yeah."

She pulled the contented kitten from her chest and held it

up in front of her face. The tiny creature let out an even tinier mewl. "What should we name you, little one?" She glanced at Kevin. "He has one white paw. You could call him Boots or Mittens."

He grinned. "Name him after an accessory? The next thing you'll suggest is that I get a murse to carry him around."

She smirked, shaking her head. "So I guess Bracelet and Toe Ring are out?"

"I don't know ... Toe Ring has a nice *ring* to it."

She groaned at his pun. "That was excruciatingly bad."

"I'm the bad boy your mother warned you about," he teased, and immediately regretted it for multiple reasons. For one, she really had thought of him as a bad boy earlier in the day, and, more importantly, the night before she'd admitted she barely remembered her mother. He'd just made light of that. "Holly. I'm sorry. Your mom—"

She shook her head. "Stop. It's just a saying. You didn't mean anything insensitive by it."

"The last thing I want to do is hurt you again."

She studied him, her eyes guarded. "If you're friends with someone long enough, they are going to hurt and disappoint you." She leaned over and put the kitten on the grass, then stood. "I think I'm going to take a rain check on dinner."

Kevin got out of his chair and stood in her path, trying to figure out where he'd screwed up.

"You don't have to stay to help with my house. You can eat and then go. You need to eat anyway."

"I'm tired and I have a lot of work to do. I think I'll just go."

"Can I walk you home?"

She laughed and glanced down at the kitten, then up into his face. "No. That definitely falls into the more-than-friends category." Then, before he could protest more, she made a beeline for the gate without a backward glance.

Chapter Twenty-Two

By the middle of Sunday afternoon Holly was sure she'd made the right decision to leave Kevin's the night before, even though her heart didn't agree. To help take her mind off it, she'd taken a break from working on the Johansen wedding and resorted to something she detested: cleaning.

She was vacuuming the living room when she heard a pounding at the front door. Killer had been barking at the vacuum cleaner, but now turned his attention to the door as Holly flipped the off switch.

Grabbing the doorknob, she wondered if she had the strength to tell Kevin no today, but when she opened the door she was surprised to see Megan. "Hi..."

Megan gave her an apologetic smile as she wrapped her hand around her very pregnant belly. "I'm sorry to bother you, but I need your help."

"Of course!" Holly said, her anxiety rising. "Are you okay?" She looked down at Megan's belly. "Oh, my God. Is the baby okay?"

"Holly!" Megan stepped forward and put her hand on Holly's arm. "I'm fine. I swear."

Holly put her hand on her chest and took a breath. "You scared me half to death."

"I know." She cringed. "I'm sorry."

She offered Megan a smile. "It's okay. What do you need?"

Megan cocked her head to the side and gave Holly an exasperated look. "I'm surrounded by a bunch of guys next door and I need you to tell them I'm right."

Holly's breath stuck in her chest. "I don't know. ...Did Kevin put you up to this?"

"No. This is just a friend asking a friend for help. They're insisting we keep the kitchen cabinets and paint them, and I need you to back me up that the kitchen needs to be gutted."

Holly grimaced. "I don't know. ..."

A warm smile spread across Megan's face. "Or you can agree with them. I just need an opinion I can trust." Then she gave her a pout. "Please."

Holly burst out laughing. "Does that work on Josh?"

"Yes, and usually Kevin, too. Will you help me? You can just come in, give your opinion, and then leave."

"Okay." But she regretted it the moment she shut the door behind her.

They walked side by side to Kevin's house and Holly struggled to catch her breath. Her nerves were getting the better of her. She kept her gaze on the tree-root obstacle course, needing to focus on something other than the fact she was about to see Kevin. Why was she so nervous? Was she more worried about Kevin's reaction when he saw her, or that she wouldn't have the willpower to walk away?

She heard Kevin's voice as well as those of several other men, along with loud banging. Josh was in the living room, prying the trim from the window. Megan walked past him like a woman with a purpose into the dining room, where Kevin was swinging a sledgehammer into the wall separating the dining room from the kitchen. A tall blond man stood next to him, shouting as he pointed to the light switch.

Kevin noticed Holly and stopped midswing, lowering his mallet. His eyes widened. "Holly...hey."

Megan looped her arm through Holly's, which Holly realized was probably Megan's attempt to keep her from bolting. "I dragged Holly over here for her opinion. We're going to settle this cabinet dilemma."

Josh walked up behind them and all three men stared at Holly like she'd just walked out of a spaceship.

"I take it none of you knew I was coming over," Holly finally said.

Megan squeezed her arm. "I had to hide my secret weapon. Now, not to put you under any pressure or anything, but what would you do with the cabinets?"

Holly dragged her gaze from Kevin's now expressionless face and turned to face the cabinets. The kitchen was a complete disaster, but she didn't feel comfortable telling Kevin to spend thousands of dollars to replace them. "Well..."

"Matt, the supposed expert here"—Megan dropped her hold and pointed to the man next to Kevin—"thinks they can be fixed."

Matt protested, "Hey, I—"

Megan cut him off. "But I insisted that the kitchen needs to be gutted. I know you redid your house, which makes you *my* expert. What do you think?"

Holly had never felt more put on the spot, and she found herself searching out Kevin's face.

He gave her a reassuring smile. "I want your opinion,

Holly. You've done this to your house. You know what you're doing."

"I've only done one house. ..."

He walked over to her, still holding her gaze. "If this was your house, what would you do?"

Somehow he made her feel like they were the only two people in the house, and that her opinion really mattered.

"Go on. What would you do?" He smiled and something in her heart melted.

She smiled back. "Gut it."

He smiled, his face lighting up.

Her stomach squeezed as regret filled her. Why did he have to be her boss's son?

"Well, there you go," Kevin said, still holding her gaze. "We'll gut it."

"Okay." Holly broke eye contact and turned to Megan. "If that's all you need..."

"We ordered pizza," Megan said. "You should stay. I'm, like, the only girl here."

"I don't know. ..."

She looked back at Kevin. He gave her an understanding smile as he asked, "Holly, can I talk to you for a minute?"

"Sure."

He led her outside to the front porch, and she suddenly wondered if he was taking her outside to tell her he didn't *want* her to stay. But he eased her concerns as soon as they were out of his sister's watchful eye.

"Holly, I'm sorry. I had no idea what Megan was up to."

"It's okay. I suspected."

"But that being said, I want you to stay."

She sighed. "I don't know. ..."

"I promise this isn't part of some devious scheme on my end."

She grinned up at him. "So Megan got all the devious genes?"

He laughed. "I suppose my mother would disagree."

Now that she was here, she didn't want to go back home to her empty house. She wanted to be here with Kevin and his sister—who was now laughing with her husband and Kevin's friend. She wanted to be part of *this*. "Okay."

He looked like he was about to reach for her, but he stopped himself. "Just friends."

Holly nodded. "Friends." Against her better judgment, she was willing to give it a shot.

She walked back inside with him, but then looked down at her shorts, sleeveless shirt, and flip-flops. "This isn't exactly demolition attire."

Megan's face lit up when she saw Holly coming in next to Josh. "You don't need demolition attire. You can sit with me and watch." She gave Josh a sexy smile. "I'm watching my husband get hot and sweaty."

Kevin closed his eyes and cringed. "Megan. Please."

"What? How do you think I got this baby inside of me?"

"Oh, my God." Kevin groaned. "Stop or I'm kicking you out—" He stopped and understanding filled his eyes. "Good try. You stay."

"Then I want my husband to take his shirt off."

Kevin laughed. "Fine. Josh, take off your shirt. Strip for us."

Everyone started laughing, and Matt shook his head, wearing a huge grin. "I thought we were demoing your house, not auditioning for *Magic Mike*."

"Speak for yourself," Josh said, pulling his shirt over his head and starting to dance while he looked at his wife.

Everyone laughed again and the men got to work. The

house was hot and the fans were set up, but with all the dust blowing around, Josh insisted that Megan sit outside. She grabbed the kitten from the basement and dragged Holly outside with her to sit in Kevin's new lawn chairs.

They watched the kitten romp in the yard for several minutes before Megan said, "I want to apologize for my mother."

"Oh," Holly said, surprised. "It's not like you can control your mother's—" She cut herself off before she said too much.

Megan gave her a hesitant smile. "I know my mother. Trust me, I spent most of my life running from my mother. Kevin, too. But when I needed her the most—when my ex-fiancé showed up at my wedding to Josh—my mother got over the shock that I'd lied to her and she stood up for me." She paused. "I know my mother puts on this front that she's cold and calculated, but there's more to her deep down. You just have to dig for it."

Holly remained silent. She was positive Nicole would become a momma lion when it came to her kids, but if Megan was insinuating that Holly would see that side of her, she was mistaken. She'd given up that hope when Nicole had turned cold months ago.

"If you'll just let me talk to Mom—"

And there it was. "No."

Megan sat up and turned in her seat to face Holly. "Mom wants Kevin to be happy. If we tell her, she'll eventually come around."

"The keyword is *eventually*. You of all people know I need this job." She paused. "My grandmother's getting worse."

Megan's eyes widened. "Holly. I'm sorry."

She shrugged, not wanting to talk about it. "We've known

it was coming. But that means I need the money I make with your mother more than ever."

"But surely—"

"Megan." Holly's tone was sharper than she'd intended. "I know you want Kevin and I to give this thing between us a chance, but it's not going to happen."

Kevin walked out the back door, having shed his T-shirt, and Holly's eyes were drawn to his bare chest. She could stare at him all day long and never get enough.

His gaze found hers and they stared at each other for several seconds before Megan interrupted.

"I take it you came out for a reason?" Megan asked.

Kevin tore his eyes from her and turned to his sister. "The pizza's here."

Josh and Matt came out the back door, carrying the pizza boxes and a cooler. They spent the next hour sitting in the backyard, swapping stories about Matt and Kevin and their friend Tyler. Holly realized she hadn't hung out with her old friends in years. They had gotten married and started families, and Holly had let those relationships drift—but now she wondered if there was a nugget of truth to Melanie's statement that she ran from relationships.

What if the reason she didn't want to lie to Nicole about seeing Kevin was more about a fear of a relationship with Kevin and less about upsetting her boss?

"Hey," Kevin asked softly as he sat down next to her. "Are you okay? You've been so quiet."

"I've been listening." Her eyes filled with tears. "Believe it or not, this is the best day I've had in ages. Thanks for letting me stay."

"Holly, don't ever question that I want you to stay."

She knew he meant more than a friendly visit, and part of her was so tempted to stay for so much more. She had a feeling they could have something wonderful. But she couldn't let herself go there. There was too much at stake.

She blinked to dry her eyes then stood. "I need to go home."

Megan gasped in surprise. "Why?"

"Megan," Kevin warned.

"I have more work to do on the Johansen wedding," Holly said. "But thanks for letting me hang out today."

Megan looked like she still wanted to protest, but Josh stood and reached out his hand to her. "Megs, we need to get going, too."

Holly was relieved that Megan backed off, but as soon as she walked into her empty house, she wondered if she'd made the right decision.

Suddenly she was questioning a lot of decisions.

Chapter Twenty-Three

The next morning, Holly woke up feeling overwhelmingly sad. She liked Kevin. But did she like him enough to risk everything for a chance with him?

She was eager to seek the refuge of her job, but thoughts of Kevin still followed her, and the woman who kept them apart was more abrasive than usual. Nicole had made a list of things that had gone wrong at the shower and how they could improve on each item next time. She wanted to go through them point by point in excruciating detail.

Holly gave her boss a forced look of patience. "While I'd really love to do that, Nicole, I need to start making arrangements for the Johansen wedding."

Nicole's mouth pursed. "Did Miranda give you her approval yet?"

"No, but given the time constraints, I thought it best to make sure the vendors could deliver before I presented the options to the Johansens. Then we aren't scrambling to come up with a backup plan. We'll look more professional and organized this way."

"Hmm…" Nicole's mouth parted like she wanted to argue, but then she closed it.

Trying not to look relieved, Holly added, "I plan to meet with the Johansens tomorrow, then I need to finalize everything for the Murphy–Douglas wedding this weekend."

Nicole looked worried. "I won't be able to help with that. I have that fund-raiser barbecue on Saturday night."

Grateful that she wouldn't be under the watchful eye of her boss during a wedding Nicole hadn't been any part of planning, Holly devoted her attention to the Johansen wedding. She had over a dozen calls to make before her presentation the next day. She'd made some progress, planning to work through lunch, when Bethany walked into the office a little before noon, clearly distressed.

"Nicole, he won't answer my calls!" She sniffed, then burst into tears.

Nicole hurried out of her chair. "There, there, Bethany. Why don't you sit down?" She started to lead her to the client table but swung her gaze to Holly. "Holly, could you get some tea?"

Holly gritted her teeth and went into the back to heat up the water, grabbing a cup for herself as well. She definitely didn't have time to be dealing with a delusional woman, and she was impatient with Nicole as well for encouraging Bethany's behavior. Minutes later, Holly put her own tea on her desk and handed Bethany her cup.

She started to walk away, but Bethany grabbed her hand. "You and I should go to lunch. We have things to discuss."

While Holly had heard her flinging around the word *fiancé* at the shower, she hadn't heard her do it around Nicole.

She shot a glance to her boss, but Nicole kept her focus on Bethany, not giving anything away.

"Why won't Kevin call me back?" Bethany asked. "Our date went so well."

Nicole gave her a sympathetic look. "You know he's just started his new job. I'm sure it's keeping him busy. Just give him some time."

Had Nicole lost her mind as well?

"And Holly's too busy to go to lunch with you. I have too much for her to do today."

Bethany dabbed her eyes. "I think I need to call my mother."

Nicole's eyes widened in alarm. "No need to do that, Bethany, darling. I'm sure we can work something out. I'd take you out to lunch myself, but I have an appointment I can't cancel."

The front door burst open and Megan pushed through, her face scrunched up in irritation. "Mother, we need to talk." She searched the room until she found her mother in the corner, her mouth dropping open when she realized who was sitting next to her.

Nicole looked more flustered than Holly had ever seen her. "Megan, darling. Now is not a good time."

Megan's brow lowered as her gaze narrowed in on Bethany. "No, I can see that."

Nicole looked at her watch, and then at her daughter and the emotional woman next to her. Worry filled her eyes. "I really need to go."

Bethany left her own self-absorption for a moment to realize that Nicole was distressed. "Nikki, I'm sorry I just barged in."

The older woman cringed at the nickname.

But Bethany was oblivious. "Megan, why don't you and

I go out to lunch instead? You can tell me all the little things I need to know about Kevin."

"Well, that might happen," Megan said slowly. "If you and Kevin were actually dating." She turned a deathly gaze on her mother.

"Megan Nicole," her mother reprimanded, but her tone lacked its usual bite.

Bethany didn't notice the mother-daughter conflict. "I know Kevin isn't ready to tell everyone about us—"

Megan's face brightened. "You know what? I think lunch is a great idea."

Nicole looked leery. "You do?"

A smile lit up Megan's eyes, and she patted her mother's arm. "Yeah, you go have a great lunch with your client and we girls will hang out."

It was clear Nicole was suspicious of Megan's offer, but another quick look at her watch seemed to settle it for her. She grabbed her purse. "If you need *anything* from me..."

Megan gave her mother a gentle push toward the door. "Go already." She flashed Bethany a sweet smile. "It's girl bonding time."

Nicole narrowed her eyes, locking a gaze with her daughter. "Call me later, Megan."

"Will do," she said with a perky bounce.

Megan watched her mother leave, then sat down next to Bethany. "How about we just order something and eat here?"

Bethany frowned. "But I thought we were going out."

"But if we stay here, then Holly can join us."

Holly was sure Megan had lost her mind, but then she turned to Holly and winked.

What was Megan up to? They decided on Chinese, and Megan offered to go pick it up from a restaurant a block away instead of waiting for delivery in thirty minutes. She was back within five minutes. "Let's eat."

"I think I'll just eat at my desk," Holly said, expecting Megan to argue. But she just handed her the container of chicken lo mein and whispered, "Start a timer."

"What?"

Her grin turned devilish before she spun around and settled at the table with Bethany. Curious, Holly opened the clock app on her phone and did as she was told.

"Just think," Bethany said. "We can have lunches like this all the time."

"I know, right. I'm so excited," Megan said, opening a package of chopsticks. "Although if you and Kevin get married, I hope you'll actually be able to leave the house."

Bethany stopped opening her container. "Why wouldn't I be able to leave the house?"

Megan froze, her face turning serious. "Oh." She sucked in her bottom lip, looking torn. "Never you mind." She waved her hand. "I'm sure you two will have it all worked out. I mean, it's not like he expects you to stay with them *all* of the time."

"What do you mean?" Bethany sounded worried as she jabbed her food with a fork.

"So have you started thinking of all those kids' names yet?"

"Kids' names?" She shook her head, looking shell-shocked. "We haven't discussed kids yet."

"Oh." Megan's head jerked up. "That's surprising. Especially since he wants so many."

"So many what?"

Megan released a giggle and shook her head. "Kids, of course. He's worried that you two are getting a late start, what with both of you in your early thirties, but thank goodness multiple births run in our family. I'm sure you'll figure out a way to have the eighteen kids he's dreaming of. And in ten years or less at that."

"Eighteen kids?" Bethany started choking on her rice.

Megan patted her back. "Are you okay?"

"I..." she stammered.

"It's all so exciting, isn't it? But I can only imagine how hard it's going to be to come up with all those names starting with the letter Q." She started counting with her fingers. "Quincy, Quinton, Queenie... What else is there?"

"Quart. Quay. Quantico," Holly added from her desk. "Or you could make up your own names. You could name the fifth one Quintuplet."

Megan's mouth pursed. "I think that would only work if there's five babies at once." Her face brightened, then she grabbed Bethany's arm in excitement. "Oh! You could take fertility drugs and have five or six at a time. Then you can get it over with sooner. Only four or five pregnancies."

"That's a great idea," Holly said, then lowered her voice. "I'm not supposed to tell you this—Kevin asked me to keep it a secret, even from his mother—but when he heard you wanted me to help with the wedding, he gave me all kinds of ideas he wants to implement."

"Oh, really?" Bethany asked, her face pale.

"He wants to have tiny little baby carriages line the aisle when you walk down, with photos of babies in each one." Holly sat up straighter and waved at her computer. "I've been hard at work trying to find them."

"Baby carriages? At the wedding?"

Megan leaned closer. "He's very eager to get started."

Holly gave her a big smile. "I'm sure you're going to be so happy in that three-bedroom, fifteen-hundred-square-foot house. All twenty of you."

Bethany stood. "I just forgot, I have a crystal client coming in fifteen minutes."

"What?" Megan asked in dismay. "But we've barely started our girl bonding time." She narrowed her eyes. "Did I mention that Kevin is adamantly opposed to his wife working outside the home? You better enjoy your time as a career woman while you can."

Bethany looked like a deer in the headlights. "Tell your mother that this is all moving a little too fast. I think I need to take some time to think things through."

"I don't think waiting is a good idea," Megan said. "You need to work on getting pregnant right away. In fact, Holly was just about to call the doctor to get your fertility treatments going."

Holly picked up the phone and held it to her ear. "Which day is good for your egg testing? Wednesday or Friday?"

Bethany didn't answer; instead she bolted out the door.

Megan turned to Holly. "Time check?"

Holly burst out laughing as she looked at her phone. "One minute and forty-five seconds."

Megan leaned back and looked at her nails. "New personal record. Damn, am I good or what?"

"Personal record?"

She picked up her food container and dragged her chair over to Holly's desk. "Getting rid of Kevin's girlfriends was a specialty of mine. I used to do it all the time when he was in high school. In fact, he stopped bringing a lot of them home. Of course, paybacks were a bitch. I couldn't bring my boyfriends home, either." She picked up a piece of chicken with her chopsticks. "Kevin told me she was gullible. But I'm still calling it a record."

"That was too perfect. Almost like you planned it."

"Not this time. Total coincidence. We'll call it serendipity."

"Just like Kevin buying the house next door to mine?" Holly asked, narrowing her eyes.

"I know, right?" Megan's eyes widened in mock innocence. "But finding Bethany here *was* a coincidence. I came by to tell Mom to butt out of Kevin's love life, and the source of my visit was right here." When Holly started to protest, Megan held up her hand. "I would have talked to her whether anything had happened with you and Kevin or not."

"Your mother is going to be furious that you ran Bethany out."

"No, she'll be relieved."

"How can you say that? She was trying to placate her."

"Yes, but did you notice the lack of enthusiasm? She was trying to figure out how to get out of this mess she created."

"What?"

Megan shook her head. "You need to learn my mother's subtle cues. She's trying to get on the holiday decorating committee at the country club, and Bethany's mother is the head of it."

Holly sat back in her chair. "So Nicole was stuck in the mess, even after Kevin told her what a nut job she was."

"Exactly." Megan shrugged. "So I did something to help all of us. Mom saves face. Kevin doesn't have to worry about Bethany popping up out of nowhere. I don't have to worry about seeing Ms. Crazy Pants at family dinners."

"Are you going to tell Kevin?" Holly asked.

"I should let him sweat it out." She looked up at Holly. "But you could tell him if you like."

"Me? I don't know when I'll even see him again." Holly studied her fork for several seconds. "Nothing else is going to happen between us, Megan. Hanging out yesterday was a one-off. Kevin wants to be friends, but..." She craved the euphoria she felt when she was with him, but it would be so easy for her to cross over that "friend" line.

Megan was silent for several seconds. "I know people." She looked down at her food and stabbed a piece of chicken. "My job in Seattle was fund-raising for a nonprofit. I learned how to read people. To spot the ones who would donate. The ones who did it to look good versus those who donated because they believed in the cause."

"That hardly seems like the same thing as our situation."

"Believe it or not, it's not that different. I watched you two yesterday."

"Can we drop this subject? Please?"

"No. He really likes you, Holly. This is big. You're different than all the other girls he's ever dated."

A sharp pain shot through her heart. "Like boring? Not sexy?"

Megan blinked at her in shock. "I'm sorry. I thought we were talking about you."

"I'm serious, Megan. I've known plenty of guys like Kevin. They date sexy women with sexy long legs, sexy smiles, and sexy hair.

Megan grinned. "Wow. That's a lot of sexy."

Holly frowned. "You know what I mean."

"If you're suggesting that Kevin's dated a lot of flashy and superficial women who care more about whether my brother has a six-pack or an eight-pack than getting to know the person *inside* my brother's body, then, yeah. He's dated a lot of *sexy* women. And he's been miserable with every single one of them. Frankly, I'm surprised he's making a play for you at all. Before he moved here, he told me he'd sworn off women altogether."

"You're kidding."

She shook her head. "No, his last girlfriend burned him

bad, although he refuses to tell me what she did. But she was just the last in a long string of self-absorbed women he's paraded in and out of his life. Maybe that's part of the reason Mom fixed him up with Bethany. Maybe she thought that was his type."

Holly sighed, suddenly confused and uncertain about her decision.

Megan leaned forward. "Holly, life is too short not to take chances. Not to take risks. Don't throw something with Kevin away because you're scared."

Holly's phone rang and she reached for it, but Megan covered her hand with her own. "You only live once. You never know how much time you have."

Holly's back stiffened. "I know that all too well, Megan." She was surprised she sounded so angry, but all the disappointment had compounded, and Megan was pushing Holly to her limit.

Megan's eyes widened with realization. "Oh, God. Your parents. Of course you do. I'm sorry."

She looked at her phone and saw Miranda Johansen's name.

Her anger softened. She couldn't hold a grudge when Megan meant well. "I know you are, but I need to take this call."

And with any luck at all, this wedding would open the door to start her own business. Then she wouldn't have to worry whether Nicole Vandemeer gave her blessing on Holly's love life.

The real question was if it would make a difference.

Chapter Twenty-Four

Y ou said what?" Kevin shouted into the phone, drawing the attention of the work crew around him. He had found an issue in the books that he needed to bring to Matt's attention right away, so he'd headed down to the job site to find him. But when he saw his sister's name on caller ID, he'd panicked. Megan usually texted.

Megan sounded distraught. "I didn't mean to upset her, and I never would have mentioned it to you at all, but I'm worried Holly will hold what I said against *you*."

Kevin took several breaths, trying to think this through. He was eager to move past this friendship and into something more, because if he was sure of anything, it was that he wanted to have her in his life. But she was shying away from even being friends. Megan might have pushed her too far.

"I can talk to her," Megan said. "I'll apologize."

"No. You need to stay out of it."

"I'm really sorry, Kevin. She seemed so happy yesterday,

and then today we tag-teamed Bethany and sent her running. I never would have suspected Holly had it in her."

"Whoa. Back up. What do you mean you tag-teamed Bethany?"

"I went to Mom's office to tell her off for trying to set you up with Bethany, and, lo and behold, she was there, crying about you."

Kevin ran his hand over his head in frustration. "What happened?"

"Mom had to go to lunch with a client, so I offered to have lunch with Bethany. I went and picked up something for lunch and we ate in the office. Then I told her that it was good to have lunch out while we could, since all the babies would keep her busy."

"*Excuse me?* Did you say *babies*?"

"Yeah, all eighteen of them. With names that start with Q. Then Holly and I offered some name suggestions and Holly said all twenty of you would be happy in your tiny house. I helpfully suggested that Bethany start fertility treatment so she could have multiple babies at once and get all that birthing over with."

"Oh, my God." He groaned, horrified. "You didn't."

"The clincher was when Holly offered to set up an egg-testing appointment and asked which day worked better for her."

"You're kidding. My sweet little Holly?" He'd suspected she had an ornery side, but he wished he'd been there to see it.

Then he realized what he'd said. She wasn't his, no matter how much he wanted her to be. But he refused to give up hope. He had to find a way to make this work. "I'm going to talk to Mom. Make her realize I can date whoever I want."

Megan was silent for several seconds. "You can't. She'll never approve. You know it, and normally I'd say too bad for her, but you're screwing with Holly's life more than your own. She needs that job."

"I know."

"So what are you going to do?"

He sighed. "Wait, I guess. What else can I do? I'm not planning on dating anyone else. You know I hadn't even planned on dating *her*. She just landed on my front porch."

"I'm sorry."

Kevin looked around the lot, his gaze landing on his friend. Matt had been talking to a small group of his crew. He noticed Kevin and waved, about to walk over, but Kevin lifted his finger to tell him he'd be done in a moment.

Kevin sighed. "I have to trust that it will all work out. In the meantime, I hope she's still willing to go this friend route, because I like having her around."

"If I can do anything to help, let me know. Okay?"

"Yeah." He hung up and stuffed the phone back in his pocket as Matt approached. "Emergency call from my sister."

"Everything all right?" Matt asked. "Megan and the baby okay?"

"Yeah, it was an emergency of another type."

"Your mom?"

"Yeah, but not how you think."

"Holly." When Kevin didn't say anything, Matt laughed. "Dude, don't look so surprised. You two aren't exactly subtle. But I have to say, I expected Tyler to be the one to cave first on the Bachelor Brotherhood."

Kevin released a shaky laugh as he rubbed the back of his neck. "I know this sounds cliché as hell, but Holly's not like the other women I've dated."

"Yeah, she works for your mother."

Kevin pushed out a breath. "You think there's a chance Mom will approve of us dating?"

Matt shook his head. "There's no way in hell she'll approve."

The hair on the back of Kevin's neck stood on end. "You think she's not good enough." His words came out in a low growl.

"No, you idiot, because Holly's her employee. How awkward would it be if you two break up? It's the same reason I won't let Carly date any of the work crew. It's a recipe for disaster." He grinned. "Dude, you were about to jump me. You have it bad for her."

Kevin grimaced.

"No denial?"

He shrugged. "You said it was obvious." He had no idea what he was going to do, especially since he could see Matt's point. "I actually came over here for a reason."

Matt groaned. "I'd like to think that frown is solely because of Holly, but I suspect you have some bad news."

Kevin nodded. "You mentioned that you had a bookkeeper before Carly."

"Yeah."

There was no easy way to break this news. "I think she was embezzling from you."

Matt's eyes flew open. "What?"

"The books say she was paying bills; the bank account says differently. I think she was pocketing the money. I'm still digging, and I'd like to have an auditor look things over. We can go after her and have criminal charges brought against her, but I doubt you'll ever recover all the money you lost. You might not recover any of it. Tomorrow I'll start calling your debtors, let them know the situation, and work out a payment plan. But I wanted to give you a heads-up."

Matt put a hand on top of his head and turned to look at his crew. "How bad is it?"

"Honestly? It's pretty bad."

"Shit." Matt took several seconds to take in the information. "Am I going to lose my business?"

Kevin hesitated. "I think you can save it, but you'll have to cut back on things. Maybe have some layoffs."

"*Fuck*. I can't afford to lose anyone."

"You might want to give it a thought and start coming up with a list." He didn't tell Matt he'd started a list of his own. And Kevin's name was at the top.

"How soon?"

"Less than a month." He hated this. "I'm sorry."

Matt gave a quick nod, then studied Kevin's face. "You're not blowing sunshine up my ass? I can save it?"

"I wouldn't give you false hope. But it might hurt for a while."

"I'll do what needs to be done. I'm not willing to let it all go." Matt started back to the job site, then turned back to Kevin, looking flustered. "Hey, I almost forgot. I saw Ken Douglas yesterday. He's getting married this weekend."

Kevin hadn't seen his high school friend since college. "Wow. To anyone I know?"

"Michelle Murphy. I think she might have been in Megan's class."

Kevin shook his head. "Don't remember her."

"Ken asked if I was bringing a date to his wedding and when I said no, he suggested I bring you. He said it'll be like a mini–class reunion."

"Go as your plus-one?" Kevin teased, hoping to help ease the sting of his news.

Matt grinned and held out his hands. "Why not? I'm not handsome enough for you?"

Kevin gave him an appraising glance that suggested Matt was lacking.

"Fine, then you can be Tyler's date. He's going, too."

"Tyler's going? Then how can I say no? The Bachelor Brotherhood, banding together at a wedding, no less. Seems poetic. Especially since it looks like I'm not revoking my membership anytime soon."

Matt clapped his hand on Kevin's shoulder. "You're in good company, my friend."

* * *

The house was hot as hell when Kevin got home, since the temperature had gotten up into the midnineties. He opened all the windows and set up the fans before he headed to the basement to check on the cat, which he'd started calling Whiskers. The kitten was happy to see him, mewling when Kevin picked it up and cuddled it to his chest. He went upstairs, wishing he'd gotten a cold beer from his minifridge in the upstairs bedroom, but he hadn't even made it upstairs to open the windows, knowing it was probably ten degrees hotter up there.

He sat on the back steps, setting the playful kitten on the grass and wondering how in the hell he'd gotten here—in a shitty house, about to lose his job, and hung up on a woman who wasn't interested in a relationship with him. The last part was a partial truth, but he saw no way to resolve it, nonetheless.

"I'm in a world of shit, Whiskers," he said, leaning over to ruffle the kitten's head.

But one problem at a time.

The job issue was a huge blow he hadn't seen coming. Matt would fight him on it, but it made the most financial sense. At least for the short term. Matt needed to pay off his debt, and he was paying Kevin a large enough salary to make a difference, not to mention he was the most recent hire.

But if he was about to lose his job, he had no idea how he was going to pay for his remodel, and yesterday he'd ripped out his kitchen. He really was in deep shit.

His phone rang and he answered it, surprised to see that it was Tyler.

"Matt called me about his bookkeeper," Tyler said as soon as Kevin answered. "I know you talked about criminal charges, but I can file a civil suit. As soon as you have anything concrete, I want the two of you to come to my office."

"If I'm still working there."

"You think Matt's going to fire you for this?" Tyler sounded incredulous. And angry.

"Matt? God, no. In fact, I expect him to fight me when I suggest that I'm on the top of the list of the people he lays off."

"*Whoa*," Tyler said. "Matt mentioned that you suggested layoffs, but he never said anything about laying off *you*."

"I didn't tell him yet. I need to get everything together first. I won't leave him in the lurch, but once I've got everything straightened up, he could hire a bookkeeper to take over for a lot less money."

"You really think he's going to do that? Sounds like his last bookkeeper was the one who got him *into* this situation."

Kevin sighed. "Even so, I think it might be a good idea for me to put some feelers out for another job. Which might mean relocation." Which bothered him more than he expected. He was happy he was part of his sister's life again, despite her meddling. He was happy he could see his two best friends more often than once every couple of years. And Holly—he wasn't ready to leave her or the possibility of something with her.

"You just got back. What about your shit hole of a house?"

"I don't know. I don't know anything right now."

"Don't do anything rash. Don't make any decisions before we've figured everything out."

"Yeah…"

"Matt's money problems aren't the only thing we discussed." Tyler's voice turned teasing. "Matt said you're going to Ken's wedding."

"Yeah. He said it would be a mini–class reunion."

Tyler chuckled. "So are you going as my date or Matt's?"

"I can ride with Matt since he's closer, but I'll keep my options open. I might find some other fella to make my own."

"Just save me a dance, big boy," Tyler teased. "I'll make it worth your time."

Kevin laughed. "Just be warned you'll have to buy me dinner before I put out."

"I'll keep that in mind. I'm pretty sure I have a coupon to Red Lobster in my junk drawer at home."

Kevin shook his head and grinned. "I bet you haven't been to Red Lobster since we went on a double date our junior year."

"You're just that special."

Kevin hung up feeling better about everything—everything but Holly. He was in the process of coming up with a lame excuse to go to Holly's house when she pushed open his fence gate and poked her head around the corner.

"Kevin?"

She'd come to him. Again. This had to be a good sign. He stood. "Hey, come on back."

She was still in her work clothes, today a fitted black skirt, a sleeveless white shirt that clung to her curves, and black heels that did incredible things to her legs. Her red-painted toenails peeked through the open toes. They'd been pink on Friday night.

Keep it together. Act like a friend. Even though his hands were aching to touch her. "I haven't been home long. I opened the windows, set up the fans, then brought Whiskers outside."

"Whiskers, huh?" She looked down at the cat with a soft smile. "Do you like your new name, Mr. Whiskers?"

"Mister? You're convinced it's a boy?"

"He looks like a boy to me."

"Want to place a bet on it?"

Her eyes narrowed. "What do you have in mind?"

"I'm not sure yet. But it has an appointment at the vet on Thursday afternoon, so we'll know for sure then."

Her smiled wavered and he knew he was in trouble. *Quick, come up with something.* Then it hit him. "I need to ask a favor of you."

She hesitated, a war waging in her eyes. "I'm not sure that's a good idea."

"You don't even know what it is yet." When she didn't stop him, he forged on. "I need to come up with a list of projects I need to complete in the house and how much money they'll take, so it would be helpful to have things like the cabinets and appliances for the kitchen and bathroom picked out."

She watched him for a second, fighting a smile, then she finally said, "You're putting appliances in the bathroom?"

He laughed. "Do a toilet and a tub count as appliances?"

"I don't think so."

"Then I prove my point: I'm completely clueless about these things. I need you to go with me and help pick them out."

"Surely Megan can help you. She's the one who got you into this."

"She's busy and I need to have the total within the next couple of days." He felt like an ass as he watched her want to tell him no yet not being able to turn away.

She looked down at her feet, then back up at him. "I don't think that's a good idea."

"Why not?"

She looked directly into his eyes. "I'm not going to date you, Kevin."

"I know. We've already agreed on that. I've moved on." He cocked an eyebrow. "Are you saying you're still hung up on me?"

Her mouth parted but she didn't respond. He added, "We would never work as a couple. You have a vicious dog who wants to eat my cat."

She started to protest, then stopped when she saw the grin spread across his face. "Killer isn't even my dog."

"Still wouldn't work."

She laughed.

He took several steps toward her. "But I really meant it when I said I wanted to be friends." He shifted his weight. "Look, I had fun yesterday, and I think you did, too. Didn't that prove we can hang out and have fun without the fringe benefits? I'll promise to pay you with more food."

Her eyes narrowed. "What kind of food are we talking about?"

"I'm open to options. But in all seriousness, you and your cousin did an amazing job on your grandmother's house. I could use your expertise and good taste."

Her lips pressed into a thin line as she seemed to be considering it. "I'd need to change clothes."

"Not if you don't want to. We can take my truck

straight to the hardware store, then we can stop somewhere to eat."

When she hesitated, he added, "I'd dress up more"—he glanced down at his jeans and sweat-stained T-shirt—"but then you might construe it as a date, which it definitely isn't. But I *would* like to take a quick shower and change my shirt before we go. So what do you say?"

She gave him a playful look. "About changing your shirt?"

"About helping me, although I'll let you have a say in that, too, if it will convince you."

She studied him for a moment. "Fine. I'll help you, but hurry. I'm hungry."

"Yes, ma'am. If you want to wait at your house, I'll come get you when I'm ready." He left her in the backyard and bolted up the stairs and took one of the quickest showers of his life. He was back downstairs in less than five minutes, surprised to find her in the kitchen with his notepad and a tape measure.

"You need measurements if you want to get an accurate list of what you need in here, so I started marking things down." She had her gaze on the wall with the window facing the side yard.

"Yeah, of course." He would have thought of that, although probably at the store.

She wrote something down on the paper. "Since you're taking out this wall, you could put a really nice island here and not only get an eating space but additional storage." She lifted her face, her gaze lingering on him for longer than a friendly glance would.

Friends. We're friends. God, he wanted her. But he was fairly sure if he made a move on her right now, he'd lose her forever. He'd rather have this than nothing at all. He stuffed his hands into his front pockets. "Yeah, Matt thinks it's a good idea and that it will increase my property value."

"I agree." She looked up at him and took a breath, glancing down at the paper for a moment, then back at him. "I took measurements of everything as well as photos on my phone."

"Oh, good thinking."

"Are you ready to go?" she asked. "No offense, but I think hell is cooler than your house right now."

He laughed. "You might be right."

For the next few hours he followed her around the chain hardware store, while she helped him pick out appliances, cabinets, countertops, light fixtures, and paint colors. He ordered the cabinets and appliances—job or not, the house had to have a kitchen—but held off on the rest, making a list of prices to add to the total he needed to finish the house. He worried that he was imposing on Holly's time, but she seemed to love every minute of it.

They went to the nearby Mexican restaurant. As they sat down, Holly glanced at him, her eyes bright with happiness. "Other than yesterday, I haven't had that much fun in ages."

He considered asking her if that included Friday night, because he sure as hell hoped not, but he didn't want to spoil the moment. Besides, he had to admit it was a different kind of fun that he'd enjoyed, too.

He couldn't think of a single woman he'd really been friends with. Maybe that had been his problem all along.

Chapter Twenty-Five

She'd fully intended to end their "friendship," but after their night of shopping, she couldn't make herself do it. Had he made a single move on her, she would have done it in a heartbeat, but he'd been a perfect gentleman. And not only that, she really did enjoy spending time with him.

They spent over an hour at the restaurant, talking about Kevin's friends, Matt and Tyler, and the time he'd spent in the marines before his enlistment ended.

He asked more about her life growing up with her cousin and grandmother. She told him stories about getting by when money had been tight. Her grandmother had been a retired widow living on social security when the two little girls moved in.

"Don't feel sorry for me," she said when she saw the pity in his eyes. "I love my grandmother. If I couldn't have my parents, then there's no one else I would have rather lived with, a family with money included."

He gave her a questioning look.

"When I was in the fourth grade, a school counselor suggested to my grandmother that she give me and Mel up to a family who could provide more for us."

His mouth dropped open. "You're kidding me."

She shook her head, surprised at the anger in his eyes. "But Grandma told her off in her own sweet way—thanking her for her suggestion, then letting her know our house was full of love and all the money in the world couldn't buy that."

"So you get your sweet disposition from her."

Holly eyed him, thinking he was hitting on her with the statement, but it was clear he meant it. "I'm not always sweet. I have my moments." She grinned. "Oh, by the way, Megan and I may have taken care of your fiancée problem."

He hesitated, then said, "So I heard."

She wasn't surprised Megan had told him. But what else had she said? "I wasn't so sweet with Bethany."

"Oh…" he drawled. "I have to disagree there. You were sweet to help me get rid of her."

"Was she really that bad?" Holly teased. "Your mother approves of her."

"Don't you think that's grounds alone to steer clear of her?" He laughed. "But since you and I are friends, maybe you should get to know her better. You could take her out to lunch and come up with a list of reasons for me to go out with her."

Grinning, she shook her head. "Trust me, I'm one of the last people Bethany wants to see after I told her that her wedding design included mini baby carriages lining the aisle."

Kevin chuckled. "She might have gone for it if they were covered in crystals." He narrowed his gaze in mock seriousness. "You don't have any weird food preferences, do you? Or any strange hobbies?"

"You just watched me inhale a burrito." She gestured to the empty plate in front of her. "Enough said about that. As for hobbies, does collecting shrunken apples carved with the faces of my old boyfriends count as strange? I have them hanging in my closet if you'd like to see them."

His eyes widened.

"I'm still trying to decide which type of apple to use for you." She held up her hands, squinting as she studied his face through a square she formed with her thumbs and index fingers. "A Granny Smith would work with your jawline, but a Fuji would be better for your forehead. Which one do *you* prefer?"

His face paled. "Uh..."

"Or maybe I should just go with a white peach to match the color of your face right now." She burst out laughing, which filled her with another happiness all on its own. She couldn't remember the last time she'd laughed this hard.

He pushed out a huge breath. "Please God, tell me none of that is true."

"Well...I *did* carve an apple face in third grade, and I *did* try to make it look like Stewart McPhee after he stole my sparkly pink glitter pen, but I don't have it hanging in my closet."

He shook his head, trying to suppress a laugh. "If you had any idea what some of my old girlfriends have done, you might not have found that so funny."

Her smile fell, jealousy burning her chest at the thought of him with other women. But there was no denying that Kevin was a sexy, single man. It was only a matter of time before he'd find a girlfriend. She wasn't sure she could stand on the sidelines and watch when that happened.

"No wonder my sister bought the house next door to you," Kevin said, shaking his head with a grin, oblivious to her change in mood. "Turns out you're just as ornery as she is."

The smile she flashed him was genuine. "I'm going to take that as a compliment." She paused, unsure what to do with her unexpected reaction. "I should get home. I have to prepare for my presentation tomorrow."

Disappointment filled his eyes, but he still grinned at her. "Then let's get you home before you turn into a pumpernickel."

"Pumpkin."

"You get your shrunken-apple heads, I get to pick what you turn into."

She laughed. "Fair enough. But I offered to let you pick what apple to carve your face with. I want to be an angel food cake."

His eyes darkened, leaving little to her imagination as to where his mind wandered. "More like devil's food."

Damn if she didn't want to live up to the title and be wicked. But then she reminded herself that she had been the one to set up the ground rules.

When they hit the parking lot, Holly's skin turned clammy from the humidity. She thought of Kevin going back to sleep in his sweltering house, then she impulsively suggested, "Why don't you spend the night at my house?"

Once the words were out, she wondered if she'd been struck with temporary insanity. Or if her subconscious was sabotaging her decision.

"Uh..." He looked shell-shocked.

Oh, God. He thought she was propositioning him.

"On my sofa," she said to remind herself as well.

"Of course, your sofa," he said seamlessly, as though he knew that all along. "We're just friends. But what about your cousin?"

"She's in Las Vegas with her friends. She'll be back on Thursday morning."

"What about Mr. Whiskers?"

She grinned. "So you're admitting he's a boy?"

"I had two gerbils when I was a kid. I named them Mr. and Mrs. Nibbles. Turns out I had them wrong."

"Is that your way of telling me you can't tell the gender of any species?"

He burst out laughing. "Some species I have no trouble at all with. You're all woman, Holly Greenwood."

She blushed, but his statement didn't come across as raunchy, and he pushed on as though trying to move past any awkwardness he may have caused.

"Even after I found out I had it wrong—after Mr. Nibbles gave birth to six baby gerbils—I still called them Mr. and Mrs. Nibbles. At least for the few weeks I still had them. My mother couldn't tolerate the idea of something procreating in our house."

"She said that?"

He grinned. "She definitely didn't want more baby gerbils."

At the mention of his mother, an uncomfortable silence spread between them. She dared to search his face. "So, will you spend the night on my sofa? I really hate the idea of you in that house."

He seemed to be considering it, then he released a heavy breath. "I have to admit that I wasn't looking forward to going back to the inferno. But I don't want you to feel uncomfortable with me there."

"I'd be more uncomfortable if you don't stay at my house."

So they'd gone back home and he'd shown up on her doorstep about fifteen minutes later with a duffel bag in one hand and Whiskers in the other. She'd already put a blanket and pillow on the end of the sofa and had changed into a pair of knit shorts and a tank top, her hair piled up on top of her head in a messy bun.

"I've already warned Melanie you're staying here until the heat wave passes, so don't worry." Melanie's texted response had made it clear that she didn't approve, but it was Holly's decision.

"If it's too big an imposition…"

"You're sleeping on the sofa. Not moving in. Feel free to watch TV, but I'll be over here preparing for a meeting tomorrow." She gestured toward the papers and laptop on her dining room table.

He froze in the middle of her living room. "I interrupted your work by asking you to help me earlier."

"No. It's good I had a few hours to kind of forget about it and tackle it fresh. I've spent all my free time over the weekend and all of today on it, so I'm ready. But it's the big job I told you about and since I have so much riding on it, it has to be perfect."

He walked over to her, looking over the plans. "What do you have left to do?"

She held her breath, pushing back the anxiety. "I have everything together. I just need to run through my presentation."

"Want to practice on me?"

She eyed him with suspicion. "You want me to present this *wedding* to you?"

"Sure, why not?" He held up the kitten still in his hand. "Mr. Whiskers is hoping to find a Mrs. Whiskers. He's looking for wedding ideas."

She shook her head, trying to keep from smiling like an idiot. "Okay. I'll pretend like you're Miranda and Whiskers can be Coraline." She picked up a glass of water and took a drink. "I need you to sit here." She pointed to a dining room chair.

Kevin did as he was told, and she sat in the chair next to him.

"Coraline, I spent some time thinking of a theme for your wedding that would work with the three-week time constraint yet be the wedding you deserve, and I think I've come up with the perfect concept." She grabbed an electronic tablet from the table and set it in front of him, sliding the screen to show him the full-page photo of an outdoor table setting with white lights strung overhead. "A Tuscan outdoor wedding will fit perfectly with the venue and hopefully it will bring a bit of sentiment to the wedding since you and Donald met and began dating in Italy." She then went on to tell him all the details, from the place settings to the menu, to the flower selection. She slid the screen as she spoke, pointing out things in the photos she planned to incorporate. "I know you're questioning whether there's enough time to get everything arranged in time, and I can assure you we can. I've already spoken to all the service providers and all of them are holding the date open for you. We'll need to go to the various places and finalize the details—the caterer will provide a sampling of options for the sit-down dinner, and the cake decorator will give us options for flavors and design, but they have fit you into their schedules. The musicians will need a list of songs to play, which you or I can come up with, or it can be a collaboration. There are a host of various other details that need to be attended to, but I have no doubt we can pull this off and give you the wedding of your dreams. Once you give me your approval, I'll move forward, but first we need to discuss the financial aspect."

She turned the page while Kevin took a sip of water. He began to cough when his gaze landed on the total. "Seventy-five thousand dollars?"

"You have no idea how hard this has been to pull off. I had to sweet-talk most of the vendors. And I need to go in with a strict guideline of what she can choose from or it will become the circus the last planner came up with. She's a spoiled rich girl who is used to getting what she wants. I just need to let her think she's calling the shots—and she will be, from a pre-chosen list of things she can choose from. Then hopefully Miranda, Coraline, and your mother are all happy."

"And what about you?" he asked. "Are you happy?"

"The wedding will be beautiful. It's a dream wedding, and I'm lucky to have the chance to work on it."

A knowing smile lit up his eyes. "Ah...but that's not what I asked, is it? This wedding plan is amazing, and I have no idea how you pulled it all together so quickly. Based on what I've seen and how much my mother feels threatened by you, it's clear that you're incredible, but I asked if you were *happy*."

"No one cares if I'm happy. My job is to make sure the bride gets the wedding of her dreams and raves about Distinctive Events, which brings the business more jobs." When he didn't respond, she added. "I love planning weddings. And I love making enough money to provide for my grandmother."

"But my mother makes things difficult." It wasn't a question.

She sighed. "I confess that I spend a lot of time anxious about whether *she's* happy or not."

"That's no way to live."

She shook her head. "It is what it is. Nothing is ideal. But hopefully this wedding will go well—I'll get a lot of referrals—and I can open my own shop. I have a plan."

He remained silent, but he looked troubled.

Holly sighed and rose from her seat. "It's been a long day and I need to get up early to head over to Olathe, Kansas, in the morning, so I think I'll get ready for bed."

He stood in front of her. "Thanks for helping me tonight. Not only do you have an eye for wedding details, but for remodeling, too. If left to my own devices, my house would look like it had been decorated by kindergartners. I owe you."

"I've loved doing it." And she had. She was beginning to think the "friend" thing might work after all. If she could forget how much she wanted more.

But sleep was elusive. Instead, her thoughts lingered on the man sleeping on her sofa and the things he'd made her feel in this bed. But now it was more than that. She genuinely liked him, and she loved how she felt around him. She felt as though she could let her guard down with him and let out the lighthearted side of her that had been locked up for years, even before her grandmother had gotten sick. He made her want to stretch out of her comfort zone and seriously consider opening her own business, once she got through the Johansen wedding. And he made her want to take a chance on love, but not with just anyone. She wanted take a chance with *him*.

But for now, she'd have to learn to be content.

Chapter Twenty-Six

Kevin had never been so thankful for a heat wave in all his life.

He'd spent all day Tuesday and Wednesday digging deeper into Matt's books, realizing the situation was worse than he'd thought. Tyler had notified the authorities, and a forensics auditor had been brought in to investigate.

Which meant Kevin might be out of a job sooner than he'd expected.

He spent Tuesday and Wednesday evening working on his kitchen to get it ready for the cabinets to be installed the next Monday.

Holly had insisted that Kevin stay at her house. He'd headed over to Holly's around eight, utterly exhausted. She fed him dinner and sat with him at the island while he ate. Then he'd watched TV while she sat at the dining room table with her laptop, working on the big wedding she'd been worried about. The wedding-dress designer's daughter had loved her plans, but Holly was still scrambling to pull off several changes in time. Kevin watched her, intent on her task, wondering if his mother had any idea how hard she worked.

Both nights he fell asleep watching TV while she still worked at the table, only to wake up in the morning and discover that she'd covered him with a blanket. Then he'd take Whiskers back to his basement before heading to work to start the day all over again.

Since the forensics auditor had taken over, Kevin left early on Thursday afternoon to take the kitten to the vet, but instead of going back to the office, he went home to work on his kitchen. He was ripping out Sheetrock in the kitchen when he heard a knock on his front door.

Checking the time, he realized it was too early for Holly to come home, but he wasn't prepared to find her cousin on his front porch. Holly had mentioned she was getting back from Vegas today. He'd expected a confrontation, but figured it would happen later tonight.

She wore black pants and a white shirt, so he suspected she was on her way to work. "Melanie."

She didn't waste any time getting down to business. "What the hell do you think you're doing?"

He wasn't surprised by her hostility after their initial meeting, but that didn't mean it didn't bother him.

She didn't wait for an answer. "I can see through this charade, so give it up. Leave Holly alone."

"It's not a charade. I want to be her friend."

"Yeah, save it for someone else—someone other than my cousin. Holly likes to see the good in people, and you're exploiting that."

His anger rose. "What reason could I possibly have for lying to her?"

"I'm not stupid, Vandemeer. I know how men think. The organ that is *really* behind their motivation."

"You think I'm trying to sleep with Holly? That this is one long con to get back in her bed?" While he had to admit to himself that it started out that way, it couldn't be further from the truth now. Sure, he wanted her in every sense of the word—and the last three nights had killed him—but he wanted her company more. And, more importantly, he wanted her to be happy. If being friends was what she wanted, he'd learn to deal with it.

"Please. Are you seriously suggesting it's not?" He paused and she released a snort. "Yeah, that's what I thought."

"It's not like that, Melanie. I swear."

"And the proof of that was when you screwed her and left? What do you hope to achieve, Lover Boy? You can't openly date her with your dragon-woman mother."

"We're friends." But he had to admit that, if the positions were reversed, he wouldn't believe him, either.

She snorted again. "You want to be her friend. Do you even know anything about being a friend with a woman?"

"No, but I'm trying."

"Holly is one of few people I know who values her principles, and she doesn't want to betray her boss, no matter how much of a bitch your mother is. So let's be honest: we both know your *real* intent is to wear her down. How do you think she's going to handle it when you do? You're only going to hurt her. *I* know it. And you know it. She's the only one who can't see it, and I can't stand back and let you do it."

He had to wonder if she might be right. He would never intentionally hurt Holly, but there was probably no good outcome from this. But, selfishly, he couldn't give her up.

"She's a good person. She deserves better than this. Leave Holly alone," Melanie sneered. Then she stomped off the porch, not stopping until she got into her car and left.

The tightness in his chest wasn't a surprise when he realized what he needed to do. It was time to look for another job, even if it meant moving away. Then again, maybe he should only look at jobs outside of the Kansas City area. Because, stay or leave, he was going to lose her.

But then he'd thrown her away, so maybe that was what he deserved.

* * *

Holly noticed Kevin's car in the driveway when she got home, and she fought the urge to go see him. She had taken her binder for the Johansen wedding to her daily visit with her grandmother, but the older woman had spent most of the visit dazed and confused.

Grandma Barb's dementia was progressing faster than any of them had expected, and Holly was scared. She was losing her grandmother, and Melanie—the only other person who could possibly understand what she was going through—refused to discuss it.

She'd never felt so alone, and the need to pour her heart out to someone was overwhelming.

She wanted to pour her heart out to Kevin. He'd been more than willing to listen to everything else.

But that was dangerous. For one thing, men tended to shy away from emotional women, and, two, if she went to him, it would only prove that she needed him.

Needing Kevin was dangerous. What if she gave in and agreed to a relationship? What if part of her appeal to him was the chase, and, once he had her, he lost interest and left her brokenhearted?

Her parents had left her. Her grandmother was leaving her. She didn't think she could survive Kevin leaving her, too.

So she stayed home and made a pasta salad—something cold to feed Kevin when he came over later. She paused, realizing that he'd spent only three nights at her house but she already was used to him being there.

And that was a very bad thing.

She poured a glass of wine and went out into the backyard, refilling the baby pool with fresh water. Excited, Killer ran around the pool and Holly's feet, playing in the water and demanding her attention. She glanced toward Kevin's house, remembering that today had been Whiskers' vet appointment. *There* was an excuse to go over and see him.

She was shameless.

But she couldn't do it. As vulnerable as she felt right now, she didn't trust herself. She was like a child told to stay away from fire. She was drawn to him despite knowing that, one way or the other, she was probably going to get burned. So she sat her butt in her chair and drank her wine. She had the Murphy–Douglas wedding to keep her busy this weekend, the rehearsal tomorrow night and wedding duties to fill up the entirety of Saturday.

Maybe that would help take her mind off the man next door.

She was going through her mental list of everything she had to get together for both days when she heard Kevin shouting through his open kitchen window.

"Shit!" The sound of spraying water accompanied his curse.

His kitchen had been completely gutted, so the sound of spraying water could not be good.

She'd put Killer in the house and was on her way through her gate when she heard him shouting again.

"Goddammit!"

Before she opened the door to his kitchen, she knew it

was bad—based on the very loud sound of gushing water. But she wasn't prepared to find Kevin on the floor in front of the pipes where the sink had been. His hand was on the turn-off valve and a hard stream of water was spraying him in the chest, the water splashing up into his face. He was completely drenched, his T-shirt clinging to the muscles of his chest and upper arms.

Focus, Holly.

"What happened?" she asked in a panic.

"I don't know." He tried to duck out of the water spray to look at her. "It just started coming out!"

"The valve doesn't shut it off?"

"I can't tell."

Bracing herself, she knelt beside him, blindly reaching for the valve. "At least it's the cold water."

"Shit," he grumbled. "I hadn't even thought of that."

She turned the valve both ways, which made no difference in the gushing water, then leaned out of the direct spray to search for the source of the leak. She found a crack in the metal pipe in the now exposed wall.

"It's your pipe," she said, sitting back on her heels. "We need to turn the water off to your house."

His eyes flew open in panic. "How do I do that? I don't know how to do that."

Holly jumped up and ran down his basement stairs, searching the unfinished walls.

Kevin was right behind her. "What are we looking for?"

"The main water line. There should be a turn-off valve."

He took off in the opposite direction but she found it first, a piece of plywood partially covering it. She grabbed the valve and pulled, but it refused to budge. There was a good chance the lever hadn't been pulled in years, if not decades.

"I found it!" she shouted to him. "But it's stuck."

He ran over and grabbed the lever, putting all his weight into it. Panic washed over his face when she heard a loud snap. "Oh, shit." Then he showed her the broken-off valve in his hand. "Now what do we do?"

She didn't answer, instead dashing up the stairs and slipping in the water that was now pooled on his kitchen floor. Kevin was right behind her, giving her a questioning look.

She ran for the front door, then down the porch steps, Kevin on her heels.

"Where are you going?" he called after her.

"To find the manhole in your yard!" she called after him, not waiting for a response as she ran toward her garage. She hadn't used the tool to shut off the main water line in years and worried she wouldn't be able to find it, but she tossed aside a painting drop cloth and discovered it underneath.

Kevin was in the yard, shaking his head as he held his phone to his ear. "I can't find it anywhere, Matt."

Holly pushed through a group of bushes by the street and found the cover, using the tool to pry it up and over to the side. Kevin was instantly next to her, helping push the heavy metal lid out of the way so she could find the valve nut and use the bar to turn it. She got the crowbar-like rod locked onto the valve, then Kevin grabbed the T-shaped handle and put his weight into it until it stopped turning.

His gaze lifted to hers. "Do you think that did it?"

"Let's go find out."

They ran back inside. The water still gushed out of the pipe, but it began to sputter, then dwindled down to a tiny stream before stopping altogether.

Holly stood in the kitchen, taking in the damage. "This is bad."

"I know," he groaned.

The walls were drenched, and an inch of water pooled

on the vinyl floor; it was now seeping toward the wood floors.

Where to start?

"Do you have a Shop-Vac?" she asked.

He looked at her and burst out laughing. "I didn't know how to turn the damn water off. Do you really think I have a Shop-Vac?"

She loved that about him—that he could be in this horrible situation, yet he could find the humor in it.

"We need to save your wood floors. Call Matt and see if he can loan you one and I'll grab a bunch of towels."

He pulled out his phone as he followed her to her house, grabbing an armload of towels along with her and following her back to his money pit. They sopped up the water on the wood floor, building a barricade at the doorway from the kitchen into the dining room.

"That's all we can do for now," Holly said apologetically. "Other than scooping out water with a bowl."

"That's okay. Matt should be here within ten minutes."

"Look on the bright side," she said. "It's a miracle your phone still works after getting drenched like that."

It was hot outside, but she was completely soaked and the breeze from the fans made her shiver. She turned to face Kevin, only to find him staring at her chest.

Oh, shit. The thin fabric of her white wraparound sleeveless cotton shirt was soaked, revealing her thin bra and her hardened nipples.

But a flood of warmth gushed through her veins as she took in his chest, his wet T-shirt clinging to every muscle.

Her breath was coming in short pants and she knew she had to get out of here or she was going to jump him, right here in the middle of his flooded kitchen.

Go. Now.

Her feet barely registered the command but they had begun to move when her foot slipped on the wet floor and she started to fall.

Kevin grabbed her, hauling her to his chest and plastering her tight against him. She looked up into his face, her breath sucked away by the lust in his eyes.

She had never wanted a man like she wanted him now. She lifted on her tiptoes to kiss him, but Kevin took over.

Burying his hand in her hair, his hungry mouth covered hers as his other hand cupped her ass, pressing his groin against her. The hard bulge in his jeans made it very clear that he wanted her.

Her hands roamed his chest, soaking in the hard contours of his pecs. But she wanted more. She wanted his chest bare. Groping blindly, she found the bottom of his shirt and jerked it up with both hands. He quickly caught on and helped pull it over his head, then he turned his attention to her.

Her fingers fumbled with the clinging cotton of her shirt, the knot at her side uncooperative.

Kevin groaned and impatiently brushed her hands away, grabbing the fabric of the deep V-neckline and ripping the shirt open to expose her bra and bare chest.

"Oh," she gasped, as her nipples tightened.

She grabbed the waistband of his jeans and tugged him closer, desperate to get his jeans undone.

He growled his impatience, cupping her ass under her skirt and lifting her up to straddle him. His mouth devoured hers and she struggled to keep up, overwhelmed by everything she felt—yet she couldn't get enough.

He dragged his mouth from hers, skimming her chin with his lips and his tongue, making her even wilder with need.

"God, Holly. You drive me crazy."

She grabbed his face between her hands and kissed, her tongue searching out his to show him he did the same to her.

"*Oh, God.* Sorry." She heard the male voice from the living room, but by the time she figured out someone else was in the house, Kevin had turned his back to the living room and lowered her to her feet. Wrapping his arms around her back, he pulled her close to hide her from view.

Oh, God. It was Matt with the Shop-Vac.

"I'll wait outside," Matt said, already heading out the front door.

Holly closed her eyes and leaned her forehead into Kevin's bare chest, her face burning with humiliation. What had he seen? Her bare legs wrapped around Kevin's waist. Her bra? But that wasn't what horrified her. Matt had seen her wild and out of control. No one had ever seen her like that. No one but Kevin.

Kevin held her close, his hand digging into her hair. "I'm sorry. I shouldn't..."

She shook her head and tried to pull free, but he held her close.

"Don't run from me, Holly. Don't run from us."

"There is no *us*, Kevin. We can't do this."

"You can't deny this," he said in exasperation. "This thing between us...I've never had anything like this. Can you say you have?"

"No." She shook her head again and pushed his arms off her. "I don't know. I have to think." A fresh wave of humiliation washed through her. "Go find Matt. You need to clean up this mess."

"Not until I know you're okay."

Tears burned her eyes. "I'll be fine."

He reached for her, lowering his face to kiss her, but she pulled back.

"Stop. We can't do this. Nothing has changed."

His eyes darkened. "You can't be serious. *Everything* has changed."

"No, we agreed to be friends. This is...No. We can't do this."

"How is this any different than being friends?" he asked, his voice tight with anger. "You said Mom wouldn't let you go out to lunch with Megan. Do you think there's any difference in her eyes? Friends with or without benefits, it's all the same to her."

She gasped. How could she be so stupid? "You're right."

But he realized his mistake, his eyes widening. "Holly."

She took a step back, the water sloshing at her feet. "I think you should stay somewhere else tonight."

Chapter Twenty-Seven

⌒

Holly was at the reception venue by seven Saturday morning, setting out the centerpieces of rosebuds—which she hoped would be semi-open by tonight—and hanging the twinkling lights and decorations she'd prepared.

By noon she was changed and at the church, making sure she was there before anyone else had arrived. She made a pass through the church sanctuary, making sure the flowers were all in place, then greeted the bride and her family when they arrived a half hour later. The wedding was at five, but there was a full schedule with hairdressers and makeup artists arriving to do the wedding party's hair and makeup, then photos.

By the time the wedding started, she'd defused two crises—the first was a salad-dressing stain on a bridesmaid's pale pink dress that Holly fixed with a stain remover she had in an emergency basket, and the second was a lost bow tie of one of the groomsmen. Holly took a bow tie from one of the ushers and replaced it with an almost identical black tie from the same basket. Once everyone was up at the altar and the service was going as planned, Holly took a moment to catch her breath.

The first half of the day was a success; now to make sure the second went just as well.

The reception was held at a local hotel. The DJ had arrived and set up, the hotel restaurant staff had everything ready for the cocktail reception, the cake was in place. Now that the candles on the tables were lit—thanks to the bride's cousins—and the twinkling lights were on, the banquet hall was more beautiful than she'd dreamed.

The wedding guests trickled in slowly at first, then in groups, getting drinks from the bar and finding seats at the open-seating tables. Holly was about to head to the back entrance to greet the wedding party when she saw him, her heart leaping into her throat.

Kevin stood with two friends—Matt and a man she hadn't met—looking more handsome than she'd ever seen him in his pale blue shirt and red tie. His friends provided competition in the looks department, but her eyes were on him. But he'd captured the attention of another woman, too. Her hand rested on one of his biceps, and the smile on his face let Holly know he didn't seem to mind the contact.

She spun around, her back to him as she tried to calm her already strained nerves. What was Kevin doing here? She'd seen the guest list and the name Vandemeer would have jumped out at her even before she'd met him.

Why was she surprised he was hanging out with a woman? A gorgeous one at that. *Was she his date?* She sneaked a look back over her shoulder to confirm her first impression. Yep, gorgeous. Tall, thin, long dark hair, and eyes only for him. All three men's eyes were glued to her.

Embarrassment washed through Holly, hot and cloying. She'd been such a fool. How in the world had she thought she could compete with someone like that?

"Holly?" The aunt of the bride shook Holly out of her reverie. "Michelle and Ken have arrived."

Holly forced a smile. She needed to get a grip. She'd never had Kevin Vandemeer to begin with. So why did it feel like she'd lost him?

She greeted the wedding party, fluffing Michelle's dress and touching up her makeup, as well as those of the maid of honor and the bridesmaids, then gave the DJ the signal to introduce the wedding party.

The bride and groom had decided to do something fun by dancing into the room to a popular upbeat song. The DJ started the song on cue just like they'd planned, and the entrance not only went according to plan, but it also started the reception off with a ton of energy, setting the stage for a fun-filled night.

Half the room joined the floor on the next dance, flooding Holly with relief. Her plan had worked, justifying the large dance floor. She couldn't help that part of her relief was from spotting Kevin at a table with his two friends, the woman from before nowhere in sight.

The plan had been to let the party kick into gear, start the buffet, more dancing, cut the cake, then back to dancing. Holly was examining the cake table, trying to avoid the groom's obnoxious brother, who couldn't take the hint that she wasn't interested, when she heard a voice behind her.

"Can I have this dance?"

Her breath caught and she turned around to face Kevin. She wasn't prepared to be this close to him, especially with how handsome he looked and how amazing he smelled. It simply wasn't fair that her heart had begun to get attached to him. Because, looking up into his warm brown eyes, she knew there was no denying it.

She was falling for Kevin Vandemeer.

He lifted his hand and then stopped midair and lowered it, as though he realized what he was doing.

She forced a smile. "I don't think that's a good idea. And besides, I'm working."

"You're not here as a guest?" he asked in surprise.

"Nope. This was my wedding." She shook her head, feeling flustered this close to him after what they'd done the last time she'd seen him. "I mean, I'm Michelle's wedding planner."

"You planned this?" He glanced around the room, awe in his eyes. "I have to say, I usually hate receptions, but this one has been fun."

"Thanks." She had to bite her tongue to stop from asking if the woman who had draped herself on him had helped make this one fun. She was jealous. But she could hardly stand the thought of him talking to a beautiful woman, let alone dating one—both feelings she had no right to.

"Surely you can still dance with me."

She shook her head, trying to rein in her emotions. "The bride and groom are about to cut the cake. I'm making sure everything's ready." Then she added, "But I couldn't dance with you anyway. I'm working. Your mother would never approve."

She wasn't sure why she'd added the part about his mother. Maybe as a reminder to herself as to why she wasn't with him.

He cringed at the reminder of his mother, but then he graced her with his sexy grin. Damn him. "But I was going to tell you if Whiskers was a Mr. or a Mrs. I never got a chance to tell you on Thursday."

Before Matt had walked in on them.

Humiliation washed through her again, but he stood there looking sexy and confident, like he was used to being caught in the throes of passion.

Oh, God. What if he was?

But she needed to pull herself together. And she really wanted to know. "He can't be a Mrs. for several reasons. *One*, he's a boy." She ticked off her fingers. "*Two*, if he *were* a she, she would have to be *married* and he is very much single, and, *three*, he's much too young to consider marriage anyway." She lowered her hand, her breath catching when she saw the grin in his eyes. "So tell me that I'm right."

"Nope. Dance first."

She put her hand on her hip, amazed that she could fall into this playful side with him when she felt sad. "That wasn't the agreement, Kevin Vandemeer. We had a bet. You need to tell me if I'm right."

"We never worked out the details of the bet." He laughed. "A little late for that now."

"Ha!" she said, pointing her finger at him. "You won't do it because you know *I'm* right."

"You're much too confident." He grabbed her finger with one hand, the other resting lightly on her hip. The contact sent a jolt of electricity skating across her skin.

"A bet's a bet," she said, trying to kick-start her brain cells into working again instead of letting her hormones take over. "Even if you already know the answer."

He cocked his head to the side, his gaze sliding from her eyes down to her collarbone. She suspected that if she'd shown any cleavage it would have continued south.

"Actually I *don't* know," he said, his attention still on her neck. "The answer is in a sealed envelope."

"What?" she asked, sure she'd misunderstood.

His eyes lit up as he returned his attention to her face. "I thought we should find out together." He winked. "So when I find out I'm right, I can truly enjoy every moment of my gloating."

Her chest warmed and her giddiness caught her off guard. She couldn't remember the last time she felt this happy over nothing. But it wasn't nothing. He'd gone out of his way to do this for her. Why? "So open the envelope." The words sounded breathless.

"Not yet. When we're alone." While his voice was slightly husky, his face remained neutral. "Later."

"Later," she whispered. *What was she doing?*

His hand fell from her hip, slightly brushing the outside of her leg and sending a jolt to her core. But if he recognized how he was affecting her, he didn't let on. He just sauntered over to his friends without looking back.

She watched him walk away from her, taking in how his broad shoulders filled out his pale blue shirt and his dress pants clung to his ass. She couldn't help wondering what she'd actually agreed to later.

Chapter Twenty-Eight

Kevin wasn't sure why he was surprised Holly was here. She was a wedding planner, and from what he'd seen so far, she was a damn good one. Once again, it confirmed that his mother bitched about her out of jealousy. Too bad his mother was too blind to see that Holly was going to bolt from his mother's chains the first chance she got. Kevin would be cheering for her on the sidelines.

He'd been on his way out of the room, needing a breather from the noise and the chaos of the reception, when he'd seen her at the table. He hadn't planned on asking her to dance—hell, he hated to dance—but he'd been desperate for a reason to talk to her.

When he sat back down at the table, Tyler wore a smirk. "Crashed and burned, huh? I thought you were going to the bathroom to take a piss."

"I was. I just happened to run into a friend."

"Run into a friend, my ass. I thought we'd sworn off women. I've held up my end of the Bachelor Brotherhood.

And let me add that I had no idea my balls could turn this blue."

"She's a friend," Kevin said, trying not to sound irritated and feed any more fuel to the fire.

"She's his neighbor," Matt said, taking a sip of his beer and giving Kevin a pointed look. "They're *friends*."

Tyler burst out laughing. "*You* got friend-zoned?"

"No," Kevin said slowly, picking up his drink, surprised that Matt hadn't told Tyler about the situation he'd stumbled upon. "*I* was the one who said I wanted to be friends."

"Why?" Tyler asked, watching Holly with a little more interest than Kevin liked. "She's hot."

Kevin tried to keep his voice even. "She works for my mother. She's the wedding planner here."

Tyler's mouth dropped. "She tolerates your mother? That has to take a special kind of woman." Then he cocked his head. "Do you know if she's seeing anyone?"

"No." Kevin's irritation grew.

Tyler stood and adjusted his tie, a smirk lighting up his eyes. "Screw the brotherhood. I think I'll go over and introduce myself."

Kevin was up in a flash. "I don't think so."

"Why not?" He looked surprised. "She's off-limits to you, but that doesn't mean I can't have a go with her. She looks like she'd be worth a short break from my hiatus from women."

Kevin stepped in front of his path, his jaw set. "Because you're a prick who will use her and toss her aside, and she deserves a helluva lot better than that."

Matt was up in an instant, grabbing Kevin's arm. "Why don't we get some air?"

"You like her," Tyler said, slack-jawed.

"Of course he likes her," Matt said. "For someone so smart, sometimes you're an idiot."

"In my defense," Tyler said, "he said they were friends."

"Okay," Matt said slowly. "When was the last time *you* convinced a woman to be just a friend?"

"Never."

"I rest my case, Counselor."

Tyler sat back down, and Matt tugged on Kevin's sleeve to get him to join them.

Kevin rubbed his temple, feeling like an ass. "I was out of line." He was ticked at himself for getting so upset, but it was a reminder of the inevitable. He was going to lose her to some other guy. It was just a matter of time. Still, he couldn't be expected to stand by and watch her get hurt. Despite their beginning, Holly was not a casual-sex kind of woman, and that was the only type of relationship Tyler knew.

"I can't believe you didn't last even a single week," Tyler said.

"He didn't last a single *day*," Matt told him. "He slept with her the night after our agreement to remain single."

Tyler burst out laughing. "For a tough-ass former marine, I expected you to be the last holdout, man. At least a week or two."

"Holly's different."

"Holly, huh?" Tyler shrugged, watching her again, but with curiosity this time. "Did your mother actually say she won't approve of you dating her?"

"No. But what do you think?"

"Yeah, no way in hell she'll go for it."

"If it was up to me, I'd just tell my mother I was seeing Holly, but this affects Holly's job. It's not my call."

Tyler clapped a hand on his shoulder. "Chin up, my not-so-young Romeo. If you love her it will all work out."

Matt snorted. "Love her? He barely knows her."

Tyler looked Kevin in the eye and winked. "Ignore him. He's just cranky because his bookkeeper stole all his money."

Kevin cringed. "Not all of it."

"Enough to make you start looking for another job."

"What?" Matt demanded, leaning forward.

Kevin released a low growl. "Dammit, Tyler."

Shrugging, Tyler picked up his glass. "If you're leaving him high and dry, the man has a right to know."

It took a good five minutes before he'd convinced Matt that his company wasn't going to fold.

"But you *are* looking for another job?" Matt asked.

Kevin considered denying it, but Tyler was right, Matt had a right to know. "I contacted a headhunter yesterday."

Matt's eyes narrowed. "Because of what I walked in on Thursday?"

That caught Tyler's attention. "What did you walk in on Thursday?"

Kevin could deny it, but that would be a lie. That was at least part of it. "I'd already considered it before that."

Tyler shook his head. "If this is about a woman, let me remind you both: We swore off women. *Remember?* They're nothing but trouble and carry around a bag of shit with them, something you're finding out firsthand, *once again.*"

Matt shook his head, grinning at his friend. "Tyler, stop trying to convince yourself. Underneath all that cynicism, I suspect you're really romantic at heart. You're just really good at hiding it from the rest of the world. Your earlier comment about Romeo and Juliet only confirms it."

Tyler laughed, but it sounded bitter as his gaze swept the room. "I suspect a long line of women would disagree with that assessment."

Their banter continued, but Kevin was lost in thought, stuck on Tyler's comment about loving Holly. He knew it had been a joke, but something had tugged at Kevin when he'd said it. He hadn't known Holly long enough to love her, but he was falling for her hard. Which was obvious when he thought about the things he'd done since meeting her.

Like asking the vet tech to write down the gender of the kitten and put it in an envelope. It never would have occurred to him to do something like that in the past. But when he'd been at the vet with Whiskers, he found himself wishing Holly was there so they could find out together. The envelope seemed like a good in-the-moment solution. The tech had given him a look that suggested she thought Kevin was crazy, but he didn't care. All he could think about was making Holly happy, and he'd been right. The happiness and excitement in her eyes proved it.

A clinking on the other side of the room caught his attention, and the newlyweds stood behind the cake, beaming from ear to ear as they prepared to cut the cake. Everyone's eyes were on the happy couple, but Kevin had eyes only for Holly, who stood to the side with a watchful gaze. He suspected she'd tried to dress understated in her pale gray dress with the high rounded neckline, trying to avoid attracting attention. But the dress only showed off her generous breasts and her full hips. Her hair was up in some kind of twist that exposed her long neck, and his eyes were drawn to the place that had made her writhe beneath him when he'd licked it a week ago.

Everyone clapped and cheered as the couple fed each other cake and drank champagne. Michelle and Ken were looking at each other as if they were the only two people in the world. Kevin couldn't stop the pang of longing that filled him. It was something he'd never had, and, given the women he'd dated, it was something he'd never expected to find.

Until Holly.

But then he realized why all his other relationships had crashed and burned. All those other women had been shallow and self-centered, incapable of real relationships. What that hell had he expected?

The dancing resumed, and Kevin was considering leaving. Matt must have suspected his discontent, and he grabbed Kevin's arm, hauling him out of his seat. "Let's mingle."

"Mingle?" Kevin snorted. "Are we in a nineteen-fifties movie?"

"Stop being such a dick. You've been gone for almost a decade. Say hello to your old friends."

Tyler laughed and finished off his beer before he stood, too. "You need another drink."

Kevin disagreed, but Matt had driven, which meant Kevin was free to imbibe all he wanted. But Kevin was also smart enough to know that getting shit-faced wasn't going to solve anything.

"Come on," Tyler groaned, heading toward the bar. "I'm buying. I need to get you loosened up for that dance you promised me."

"Like hell I did. You promised a Red Lobster dinner first."

Kevin laughed, grateful that his friendship with Matt and Tyler was slipping back into something familiar.

Matt made the rounds, reintroducing him to all their old high school friends and stopping when they ran into a couple who caught Kevin by surprise.

Randy Harris had been a friend in high school, and now he practiced law in the same firm with Tyler. But what Kevin found surprising was his fiancée. Brittany Stewart had been in their graduating class, but she'd always been shy and reserved and had a different group of friends than the four men. Brittany had been studious and was in the marching band and math club—a total opposite from the popular football player and partier she was now engaged to. When Kevin voiced his surprise, both of them laughed.

"I never would have considered her in high school," Randy said, casting a sly glance at the woman at his side. "I wasn't good enough for her back then."

Brittany laughed. "Good enough? You're right about that. You acted like a fool then, but good thing you grew up so I can overlook your previous stupidity." She turned her amused gaze to Tyler. "Now if we can get this one to grow up."

Tyler winked. "Not a chance."

"I hope you're ready for our wedding festivities," Brittany said, taking a sip of her drink. "The couple's shower is in August."

"Like hell I'm going to a couple's shower," Tyler snorted.

Brittany gave him an amused look that should have warned Tyler he was in trouble, but he seemed pretty clueless as she turned her attention to Kevin. "Hey! I just put it together." Brittany snapped her fingers and pointed at Kevin. "Your mom has the event-planning business, right?"

"Yeah."

"Her employee is doing my wedding."

"Holly?"

"Yeah, she's amazing. The wedding is going to be gorgeous. She knows how to work wonders on a budget. She's sweet, too, and she just happens to be single." She gave Tyler a sidelong glance. "You could do worse, Tyler. It's time for you to settle down."

Tyler grinned. "I was just mentioning to Kevin that I should introduce myself." Kevin stiffened, and Tyler added, "But she's not my type. Too straightlaced and stuffy for me."

Tyler didn't even know her, and Kevin was sure his answer was meant to get him off the hook without outing

Kevin's interest in her, but damned if his criticism of her didn't sting, too. What the hell was wrong with him?

He needed to get out of here for a few minutes.

He excused himself and went outside. Pressing his back to the wall, he stared up into the now star-filled night. The heat had broken and the humidity had decreased, and it was one of those rare summer nights when it felt better outside than in the air-conditioning.

The door opened and he turned his head, prepared to go back inside, but the woman walking outside made him change his mind.

Holly let the doors close behind her as she stood on the sidewalk. She closed her eyes with a loud sigh and leaned her head back, exposing her neck to the moonlight.

God, he wanted her.

Of course, that had never been in question. He'd wanted her since their first encounter, even in all her awkwardness. It was the intensity that stunned him. The grief he felt when faced with the idea that she might never be his. He had to find a way to make this work. He had to find a way to make her his.

"Hey," he said softly, so as not to startle her.

She opened her eyes and turned to him, wariness quickly replacing her surprise. "What are you doing out here?" She looked like she was ready to bolt.

A wry grin lifted his mouth. "I needed a moment alone."

"You needed a break from your friends?"

He hesitated then said, "I've got a lot on my mind."

"Oh." She tilted her head toward the door. "Do you want me to go back inside and leave you alone?"

"No. As cheesy as it sounds, you being here makes me feel better." He hoped she didn't think he was feeding her a line.

Her shoulders relaxed, and she looked more at ease. "Me, too."

Those two words filled him with more hope than their hot makeout session in his kitchen.

They were silent for several seconds before she nudged his arm with her shoulder. "So, where's this mysterious envelope?" she teased. "I figured you'd whip it out so you could gloat."

He grinned. "I don't just carry it around in my pocket, and I had no idea you'd be here." He turned to face her. "We can open it later. After you finish here. How much longer will you be?"

She sighed, her exhaustion evident. "The party's in full swing and I don't see any chance of it ending for at least another few hours. Then I need to pack up all the centerpieces for the bride's mother to take home and take down the decorations."

"Don't you have an assistant who can do it for you?"

She released a soft chuckle. "Everyone thinks *I'm* the assistant, remember?" Still, there was no bitterness in her comment, only sad acceptance.

"I'll help you."

She glanced up at him, her expression wary. "You don't have to do that, Kevin."

"I know, but I want to anyway." He gave her a grin. "Just think of me as your assistant."

She shook her head, looking at him like he was a naughty schoolboy. "*You* working as an assistant to a wedding planner?"

"Why not? Are you worried I'll be a difficult employee?" he teased. "I promise to obey your every word."

She laughed softly, and he decided there was no better sound than her laugh.

Her smile faded, but her eyes remained soft. "You don't have to help me, Kevin. It's part of my job."

"I know, but I want to open the envelope and I can't do it until you go home, so it's a selfish motive."

She playfully cocked an eyebrow. "So either way, it's all about you."

"Of course. But Matt drove me and I have a feeling that packing up centerpieces isn't his thing, so will you take me home?" He flashed her a mischievous grin. "It's not that far out of the way."

She laughed again, and it warmed his heart more than a laugh should. It only confirmed that he was falling for her. Hard.

"I can't let you help me, then make you walk home, can I?" She was silent for several seconds, then looked back at the door. "I suppose I should go back in." But she didn't budge from her spot.

As much as Kevin wanted to believe he was the only thing keeping her here, her exit from the building led him to believe there was something else going on. "What are you doing out here?"

She hesitated. "I needed a breather, too."

Anyone else might have bought it, but Kevin knew there was more to it. "What aren't you telling me?"

Guilt filled her eyes.

"What happened, Holly?"

"It was nothing I couldn't handle." Her gaze held his and he believed her, but he still wanted to know what had happened. Thankfully, his silence worked her tongue loose. She looked away. "The groom's brother has shown a great deal of interest in me throughout the day, and he's had too much to drink tonight."

His chest seized and he forced out through gritted teeth: "Did he do something inappropriate?"

She turned back and studied him, her wariness returning. "I made sure it didn't get out of hand, but it's a tricky balance, trying to make sure I don't offend the clients while also making sure the guy is convinced nothing is ever going to happen between us."

"Did he touch you?" His mind was shuffling through his high school memories, trying to remember how many brothers Ken Douglas had.

She grinned up at him and shook her head. "He tried to kiss me, but I avoided it. I lied and said I have a boyfriend. But he's drunk enough it could have turned into... a situation."

"If he bothers you again, I want to know."

Her eyes narrowed. "Why?"

"So I can back up your story."

She sighed and her gaze dropped. "While I appreciate you corroborating my lie, that's really not necessary." It was obvious that the lie—told to smooth out a potentially disastrous encounter—bothered her.

He started to tell her he could ease her guilt—that it didn't have to be a lie—but wisely choked back the words. "Hey, we're friends," he said. "Friends have each others' backs."

She smiled up at him, but he saw the sadness, too. "You know we can't be friends. We tried that and it doesn't work. In fact, you should just go home with Matt. I never should have agreed to let you help me."

"I miss you, Holly," he whispered.

"I miss you, too." She stared straight ahead, blinking. But then her back straightened and she was back "on," ready to face her clients. "We need to go in separately," she said, taking a step away. "Otherwise, people might talk."

He had no problem with that, but then *his* reputation had never been the issue. "Okay."

"And if you change your mind about helping me clean up later, I understand."

Even if he hadn't seen the exhaustion on her face now, his answer still would have been the same. "I won't."

He watched her walk back in, unable to stop his gaze from wandering over the sexy body she tried to hide in her utilitarian gray dress. But as soon as she left his sight, he sent a group text to Matt and Tyler.

Is Ken's only brother Pete?

Yeah, Tyler responded.

Why? Matt asked.

He didn't answer. Instead he made his way back into the reception, and it didn't take him long to find the drunken bastard. Pete was leaning against a wall, and it looked like he'd trapped a woman into a conversation she didn't want to be in. The observation appeased any guilt he might have felt when he approached and caught the woman's eye. "If you'll excuse us for a moment, Pete and I need to have a word."

"Sure." Then she shot him a look of gratitude before she ran off.

"Hey," Pete said, taking a step toward him and nearly falling on his ass. "I was about to score with her."

"Like you were about to score with Holly?"

"Who?"

Rage washed through Kevin. Jesus Christ, he didn't even know her name. He grabbed a handful of Pete's shirt and moved his face closer, nearly gagging from the man's breath. "Stay away from her, do you hear me?"

"Which one?" He sounded confused.

His grip tightened. "The wedding planner."

"Oh!" His eyes widened but remained unfocused. "She told me she's got a boyfriend, but between you and me,

I think she's playing hard to get. I just need to wear her down."

Kevin pushed Pete hard against the wall, part of him thankful the music drowned out the thump and the rest of him not giving a shit. "She *does* have a boyfriend and you're looking at him, you sorry piece of shit. If you go near her again, it won't be a warning, you got it?"

The man's eyes were wide with fright, but he nodded.

"He got the message," Tyler said, prying Pete's shirt out of Kevin's fist. "I think you can let go now."

Pete scurried off like the rat he was while Kevin turned slowly to look into the stunned faces of his two friends.

"I told you he had it bad," Matt said with a sidelong glance at Tyler.

"Talk about the understatement of the year," Tyler said. "I think we just lost one of the Bachelor Brotherhood charter members."

Not yet, but Kevin was determined to make Tyler's statement true.

Chapter Twenty-Nine

Holly wasn't sure what was going on, but Kevin's two friends were huddled around him by the back wall. But then a glimpse of Pete Douglas running out the back door clued her in.

What had Kevin done?

She'd told him she had handled it on her own, but obviously he'd intervened. She knew she should be pissed, but she couldn't stop the giddy feeling rising in her chest.

What was that about?

For nearly thirty years, she'd taken care of herself. She sure didn't need someone to take care of her now. But she had to admit that Kevin's gesture filled her with a sense of gratitude that took her breath away. It was nice to have a friend who cared.

A *friend*. She wanted him to be more than a friend. Kevin Vandemeer made her happy. And that terrified her.

"Holly, the DJ hasn't played 'The Chicken Dance' yet," the bride's mother said, interrupting Holly's thoughts. She hadn't even realized Mrs. Murphy had walked up to her. "And the party is almost over."

Holly forced the smile she reserved for troublesome clients and bosses—the one that looked warm and inviting even when she didn't actually feel that way. "I'll go talk to him now."

The party lasted another two hours, going forty-five minutes longer than scheduled, but the father of the bride made some under-the-table arrangement with the DJ to keep it going. And although Holly worried that the hotel staff would get upset, since they knew her they let it slide. A successful reception was only a good endorsement for her. In fact, a wedding guest scheduled an appointment to discuss using Holly for her wedding next spring.

But Holly kept sneaking glances at Kevin, sure he would renege on his offer to help, not that she could blame him. His friends were still there, close by and acting like his bodyguards, or perhaps as protection for the groom's brother. But it was obvious they were bored.

Time to be a big girl.

After she reminded the DJ to play the requested song, she walked over to Kevin and his friends and took a seat next to Tyler. She turned to Kevin, who held a bottle of water in his hand. Come to think of it, she hadn't seen him with anything but water since they came back inside. "This party will be going for a while longer, so why don't you boys go ahead and go." She held Kevin's gaze. "I'll see you tomorrow."

His two friends turned their attention to him, but he shook his head. "I told you I would stay and help you, and that's what I'm doing."

Why did he seem so determined to stay? The worried glance Matt shot toward the groom's brother confirmed her earlier suspicions. "While I very much appreciate the offer, your friends are ready to go and it's obvious they aren't leaving you alone." She lifted her eyebrows. "I can handle myself." She cast a quick glance at Pete Douglas, then back to Kevin. "I promise."

"That much is obvious," he said, his face giving nothing away. "But sometimes you need to accept help, even when you don't think you need it."

Both of his friends grunted.

She stood and moved behind Kevin. Resting her hand on his shoulder, she squatted next to him and whispered into his ear, "Give your friends a break and go home, Kevin." Then she kissed him on the cheek and walked away.

Five minutes later, all three men got up and left. Holly stood in place at the cake table, where she'd been packing up the wedding cake. She took a breath and placed the top tier into a box, trying to ignore the ache in her chest as Kevin walked to the door without a word good-bye.

Why was she upset? He'd done exactly what she'd told him to do.

Shortly after midnight, the crowd had finally dwindled and the DJ called it. The bride and groom had already left. The presents and cake had been packed into the mother of the bride's car. All that was left were the centerpieces, most of which the bride's mother had handed out to friends, and the lights around the room.

"It was absolutely beautiful," Mrs. Murphy said, pulling Holly into a hug. "Thank you for everything."

"You are so welcome. I loved every minute of it." Which was mostly true.

"Michelle's father and I would like to give you a big bonus for all your hard work. Twenty percent."

A twenty percent bonus? "Mrs. Murphy, I don't know what to say. Thank you."

She patted Holly's arm. "We'll mail the check to your office."

Holly kept the smile plastered on her face, even though the surge of disappointment brought tears to her eyes. Nicole would confiscate the check and deposit it in the business account, giving her only a small portion. She'd done it before. "It's been a long day, so why don't you take off and I'll take care of everything else. I'll drop the remaining centerpieces at your house tomorrow."

The woman gave her a weary smile. "I already took what I wanted. You keep the rest or throw them away."

The last couple left, leaving Holly and a few of the hotel staff to clean up the mess. The bride's father had bribed the bartender and the waitstaff to stay longer, too, but they had been keeping up with the cleanup and were soon gone, leaving Holly alone. She picked up the last centerpiece and tears stung her eyes as she looked at the arrangement of pale pink roses in a small round vase. She had a job she loved and she'd just made a bride's dreams come true. Why was she so melancholy?

"I see you got started without me," Kevin said as he stood in the open doorway.

The vase still in her hand, she spun around, gasping at the sight of him. He'd changed into jeans and a T-shirt with the U.S. Marines logo. She swiped an errant tear from the corner of her left eye. "What are you doing here?"

His warm eyes held hers as he walked toward her. "I told you that I was going to help you."

"But you went home."

"And I came back. Just like I said I would." He moved closer, standing in front of her. "I won't let you down again, Holly. If I tell you I'm going to do something, I'm going to do it."

She broke his gaze, her face burning when she realized what he was talking about. "Kevin..."

"Dance with me."

Her eyes snapped back to his. "What?"

"You said you couldn't dance with me earlier because it would be unprofessional. Well, there's no one here now. Dance with me now."

She gave him a grin, but the flowers shook in her trembling hands. She wasn't sure she had the strength to refuse him. She might be naive, but she knew he wanted more than a dance. "I'm not sure that's a good idea," she whispered.

"I think it's the best idea I've had since the envelope." His voice was steady as he pulled his phone from his front jeans pocket and opened his music app. The sounds of a Sara Bareilles song filled the space around them.

Holly released a soft laugh. "I find it hard to believe a big tough guy like you listens to Sara Bareilles."

"I don't," he said, setting the phone on the table, not taking his eyes from her as he took the arrangement from her hands and set it next to the phone. "I downloaded it for you." He reached for her, putting his hands gently on her hips, letting her know exactly what he wanted, yet giving her every opportunity to bolt.

She was mesmerized by his eyes. They were dark and burned with unspoken promises. Promises she very much wanted to accept.

"Dance with me, Holly," he whispered into her ear, his voice husky with desire.

She should tell him no. The smart thing to do was to tell him no. But instead, she found herself whispering back, "Okay."

The muscles in his arms and shoulders were so tense she expected him to take charge and pull her to his chest and kiss her, and she was ready for it. Ached for it. But his hand was gentle as it slid up her back, pulling her ever so slowly to his chest.

He began to sway, and she was aware of every part of him. His firm muscles against her breast, the strong arm that held her pressed tightly against him, so tightly she could feel the beating of his heart. His scent—oh, his scent—she'd come to know so well. Too well. How had she let this man get under her skin? She'd only known him for a little over a week.

She closed her eyes and rested her cheek on his chest, her heart aching even more as she realized he'd picked a song about lost love. She should take a step away from him, end this now.

But her body refused to listen to her head. She slid her fingers up his arms, resting them on his tense shoulders, kneading gently before moving on to trace the outline of his jaw.

Reaching up on tiptoes, she lightly pressed her lips to his.

He stopped moving, his body still as she ran her tongue along his bottom lip. When he began to sway again, his lips brushed hers tenderly as he pulled her in tighter.

The kiss deepened but remained unhurried, slow and leisurely, as though he had all the time in the world. But his tongue worked magic, finding hers and coaxing it to join his dance of slow seduction.

He lifted his hand to her face, tilting her head back to give him better access to her mouth while his thumb made slow strokes along her jaw.

She lost herself in him, their bodies connected by hands and mouths, but also hearts. She felt alive—so alive—from the tingles on her skin, to the ache in her core, to the lightness in her heart. He made her heart sing, and she felt more cherished and desired than she'd ever felt in her life.

He lifted his face and she lost herself in his warm brown eyes, so full of adoration it stole her breath away.

It took her several seconds to realize the song had ended.

Leaning down, he gave her a gentle kiss, then lifted his head. "Thank you for the dance."

She smiled softly, incapable of forming intelligible words. Twice they had gotten swept away with passion and hormones, but this tender moment with him meant more to her than any other in her life.

He slowly released her, giving her a gentle smile. "Let's clean up and go home."

Her stomach fluttered with anticipation as they worked together to dismantle the room, and within fifteen minutes they had everything they needed packed up in boxes. Holly slipped her pumps back on, grabbed her purse, and looked around the room, making sure she hadn't missed any decorations.

Kevin stood next to her holding both boxes. "We good?" he asked softly.

She looked up at him, still in awe of just how much she felt for him. "Yeah, you saved me a ton of time. Thanks."

He grinned. "So do I get the assistant job?"

"Yeah, you have it," she teased. "The pay is crap, but it's yours."

He leaned over and gave her a tender kiss, then turned toward the door. "Then let's get you home."

He'd parked next to her small SUV, and after he'd put the boxes in the back, he shut the hatch and looked down at her. "You still up for opening the envelope?"

She grinned. "I've waited long enough, don't you think?"

"It's at my house. We can open it there."

"Sounds like a plan."

He opened her car door, then pulled her to his chest, kissing her again, leaving her breathless and weak in the knees. "I'll follow you home."

"Okay," she whispered, wondering if she should try to be more coy about the effect he had on her but not wanting to. She was tired of fighting her feelings for him.

When she got home, Kevin was in her driveway, waiting for her to get out of the car. He insisted on carrying the boxes of lights into her garage, but she told him to leave the centerpieces in the trunk.

"You want to open the envelope tomorrow?" Kevin asked. "You look exhausted."

She grinned up at him. "You can't get out of it that easy. Want to get the envelope and meet me in my backyard?"

"Sounds good."

She went into her house, kicked off her shoes, poured herself a glass of wine, and grabbed a bottle of beer. When she came out the back door Kevin was already sitting in one of the Adirondack chairs, his shoes off and his feet in the wading pool. The kitten was nervously pacing around on his lap.

She laughed as she handed him a beer and stepped into the pool. "I see you've figured this part out."

He accepted the bottle and took a drag. "It's a unique setup, but I can see the benefits."

After she settled into the chair, she released a contented sigh. "This is one of my favorite places in the world."

"With your feet in a kiddy pool?"

"In my grandma's backyard. It's hard to be unhappy when you're surrounded by flowers."

He was silent, taking another sip as he watched her.

"Gran's always been a gardener. She taught me how to

plant and prune, but she had a magical touch that I don't seem to have. The garden is already looking worse for wear this year. Next year it won't be the same."

He was silent for several seconds, and when he spoke, he seemed hesitant. "I know you feel like you're losing her with her dementia. I would guess that you'd want to try to keep this part of her."

She glanced over at him, tears filling her eyes. How did he understand her so completely? She nodded, taking a second for the lump to clear from her throat. "You're lucky that you have so much extended family. Nicole talks about them."

"Family is overrated," he said and, though he said it jokingly, she had to wonder at his tone.

"You and Megan seem to have a great relationship. Strong enough to survive that disaster," she said, waving her hand in the direction of his house, hoping to lighten the mood.

"Don't remind me. At the rate I'm going, I'll be stuck in that place forever." For some reason he didn't sound so depressed about that fact.

"Okay, enough stalling. Did you bring the envelope?"

He reached into his pocket and pulled it out. "Why don't you do the honor?"

"Whiskers is *your* cat. You should do it."

He ran his hand down the kitten's back. "I've got my hands full. You do it."

She took the envelope and broke the seal. "I feel like we should have a drumroll or something."

He tapped his fingers on the armrest in a mock drumroll and grinned.

She pulled out the paper and held it up. "I can't read it."

"Why not?"

She squinted. "It's too dark. It's practically illegible. Take your pick."

"I'd let you use the flashlight on my phone, but I left it home."

"I've waited forever and I *have* to know." She stood up, her foot catching on the edge of the pool, and she started to wobble.

Kevin was up in an instant, dropping the kitten in the chair as he stood and reached for her. But his foot slipped and he fell, taking her down with him. He twisted just before they reached the bottom of the shallow pool, turning her to the side so he didn't land on top of her.

They lay there for a second before she said, "I never realized these inflatable sides made such a comfortable pillow."

He grinned and she burst out laughing as they lay in the cold twelve-inch-deep water, their faces inches apart. But after a few seconds their laughter died and the amusement in his eyes turned to desire. Slowly he began to slide his hand up from her hip toward the curve of her breast.

The light in Melanie's upstairs window flipped on and Holly giggled. "Mel's gonna be pissed that we woke her."

Kevin's hand froze, and he looked worried.

But Holly suddenly remembered how they'd ended up in their predicament. "The paper!" She bolted upright and twisted around to find the paper floating on the water behind her. She picked it up and groaned when she saw that the ink had bled, then handed it to him. "Please tell me that you really know and you're just teasing me."

He sat up next to her, grimacing as he squinted at the slip. "I don't."

"Can you read it?" she pleaded.

"I don't think so."

The back door flew open and Melanie stood in the opening, glaring at them with a hand on her hip. "What are you doing out here?"

Killer ran out and jumped into the pool, landing on Holly's lap.

Holly gave her an innocent look. "We're taking a midnight swim."

Kevin laughed, but Melanie did not look amused. "It's one thirty in the morning. Get inside before you wake the whole neighborhood and Mrs. Darcy calls the cops."

"We're doing something important."

Her cousin scowled, then said sarcastically, "Yeah, I can see that."

"No, seriously. We were about to find out the sex of Kevin's kitten, but the paper got wet." She snatched it from Kevin's hand and held it up.

"Is this some new sex game? Because honestly, it sounds a little perverted."

Kevin burst out laughing.

Holly started to stand and her foot slipped again, making her land on Kevin. Hard. He grunted and she burst out in giggles.

Melanie groaned, walking down the steps.

Holly pushed out a sigh. "He took the kitten to the vet and they put its gender on a paper in an envelope but now we can't read it." She waved the paper, showing the bleeding print.

"Oh, for God's sakes." Melanie scooped the anxious kitten out of the chair and walked to the back porch, then held its butt up toward the porch light. "It's a boy. Happy now? Come inside."

"How could you tell?" Holly asked, her mouth gaping.

"It's called anatomy, Hol. Maybe we should have a refresher course before Mr. Handsy goes for Round Two."

Holly looked down and realized that Kevin's hand had a firm grip on her ass.

Kevin stood and reached down to Holly, helping her onto the grass, before he leaned over and gave her a gentle kiss. "I'll see you tomorrow."

Then he took the cat from Melanie and left.

Chapter Thirty

Kevin spent the morning working on his house, purposely leaving Holly alone. Something had happened at the wedding reception—a switch had been flipped inside him. Holly was worth fighting for. Worth waiting for. They'd moved at light speed when they met, but he was willing to slow things down and prove this wasn't just about sex. He wanted *her*. If he had to wait until after her big wedding to have her, he would simply bide his time.

In the meantime, he planned to court her.

Tyler and Matt were sure to get a good laugh over that.

By one o'clock he'd showered and changed, coming up with a lame-ass excuse to see her, finally coming up with settling the bet over Whiskers' gender. Not that they'd ever come to an agreement about the particulars of the bet, but that could work in his favor since Holly had won. So he didn't have *all* the details worked out—he'd just wing it.

He stood on her front porch and was about to knock when he heard Melanie's angry voice inside.

"It's not her anymore, Holly."

"Sometimes it's not," Holly agreed. "But sometimes it is. And when it is, Grandma Barb asks for you. She misses you, Melanie."

"*I can't do it!*"

"You can't run away every time we have this conversation, Melanie!" Holly's voice rose. "You accuse me of running away from relationships, but you're the one running right now."

"You think I'm running?" Melanie responded in a hateful tone. "How about if I run to Kiera's?"

The front door opened and Melanie stood in front of him, her purse slung over her shoulder. Her eyes narrowed when she saw him. "Holly, your booty call is here."

He expected her to get in a few more jabs, but she bolted for her car and drove away.

Holly stood in the doorway, looking up at him in surprise.

"Are you okay?" he asked.

"I'm fine."

"Are you sure? You don't look fine."

She released a loud sigh. "I'm sad for my grandma. I'm not sure I can face the disappointment in her eyes when she asks about Melanie, but I can't not see her."

"You're between a rock and a hard place," Kevin murmured, studying her face.

"Yeah." She walked back in and snagged her purse off the table.

"I take it that you're headed to see your grandmother now."

"I thought I could give her one of the centerpieces from the wedding and then the nursing staff could maybe pass out the rest or put them in the dining hall. The residents really love it when they get flowers."

It was so much like something she would do, it didn't surprise him. "Need help when you get there?"

She glanced over at his house and smirked. "Trying to get out of working on your house?"

"Is it that obvious?" He laughed. When Holly looked uncertain, he added, "Have I mentioned how awesome I am with older people? You saw me with my Gram."

"Why would you want to come?"

He hesitated, worried his answer would scare her off. "The truth?"

"Yes."

He studied her face. "I want to meet the woman who is so special to you. I want to know the woman you're talking about when you mention her with so much love in your eyes."

Her eyes glistened with tears. "Really?"

"Yeah. Really."

She put her hands on his shoulders and gave him a soft kiss. "Thank you."

He'd do just about anything to see that look of happiness in her eyes.

They took her SUV, Holly driving and telling him about some of the residents in the home until she pulled into the nursing home parking lot. Then suddenly her gaiety faded to seriousness.

"It's hard for you to visit?" he asked softly.

"Every time I see her, I'm flooded with guilt."

"Why?"

"I put her here."

The devastation in her voice rocked him to his core. "Holly, from what you told me, you didn't have a choice."

"It still doesn't make it easier."

"How often do you come to see her?"

"I try to come every day, but sometimes I miss a day, like I did yesterday."

He stared at her in surprise. How had he known her a week and a half—seeing her almost every day—and not known this?

She looked over at him with tears in her eyes, reading the shock on his face. "You couldn't know. I don't talk about it. It's too hard." Then she opened the door and climbed out.

Kevin met her at the back of the car and pulled the box out of the back while she swiped at her eyes.

"Is my mascara smeared?"

"No, Holly. You look beautiful." And she did. She was wearing a pink summer dress that made her pale complexion rosy. Her hair was in a ponytail, high on her head. If she heard the longing for her in his voice, she didn't let on.

"Okay. Let's do this."

He followed her through the front door, waiting for security to buzz them through the second door. She glanced over at him. "She has her good days and her bad. If it's bad, we probably shouldn't stay long. You might confuse her."

"Okay."

They walked past a sunny room with several older people playing board games and making art projects before they went down a hall and then stopped at a door that had the name Barbara on it. There were pictures of an older woman decorating the door, and he noticed that Holly was in several of them.

Holly took a deep breath, steeled her shoulders, and walked in.

An older woman sat by the window, looking out onto a small garden.

"Good afternoon, Grandma!" Holly said in a cheerful voice. "I brought you presents!"

The woman turned to face them, a bright smile on her face. "There's my Sunshine."

Holly leaned over and gave her a long kiss on the cheek, then glanced out the window. "Oh. The yellow roses in the garden are fading."

"It's a wonder they lasted this long." Her grandmother looked up at Kevin. "I see you've brought a young man with you. I approve."

Holly laughed. "Grandma, there's nothing to approve. Kevin moved in next door."

"Did the Fergusons move?"

"No, the other house."

Her eyes widened. "You moved into that rat trap?"

He laughed, shifting the box to his hip. "It's a long story, but yes."

She shook her head and looked at Holly with pity. "So your new friend's crazy."

Holly laughed, then graced him with a dazzling smile that stole his breath. "Yeah," she told her grandmother. "One could argue that he is, but I'll keep him around."

Holly tried to take the box, but Kevin held tight and asked, "Where do you want me to put it?"

"I can take it, Kevin."

He still held on. "I know you can, but there's no need to when I can put it wherever you want it."

"Fine," she said, sounding exasperated. "On the table."

Kevin set the box down and turned in surprise when he heard Holly's grandmother chuckling.

"I see you finally met someone you couldn't boss around."

Holly rolled her eyes. "What are you talking about? There's plenty of people I can't boss around. My boss. Melanie. You."

The older woman waved off her statement. "I'm talking about the men in your life. All a bunch of spineless ninnies."

"Grandma!"

Kevin laughed. "She bosses me around plenty. Sometimes I obey her and sometimes I don't."

The older woman laughed again, then broke into a phlegmy cough. When she settled down, she winked at him. "Choosing your battles, young man? Wise."

He nodded with a grin. "Yes, ma'am. My own grandmother taught me well."

"So why aren't you dating this handsome man?" she asked Holly.

Holly reached into the box. "Because that's not an option, Grandma."

"Well, why the hell not?"

"Grandma!"

She narrowed her eyes at Kevin. "Why aren't you dating my lovely granddaughter?"

He paused, certain that Holly didn't want her to know the full reason. He turned his questioning gaze to Holly.

"Grandma, men and women can just be friends. Sometimes they work better that way."

"I call that bullshit, but I'll let it drop"—she pointed her finger at Holly and then Kevin—"for now."

Kevin laughed, but Holly groaned. "You'll just be disappointed with my answer next time." She grinned. "Now behave, or Kevin won't ever come back to see you."

Kevin tried to hide his surprise that she was considering bringing him back.

The older woman's face lit up. "What's in the box?"

"Something pretty for your room." Holly handed her a vase with the roses, and the older woman set it in her lap, tears filling her eyes.

"They're beautiful."

"They're left over from the wedding reception yesterday. Remember the Murphy wedding?"

Her grandmother's eyes lit up. "I should have recognized them from your notebook. They look just like you planned."

"Well, the bride's mother didn't want them, so I decided to bring them to you. I was so happy when the bride picked them out. I know they're your favorite rose."

"Pashminas," she whispered, lifting the vase up to her face, then looking up at Holly. "How are mine doing in the yard?"

Holly shot Kevin a panicked look. While she hadn't told him the Pashmina roses hadn't done well, it wasn't hard to figure out they were included in the group of suffering plants.

"They're gorgeous," Kevin said, leaning against the wall. "Stunning."

"Really?" she asked, looking relieved. "My husband gave them to me when we were first married. A wedding gift."

"What?" Holly asked. "You never told me that."

The older woman didn't answer, just looked at the flowers on her lap.

Holly looked upset, and Kevin resisted the urge to pull her into a hug. Instead, he turned his attention to her grandmother. "How long were you married?"

"Thirty years. Not long enough before his heart attack. And then my two boys were killed a year later." Her eyes filled with tears again, and she wiped her cheek with the back of her hand. "My Sunshine and Storm Cloud got me through the pain. I don't know what I would have done without them."

"No more of that kind of talk. Mel and I..." Holly sniffed, looking dangerously close to crying. She took a breath and pulled out another vase. "I have fourteen more of these. What would you like to do? I can set them up around your room so you're surrounded by them."

Her grandmother shook her head. "That would be selfish of me. Let's share them. Help me up."

Holly smiled and looked toward Kevin. He picked up the box and followed them through the halls, giving out flowers to her grandmother's friends like he was Santa. The residents squealed in delight and Kevin was filled with more contentment than he'd felt in ages. When they'd finished, they went outside and sat in the garden while Holly told her grandmother about last night's wedding reception, answering her many questions. Kevin piped up from time to time, adding details that Holly glossed over.

"I wish I could have been there to see it," the older woman said.

"I would have taken pictures with my phone, but I was too busy," Holly said, sounding apologetic.

"But she'll have some next time," Kevin said. "I'm her new assistant, so I can take them."

Both women gaped at him, Holly looking more surprised than her grandmother.

"That was a joke, Kevin."

"Not to me." Then he changed the subject, telling the older woman about his Gram and her current career as a yoga instructor.

"I wish we had something like that here," she said with a frown. "Something other than painting."

Kevin grinned. "I bet Gram would love to teach a class before she goes back to Wisconsin or wherever she's going next. But I have to warn you. My Gram's a wild one."

The older woman clapped her hands together. "The wilder the better."

They walked her back to her room and she cast a glance at Kevin, then pulled Holly into a tight hug. "You remember what I said. You hear?"

"Yes, ma'am," she said dutifully as she stepped back.

The older woman reached for Kevin and gave him a hug.

"It was wonderful to meet you, Mrs. Greenwood."

"None of that Mrs. Greenwood nonsense," she said. "Either call me Barb or Grandma." She patted his face, searching his eyes. "Promise me I'll see you again."

His smile fell and he turned serious. "I promise."

"Good." Her hand dropped. "Now I'm exhausted, so help me to my chair."

They got her settled and her eyes drooped.

Holly was silent until they got into her car, and then she turned to him, looking angry. "Why would you promise her such a thing?"

"That I'll come back? Because I will."

"But..." She frowned. "Why did you tell her you were my assistant and that you'll take photos for her?"

He said patiently, "Because I asked if I could try out for your assistant position."

"There *is* no assistant position."

"Well, there should be. That's too much for one person to do. I plan to talk to my mother tomorrow."

"What?" Panic filled her eyes. "You can't do that! She'll think I'm incompetent."

"That's ridiculous, Holly."

"You can't say anything. You have to stay out of it."

"Fine, but you have to let me help you with your next wedding."

"That's my big one. The Johansen wedding."

"The wedding-dress designer?" he asked. When she

looked surprised, he grinned. "I pay attention. And if there was ever a wedding you needed help with, it's that one."

"You can't be my assistant, Kevin. There's no pay."

"I know, but let me help you anyway."

"Why?"

"The truth?"

She looked flustered. "Of course."

He turned in his seat to face her, taking both her hands in his. "I like you, Holly. I'm not sure you fully grasp how *much* I like you. I want to have something with you. I want to see where this goes."

She pushed out a groan of frustration. "You know I can't—"

"Yes, I know all too well about my mother. But you told me there's a light at the end of your indentured servitude: the Johansen wedding. When you pull that off without a hitch, you should get enough referrals to start your own business, right?"

"A lot of things have to fall into place. ..."

"You don't want to date me while you work for my mother."

"She'll fire me, Kevin."

"So we spend the next two weeks as friends, and then, after the wedding in two weeks, we can be out in the open and we can give this a real try."

Wariness filled her eyes. "You would wait two weeks?"

"Jesus, Holly." He grinned. "You make me sound like a horn dog."

She laughed. "Well, aren't you?"

"When it comes to you," he leaned into her ear and whispered, "I think about sex with you All. Day. Long."

She sucked in a breath, and he started to get hard, thinking about taking her to bed.

"But I'm willing to wait," he said, nibbling her earlobe. "Because the prize at the end is more than worth it."

"I thought we were waiting." Her voice was breathless, turning him on even more.

"We are," he murmured against her cheek as he trailed kisses to her mouth, then sucked her bottom lip between his teeth.

She pulled her hands from his, linking them behind his neck. "This is waiting?"

"I never said we couldn't kiss," he said against her lips. "We'll just stay at first base until the Johansen wedding. It seems like a good compromise."

She laughed. "You think you can stay at first base for two weeks?"

"I'll do whatever it takes to keep you. Now, I need to ask a favor."

"You know you have me at a disadvantage, right?" she said breathlessly after he kissed her again. "I'd agree to just about anything."

"I need to go to the grocery store. I want to grill for you."

She grinned. "Sounds like I'm getting the better end of the deal."

They drove to the grocery store, and after they got a cart they headed to the produce department. Holly checked out a display of strawberries while Kevin looked for the ingredients to make a salad. He was grabbing an onion when he heard a man exclaim, "Oh, my God. Holly Greenwood. Is that you?"

"Tony!" she said, sounding excited.

Kevin stood back, getting pissed at the jealousy rising up when he noticed the guy standing a little too close.

"You look really good." Tony's gaze stayed on her legs and chest longer than appropriate.

"Thanks." She swiveled to look at Kevin, but he pretended to be interested in the potatoes as he waged a massive inner battle not to go over and stake his claim.

"What are you up to?" Tony asked. "Still at the Marriott?"

"No," she said with a shy smile. "I'm working for an event planner. I mostly work on weddings."

"No kidding. I remember you used to give the brides advice when they booked the reception room at the hotel. Glad to hear you're getting paid for it now."

She cocked her head. "Yeah. Mostly."

Mostly. What did that mean?

"So does that mean you're busy most weekends?" he asked.

"Some. I don't have that many weddings scheduled yet. Most are booked out into next fall and winter. What are you doing back in town?"

"I'm working for a stockbroker in Kansas City now. And Mara and I broke up."

"Oh." Then a second later it seemed hit her. "*Oh.*"

"You still at the same number?"

She looked flustered, and it took everything in Kevin not to walk over and tell the asshole she was taken, but he wouldn't. Because she wasn't. Not officially. And that pissed him off so much he literally saw red.

But Mr. Oblivious caught none of it. "Great. I'll give you a call sometime."

"Yeah…"

"It's really great to see you, Holly. You look *really* good." He pushed his cart toward the bread section and Holly's gaze followed him, making Kevin even angrier.

Was she interested in him?

"Who was that?" he asked, trying hard to sound casual and nonchalant but failing miserably.

"Tony. We used to work together at the Marriott."

"So he broke up with his wife?"

"Girlfriend."

"He moved away somewhere with her?"

"Wichita. She was in grad school."

"And now he's back and wants to take you out on a date."

"No." Wariness filled her eyes. "He just wants to catch up."

"He wants to catch up, all right. He wants to catch up on your legs."

Her eyes flew wide and a middle-aged woman picking up a head of lettuce next to them stopped and stared open-mouthed.

"What are you talking about?" Holly asked, her hands on her hips. "He's an old friend that wants to catch up. You know...talk." But she seemed less sure.

"I saw him checking you out, Holly. He wants to do more than talk. Much, much more."

"You don't know that."

"He'd have to be a fucking idiot to not want to. Do you even have any idea how gorgeous you are?"

"Why are you getting so mad?" she asked, getting irritated herself. "We worked together for three years. I haven't seen him since he moved. We just said hello. That's it."

He counted three full seconds before he said, "I don't like that guy."

"Why?"

He swallowed and asked in an even tone, "You want to go out with that guy?"

Her eyes blazed with anger. "No, you moron. You really think I'd make out with you ten minutes ago, then arrange a date with someone else in the grocery-store produce aisle with you standing four feet away?"

She was right. He was an idiot, but he hesitated long

enough that she mistook his silence. "Find your own way home." Then she spun around and stomped out of the store.

The woman who had been eavesdropping moved closer to him. "I hear picking up women in the produce aisle is the new dating trend." Then she batted her eyelashes. "I'm available."

"Thanks," he told her, "but we're going to work it out." He hoped.

Sighing, he pulled out his phone, trying to figure out whether to call Megan or Matt—which one was less likely to give him grief over this?

The answer was easy: neither. He was better off walking home.

Chapter Thirty-One

Holly was surprised to see Melanie sitting on their couch watching TV when she walked in the door. "You're home. I thought you were going to Kiera's."

Sitting up, Melanie grabbed the remote and turned off the TV. "I've been thinking about what you said." She paused. "You're right. I keep trying to run away from what's going on with Grandma. Like, literally. It's time to face it head-on."

Holly shut the door and sat down beside her. "What exactly does that mean?"

"It means I can't handle the thought of losing Grandma, so instead of facing the truth, I pretend she's not sick. Even if she's not here."

"I get it, Mel. It's hard. But she misses you something fierce."

"I know." Tears filled her eyes. "I was thinking about going to see her tonight. Will you go with me? Do you have plans?"

"Not anymore." Kevin had overreacted to her conversation with Tony, but she had, too. There was little chance Kevin would want her to come over for dinner when she'd left him stranded in the produce aisle.

"Will you go with me?"

"Of course." She gave Mel a hug, then headed to the staircase.

"Who's Tony?" Melanie asked.

Holly froze on the bottom step. "Why do you ask?"

"You left your phone on the kitchen counter. He sent you a text asking you out to dinner. So who is he?"

Holly's face burned. "I used to work with him at the Marriott."

"The assistant manager? The hot one?" She handed Holly her phone. "Good thing, since I told him yes for you. He's picking you up tomorrow night at seven."

"You did *what*?"

Melanie sat up, swinging her legs over the edge of the sofa. "What's going on with you and Kevin?"

"It's complicated."

She held her hands out at her sides. "Well, then there's no reason you can't go out to dinner with Tony."

"This is not a good time for me to go out with someone."

"Yeah, because of the guy next door."

"Melanie. That's not for you to decide!"

"It's too late. I already told Tony yes for you."

How was she going to get out of this one? She needed to call him later, explain that her cousin had answered for her, and tell him she needed to cancel. Surely he'd understand.

* * *

Holly waited for Kevin to come home, but she didn't see any sign of him until later that evening. She considered going over to apologize, but she was still emotionally drained from the visit with their grandmother. Melanie had been jittery and nervous, but at least she hadn't been sad, and, best of all, Grandma Barb had recognized them both.

The next morning, Nicole quizzed Holly about the Murphy–Douglas wedding, seeming pleased with her answers.

"How's the Johansen wedding coming along?"

"Good. Coraline still seems happy."

"That's a small miracle," Nicole muttered to herself. Holly wondered if it was an insult to her ability to keep the bride happy, but then Holly realized Nicole really did see how difficult the woman was. "Keep up the good work."

Maybe Holly had been viewing Nicole through the wrong lens. What if she wasn't as nitpicky and self-absorbed as Holly thought?

But she had little time to think about it as she got busy setting up appointments with two other brides-to-be from the Murphy wedding.

She stopped to visit her grandmother after work, finding her in the dining hall, where she was finishing her dinner. Her grandmother looked past Holly. "Where's your young man?"

"Kevin couldn't come. The visit with Melanie last night was great, wasn't it?" she asked, hoping to get her grandmother off the Kevin topic.

But Grandma Barb was clearly focused on just one thing. "Yes, the visit with Storm Cloud was lovely. But I'd really like to see your handsome young man. Maybe he'll come next time," she said hopefully.

Holly sighed. "Probably not, Grandma. He's very busy working on his house. Yesterday was probably a one-time thing."

"Don't let him get away, Holly." Her eyes were clear and bright. "You really like him and he likes you."

"It's not that easy." Holly sighed. "His mother is my boss."

"Dragon lady?"

Holly grinned. "Yeah."

Her grandmother was silent for several long seconds, then she grabbed Holly's hand. "Love is a very precious gift, Holly. Some people are fickle, falling in and out of love. But that's not really love." She waved her free hand back and forth. "But once you find real love, something so deep it sinks to your toes, a love that fills you so completely it makes you a better person than you were without him—once you find that love, don't let it go."

Holly looked down at her lap. "Grandma, it's not that easy."

"Nothing worth having in life is easy." She tilted up Holly's face to look into her eyes. "Life is short, my precious girl, you and I know that firsthand. You never know how much time a person has left in this world, so don't squander it. Hold on and enjoy the ride while you can." She winked. "And I do mean the ride."

Holly gasped. "Grandma!"

"Kevin's Gram came and gave a yoga demonstration today. We had a chat." Her grin spread. "I like her."

Holly spent a bit more time with her grandmother, then left, realizing on the drive home that she hadn't cancelled her dinner with Tony. She sat several seconds through a green light as she dealt with a mini panic attack. Was it too late to cancel? What would Kevin think? But she hadn't talked to

Kevin since she'd left him at the store. Besides, she and Tony had never been anything but friends. She wasn't interested in starting anything with him now, and she'd make sure he knew it.

The rest of the drive home, she thought about her grandmother's advice. When she got home, she sent Kevin a text, telling him she was going out for the evening but when she came home, she wanted to come over to his house and talk.

He sent a text back within seconds. *I'll be home.*

Tony picked her up minutes later, and she met him in the driveway, eager to get the evening over with. But their dinner went better than she expected. The conversation flowed easily, and Tony was genuinely interested in hearing about Distinctive Events and how she'd gotten her job there.

"A friend of a friend," she said, taking a sip of her water. "Nicole had just started her business last fall and she held an event at the Marriott. I helped her with a few things and she offered me a job."

He laughed. "You mean you did what you usually did when the brides came to book the rooms for receptions—you planned half the wedding."

She grinned. "I wasn't *that* bad."

He looked worried. "It wasn't an insult, Holly. Those brides loved you. You saw that they were worried and confused, and you stepped in and helped them. That's what you do. You help people."

"Nicole as a client is a whole lot different than Nicole as a boss."

"Who was the guy in the grocery store?" Tony asked, giving her a wry grin.

"What?"

"The guy who looked like he was about to crush an onion

with his bare hand. If he had laser eyes I would have been vaporized on the spot."

"Oh." Her cheeks heated. "That was Kevin. My next-door neighbor. We stopped at the store after we'd gone to the nursing home to visit my grandma."

"You took a guy to see your grandmother? It must be serious. You protect her like she's the Hope Diamond."

"Oh, no," she said, getting flustered. "We're just friends."

"Hate to break it to you, Hol, but the looks he was giving you were not the looks of a friend."

Holly looked into his eyes. "His mother just happens to be my boss."

"Oh," he said in a knowing voice. "And if she's half as bad as the stories you've told me tonight, she'll never approve."

"No. And I need this job."

"For your grandmother."

"Yeah. That, too." Her job used to be the most important thing in her life.

But now she wasn't so sure that was true anymore.

Chapter Thirty-Two

Kevin told himself for the tenth time that watching out the bedroom window to see if Holly had gotten home didn't make him a stalker.

"I'm just being a concerned friend," he told Whiskers, who looked up at him like he wasn't buying it for a minute.

Of course, it was early for Holly to be home from a date. She could be gone for hours. Or she might not come back at all. She hadn't told him she was on a date, but Kevin had seen the guy Tony from the grocery store pick her up. It wasn't hard to put two and two together. He didn't like the burning in his gut at the thought, but he reminded himself that he couldn't make her choose him. Maybe she'd rather be with the shit head from the grocery store.

But that didn't mean he had to like it.

He didn't blame her for leaving him at the grocery store. He'd been an ass, which Megan had been eager to point out multiple times the night before, after he'd caved and asked her to pick him up. He'd started to go to Holly last night, but he'd decided to apologize tonight and maybe try again to make her dinner.

Of course, she came up with other plans.

It occurred to him that he'd told her what *he* wanted for them, but he'd never asked her what *she* wanted.

He was looking out the window for the third time in ten minutes when he saw the guy's car in the driveway.

She'd been gone an hour and twenty minutes, which included drive time. The date must not have gone very well.

He bolted down the stairs, making sure the front door was closed behind him, and stopped on his porch, his chest squeezing when he saw the two in an embrace, Tony's face lowered to hers.

Was he kissing her good night?

Kevin might have to move in with his mother after all, because he wasn't sure he could handle watching Holly with another man.

Tony walked back to his car and Kevin warred with himself. Should he go to her, making it obvious he'd been watching for her? Or should he wait for her to come over like she'd asked before her date?

His feet decided for him.

He was halfway across the yard when she started down her porch steps, stopping short when she saw him.

God, she was so beautiful. She was wearing a peach dress that made her skin glow and her blonde hair was down, loose and wavy. She wore a pair of white sandals with a small heel that made her calves look incredible. He was blown away that Tony had brought her home so soon when she looked this amazing.

"You went on a date." It wasn't a question.

She hesitated. "We went to dinner and caught up."

"Do you like this guy?" He struggled to get the words out. "You want to see him again?"

"Yeah, I plan to see him again," she said quietly, looking into his eyes.

A vise tightened around his chest, cutting off his oxygen.

She paused. "We're friends."

"Friends." He climbed the steps and stood in front of her, his voice husky. "Friends like you and me?"

She backed up a step, the front door stopping her as she looked up at him with so much emotion in her eyes he couldn't make heads or tails of it.

She shook her head slowly. "No, Kevin. Nothing like you and me. I've never had anything like you and me."

He reached for her and pulled her to his chest, kissing her with a raw hunger that caught him by surprise. He started to pull back, worried that he'd scared her with his intensity, but her fingers threaded through his hair, holding him firmly against her mouth.

He cupped her cheek and tilted her head back, his tongue searching for hers, which made her cling tighter. She slid a hand down to his chest, grabbing his T-shirt in her fist.

Encouraged by her response, he had run his hands over her ass, then down to her outer thigh, and he started to bring her leg up to his waist when he realized what he was doing. On her front porch.

"God, Holly. I'm sorry." He dropped her leg and tried to step back, but her hold on him tightened.

Her eyes blazed with passion and defiance. "I'm not."

He wasn't sure he'd heard her right.

She took a breath. "I like you. I *really* like you." Her voice trailed off as she reached for his face, then trailed her fingers along his jaw.

He searched her eyes. "I told you I would wait for you

until your big wedding, and then we can be open about being together. But it occurred to me that I never asked if that was what you wanted."

She studied him, her expression giving nothing away. "Are you asking me if I agree with your proposition—that we wait two weeks before we announce to the world that we're together? And we only kiss until then?"

He nodded. "Yes."

She slowly shook her head. "No. I'm not okay with that."

He struggled to deal with the disappointment cascading through him, and he took a step back. He *had* to be okay with this.

Her hands fisted the material of his T-shirt, and she tugged him back to her. "I'm not finished."

Kevin rolled his head back, releasing a defeated groan. "*Holly.*"

"I don't want to be with you for two weeks with the rule that we kiss."

His hope latched on to her words. He could work with this. "We don't have to kiss. We can—"

But she cut him off as she placed a small kiss at the corner of his mouth, then left a trail of kisses as she moved to the center of his mouth. "I *want* to kiss."

His erection throbbed against the tight confines of his jeans. "I'm confused about your opposition."

She held his face between her hands, their mouths inches apart. "Let me tell you what I *do* want."

Her voice was so sultry that a wave of desire surged through him, and he fought the urge to press himself against her. Which was definitely against the rules he'd proposed yesterday. "I am dying to hear what you want."

"I agree to your two weeks together before the wedding." She kissed him again, covering his mouth with hers.

"Okay."

"I agree to go public if the wedding goes well."

"It will."

"But I want more than first base during our two weeks. I want it all."

He leaned back, taking in her hooded eyes and her swollen lips, her words making him ache to be inside her. "You want it all?"

"Everything."

He pushed her against the door, kissing her as his hands roamed her body, but then he stopped. "Inside. Now."

"Yes."

He opened the door and nudged her backward into the living room, then shut the door. He grabbed her ass and tugged her flush against him as he kissed her. She pulled his shirt up and over his head, leaving him bare chested. She let out a tiny breath as her palms covered his pecs.

"I love your chest," she said, pressing her lips over his sternum. Then she placed open-mouthed kisses down to his left nipple and drew it into her mouth.

"Holly."

Her mouth moved across his skin to his other nipple.

Her hands found the button to his jeans, unfastening, then unzipping. Then she pushed the fabric over his hips and down, pulling his briefs with them. When she got to midthigh he tried to take over, but she pushed his hands away, bending to pull them down the rest of the way, then dropping to her knees. He'd kicked off his shoes and had just stepped out of his jeans when she reached for him and ran her tongue along his tip.

"Oh, God." He grunted, his hands sinking into her hair.

She sucked his tip into her mouth, licking, then taking him deeper.

His grip on her hair tightened, and he forced himself to be gentler—easier said than done when she was driving him out of his mind.

It didn't take her long to bring him to the brink. He grabbed her upper arms and hauled her up, his mouth searching hers. He reached behind her, finding the zipper of her dress. He had it down to her waist within seconds, before he came to his senses. "Your cousin?"

It took her a second to understand what he meant. "She's at work."

Her words set him free. Her dress was at her feet, her bra quickly following it, leaving her in only her lacy panties.

His palm pressed flat against her abdomen, sliding down to her mound as he lowered his face to the nape of her neck. He backed her up to the sofa and pushed her down. "You're so beautiful, Holly."

She gave him a shy smile.

"I want you."

She pushed out a breath, her breasts rising and falling. He wanted to kiss every inch of her body. He hooked his fingers on the top of her panties and tugged them over her hips and down her legs, leaving them on the floor. He knelt between her knees, spreading her legs apart, then lowering his mouth to her breast, finding her nipple and drawing it into his mouth. Sliding his hand down between her folds, he found her slick and wet. Her hips lifted up as she released a tiny moan.

He smiled as his mouth glided over her abdomen, his tongue leaving a trail to her mound. He pressed her legs wider, his hands firm against her inner thighs as he lowered his mouth between her folds, his tongue finding her sensitive spot.

Leaving a hand on her thigh, his other hand moved to her

core, then he pressed two fingers inside her as his tongue brought her higher.

He looked up at her, the peaks of her breasts rising and falling with her rapid breath, her mouth parted. Her hands held on to his head, then pulled him up.

"I want you," she said breathlessly as she looked at him. "I want you in me now."

He loved her confidence, his erection twitching with the ache to be inside her. "I need to get a condom."

Her eyes found his. "I'm on the pill."

He grabbed her shoulders and turned her so she was lying on the sofa, then he climbed between her open legs. "Are you sure?"

She grinned. "That I'm on the pill?"

He grinned, too. "I trust you on that. I meant are you sure you trust *me*?"

She looked deep into his eyes. "I trust that you would never hurt me."

He sucked in a breath at the significance of her gift. Her trust was everything.

Hooking his hand around her thigh, he lifted her leg around his waist and entered her slowly, losing himself in the sensation.

She lifted up to him, taking him deeper as he buried himself inside her in slow, deep strokes.

Writhing beneath him, she pressed herself to him and he increased the pace, holding her hips to steady himself. She tightened even more around him as she climbed higher, releasing soft moans that drove him mad.

He leaned over her, then gave in to his desire, thrusting fast and hard, so close he had to grit his teeth until she cried out beneath him, calling out his name.

And that was when he came, burying himself deep inside

her, his name on her lips. He slowed his pace until he rolled to his side, pulling her to his chest, still inside her.

He brushed her hair from her sweaty face, searching her eyes. This was too good to be true. His fingertips softly stroked the side of her cheek. He'd never felt this tenderness before, and it caught him by surprise. "What made you change your mind?"

She smiled at him. "My grandmother."

He laughed. "She told you to have sex with me?"

"No." She grinned. "She told me once I found a love that I felt all the way to my toes to never let it go."

His breath caught on the L word.

She released a soft chuckle. "I don't know what this is between us, but I've only felt it with you. I'd be crazy to let you go, Kevin. I want you. I want this. We'll make it work."

He kissed her, still in disbelief that she was his, but now that she was, he would do everything in his power to keep her.

Chapter Thirty-Three

~

The next two weeks were bliss. Kevin and Holly spent every night together, they'd wake up in the morning, and then he'd kiss her good-bye as they left to start their days—although Kevin was only working half days while Matt's company worked through the embezzlement issues. Tyler had found an investor who was willing to give Matt's company the capital it needed to stay afloat for several months, including retaining Kevin's position. They were just waiting for the funding to come through. In the afternoons, Kevin came home and worked on his house. The pipe in the kitchen had been fixed and the cabinets had been installed, but there was still a lot left to do.

And later in the evening, Holly and Kevin would spend hours exploring each other. Sex with Kevin was amazing, more amazing than Holly could have ever imagined, but it wasn't just sex. He made her feel like she was the most cherished and adored woman in the world. Some nights they sat in her backyard, surrounded by her grandmother's flowers.

Wrapped in his protective arms, she wondered how she almost gave him up.

As the Johansen wedding grew closer, Coraline Johansen became more demanding and harder to please. Holly tried to chalk it up to nerves, but the crabbier Coraline got, the more worried Holly became.

One night before the rehearsal dinner, she and Kevin lay in bed talking. Her head rested in the crook of his arm while his fingertips lazily stroked her arm, and she finally found the courage to ask, "What will we do if this wedding goes wrong?"

His fingers stilled. "What could go wrong?"

She didn't want to worry him, but she had to know what he wanted. "Coraline is becoming unstable. I'm worried she might cancel the wedding."

He turned slightly to study her face. "Do you think she will?"

She sighed. "I don't know. Maybe?" She tried to push down her fear. "What will we do if it happens?"

"We'll tell my mother."

"She'll fire me."

His eyes hardened. "Not if I tell her that she'll lose me as a son if she does."

She shook her head. "I can't let you do that, Kevin."

"Holly." He lifted her chin so she would look up at him. "I would do anything for you. Haven't you figured that out yet?"

She had. She just couldn't live with the guilt. "I would give anything to have my mother. I will never let you willingly give yours up."

"Holly."

"I'll quit." She'd already given it some thought. Too bad she didn't have the financial details worked out yet.

Kevin gave her a gentle kiss. "You love your job."

I love you more was on the tip of her tongue, but thankfully she kept it to herself. Could you love someone after three weeks? Was it real? But one look into his worried face was all the confirmation she needed. She loved Kevin Vandemeer.

She'd give up her job to keep him. She just had to figure out how to take care of her grandmother if she did.

* * *

Nicole was feeling the stress of the wedding, too. Holly realized her boss had a lot riding on the wedding as well. The reputation of her business was on the line.

On the morning of the rehearsal, the tension in the office was thick. Holly was making sure she had everything prepared for the rehearsal dinner when the phone on Nicole's desk rang.

Nicole answered, then entered a very one-sided conversation.

"Uh-huh...yes...uh-huh...I see...yes, I'll take care of it." She hung up and turned to Holly.

Nicole's mouth was puckered as though she'd eaten a lemon, which was always the first clue that Holly was in trouble. Holly steeled her back, preparing for the brewing storm but not sure how much more stress she could take. She already felt close to snapping.

"I just received an interesting call," Nicole said.

"Oh?"

"From Coraline Johansen. She's very unhappy with you."

Holly sighed. "I'll call her and smooth things over."

"You were late to an appointment with the caterer yesterday."

"There was an accident on the highway, Nicole. Traffic was at a dead standstill. I got there as quickly as I could."

"You should have planned for such events."

Holly had had enough. "I know for a fact you were late to a meeting last week. A half hour late. The client called looking for you, and I covered for you, telling them I wrote down the wrong time. And we won't even mention that you were late to the Johansen meeting due to a car accident. Maybe you should have planned for such an event."

Nicole gave her an indignant look. "The first incident was probably your fault. You must have written it down wrong."

Holly was losing her patience. "How could I write it down when I don't have access to your digital calendar?"

"Well...I don't know." She looked flustered, then turned angry, pointing her finger at Holly. "You've been distracted the last several weeks, and I know that you've left early several days."

"I do work at home, Nicole. Often hours of it to get everything done."

"What you do at home is not my concern. What about the call you received a few days ago and then you went running out?"

That had been the care center calling about Holly's grandmother. She'd had an episode of memory loss that had made her violent, something that had never happened before. Holly left to try to calm her grandmother down. But there was no way Holly would tell Nicole that. She lifted her chin. "I took some personal time."

"Well that personal time is coming from your paycheck."

"That's not fair." Holly had easily put in fifty hours the week before and gotten paid a salary for only forty hours. This week—including the wedding—would be around sixty.

"It most certainly is." Nicole's jaw tensed. "You're seeing a man, aren't you?"

Holly froze. "*What?*" Did she know about Kevin?

"I know that look...the look of a woman in love." Her eyes narrowed. "I don't have time for you to be in love. I need you focused at work."

"Nicole, my love life is none of your concern."

"It is if you're taking personal time to meet your lover."

"What?"

"I'm sorry. That was so uncalled for, even from me." Tears filled Nicole's eyes. "I'm sorry I've been impossible. I just can't afford for anything to go wrong, Holly. You have no idea how much I have riding on this wedding."

Nicole had hinted at it multiple times over the last two weeks, but this was the first time she'd been this direct. Holly's anger softened. "I assure you that I'm doing everything I can to make sure this wedding goes perfectly. I know your reputation is on the line."

"It's not just my reputation, Holly. I have multiple clients threatening to cancel if this doesn't go well. They don't want to be known as hiring the event planner who wrecked the Johansen wedding." Her mouth pursed. "Trust me, Coraline has a reputation. There are a lot of eyes on this, and if anything goes wrong, we risk losing over half our future income."

Holly gasped. "What?"

"If this wedding doesn't go well, you'll lose your job, not because I'm firing you, but because I'll have to lay you off."

Oh. God. "Nicole," Holly said, starting to panic. "I assure you I'm doing everything I can to—"

"I know." Nicole sank back in her chair. "And I know Coraline Johansen is a self-centered brat who is impossible to please. That's why *I* wanted to be the planner. So *I* would take the credit if it failed. So you could get a job somewhere else without the failure of a high-profile wedding on your résumé."

Holly shook her head in disbelief. "Why didn't you tell me?"

Grabbing a tissue, Nicole dabbed the outer corners of her eyes. "At first, I was hurt and furious they chose you over me. And I confess that part of me felt relieved that I wasn't dealing with her."

"Then why did you want the job in the first place?"

"It was a gamble. One I was willing to take. I set my son up on a date with that twit of a girl all in an effort to get on that stupid country club committee, with no return on that risk, and now this. And I didn't tell you any of it because I didn't want you to deal with the added stress along with the stress of the wedding. *I* was the one who went after the Johansens. This is *my* doing."

"I swear I'll do my best, Nicole."

Nicole turned her back to Holly, staring at her computer screen. "You wouldn't be handling the wedding if I didn't think you could. Now you better head out to the vineyard if you're going to have everything set up in time."

*   *   *

A couple of hours before the rehearsal, Holly was on a ladder replacing a burned-out bulb on a string of twinkle lights hanging from a tree branch at the vineyard. She had just gotten the bulb shoved into the socket and the strand had come to life when she heard Kevin's voice behind her. "Isn't that a job for your assistant?"

Her mouth parted and she looked down at him in shock as he moved next to the ladder. "What are you doing here?

I thought you and Matt were having an impromptu meeting about his new investor?"

"Yeah...well..." He grinned. "It finished early, so I figured I'd head over to my second job."

"Third job, when you count fixing up your house as your second," she said with a frown, climbing down. "If you insist on helping me, why don't you go home tonight and get some rest and you can help me tomorrow after you've had a good night's sleep."

"I'm already here and you need help. Besides, this job has perks." He pulled her to him, and she acquiesced, meaning to make it a quick kiss, but his lips lingered longer than she'd planned.

"I needed this," he murmured against her lips. "I need you."

"I need you too." And not just sex. He made her believe everything would be okay. No matter what they faced.

"Someone could see us," she said against his lips.

He lifted his head. "Is my mother here?"

"No."

"Then I don't care." He tugged her against him and deepened the kiss.

She leaned back and swatted his chest. "If you want to help me, I need less kissing and more light hanging. The wedding party's going to be here for the rehearsal in less than an hour."

He grimaced. "The last wedding rehearsal I went to didn't go so well."

She cocked her head and sounded worried. "And whose wedding was that?"

"My sister's, but it all worked out in the end." He shrugged. "Although I might have threatened the groom."

Her brow furrowed. "I heard her wedding reception was a disaster, too. Maybe I should send you away."

"I'm feeling lucky. Let's see what happens."

Holly shook her head. "I really need this wedding to go well." She considered telling him how much his mother's business needed this wedding, but it fell into that murky no-man's-land of what was appropriate to share—while he was her boyfriend, she thought it was up to his mother to tell him that her business was flailing. "I'm about to start looking for four-leaf clovers to help make that happen."

He took the strand of lights from her. "No luck needed. You've got this. What are we doing standing around here talking, then? Start bossing me around."

Chapter Thirty-Four

The day of the wedding, Holly woke up bright and early, worried about the million and three things that could go wrong. The rehearsal had been like a powder keg waiting to explode. Coraline had been paranoid and confrontational, and the groom had threatened to leave before the appetizers were even served.

Kevin was still asleep, and she watched him for nearly a minute, basking in the happiness of the past two weeks. She started to get out of bed, but Kevin cracked his eyelids and snaked an arm around her waist, tugging her back so they were face-to-face.

"Where do you think you're going?"

She laughed. "I was going to take a shower. I have a busy day."

"As your assistant, I have a busy day, too."

She studied his face. "You seriously plan on helping me today?"

"Holly, I saw how hard you worked at Ken Douglas's

wedding. If you won't ask my mother for an assistant, then let me be one."

"And what if she finds out?" While Nicole had admitted that she appreciated Holly's work the day before, Holly wasn't sure how far that generosity would extend toward her relationship with her son.

He paused, then looked deep into her eyes. "She'll never know. But if she finds out somehow, I'll come up with a story that won't bite you in the ass." When she didn't protest, he gave her a huge smile and then a kiss. "Just think. More bossing me around."

She laughed, but he'd been more helpful the night before than she could have hoped. And if there was ever a wedding she needed help with, it was the Johansen nuptials. If anything, Holly was shocked that Nicole hadn't insisted on being on-site. "Okay. Deal."

He cupped her face, his thumb tracing her jawline. "I have to run an errand before I head out there. Do you need me to do anything right away?"

She shook her head. "No. All the big stuff is taken care of, so I'll just go to keep an eye on things for a few hours before the bridal party starts arriving and help the people from the bridal magazine get set up. This wedding has to be perfect."

He grinned as he kissed her. "I know. You've told me a million times."

"I think I'm just reminding myself."

"Trust in yourself. I do."

She kissed him, then sat up. "Thank you. Keep saying things like that and I just might keep you around."

* * *

Kevin made Holly a pot of coffee and prepared a travel mug for her while she finished getting dressed. He'd just finished putting on the lid when he heard her heels on the stairs. He turned to face her, once again sucking in his breath at the sight of her. Today she was all business in her pale pink blouse, black pencil skirt, and shiny black pumps. She'd put her gorgeous hair up in a twist.

He pulled her into his arms as soon as she hit the bottom step.

She gave him a teasing look of reprimand. "You can't do that today at the vineyard, Kevin. You have to keep your hands to yourself."

He dropped his hold, took a step back, and leaned over to kiss her. "I know how to keep my hands to myself." His mouth skimmed to her neck.

"*And* your lips."

"This will be very hard." But he lifted his face and smiled as he saluted her. "I can handle the mission, Captain."

She grinned and poked his chest with her finger. "You'd better or you'll be fired." Then her grin fell away. "I'm nervous."

"Babe, it's going to be stunning."

"I'm more worried about the bride."

He cringed. "She *did* seem a little temperamental." She'd thrown a few fits the night before, making him wonder why the groom was marrying her. Especially when Kevin saw him and the maid of honor coming out of a dark room together. Kevin would have guessed he was marrying her for the money, but the groom's family seemed to be loaded, too.

Holly let out a sigh. "Understatement of the year."

"If anyone can handle it, you can."

She gave him another quick kiss. "And with that note of confidence, I'm off."

As soon as she was out the door, he pulled out his phone and called his father. "Dad, did you get my text last night?"

"You want to meet for breakfast?"

"Yeah, but without Mom. She can't know. I need to ask your advice on something."

"Tell me when and where."

"Half an hour at the Big Biscuit?"

"See you there."

Kevin hung up, then jumped when he heard a voice behind him.

"You really care about her, don't you?"

He spun around to face Melanie, who was sitting on the stairs in her pajamas.

He squared his shoulders. "Yeah, I do. I'm trying to make this right for her with my mom."

"Why? So you're not caught in the middle?"

"No, because she deserves better than how my mother treats her. I'm going to see if my dad has a suggestion for how to handle this. I'd just confront my mother, but Holly has begged me not to, and I want to respect her wishes."

She made a face. "I've tried to get her to stand up to your mother since she started working there, but Holly refuses. She just keeps saying she's grateful to Nicole for hiring her." She paused. "I've told Holly she needs to figure out when people are using her and use them in return, but she won't listen. She says she won't stoop to their level, but she's only hurting herself."

Kevin disagreed, but kept it to himself. He loved that Holly lived by a moral compass. He'd dated too many women who didn't.

Melanie stood and walked down the steps toward him. "And if Holly broke it off right now, would you still help her?"

"I care about her. I only want her to be happy, whether

she's with me or not. But there's a good chance this wedding is going to fall apart today. I need to make sure Holly's job is protected."

Melanie broke out into a big smile and pulled Kevin into a hug. "Then welcome to the Greenwood family."

* * *

Half an hour later, Kevin's father was waiting for him at the restaurant.

"Thanks for meeting me, Dad." Kevin held out his hand, but his dad pulled him in for a hug.

"Of course. I'm just sorry it's taken us this long to see each other."

"Yeah. I still can't figure out how you got out of Megan's shower. You need to teach me your tricks for saying no to the women in our family." Kevin grinned, but he was dead serious.

The hostess led them to a table then left a pot of coffee with the menus. Once they placed their orders, his father gave him a wry smile. "This is obviously about your mother. What has she done now? You're not here on Megan's behalf, are you?"

"What? No. This is all me." Kevin took a deep breath, hoping he wasn't breeching Holly's trust. "I love Mom, but you know she's not always the most fair and unbiased person. I need to protect someone I care about."

His father hesitated. "*Who* are you trying to protect?"

Kevin had weighed the risks of what he was about to do, but it was still hard to spit out her name. "Holly. Her assistant." He shook his head. "Her employee."

His father groaned, leaning back in his seat. "What has that woman done this time?"

Kevin tried to contain his rage. "I have no idea what Mom tells you, but Holly is the sweetest, kindest woman I have ever met. She's brilliantly talented. Mom's threatened by that and treats her like crap."

"I was talking about your mother." His father released a soft laugh. "I had no idea you even knew Holly, let alone cared about her so much."

"I love her." He said the words without thinking, but he knew it was true. There was no way he could stand by and let his mother hurt her anymore. "If the wedding Holly's working on today crashes and burns like I suspect it might, Holly will have a hard enough time dealing with it without the added stress of worrying that Mom is going to fire her. Which means someone has to shake some sense and decency into Mom. The only person I know capable of such a feat is you."

His father was silent for several long seconds. "Maybe you should start at the beginning. Like how you two even met."

Kevin gave him a condensed version of Megan buying his house, his meeting Holly, then finding out at the shower how she was connected to his mother. "A lot hinges on this wedding today. Holly won't keep our relationship a secret from Mom after the wedding. It's killed her to hide it the last few weeks. We both know Mom will probably fire her. She wouldn't even let Megan go out to lunch with Holly."

His father grimaced and shook his head. "So you know that if the wedding doesn't go well, Holly likely won't have a job?"

Kevin's mouth dropped open. "Mom admitted it? Even knowing how temperamental the bride is acting?"

"The threat is because of the bride's behavior, not your mother's."

Kevin stared at his father in disbelief. "You know about this? And you condone it?"

His father picked up his coffee cup, looking confused. "How is your mother responsible for the spoiled woman's behavior?"

"Exactly!" Kevin said, his frustration mounting. "If Mom can't be held responsible, then how can Holly?"

"What are you talking about, son?" Bart Vandemeer shook his head. "I'm pretty sure we're talking about two very different things."

"What are *you* talking about?" Kevin asked.

"*I'm* talking about how much is riding on this wedding for your mother's business. If this wedding crashes and burns, she's set to lose half her upcoming functions. No one wants the stink of the Johansen failed wedding attached to their event planner. And if that happens, your mother will be forced to lay Holly off, no matter how much it kills her."

Kevin sat back in his seat as shock washed through him. "Why didn't Holly tell me?"

"For one thing, I suspect she doesn't know. Your mother was trying to keep it from her. She didn't want to give Holly any additional pressure. And, second, I can imagine if your mother told her, she swore her to secrecy." He took a sip of coffee, then lowered the cup. "Your mother only confided in me last night."

"But she's been so awful to Holly. ..."

"Your mother is unbelievably stressed. You of all people should know she doesn't handle stress well."

"Maybe so, but that doesn't make it right."

His father shrugged. "I never said it did."

"And what about Holly and me? I love her. I know she's the woman for me and I don't want to hide it from Mom. I want to tell her, but I don't want to jeopardize Holly's job—presuming she still has one when this is over."

His father chuckled and lifted his hands in surrender. "You don't have to try to convince me. I'm onboard. I'm trying to figure out the best way to handle this."

"So you'll help?"

His father smiled, his eyes lighting up. "I've never heard you say you loved a woman. And I've met Holly, so I know how special she is. I'll help you make this right."

"Dad. Thank you."

"Don't thank me yet. I still have to figure out how to handle this. Experience has shown it usually works better when your mother thinks it was her idea to begin with." His father winked. "The trick is in planting the seed."

Chapter Thirty-Five

Holly knew everything had been going too well. Everyone in the bridal party had arrived on time, even the maid of honor, who kept sneaking away, returning a couple of times with red eyes.

Coraline had refused to take photos before the wedding, saying it was bad luck for the groom to see her in her wedding dress. The dress that was still on its padded hanger on a hook on the wall in the changing room—even though the ceremony started in thirty minutes.

Holly gave Miranda a worried glance, and the older woman scowled.

Miranda approached her daughter as if approaching a skittish horse. "Coraline, darling, if you would just tell us what the problem is, then maybe we can fix it."

The bride paced, her white satin dressing gown billowing behind her. "And I told you, I *don't know* what's wrong. But there's something wrong. I just *feel* it."

The maid of honor bolted from the room again, muttering "Bathroom issues" as she ran out the door.

"Eww..." one of the bridesmaids sneered. "TMI."

Coraline glanced at the door and took off into the hall.

"Coraline!" Holly called after her. "The guests will see you!" But as soon as she started after the bride, the flower girl tripped and fell flat on her face, letting out a shrill cry of pain as blood started pouring from her nose.

"Oh no!" Holly exclaimed as she scooped up the child, and then she had her lean her head back while Holly pinched her nose. "Someone get me a towel!"

One of the bridesmaids held out a small hand towel between her thumb and forefinger, as though the blood from the child's face would jump off and land on her dress.

Holly swiped at the blood while trying to comfort the four-year-old. "Can someone find her mother?"

Everyone stared at her like she'd asked them to run outside naked.

"I want my mommy," the girl wailed.

Holly's phone vibrated against her thigh, but she ignored it. "You!" She pointed to one of the bridesmaids who she'd seen talking to the little girl's mother earlier. "Go get her mommy."

The woman sighed and grabbed her phone from her purse and sent a text.

Holly's phone stopped buzzing, then began to buzz again, but the flower girl was still crying, and now one of the bridesmaids looked close to fainting as she stared at the bloody towel in Holly's hand.

"Someone get some wet paper towels." When no one moved, Holly pointed to the pale woman. "*You*. Go get some towels."

"Her mom won't answer." The bridesmaid with the phone said, sounding aggravated.

"Then go find her yourself."

"But someone might see me!"

Holly fought the urge to roll her eyes. "No one cares if they see you. They're here to see the bride. Now go get her mother!"

"The wedding planner's kind of cranky," the third bridesmaid grumbled to the woman leaving the room.

Ordinarily the snide remark would have stung, but at the moment Holly had bigger issues to deal with.

Her phone began to vibrate again. Holly reached into her pocket to pull it out, but her hand caught on the edge of the seam. Once she had it free, she answered without looking at the name on the screen. "This better be an emergency."

"I think this counts as one," Kevin said. "You need to get in here right away."

"Oh, crap." Holly stood, balancing the phone on her shoulder and handing the little girl to Bridesmaid Number Three. "Where are you? What happened?"

"Groom's room." Kevin's voice sounded strained and Holly heard yelling in the background. "Now."

She took off sprinting down the hall, running into the flower girl's worried mother. Her eyes widened as she stared at the blood smeared across Holly's left breast.

"What happened to my baby? Is she okay?" her mother cried out. "Tonya said she was bleeding out."

Holly gave the mother a comforting pat on the arm. "Oh, no, I promise she's fine. She fell and got a bloody nose. It's almost stopped now, but she's scared and wants her mommy."

A loud bang shook the hall wall, followed by a woman's unintelligible shouting coming from the groom's room.

Oh, crap.

"If you'll excuse me..." Holly hurried past the woman

and took a deep breath before she opened the door—just in time to see Coraline throw a chair across the room.

"*How dare you?*" the bride shrieked, stalking toward the cowering groom. "How dare you sleep with my best friend!"

Holly put a hand on her chest, suddenly feeling light-headed. "Oh, shit."

Kevin was beside her in an instant. "I'm sorry. I had no idea what you wanted me to do."

The groom held up an arm in defense. "My little Cora-bean. It's not what you think."

"How can finding your tongue halfway down her throat not be what I think?" He started to say something, and she jabbed him with her long, pointy nail. "And if you give me an excuse like you did in Spain last month about giving that woman mouth to mouth, I will *kill you.*"

"You were kissing someone in *Spain?*" the maid of honor asked in dismay from the other side of the room, hiding behind two of the groomsmen.

The groom grimaced as he glanced over at the maid of honor. "I was saving her life. I'm certified in CPR!"

"*She was standing up!*" Coraline shouted.

The groom held out his hands and gave her a cocky grin. "I'm just that good."

Coraline screamed in frustration, then picked up the first thing she found—a duffel bag—and began swinging it at the groom's head.

That sparked Holly into action. "Coraline, I know you're upset, but this won't help anything." She tried to reach for the bag, but the bride turned her attention on Holly. "This is all your fault!"

"How is your cheating, asshole fiancé *Holly's* fault?" Kevin demanded, stepping between them.

Holly pushed him to the side. "Kevin, I've got this."

Coraline burst into tears, covering her face with her hands. "How could he do this to me?"

Holly grabbed the strap of the bag and tugged it away from the crying woman, then wrapped an arm around her shoulders. "Let's get you back to the changing room."

The groom tried to reach for her, but Kevin held him back. "I still love you, Cora-bean!" he called after her. "This was a huge misunderstanding!"

"*I hate you!*"

Holly glanced over her shoulder at Kevin. "Don't let him leave."

"I've got it covered," he said, pushing the groom backward into a chair.

Holly led the now hysterically crying bride back to the changing room. Unfortunately, the hall was now full of guests who had heard the commotion and had come to investigate. They watched Coraline's walk of shame with looks of horror and amusement, snickering to each other, a few taking photos with their phones.

Some friends.

"*Where's security?*" Holly asked no one in particular, pulling out her phone and calling the man in charge of the guards. "I need you to clear the hallway to the bridal party and groom's room. *Now.*"

"Go back to your seats," Holly said, trying to hide Coraline with her body as she motioned for the guests to leave the hallway. She cracked open the changing-room door and pushed the bride inside. Everyone in the room stared at Coraline with wide eyes and open mouths. To be fair, she was a sight, with a bright red nose and snot dripping over her upper lip.

Holly led her to the sofa, then snatched a box of tissues, grabbing a handful and mopping up the mess on the bride's face as best she could. Coraline's makeup was a lost cause, although that was probably the least of their worries.

"Where's Piper?" Miranda asked, glancing around the room for the missing maid of honor.

"She's with that lying, cheating bastard!" Coraline threw herself down on the sofa, her chest heaving with sobs.

Miranda gasped and looked up at Holly. "What on earth is going on here?"

"Your daughter just caught her fiancé kissing the maid of honor. Apparently they've been sleeping together."

"I see." Miranda's face paled, and Holly knew she was thinking the same thing she was. There would be no wedding. There would be no magazine spread. Everything Miranda had been striving for had come to a grinding halt. But, to her credit, Miranda sat on the sofa by her daughter and pulled her into her arms. "There, there, Cora. Everything will be okay."

"How can you say that?" Coraline asked as she pulled away and looked into her mother's eyes. "He cheated on me."

"Better to find out now than after your ceremony."

"I can't marry him, Mom."

Miranda pulled her daughter's head to her shoulder. "Of course you can't. I wouldn't let you even if you still wanted to."

"But your magazine photos..." Coraline's voice trailed off and she started crying again. "I'm sorry."

Holly nearly fell over from shock.

Miranda stroked her daughter's head. "You're much more important than a magazine spread, darling." But Miranda had a gleam in her eyes as she looked Holly over.

She knew she was a sight—covered in blood, snot, and tears—but Miranda's look wasn't one of disgust. She looked...hopeful.

"Never fear, darling. There's going to be a wedding. Just not yours."

Chapter Thirty-Six

Kevin had assigned the groomsmen the task of guarding the groom, not that the groom looked like he wanted to leave. He was sitting on the floor, rocking back and forth and mumbling about his grandfather and a trust fund.

Right now Kevin was more worried about Holly. He was halfway down the hall when his phone vibrated. He pulled it out, worried that it was Holly, but it was Tyler's name he saw on the screen.

"Now's not a good time, Ty."

"I'm just checking on your second job."

"Turns out this job is harder than it looks. I've got a wedding to fix."

"You *what*?"

"I'll fill you in later."

Kevin knocked on the bridal-party changing-room door, and one of the bridesmaids cracked open the door, then looked him up and down. "You're the wedding planner's assistant, aren't you? You can be my assistant anytime."

He cringed. "Sorry, but my position with Holly is pretty exclusive," he said, hoping to get the double meaning across.

She gave him a coy grin. "Well, if you ever change your mind…"

He felt sick to his stomach. He'd always wondered why his relationships had never lasted, and this woman was a perfect example of why they were doomed. He used to date women like her—shallow and opportunistic. Women who thought nothing of sleeping with their best friend's fiancé. The exact opposite of Holly.

"I'm pretty damn sure that's *never* going to happen." He pushed the door open the rest of the way and saw the bride on the sofa in her mother's arms, while Miranda was giving Holly an odd stare.

Kevin moved next to Holly, resisting the urge to grab her hand or put an arm around her. She needed to look professional and in charge, but it was pretty damn hard when all he wanted to do was comfort her. Especially when he knew what this would mean for her job at his mother's business.

But Holly didn't even seem to notice he'd entered the room. Her complete focus was on the bride's mother. "What are you talking about, Miranda?"

"The magazine needs photos."

"Of your *daughter's* wedding."

Miranda dropped her hold on Coraline and stood. The bride had stopped crying and was now watching her mother walk toward Holly.

"No, of my dress," Miranda said, sounding perfectly reasonable. "Think about what a story this will be! How sensationalistic. Social media will love it. Publicity for us both."

Holly shook her head, her eyes wide. "What are you talking about?"

"The replacement couple. They are stunningly gorgeous

and they are desperately in love. It's like a fairy-tale wedding."

"Miranda, who are you talking about?" Holly asked, sounding bewildered. "Who's getting married?"

The woman gave her an irritated look. "You, of course." Then she pointed to Kevin. "And him."

Kevin was shocked by the announcement, but immediately warmed up to the idea. It was a win/win as far as he was concerned. He would help Holly salvage the wedding and in turn save her job. But the real reward was her. He knew without a doubt he wanted to marry her, whether it was in a half hour or another year.

Holly, however, wasn't taking the suggestion as well. She held up her hands in protest. "Whoa, whoa, whoa. Slow down. What makes you think we're in love?"

Miranda rolled her eyes in an exaggerated movement. "Holly, it's so obvious. The way you two look at one another. The way he can hardly stop himself from touching you now." She motioned to Kevin's right hand, which was hovering near Holly's waist.

He looked her in the eye. Guilty as charged.

The designer gave her a satisfied grin. "And I know you'll fit in the dress perfectly. It's like serendipity."

"Miranda," Holly said slowly, "we're not even officially dating. ...*This is crazy!*"

Kevin looked down at Holly, then over to Miranda, wanting to make sure he had all the facts. "So all you need to do is have a fake wedding, and you're good. You get the photos and the publicity you need. The wedding looks like a success?"

"Well...there's a catch," Miranda said. "It has to be real."

"*What?*" Holly asked.

"This will be big entertainment news. Either way, it will probably be on TMZ and at least a couple of gossip magazines. We can't have a fake wedding. Besides, the whole premise of this photo shoot is that it's a *real* ceremony."

"We can't do this." Holly shook her head. "I could never ask Kevin to do such a thing."

"I'll do it," he said without hesitation. "I'll marry you."

She spun around to face him. "I can't ask you to do that, Kevin. Don't get sucked up into my mess."

"You *didn't* ask. I'm offering."

"Why on earth would you agree to this craziness?"

He lifted his hand to her cheek, looking into her green eyes. "She's right, Holly. I love you."

She gasped. "What?"

He kissed her lightly, then looked into her eyes. "I love you, Holly. There's only you. So marry me."

"But your mother..."

"Might have a fit. And you might lose your job, but after talking to my Dad this morning, if this wedding didn't work out, I found out you were going to lose it anyway. But if my mother ever wants to see me again, she'll let her daughter-in-law keep her job or wish her well when she starts her own wedding-planning business."

She shook her head as tears filled her eyes and a new horror hit him. What if Holly didn't love him? What if this was completely one-sided?

"Tell me what you're thinking, Holly."

"A lot of things." She looked utterly panicked as she searched his face.

"I'm not going anywhere. Tell me."

"First"—her voice broke—"that I love you, too."

"Oh, thank God." He kissed her, unable to resist, but then he pulled back and took her hands in his. "What else?"

"How can you be sure you want to marry me? We've only known each other a month."

"Sometimes you just know something, and I know. It's like I was only half a person until I met you. And now I'm whole."

"Really?"

He smiled, his chest aching with the need to hold her, reassure her, and convince her how much she meant to him. "What other protests do you have?"

"What about our friends and family? Don't you want your parents here? Your sister?"

"We'll have our own private wedding with them. In your grandma's backyard if you want. We'll bring her home so she can be part of it, too." He dropped to his knee. "Holly Greenwood, will you marry me?"

She looked wary. "Are you doing this because you feel sorry for me and you think your mother will fire me if this wedding doesn't happen? Because she and I discussed this yesterday. I'll lose my job, but not because she's firing me. But that's still not a reason to marry me."

He grinned. "I can assure you that I'm doing this for purely selfish motives. If anything, I'm being completely opportunistic. I love you. I don't want to lose you. We have a chance to get married in the most beautiful wedding ever, and it was planned by you. Feeling sorry for you never enters the picture here."

"Are you sure?" she whispered. "Like *really* sure?"

"I've never been more certain of anything in my life." He paused and got to his feet. "But what about you? This is pretty fast. But maybe you want to wait. I don't want to rush you into something you're not ready for."

She shook her head, a tear sliding down her cheek. "I love you, Kevin. You're the only man I've ever wanted. I want to spend the rest of my life with you."

"Then you'll marry me?"

She nodded, and the smile spreading across her face filled him with more happiness than he thought possible. "Yes."

He couldn't wait to make this woman his wife. "Then let's get married."

* * *

Holly stood in the hall, waiting for the song for the wedding party to start. Closer to the exit, three bridesmaids were huddled together in a clump of pink silk, occasionally casting looks of disbelief in her direction. The maid of honor had sneaked off soon after getting caught.

The wedding guests had gotten restless waiting, but they were mostly Miranda's friends, so when she explained to them the last-minute change of plans they were more than happy to help her.

But now Holly was waiting to walk down the aisle alone to the only man she'd ever loved, and part of her heart ached for her father. What would he think of the man she was marrying? What would he think of *her*?

Her grip tightened on the stems of the bright pink bouquet and she started to pace, trying to calm her nerves. While she had no qualms about marrying Kevin, she was a bundle of nerves when she thought about being the center of attention in front of several hundred people she didn't even know.

A gentleman cleared his throat and Holly turned to see Kevin's father, her mouth dropping open in surprise.

"Mr. Vandemeer. What are you doing here?" She and Kevin had both agreed not to tell either of their families, since it would be impossible to get everyone together. They would break the news after the fact. Had Kevin gone against their agreement?

He took her arm in his hand and gently tugged her away

from the curious bridesmaids. "Nicole called me and told me to get here right away."

Her breath caught as her hands turned icy. "So you can stop the wedding?"

"No. So I can give you my blessing. And if you're marrying my son, then you need to call me Bart. Or Dad."

"*What?*"

"I would never think of trying to replace your father, and I would never try. But I would love to be the best damn father-in-law I possibly can." The grin spreading across his face filled her with as much reassurance as his words. "Once you marry into this family, you're as much a part of our family as Megan or Kevin or Josh."

"But Nicole—"

"Will come around."

But what if she didn't? Would that eventually cause a rift between Holly and Kevin? "But how did you even know what was going on?"

He laughed. "Apparently the bride's mother called Nicole to come take over the wedding-planner responsibilities. To say Nicole was surprised is an understatement."

Unbelievably, for the first time since saying yes, she was having her first doubt. And over Kevin's mother, no less. "Is she furious?"

Bart chuckled. "No. Confused and blindsided, but not furious. She just needs to adjust to the idea."

Holly had always hoped to marry into a warm and loving family but was willing to accept a belligerent mother-in-law as part of the package if it meant marrying Kevin. Nicole's reaction was more than she could have hoped for. "Thank you."

He smiled. "You make Kevin very happy. I can love you for that alone." He kissed her cheek. "You ready?"

Was she? She was getting married in front of a bunch of strangers, but the only thing that mattered was the man waiting for her at the end of the aisle. She smiled, her heart bursting with happiness. "Yes."

"Then I'll go cue the music."

"Not yet," Nicole said in her no-nonsense voice from behind Holly.

Bart gave Holly a hug, then disappeared toward the guests.

Holly's knees began to shake as Nicole moved next to her, giving her a tight smile. "Let me fix you up," Nicole said, lifting a makeup brush. "We can't have you walking down the aisle and having photos taken with a shiny nose."

Was this some kind of trick? "Nicole...I..."

Her boss kept her focus on her task. "Since the original wedding planner is getting married," she said in a tight voice, "I obviously need to step in."

"I..."

Nicole's gaze locked on hers. "Kevin and I just had a chat. There's no doubt that he loves you, and that you've made him happy. And while I'm still upset that you two hid this from me, he deserves someone who fills him with such joy. And..." She paused, giving Holly a warm smile. "You're a sweet girl. The sweetest woman he's ever dated...as far as I know."

She stared at Nicole in shock.

"Just promise you won't steal my party and shower clients when you start your own shop, and I won't plan any weddings."

"What?"

She lifted her chin and said in a controlled voice, "I think it's best if we split our businesses. We don't want any nepotism. And I can't very well compete against my own daughter-in-law, now can I?"

"I don't know what to say."

Nicole smiled. "Say you'll try your best to make my son happy."

"I love him. I *want* to make him as happy as he makes me."

Nicole gave Holly's nose one last swipe and nodded. "I'll cue the musicians to play the bridal processional." And then she was gone.

The music changed, the violins of the small orchestra playing the classical piece Holly had picked out, and the first bridesmaid headed down the aisle. The other two bridesmaids whispered in hushed, nervous tones until the second one followed the first.

The third bridesmaid—Coraline's younger cousin—glanced back at Holly. "You're much more beautiful than Coraline in that dress." She grinned. "But if you ever tell her I said that, I'll deny it." Then she left, too.

Holly released a nervous laugh, telling herself she only needed to ignore everyone else and focus on Kevin.

The music changed and the door opened. Nicole graced her with a warm smile as she walked by. "May you have a beautiful future."

The large crowd made Holly pause, but she focused on the man waiting at the end of the aisle, standing under the white-and-pink-rose-covered arch that opened to a long vineyard row. The look of happiness in his eyes was nearly her undoing.

They may have been surrounded by a sea of strangers, but all she heard was the soft sounds of the violins and the cello. All she saw was Kevin—the one person who made her feel alive and loved. The man who believed in her enough to convince her to believe, too.

And in that moment, of all the decisions she had ever made, she knew this was by far the best.

* * *

When Holly appeared in the open doorway, Kevin was overwhelmed with gratitude. He was sure he'd never seen a more beautiful woman in his life—both inside and out—and she was walking toward *him*. She wanted to marry *him*.

Her gaze locked on his as she glided toward him, her silk-and-lace wedding dress floating around her and trailing behind like a billowing white cloud. She gave him a shy smile and he beamed, eager for her to reach him.

When Holly stopped in front of him, he reached out to her. She took his hand and he gripped it gently as she moved to his side.

Holly kept her gaze on him the entire service, as though she were ignoring that anyone else existed except for the two of them.

When the minister got to the vows, he cleared his throat. "The original bride and groom wrote their own vows. Would you like me to use the traditional vows?"

Holly's eyes widened, but then she leaned closer to him and whispered, "I don't. Do *you*?"

He shook his head. "There's nothing traditional about us, so why start now?"

She laughed and nodded, her face flushing a pretty pale pink. "Then I'll go first."

He nodded, unable to wipe the smile from his face as he took her hands in his.

"Kevin, I never wanted to open my heart to love until I met you. I was never even tempted. But you make me feel light-hearted and adored. You fill me with more joy than I ever thought possible. We may have only known each other for a month, but we could wait a thousand months and I would have no doubt that there is only you."

He'd never wanted to kiss her more than he did right now, but instead he squeezed her hands and smiled. "Holly, I wasn't looking for love. In fact, I was determined to avoid it. But then you showed up on my doorstep with your reheated lasagna and your sweet, shy spirit and I was hooked. I knew my life would never be the same. I know you're worried that I feel pressured into this, but I have no doubts—not a single one—and I am so honored that you agreed to be my wife. You've just given me the greatest gift I could ever hope to get in my life."

She blinked back tears as the minister said it was time to exchange rings, and then suddenly her eyes filled with worry.

He gave her a reassuring smile and whispered, "I've got it covered" as he pulled two rings from his pocket. "Gram's and Gramps'. Dad got them before he came."

After the wedding, they took photos for the magazine with the bridal party and then alone, setting up exaggerated shots for the magazine layout. The writer from the magazine asked Kevin and Holly endless questions about their relationship and what spurred them to agree to an impromptu marriage. Then a local newspaper heard about the wedding on social media and showed up to take photos and interview them as well.

As soon as they had fulfilled their obligations, Holly found Miranda Johansen to let her know they were leaving. She grabbed both of their hands and smiled. "Thank you both for what you did. I realize it was unfair of me to put you on the spot like that."

Kevin put an arm around Holly's back, his hand resting on her hip as he pulled her close. "You helped make me the happiest man alive, so thank *you*."

She smiled at Holly. "I guess we have Holly to thank for that, don't we?"

Holly looked up at him with eyes so full of love he wanted nothing more than to take her home and make their wedding official in the biblical sense. Kevin turned to Miranda. "If you'll excuse us, I'm ready to take my wife home."

"Of course," the woman said. "And congratulations to you both."

Kevin took Holly's hand and stared into her eyes. "I meant what I said. You have made me the happiest man alive, Holly Vandemeer."

"You've made me happy, too." She looked into his eyes. "I know you said we were going home, but where is home? Your house? Mine? Where's home for us, Kevin?"

He smiled and lifted his hand to her face and gave her a kiss. "That's simple, Holly. Home is wherever you are."

Look for the next book in the
Bachelor Brotherhood series, *Until You*.

A preview follows.

Chapter One

⟋

"Tyler Norris...this is the *last* place I ever expected to see you."

Tyler leaned back in his patio chair and sipped his beer, hiding his annoyance with a smirk. This was the fourth woman to approach him tonight, and while he was used to women hitting on him, this seemed to be a bit much given he was a single man at a *couple's* wedding shower.

Still, he was in the middle of a self-imposed dry spell from women, and over the last few weeks, he'd been dying of thirst. For a man who was used to having sex on a regular basis, going five months without it had been torture. However, after the disaster with his last girlfriend, he couldn't bring himself to take the plunge again. Even for a simple one-night stand. But he was safe from temptation with the blonde eyeing him like he was the last margarita on Ladies Night at LaFeunte Bar and Grill.

"How'd you get roped into it?" she asked, her right hand on her hip.

Theresa Fink. He hadn't seen her since high school, but

the look in her eyes told him she was *very* happy to see him. She lifted the wine glass in her left hand, spotlighting her bare left ring finger, even going so far as to slightly wiggle it to catch his attention.

She continued studying him with lust-filled eyes, apparently expecting an answer. He finally shrugged his nonchalance. "Turns out being groomsman means the bride can strong-arm you into anything she wants." That wasn't entirely true—he had a soft spot when it came to Brittany—but no need to tell Theresa that.

Her eyes lit up. "Maybe she can spill some of her secrets. Your legend precedes you, Tyler Norris."

Chuckling, he took a drag of his beer. "And which legend is that? I hear there are many." He winked. "And the ones about my size and endurance are *all* true."

Theresa flushed, pressing her hand against her chest and fluttering her eyelashes.

Jesus. Why did he tell her that? Old habits were still hard to break, but now she looked like a barracuda ready to gnaw off his leg. Or, more specifically, another body part in very close proximity.

"Tyler," a deep voice said behind him. "Holly needs your help with the ice."

Tyler tried not to look so relieved when he jumped to his feet and turned to face Kevin Vandemeer, one of his two best friends. "Yeah. Be more than happy to."

Disappointment washed over Theresa's face, but he ignored her as she called after him. "Want to get drinks later?"

Tyler walked through the suburban backyard, feeling like he was about to break out into hives just being here, let alone sitting outside in the Missouri hot and humid August evening for the last hour. He tugged at his collar, regretting his decision to leave on his tie.

"Thanks for the save," he said as he followed Kevin to the back deck, then stopped to grab another beer from a bucket of ice water.

"The save comes at a price," Kevin said with a chuckle. "You're refilling the drink tubs with ice."

"Me?" Tyler asked, standing upright and turning to face his friend. "Shouldn't that be your job since *your wife* is in charge of the party?"

Kevin's wife. Damn, that was hard to spit out. Not that he had anything against Holly, he actually liked her, and if Tyler was honest, she was a good fit for the ex-marine. But of his two best friends, Kevin had been more like Tyler when it came to women. Lots of girlfriends that never lasted. So when Kevin moved back home two months ago after his last tour in Afghanistan, the three friends had commiserated on their extremely unlucky love life and decided to give up on marriage, imposing a ban on women and forming the Bachelor Brotherhood.

Kevin Vandemeer had lasted one fucking day.

"My *wife*," Kevin said in a warning tone, "was the one to suggest I save your ass, you dickweed. So get your ass out to the garage and grab a couple of bags of ice out of the freezer or I'll tell Theresa Fink that you want to leave the shower and go out for a candlelight dinner. Just the two of you."

"You suck, Vandemeer," Tyler grumbled.

Kevin's answer was a shit-eating grin.

Tyler would have loved to kick his friend's ass right then and there, but Brittany would have killed him. And while he considered doing it anyway, instead he went into the dark, cooler garage, deciding this wasn't such a heinous task after all. It had to be ten degrees cooler in the two-car garage and he was alone. Maybe he could hide in here for ten minutes or so, then tell Britt a work emergency had come up and he needed to go.

Only her fiancé worked at his law firm and pretty much knew every case Tyler was working on. Randy would bust his ass in a New York minute.

Shit. He was stuck.

Tyler had been at Randy's house enough times to know the garage refrigerator was stocked with beer, some of which were Randy's precious import beers. Tyler opened the door and grinned. Jackpot. He replaced the bottle in his hand with a Stella and screwed off the top, then took a long drag, letting the cold beer coat his dry mouth.

"I see you found Randy's import stash," a woman said in the darkness.

Caught off guard, he choked, spitting beer down his shirt. He spun around and found her sitting on Randy's workbench with her own bottle of Stella. She leaned to her left side, bracing her body with her outstretched arm. Unlike every other guest at the shower with the exception of him, she was still dressed in business attire—a light gray, nearly sleeveless dress with tiny pleats from her hips that ended just above her knees. Her legs were crossed and she bounced her black three-inch pump as she watched him, lowering the bottle from her mouth. Long dark hair hung down her back, several strands lay over her shoulder and covered her breast. He forced his gaze to rise to her face.

"Didn't mean to startle you," she said, her dark eyes dancing with amusement.

She was gorgeous, and damned if he wasn't intrigued. "I didn't see you over there."

She grinned. "Obviously."

He moved toward her, unable to stop himself. "Looks like we both have the same idea."

She laughed. "If your idea is hiding from Brittany and drinking Randy's import beer, then we do."

He gestured to the empty spot on the workbench next to her and she lifted her shoulder into a half-shrug invitation. Tyler hopped up on the bench and perched next to her, leaving a few inches between them. "So what's a nice girl like you doing in a musty garage like this?"

She laughed again, uncrossing her long legs and turning toward him, her eyes full of mischief. "I bet you use that line on all the girls."

"Only the ones I find in musty garages." Up close like this, he could see that her dark eyes were a milk chocolate brown and framed by long, sexy eyelashes. She lifted her beer and took a sip, and he suddenly found himself jealous of the bottle in her hand.

"I know why you're hiding," she said as she set the beer next to her on the table.

He smirked. "Okay, tell me why I'm hiding."

"Brittany. She's playing matchmaker again." His eyes widened and she gave him a knowing smile. "It wasn't that hard to figure out. For the last hour, she's been sending women to you like they're going through the turnstile at a ride in Disneyland and you keep sending them away." She flicked her fingers to demonstrate.

He lifted his eyebrows as he studied her face, then teased, "You've been spying on me?"

She cocked her head to the side, rolling her eyes. "Amateur. You obviously haven't known Brittany for long."

"About a year." And while that was true, it had been about six months ago when he'd really gotten to know her. When he'd gone through his ordeal with his last girlfriend, she and Randy had shown him more support than he'd expected.

She laughed again. "I have about thirty years on you."

Thirty years? Tyler had graduated with Brittany, which meant Britt had to have met her when they were babies.

She gestured to his beer. "Since you have exceptional taste in beer *and* hiding spots, I'll be generous and give you a few pointers."

"Should I be taking notes?" he teased. While she was flirty, she wasn't coming on to him, and it only intrigued him more.

She shrugged. "It wouldn't hurt, but I suspect we'll be seeing each other again in a month, so I can give you a refresher course at the wedding."

Finally. Something to actually look forward to at the wedding.

"First," she said in a conspirational tone, "Britt comes across as this sweet and unassuming woman, but don't let that fool you."

"No?"

"*No,*" she said, pointing her finger at him. "She uses it as her ultimate weapon to get you to do what she wants." She stabbed her chest to make her point. "Look at poor Randy."

Tyler was loyal to the people who stood by him, and he was about to defend Britt until he saw she was teasing. There was no doubt that Randy had been ensnared by Brittany, but it was just as obvious the adoration went both ways.

"You have to be firm." She brought her hand down sideways onto her open palm, like a karate chop. "If you show the slightest ounce of waffling, she'll pounce on it."

"So," he said slowly. "You're saying I haven't been firm enough? That I can't hold my own?" He gave her an arrogant grin. "Because I have a nickname that disputes that."

"Oh really?" she asked, her face lighting up in mock surprise. "Are we talking about cute nicknames that your *guy* friends have given you? Like The Terminator? Or Maverick?"

He shook his head and laughed, trying to think of the last time he'd enjoyed a woman's company so much. "Have you been binge-watching eighties' movies on Netflix?"

"Busted." She laughed, leaning her head to the side and exposing her long neck.

A wave of lust washed through him and he struggled to control it. It was obvious she wasn't an easy conquest. Oddly enough, he considered playing the long game with her.

What the fuck was wrong with him? He wasn't supposed to be playing the game at all.

She shook her head, her grin tugging at the corners of her full lips. "So what's this awesome nickname of yours? I take it my suggestions came from the wrong decade."

He gave her a long look, now reluctant to share. "The Closer."

Her eyes widened in amusement. "Because you're so good with *the ladies*?" She waggled her eyebrows.

He laughed, feeling like an idiot. "And because I can close a case before it goes to trial."

"Uh huh. Sure.". She hopped off the bench and wobbled a little on her heels, cluing him in that she'd had more than the one beer tonight. "Well, *Mr. Closer*, Brittany Stewart is much more subtle than that." She pushed his legs open and stood between them, grabbing a handful of his tie and pulling his face inches from hers. "She sees you as a challenge. She thinks everyone in the whole wide world needs to be in love and she won't rest until it happens. And *you* are the perfect challenge." She dropped her tie and spread her hands out. "Big bad womanizer who can't bring himself to let his guard down and let a woman in, much less love her. Why Britt just can't resist." She laughed and grabbed his tie again, slowly leaning closer. "The more obstinate you are to her efforts, the more determined she becomes."

Her breath fanned his face, and it took everything within him to keep his hands to himself, because instinct told him that if he made a move, she'd give him a brush-off so epic an 8.0 earthquake would pale in comparison.

And he definitely did *not* want her to give him a brush-off.

"And how do you know all this?" he asked, proud that he sounded so in control.

Her lips hovered inches over his, and she whispered, "I've been her number one project for years. Looks like I've just been usurped." She dropped her hold on his tie, then smoothed it down his chest, her fingertips trailing to his abdomen in small sweeps.

A fresh jolt of lust rushed through his blood and he gripped the sides of the table, hoping she didn't see how much she affected him when her eyes lifted to his.

"So why didn't she try to fix me up with you?" he asked, his voice husky despite his intentions.

Her smile became sardonic. "Because she's figured out that I'm a lost cause." Then she turned and walked back into the kitchen, her tight dress hugging her rounded ass so perfectly another wave of desire scorched him.

Tyler waited a good minute before he could go back into the kitchen without looking like he was auditioning for the role of a circus tent center pole. As he took the last drag of his beer and tossed the bottle into the recycling bin, he realized that never in his thirty-three years had he been so turned on by a woman.

And he didn't even know her name.

ABOUT THE AUTHOR

Denise Grover Swank is a *New York Times* and *USA Today* bestselling author who was born in Kansas City, Missouri, and lived in the area until she was nineteen. Then she became a nomadic gypsy, living in five cities, four states, and ten houses over the course of ten years before she moved back to her roots. She speaks English and a smattering of Spanish and Chinese, which she learned through an intensive Nick Jr. immersion period. Her hobbies include witty (in her own mind) Facebook comments and dancing (quite badly, if you believe her offspring) in her kitchen with her children. Hidden talents include the gift of justification and the ability to drink massive amounts of caffeine and still fall asleep within two minutes. Her lack of the sense of smell allows her to perform many unspeakable tasks. She has six children and hasn't lost her sanity. Or so she leads you to believe.

You can learn more at:
DeniseGroverSwank.com
Twitter @DeniseMSwank
Facebook.com/DeniseGroverSwank

Sign up for Denise's newsletter to get information on new releases and free reads!
http://DeniseGroverSwank.com/mailing-list/

Fall in Love with Forever Romance

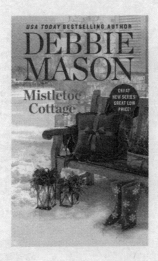

MISTLETOE COTTAGE
By Debbie Mason

The first book in a brand-new contemporary series from *USA Today* bestselling author Debbie Mason! 'Tis the season for love in Harmony Harbor, but it's the last place Sophie DiRossi wants to be. After fleeing many years ago, Sophie is forced to return to the town that harbors a million secrets. Firefighter Liam Gallagher still has some serious feelings for Sophie—and seeing her again sparks a desire so fierce it takes his breath away. Hoping for a little holiday magic, Liam sets out to show Sophie that they deserve a second chance at love.

Fall in Love with Forever Romance

ONLY YOU
By Denise Grover Swank

The first book in a spin-off from Denise Grover Swank's *New York Times* bestselling Wedding Pact series! Ex-marine Kevin Vandemeer craves normalcy. Instead, he has a broken-down old house in need of a match and some gasoline, a meddling family, and the uncanny ability to attract the world's craziest women. At least that last one he can fix: He and his buddies have made a pact to swear off women, and that includes his sweetly sexy new neighbor...

THE BILLIONAIRE NEXT DOOR
By Jessica Lemmon

Rachel Foster is surviving on odd jobs when billionaire Tag Crane hires her and whisks her away to Hawaii to help save his business. As things start to get steamy, Rachel falls for Tag. Will he feel the same, or will she just get played? Fans of Jill Shalvis and Erin Nicholas will love the next book in the Billionaire Bad Boys series!

Fall in Love with Forever Romance

HEATED PURSUIT
By April Hunt

The first book in a sexy new romantic suspense series from debut author April Hunt, perfect for fans of Julie Ann Walker, Maya Banks, and Lora Leigh. After Penny Kline walks into his covert ops mission, Alpha Security operative Rafe Ortega realizes that the best way to bring down a Honduran drug lord and rescue her kidnapped niece is for them to work together. But the only thing more dangerous than going undercover in the madman's lair is the passion that explodes between them…

SOMEBODY LIKE YOU
By Lynette Austin

Giving her bodyguards and the paparazzi the slip, heiress Annelise Montjoy comes to Maverick Junction on a mission to help her ailing grandfather. But keeping her identity hidden in the small Texas town is harder than she expected— especially around a tempting cowboy like Cash Hardeman…

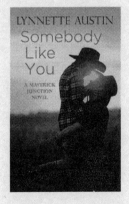